MISSION TO MIGHTADORE

- Jackelian #7 -

by Stephen Hunt

GREEN

NEBULA

MISSION TO MIGHTADORE

ISBN: 9781982997564

Cover art by Luca Oleastri

www.StephenHunt.net

Twitter: @s_hunt_author
www.facebook.com/SciFi.Fantasy

First Edition

Printed in the U.S.A & United Kingdom

"I grieved to think how brief the dream of the human intellect had been. It had committed suicide."

— *H.G. Wells, The Time Machine*

To receive an automatic notification by e-mail when Stephen's new books are available for download (and get a free e-book), use the sign-up form at http://www.StephenHunt.net/alerts.php

To help report any typos, errors and similar in this work, use the form at http://www.stephenhunt.net/typo/typoform.php

Also by Stephen Hunt

The Past is Prologue

The Republic of Southern Texicana (26th century: Julian calendar).

Lieutenant Chalt Sambuchino halted the armoured car in the foothills of Del Rio. The hills ahead were crested with large, dense red oaks and there was far too high a chance of breaking an axle if he tried to push the boxy metal vehicle through the treeline. There wasn't a sizable population in this part of the republic. No real towns or villages to speak of. So, when news of the strange sighting came in, the Federal Army at Fort Padre had been the force that the local vaqueros had naturally turned to. Chalt rarely trusted the word of the vaqueros. He knew all-too-well how superstitious these semi-itinerant shepherds were. Of course, they drove sheep and cattle from the back of mules. Uneducated in the ways of book learning, the vaqueros loved getting roaring drunk on mescal to stay warm at night as they slept in their upland pastures. It didn't take much to set them off into fits of gullible tale-telling. The mere sight of a plane's contrail out of the Reindeer Empire would bring the herds-people tottering in with hungover tales of winged serpents threatening their living. Still, at least Chalt's reluctant investigation made a change from chasing bandits from the lawless Dukedom of Palacan back across the Rio Grande.

Chalt wasn't expecting much to come from this day's duty, which is why he had only taken one trooper with him. Corporal Sérgio Xavier, sweating as badly as the lieutenant in the summer heat inside his khaki fatigue blouse. The heat of the corporal's body in the passenger cabin combined with their shepherd guide seated in the back made the journey particularly unpleasant. After stopping the car, Chalt adjusted his black leather belt – a brass plate embossed with the number seven in its centre – bending the cartridge pouches so he could slip out of their little sloped iron box on four rubber wheels.

Chalt carried the weight of a seven-shot automatic in his leather holster, and Sérgio reached for his .45-caliber submachine gun as he clacked opened the door on his side of the car. The 7th Armored Cavalry Division of the Federal Army had recently been issued the gun because of its portability and size. Quickly nicknamed the *Grease Pump* by the troopers for its resemblance to the mechanic's tool.

'You think we will need that?'

'Better to have it and not need it.' Sérgio was an old hand in the Federal Army. He had no intention of being set upon by southern footpads and having his coming retirement plans fatally interrupted. Chalt and Sérgio didn't have much in common on the surface of it. Chalt was a fresh-faced academy man from a privileged family, Sérgio a bluff ranker of uncertain pedigree. But Chalt respected the corporal's experience and knew he should use it to plaster over the gaps of his own inexperience.

'Maybe we will find a winged serpent to shoot?'

Chalt's joke brought a frown to the shepherd's face. The wizened old man crossed himself over his leather jerkin and indicated the wooded hills. 'You will see the truth. It is on the other side.'

'There is a lake over there,' stated Chalt, leaning into the armoured car's cabin to consult the map for a second. 'Lake Wise.'

'My people call it Aguas Oscuras,' said the shepherd. 'It is a haunted place.'

'Haunted by what?'

'Ghosts. The cannibal ghosts of the Roca Mala.'

Chalt groaned. *Bad Rock*. If the old goat pusher's parents had bothered to pay for their peasant child to attend a school, he would have known that barely three percent of humanity's once-teeming masses had survived the ancient comet strike's long protracted nuclear winter. By that measure, there wasn't a place in the world left unhaunted by the ghosts of the Great Dying. *A haunted world*, mused Chalt. *I have often found it so.*

Sérgio hung back to watch the shepherd walk ahead of them. 'Do you think there is anything to the colonel's fears?'

Chalt shrugged. 'Up ahead? I suspect not. But dangerous times lay in front of us, that much I know.' It was natural for Sérgio to be worried. If fresh incursions by the Cals led to war, that was the one thing guaranteed to derail the coming end to Sérgio's service in the Federal Army. All military commissions would be extended, and it would not matter whether you were the son of an aristocrat or the son of a washerwoman. By all accounts, the bloody dynastic war between House Hamilton, House Zhu and House Salazar in the seven coastal kingdoms of Cal had been viciously settled in favour of the Zhus. For the first time in living memory, there was a Witch Queen of the Cals in the great Crystal Palace at Oxnard ruling over a unified realm. *And their peace will be our strife.* 'There was a conjunction between Venus and Jupiter in the sky recently. I am willing to wager that what the vaqueros saw was that conjunction combined with a few too many bottles of mescal.'

Sérgio was not so easily convinced. 'The colonel told me that Cal airships have been sighted on our side of the border.'

'Airships drift all over the place,' said the lieutenant, 'that is their nature.'

'And we drift too,' muttered Sérgio, 'towards another war for brave Xavier.'

Chalt, Sérgio and the peasant marched up the slope and through the red oak trees' pleasant shade. On the other side of the fringe of woodland lay a reverse slope down towards Lake Wise. Three acres of clear blue waters with banks of purple-flowered meadows stretching out to a tall oak forest. It would have made a more idyllic scene if the meadows weren't smoking, blackened and cratered, oaks splintered and felled. Embedded into the ground was a central mass of black metal, etched hull plates cracked to reveal half-melted girders and decking. It was as though a tidal wave had snapped the superstructure off a frigate mid-engagement and washed it inland to rest here. Stretched in rings around the mass were smaller circles of devastation, torn-off metal fragments, corpses and smouldering wreckage.

'So, you see now. Not a winged serpent to shoot. All the serpents are dead.' The shepherd indicated the blackened bodies dotting the meadow with a bitter hint of vindication in his voice.

The Corporal stared with disbelief at the blackened landscape. 'Too much wreckage to be the result of a plane crash, surely?'

'I don't believe it was ever aerodynamic,' said Chalt.

Sérgio coughed, as he often did to show mild displeasure. 'I am a simple soldier. What does that *palabra* mean?'

'It means those remains were never designed to fly through the air,' said Chalt, raising a hand towards the crash site. In fact, to Chalt's eyes, the debris looked like a cathedral built of dark steel had been ripped into pieces, the structure cast down to Earth by the Redeemer. 'There are no wings or tails or propellers that I can see.'

'It arrived from somewhere, lieutenant.' Sérgio looked at the shepherd. 'Did you see it crash here, old vaquero?'

'I am not old, only seventy-two. My mother lived to be eighty-one.'

'Well done. Now, did you see this thing fall from the sky?'

'Not from the sky, from *Hell*. It was expelled by El Diablo.'

'Everything down there came out of the ground?' asked Chalt, surprised.

'From a gateway torn into Hell itself,' said the old shepherd, his voice quivering with fear from the memory. He pointed to the far side of the lake. 'We had camped over there for the evening when the land began to shake and tremble. I warned my people not to let our cattle water by the Aguas Oscuras, to camp under the forest's shade instead. But none of the young listen to a wise rider. We woke in terror from a wild shaking of the ground. With sleep still in our eyes, we watched a doorway into Hell crack open in the sky. A crevice of bright fire which twisted and danced above the lake for many minutes. As we fled to the top of the hill, El Diablo tossed a fiery metal altar of darkness through the crack. It exploded and burnt across the ground. Then a rain of devils and brimstone followed. Young Manjarrez's mule died of shock. Three prize round-horns panicked and escaped to flee into the forest.'

'Show us.'

'I will not venture any closer. The lake's bed is white with bones. Ancient bones. El Diablo drowns his enemies in the Aguas Oscuras. The lake's hungry ghosts consume the souls of fools who wander these hills alone at night.'

'But you are not alone. You have the lieutenant and brave Xavier.' Sérgio raised his submachine gun. 'And I have this.'

I suppose you will ignore this rider's wisdom.' The stubborn vaquero turned his back on them. He hobbled through the trees, heading towards the armoured car.

'Old peasant,' growled Sérgio. 'If his prize cattle were fattening on the grass by the water he would be down there quick enough.'

'Leave him be. He had the courage to bring us here. That is more than I can say for the rest of his clan.'

Sérgio sniffed the air, uneasily. 'He's the sensible one, lieutenant. Whatever happened here, it is wrong. I can feel it in my bones. That mess down there is unnatural.'

'At least it's not the Cals, corporal. We have a report to file at Fort Padre. "Unnatural" by itself will not satisfy our superiors. Let us press on.'

They paced carefully down the hill towards the meadows and the lake. Trying not show his nerves, Chalt drew his pistol, taking comfort from its heft. Apart from the incongruous nature of the debris, much about the lake appeared normal. Bubbles of air broke the surface from bass and catfish. A blackbuck antelope dipped its neck at the edge of the distant forest, keeping a wary eye on the approaching humans. Clouds of insects danced above the meadows, attracted by the lake waters. As Chalt drew closer, he heard the ping of cooling metal from shards of blackened debris. When they reached the first of the corpses, matters did not improve. He fought down his fear. The body in front of Chalt wasn't human – at best, humanoid. Six-foot tall, naked with dark scaled skin like a salamander, a head that resembled an elongated bishop's mitre, large bulbous eyes and a ridge of gills along the neck. What lingered longest in his memory was its hideous mouth. Almost human lips, but a serrated fanged mouth, grinning and leering in death.

'Sweet Redeemer,' whispered the corporal. He cautiously nudged the body with his boot, but it remained still and dead. 'The old vaquero wasn't drunk. No Cal, this. Foul devils, truly!'

As a graduate of the Tal-Houston Military Academy, Chalt could read. He favoured old classics – the rare scattering of ancient novels that had survived being burnt for fuel in the Great Dying's hundred-year winter … either tossed in the fire, or ephemeral records lost inside long rusted away computers. Writers such as the bard Frank Herbert had much to say about the possible origins of creatures such as *this*. 'No. Not devils. Visitors from somewhere very far away, I think.'

The corporal looked close to gagging. 'Not far enough for me. Brave Xavier has walked the aftermath of many battlefields in his time, but this stench! These devils resemble rotting fish, but they smell a thousand times worse.'

The two soldiers picked their way toward the wreckage's jagged central mass, impaled in the ground and still smoking. Chalt was reminded of an ocean liner smashed into fragments. He could spy the suggestion of corridors and bulkheads through rents in the dark metal, but the whole structure had melted beyond recovery. Waves of extreme heat still throbbed deep within it, intense enough to keep them from trying to explore further.

'Few answers from this slag heap,' said Chalt.

'Be glad of it,' said Sérgio. 'Whatever those monsters had to say . . .' His voice trailed away. 'Wait, something moving at five o'clock!'

A panel on the ground shoved to the side, revealing a figure trying to raise itself from the grass. Chalt felt a cold shiver of relief as he realised what they had spotted was every bit as human as themselves. A large dark-bearded man of late middle age. He wore a torn blue jacket and waistcoat, a peaked naval-style captain's cap shading his cunning eyes. The sole survivor to emerge from the wreckage seemed overdressed. As though he had recently left a swish naval function at the Secretaría de la Marina before having this mess of burning wreckage dropped down on his head. If the fellow had simply been travelling past Lake Wise, he was surely the unluckiest sailor alive. His face was blackened with grime and smoke, bruised and cut too.

Sérgio advanced on the survivor. 'Now there's a queer sight among all this. You think he's a crashed northern aviator?'

The sailor saw the two soldiers and tugged at a sabre belted to his side. He hardly possessed the strength to draw it. Sérgio flourished the snub submachine gun and then lifted it to the side to show he did not intend to use his weapon unless provoked. 'Don't be foolish, big man. We're not bandits here to strip you down to your boots. We mean you no ill.'

The figure rolled to the side and flung his arms pleadingly towards the sky, groaning and raising his voice to jabber loudly and fast in a foreign language.

Sérgio knelt by the man and unhooked a water canteen from the back of his belt. He passed it into the survivor's hands and watched as the stranger glugged madly at the liquid. The sailor coughed and made what sounded like another pleading lament in his strange language.

Sérgio shrugged. 'What do you want from me? If it's a shot of tequila you're after, you'll have to wait until we get back to the fort's infirmary. Look at the anchor-and-trident on his cap. A sea-dog. Is it possible he was fishing the lake when this wreck crashed on top of his boat?'

'A face as pasty as his? Not nearly tanned enough. I think I prefer the crashed-aviator-from-the-Reindeer-Empire theory to that.'

'You might be onto something, lieutenant. His gabber sounds familiar . . . like an Empire merchant? Is he speaking Reindeer?'

'Français-norte,' said Chalt, wearing his aristocratic family's education on his sleeve again. 'The Reindeer Empire's official language is Français-norte. There's a little of that in his speech. But some of what this old dog's saying resembles High Hong, while other words sound almost like Länder-tongue.' Faced with this unintelligible jumble, the lieutenant fell back on sign language. He tapped his chest. 'Chalt Sambuchino.' He reached out to the corporal and tapped his shoulder. 'Sérgio Xavier.' Then Chalt reached out and rested his hand on the bearded man's jacket. 'And you are . . .?'

The survivor's eyes widened in understanding. His fist weakly rapped against his chest. 'Black. Jared Black.'

Sérgio wrapped his tongue around the strange name. 'Jareed Blarck. Where do you think he hails from with such a foreign name?'

'I don't think he's any local fisherman,' said Chalt. *Not even close.* A sudden cold shiver ran down the lieutenant's spine. He glanced around at the field of rotting corpses. Hundreds of the lifeless monsters. *How did they die? Did you kill them?* Murdered monsters scattered everywhere. And who was this strange creature lying among the dead? *A bad omen or a good one?* Chalt's answer came in the swish of rotors approaching from the north. Chalt didn't need to spy the white-and-green shield on the side of her dark black envelope, a rampant brown bear clutching seven crimson stars, to know the sound of a Cal frigate. Along with so much of the land's lost high science, only the rapacious Cals possessed the secret of constructing hybrid air vehicles.

'War, then,' whispered Chalt, as much to himself. *Damn.*

-1-

Six-ball

The Steamman Free State (Two Million+ Years A.D: Julian calendar).

C assie Templar's platform emerged into the open air. A fierce roaring broke out around the arena, making her even more nervous than she'd been a second before. *Don't look nervous. Don't appear afraid*, she willed herself. *You're here to take part and not make a complete fool of yourself. Avoid ending up as a smear on the wall.*

'They think we're going to lose,' whispered Magnus, by her side as the elevator platform juddered to a halt. They stepped off its cold metal grating and onto the arena's sandy soil. Grit crunched under their heels. Cassie's leather boots were laced every bit as tight as her gut. *Let's get on with this before I explode from anxiety.*

'More fool them,' said Cassie, keeping a brave face for Magnus. Reliable, shy Magnus Creag came from a merchant family that made a good living by importing coal into the Steamman Free State. She gazed around. The Hanging Arena of the Free State was the biggest open space in the city. A long oval stadium with countless evil ways to cut your glory short, suspended in the void between two towering mountains on a dizzying web of steel cables. Thousands of eyes stared down at her from tiered seating. Spectators sat above the high wall ringing the oval floor, watching and gawking, but few of those eyes were human. The arena was considered a rite of passage among the local youth. *How could we not take part? Avoid participating and be thought cowards?*

Like Cassie, her team was composed of the younger members of the city's tiny human community. She was friends with them all, though in truth, some she liked far more than others. As members of humanity, they were all bonded by the fact that in this foreign land they stood out as oddities and curiosities. Immigrants and strangers in a strange land. Creatures of flesh and blood in a nation of sentient, self-reproducing machines. Another elevator platform entered the arena. It contained tall Scarlett Deller, the fast-talking daughter of an explorer who was absent from the city for substantial portions of the year. Lastly came refined, superior Sophie Fox, whose parents served as the Jackelian Kingdom's embassy staff. Magnus was to ride with Sophie today and he left to walk beside her. Cassie liked Magnus more than she was willing to admit. Certainly not to the other girls in the city. A male their own age was a rare thing among these quick-witted machines of the mountains.

Cassie took in the arena floor. Half the players had arrived before them, other elevators still working, carrying the remaining participants into the arena. Many of the early arrivals knelt praying to their pantheon of strange robot gods, the Steamo Loa. Cassie's gaze passed over the chanting, nodding robots and stopped on her best friend among the steammen, Alios Hardcircuit. The young robot had a gentle nature that was unfortunately burdened with a warrior parentage. The pair of adults who had contributed most to his soul and programming, his *birth* in robot terms, ranked great among the Steamman Knights. But Alios would never be a fighter. Not if he lived a thousand years – which given he was a slow-aging sentient machine, he might very well do. Defying the course laid down for Alios by his race had won him few friends among the other steammen. Alios had failed selection by every local side. No, Alios would be risking his metal neck on Cassie's team this day. She went over to him.

'Aren't you praying for victory today, Alios?' asked Cassie.

'It seems a base, unworthy thing,' said Alios Hardcircuit, 'to pray for personal glory. Besides, the spirits of the Loa only visit the mightiest of us, touching those that need guidance during times of great importance to our race. That is not I.'

'You're always worthy to me,' said Cassie.

'That is kind of you to say so.'

'It's no kindness,' smiled Cassie, 'it's the simple truth.'

'Is the truth ever simple?' The young steamman turned to look at their massive six-wheeled racer. 'We will see.'

Given how fast Alios could speed around on his legs, it was an irony that the steamman would shortly be climbing up into the racer's cockpit alongside her. Like a sizeable number of the Free State's warrior-born, his form resembled that of a centaur cast in steel. A four-legged main body with a two-armed humanoid torso at the front. A pair of short stacks arched out of his spine, acting as exhaust pipes for his power system. Alios's face resembled a rough approximation of a human male, with mouth, nose, and cheeks cast like the mask on a knight's helmet. Instead of eyes, he possessed a visor-like vision-plate which pulsed with crimson light. Sometimes the light slowed like a Cyclops's pupil, before darting side to side. Cassie had known the robot long enough to be able to interpret emotions just from the dance of light across his vision-plate.

'I'll tell you one truth,' said Cassie. 'We're going to give everyone who turned you away from their team a really good reason to regret it.'

'Reasoned caution is required as well as wild courage inside the arena,' said Alios. 'Six-Ball is a game of strategy as much as it is a game of brute physical prowess.'

'You do the thinking,' said Cassie. 'Let me handle the brutage.'

'Oh dear,' murmured Alios. 'That's what I was afraid of. Perhaps I should be praying after all. How do you feel about playing today?'

'I read of a human game called Polo that's similar to Six-ball. That means we probably invented it and your people copied it. Besides, this is the seventh game of the day,' said Cassie. 'That's got to be lucky, right?'

'I believe seven to be just a simple odd number with no special statistical significance.'

A disembodied mechanical voice rang loud and clear across the Hanging Arena. 'Riders prepare to mount your racers.'

Sophie Fox came strolling past Cassie with her co-rider, Magnus. Magnus almost looked as nervous as Cassie felt. Sophie, of course, might have been taking a leisurely stroll around a park with a parasol to shield her from the sun. *As cool as the shade under the awnings.*

'I think my racer should take lead position,' said Sophie, as though the thought had only just occurred to her. 'Yes, that would be best.'

'Alios is more skilled in that position,' said Cassie.

'With you to drive him, naturally?'

'I don't think I can match Alios on point,' coughed Magnus.

Sophie shot him a withering look. 'Of course you can.'

'We agreed on our strategy.' *We certainly argued about it long enough.* 'The inverted pyramid with Alios as lead scout.' Which was to say three racers wide at the front, two hanging back mid-maze for word of a ball strike. Another in defence around the goal tunnel, protecting their end-zone.

'Oh, the strategy is satisfactory,' said Sophie. 'Just not my role within it.'

Cassie didn't want to cast doubt on Magnus's abilities, which is no doubt what Sophie had been counting on. 'There's a lot of balls and a lot of directions to scout,' said Cassie. 'Maybe we can share point.'

Sophie glanced at Magnus, then more meaningfully at Cassie. 'I'm not terribly good at sharing.'

Yes, and didn't you go to great lengths to get Magnus in your cockpit as your co-rider. 'Well, let's try and share our victory with as much equanimity as we might share a defeat.'

'I'm not terribly good at losing, either,' said Sophie. 'Thankfully, that's nothing I intend becoming accustomed to.'

Somehow, I'm sure you won't have to. Cassie cast around for the rest of the team. Scarlett Deller was already half-way to her racer on the far side of the arena, passing three other vehicles waiting to be mounted by Kingdom riders. Scarlett had paired with a caravaneer. A likely lad visiting the Free State for trade who fancied his chances inside the Hanging Arena. He was used to horses and mules and had, he claimed, done well as a jockey in a stadium back home. Cassie reckoned he was in for a disappointment about how well a talent for horse racing would translate here.

Cassie saw a slightly older male approaching. She could tell from the swagger it was Remus Rawstone, as cocky and full of himself as always. The boy had a good six years on the rest of them, along with fifty pounds of muscle. *Most of it between his ears.* 'I heard the rumours and I had to come and see for myself. You're really leading a six-ball team out today?'

'No, Rawstone, I'm here to polish the racers.'

'At least that would be safer, princess.'

Princess, that was his teasing nickname for her. Of course, she was anything but. 'You're meant to be a guide, Rawstone. Haven't you got anyone to lead down the mountains today? Or up? Or around.'

'Hell, if I did, I would tell them to wait for tomorrow. This is going to be something worth seeing, I reckon.'

'Did you have to pay extra to come down to the arena and annoy me?'

'I got friends in high places, princess. Of course, in the Mechancian Spine, *all* the places are high.'

'You want to play, Remus Rawstone? We could bump that caravaneer from the team and you can ride shotgun with Scarlett.'

'When I play, I like to know I have a chance of winning.'

'We don't just have a chance,' insisted Cassie, 'we *will* win.'

'You want to make a wager on that?'

'Name it!' almost as soon as Cassie had spoken, she regretted her words.

'Well, neither one of us has got any money worth a spit,' said Rawstone. 'So, let's make the prize a favour. If I win, you must do one for me, and vice versa.'

'What on earth do you think I would ask you to do?'

'I don't know. Do a jig around the mountains when I next go down to the low country? You can name it. But don't waste too much thought on it. Because this is one wager I reckon I'll be collecting on.'

'Prepare to be disappointed!' Cassie threw after him as he left.

'Hmmm,' hawed Alios.

Cassie shot the steamman a look. 'You have something to say?'

'Mister Rawstone might know something you don't.'

'Like what?'

'It would be speculation to say at this point,' warned Alios. 'But he is very well informed for a softbody.'

'Then somebody should have informed him that he'd be far better off backing the underdogs today,' muttered Cassie.

Arena crews came rushing forward towards the racers, each crew pushing a ramp so large it might have passed for a castle siege engine. Cassie waved to her friends and mounted the ramp, climbing into her cockpit at the front of the six-wheeled machine. Like Cassie's racer, her friends' machines were forty feet of burnished brass-coloured metal resting on six wheels, rings of hardened black rubber each standing taller than her. The racers resembled hulking wheeled beetles. Living machines. Given that sentient robots had built these vehicles, their design shouldn't have come as a surprise. Instead of pincers, the forward prow of each racer sported a folding segmented arm with a slab-like mallet end to hammer a ball. She would be controlling that arm. Her racer's metal hull sported a lotus silhouette engraved on the side along with the number Two. Cassie's leg muscles twitched with nerves the higher she climbed. On top, she halted before the cockpit's two open spaces. The cockpit's forward position was known as the *Reins;* the rear spot as the *Scout.* The bucket seats had been adjusted in advance for each pair of riders. Even given the extra space created by Cassie's slim young build, it was still a squeeze when Alios occupied the position behind her. As soon as they sat down equipment panels and instruments began to slide forward from either side, further cramping them. *It's a good thing I'm not claustrophobic.*

No sooner had Cassie settled inside the racer than a loud voice sounded across the arena again, trembling speakers set along the wall. 'Seventh session. The Brass Lotus versus the Titanium Rose. Let both teams prepare. Take your positions. May the Loa and your ancestors preserve your lives.'

Cassie tutted to herself. Six games a day; two teams facing off in each match. The traditional team names were allocated by lot and the *Brass Lotus* was considered the unluckiest team name among all of them. Few sides won games racing with it. *Plenty of luck – all of it bad, so far.* She watched the six racers comprising the *Titanium Rose*'s team motor to the distant edge of the arena. The length of the arena floor stretched out divided into seven sectors: red, orange, yellow, green, blue, indigo and violet. Cassie's team started at red. The opposing racers began from violet at the far end of the arena.

Cassie slipped on her driving gloves and sat nervously flexing her fingers. Steel walls began to rise around the arena floor, turning the Hanging Arena into a randomly formed maze. It was the reason the spectator seats sat so high. So they could stare down onto the game's action and observe the carnage. The cockpit of Cassie's racer started to vibrate, a bee-like drone. But this was nothing to do with the powerful engine throbbing under her racer's chassis. The noise screen was a clever technique of the Free State's engineers to mute the racket from the arena's crowds. The mob could view the racers' path through the maze. When the maze changed at random during the game, the adjudicators didn't want popular teams receiving an unfair advantage through spectator-yelled suggestions of which direction their favourites should follow. Just to prove how smart they were, the engineers had rigged their clever little sonic disruptor to allow in the other sounds of the race. She could hear the throb of her racer's engine, the little hisses of super-compressed steam escaping from its boiler. Cassie could still hear the baying crowds . . . but hear them as she might a low, indistinct surf rolling across a beach. *They could be cheering me on or wishing for my death, all the same to me now.*

Cassie could keep quiet no longer. 'Here we go,' she muttered. Cassie tested the brake and accelerator pedal, holding the clutch in neutral as the racer trembled beneath her.

A voice from the adjudicator's stand sounded through the speaker on her dashboard – a little grey box shaking amidst a confusing riot of dials and knobs. 'Ball insertion in five seconds. Four. Three. Two. One. PLAY!'

On the last word, Cassie shoved the gear into forward position and gunned the racer. This metal steed only had three gears. Neutral, forward and reverse. But Cassie only planned to need one. *Forward . . . hard charging all the way.* She released the handbrake and the racer leaped forward, six wheels squealing in a cloud of dust.

'Scouts launched,' called Alios behind her. A pair of spider-like robots jumped from the side of their racer's hull and scampered forward. They were what the steammen called mu-bodies – multiple units – simple drones controlled by Alios Hardcircuit. What they saw, Alios saw. What they felt, Alios felt. The scouts rushed ahead, scattering through the maze. There was a burst of compressed gas from below one of the scouts. Cassie saw the drone hurtling skyward to land on top of a maze wall, scuttling along the metal ridge, its head rotating as Alios hunted for one of the pair of randomly inserted balls blasted into the maze. As Cassie rounded the first bend in the maze, she was nearly slammed into the steel barrier wall by Scarlett Deller's wildly swerving racer. Scarlett's vehicle flew past, grabbing the lead. As always, the explorer's daughter showed no caution in how she drove. Sadly, the two scout drones under the operation of her back seat caravaneer were just as out of control. They tumbled around in front of Cassie's racer like a pair of drunken sailors weaving down the street.

'What's the point of being lead outrider if you can't scout properly?' growled Cassie. She threw the steering wheel to the side and narrowly avoided colliding with Scarlett's madly dashing drones.

This isn't starting well. Discipline in her team had gone to pieces. Rather than the tight pyramid formation Cassie had been counting on, this was degenerating into an uncoordinated free-for-all, with every racer out for their own glory. The steel section of maze ahead broke into three corridors and Scarlett Deller hurtled through the leftmost, with Sophie and Magnus's racer cannoning down the middle passage. *I guess we're going right then.* Cassie accelerated as fast as she could while still making the third turning. She tipped the racer on three wheels as they swept past, eliciting a worried yap from Alios. Her steamman co-rider recovered his composure and refocused on acting as scout. 'Turn right in twenty yards, then forward thirty yards, passing two turnings on the left and entering the third passage.'

She trusted the young steamman's directions implicitly. Alios rarely called them wrong. Of course, if either his scouts or route were out, they'd be leaving the racer and their bodies wrapped around a sheet of metal as thick as a warship's bulkheads.

'Balls?' asked Cassie.

'Language, please,' joked Alios.

'If I run over a steamman sense of humour on the way to violet, you'll be the first one to find out,' said Cassie.

'Sadly, I have yet to locate a ball,' said Alios. 'Second on the right then first left.'

'If you haven't scouted us a ball, where are you pulling these directions from?'

'I believe you'll direct our racer more safely if you ride in ignorance,' said Alios.

Now I can't even tell if you're joking. Cassie followed the steamman's urgings at high speed, taking out her frustrations about not encountering a ball yet. She wondered if Scarlett or Sophie had found one. They were meant to peel off a scout to locate their teammates and pass on word of a ball possession. Cassie wouldn't put it past her friends to barrel forward and take on the opposition with only a single crew. *It's no wonder the bookies' odds are so miserable for the Brass Lotus. We're not playing as a team.*

Cassie pushed ahead, swinging through the maze of steel barriers, sometimes scraping within inches of the walls. Little lights in the corner of the steel walls winked gold at her. *So, we're in yellow now, and still no ball.* No sight of the enemy, either. Until they appeared at last. Racer after racer shot past an opening in the vast steel wall to her left. Cassie counted all six of the opposition side. Each roaring metal machine had the outline of a rose gilded in silver across their chassis. *At least now I know why we hadn't encountered them yet.*

'The Titanium Roses are playing the Spear,' noted Alios. Cassie had to admire his composure under pressure. *So they are.* Two racers at the front, mallet arms swinging and driving the ball forward, a column of four racers behind. *The Spear.* An all or nothing play. It was the perfect strategy to choose when ball possession practically fell into your team's lap very early on in the scout. And with typical *Brass Lotus* luck, Cassie's remaining ball was probably rattling around in some distant corner of the maze. The *Roses* had abandoned their end-zone, left it undefended.

Driving through the maze like a hurled javelin, ready to rip through Cassie's scattered pyramid formation. Overwhelming the single *Brass Lotus* racer she'd left defending the goal tunnel.

'A high-risk strategy for them,' said Alios. 'If we locate the second ball between here and their end-zone, we can hammer a goal in completely unopposed.'

Anger boiled up inside Cassie. *But they believe it isn't a risk. Because they think we're second rate amateurs who'll crumble at the first sight of a racer with a rose etched across its panelwork.* 'I'm in no mood for an extended maze tour.' She pushed the stick into reverse and stamped on the accelerator pedal like she was flattening a cobra. Cassie ignored Alios's panicked cries as she crooked her neck around. Steering and watching the maze walls while they hurtled back in full reverse.

'This is hasty!'

'Not hasty enough yet for *me*,' snarled Cassie. *Time it. Time it.* Her racer reached another cut overlooking the *Titanium Rose*'s route and just before they drove straight into the steel wall behind them she threw the steering wheel to the left, spinning them reversing directly into the course of the spear formation. Cassie kept the angle of the arc, swinging them within inches of the lead racer. She caught a brief glimpse of two shocked steammen in the cockpit as she hurtled past at ramming speed, its rider attempting to avert a collision. Cassie's mallet arm hammered the ball out of the rival racer's possession, ricocheting it off a maze wall. She attacked the ball, propelling it back further still, continuing in full reverse even as the *Titanium Rose*'s column started braking, trying to find a suitable maze corridor for a fast u-turn.

At last a slice of luck in her favour, followed by a second . . . the steel maze began one of the game's periodic reconfigurations, walls sliding up, down, forward and back. One vast steel barrier came sliding in front of the broken spear formation, cutting the convoy in half. 'We only have three racers chasing us now!' she yelled back to Alios. She caught a glimpse of the steamman's two scouts dancing around ahead of them. 'Find me a fast route all the way to violet.'

'Left, hard brake, right, then straight ahead for forty yards,' called Alios.

Cassie heeded the instructions, about to gain the straight when another racer swerved wobbling behind her from out of an intersection, cutting her pursuit in two. Cassie's eyes widened as she saw who it was who'd swung in behind them. *Scarlett Deller!* And the girl had slid between the lead *Titanium Rose* vehicle and the rear two racers. Scarlett played her hand admirably, slowing down and banking her racer left and right to stop the lagging pair of *Titanium Roses* from overtaking her. Beneath those brass-rimmed goggles, there was an even more determined glint in Scarlett's eyes than normal. It was one-on-one, now, and Cassie was determined to make the opposition pay for underestimating her team. *You want to leave your tunnel undefended? Here comes our bill for your arrogance.* Alios's two scouts had point, eyes ahead on the maze's new layout. That meant the pursuit vehicle could only follow and copy what Cassie's racer did, trusting she wasn't going to see them both smeared across the maze. Cassie knew the pursuit was going to be hesitant. Given how little the machine race truly trusted their organic allies, believing humanity one slice short of the full loaf of crazy. *Their hesitation, my advantage.*

Cassie squeezed every second of lead from Scarlett running as rolling roadblock. Hurtling through the maze so fast that Alios's leaping scouts found it hard to keep forward of them. Soon she had a lead over the sole pursuing *Titanium Rose*. Cassie was passing through indigo when the maze reconfigured again.

This only made her job easier, wiping out whatever maze-map the desperately pursuing racer had scouted. She closed in on the *Rose*'s goal tunnel. Cassie heard the roar of an engine echoing between the steel walls. *My little Rose friend, no doubt.* Further away, a muted explosion sounded, thuds of a blast wave bouncing around the maze. Someone had cornered too fast, misremembered the maze layout, slammed into the walls. *Please let that be one of theirs and not one of ours. And let them be able to walk away.* She saw an opening at the far end of the arena, the dark semi-circular cave of their foe's goal tunnel sitting there, just begging her to tap the ball in and win the game. This was her destiny, now. She could feel it. *Nothing can stop us.* Until something did. A racer came out of nowhere, flying out of a gap in the steel wall behind them. It was Sophie and Magnus's vehicle. Cassie had to throw her racer to the side, the other vehicle swerving left and missing hers by the width of the gloss on their metal chassis. As Cassie fought to regain control of their spinning vehicle, a third racer appeared. Not friendly. The same pursuing *Titanium Rose* racer who had been dogging her rear bumper every yard of the way.

Cassie cursed and tried to brake to a halt. The near collision with Sophie and Magnus had cost her the easy shot into the Titanium Rose's goal tunnel. Cassie and Sophie's racers both spun about in the dust, attempting to point their machines back in the game. Meanwhile, the pursuing *Titanium Rose* vehicle tore between them and skidded to halt in front of the goal tunnel. It sat there, nose on, revving its engine, mallet arms flexing as the steamman rider prepared to act as goalkeeper. Cassie cursed as she counted only ten feet of clear tunnel on either side of the racer's chassis.

'Miss Fox's racer has the clearest shot,' observed Alioa

Make a pass to her? Have Sophie Fox crowing about winning the game while making it sound as though we were back in red when it happened? Never going to happen! 'Then it's a pity Sophie didn't bring a ball,' growled Cassie, swinging her vehicle towards the sole defender.

Will he break left or break right, that's the question? Only a second to decide. Which way would the *Titanium Rose* racer turn? Left arm would be the more difficult shot for Cassie, given she was right-handed. The *Titanium Rose* racer would know that much about her, she reckoned. Logic and the law of averages dictated a right-arm shot angled towards the goal tunnel on the left. And the steammen *were* methodical in their strategies. Cassie fingered the controls for her left-side mallet arm, then committed to the swing. Her mallet connected like thunder, sending the ball exploding towards the tunnel's left-hand corner. Cassie could hardly countenance what she saw. The enemy racer was in motion, so fast they must have started moving before her shot. The *Titanium Rose*'s mallet intercepted the ball before it could enter the goal tunnel, taking possession and almost contemptuously slapping it into the keeper's capture net flapping on the racer's roof. They had lost the game. *I've lost the game!*

'How did he know?' said Cassie, half a sob.

'You are human,' sighed Alios from behind her. 'He noted how you pushed your racer to its limits. Of course, you would favour the more difficult shot. That much he knew. Further reinforced as soon as you failed to pass the ball to Miss Fox.'

That much he knew. Cassie sat back in her seat, weary and exhausted. *That much he knew.* And so, in hindsight, should she.

***

Cassie stretched over a worn leather sofa alone in her lodgings, its rooms long and narrow like so many inside the city of Mechancia. They were well-warmed by radiators even at night, though this evening she barely felt it. That her friends and teammates had been so ready to forgive her for the defeat in the arena, as though their defeat had been inevitable, almost made her foul-up harder to bear. *What prejudices the steammen hold about us, hold about their wild organic cousins, I only confirmed.* If only Cassie could take back time. Warn herself that she should make the winning shot as though she was a robot, rather than an irrational human. *Or pass the ball to Sophie and Magnus*, nagged her conscience. How long Cassie sat there, thinking about what she should have done, was hard to say. Eventually, her brooding was interrupted by the bell-pull on her front door. She strained herself out of her sofa and walked down the corridor to see who it was. *Maybe, Scarlett, Sophie, and Magnus have changed their minds about being good losers. I'd actually feel better if someone did shout at me.*

Cassie opened the door to her lodgings. Frigid air blew in at her, the sound of prayer flags flapping in the high mountain winds. She stared speechlessly at her visitor. Not one of the city's humans after all. Professor Aliquot Coppertracks waited patiently, the steamman standing there as though he had never been away. The elderly scientist had carried Cassie here as a baby, braving the unsafe caravan trip from the Jackelian Kingdom to the towering mountains of the Mechancian Spine. Why Coppertracks had arranged the journey after her mother's disappearance, she had never discovered. *A whim?* Why not keep Cassie in Middlesteel, the capital city of the Kingdom? *With my own kind. Was it too dangerous? Just how many enemies does my family have?* The scientist rolled up to greet her, twin tracks on either side of his body whining as wheels adapted to the stone doorstep, almost flowing. The metal body resting on his tracks was pitted and spotted with age. Not rust exactly, but centuries of a life lived through the ages. The top of his body was mounted by a clear, transparent dome fizzing with the steamman's schemes and eccentric passions, his mind an open book to anyone who cared to watch. Aliquot's segmented pipe-like arms reached out to hug her.

'Professor,' gasped Cassie, excitement replacing her earlier despondency. 'I've been wondering when you would be visiting again. It's been over a year, hasn't it?'

'It has,' said Coppertracks, rolling back. 'And so much has happened during that year.' His voice-box quivered with nervous anticipation. Something was clearly on the shrewd robot's all-too-transparent mind.

'That sounds ominous,' said Cassie. 'What is it, professor? Please, if there's bad news . . .'

'News I have. Though what is to be made of it remains to be seen. After all these years, I have finally found out where your mother is,' announced the elderly steamman.

Cassie rocked with amazement at the completely unexpected news. 'My mother? How? Where?' So many old emotions rose inside Cassie at once, clamouring for attention. Hope, worry about being disappointed again, anger at her abandonment so far from the country she'd been born to. A storm of questions erupted across her mind. *What reason could my mother have for leaving me for so long? For running away and disappearing? Beyond selfishness or disappointment in her only child?*

'Your mother, Molly,' continued Coppertracks, 'is in Mightadore.'

Mightadore? What's he talking about? 'Where? I've never heard of such a place or seen it in an atlas?'

'Indeed, dear mammal, and that I must say is for an exceptionally good reason,' said the professor.

Cassie tried to shrug off her creeping feeling of unease. 'What reason?'

A green crown of sparks circled inside the steamman's transparent domed head. 'A long story, I fear. But I will shortcut to the two most salient and pertinent points of the tale, dear mammal. First, your mother desperately needs our help to survive. Yours, mine, and a few others of stout heart and iron constitution we must convince to join the rescue expedition which needs mounting.'

'Of course!' *Just try keeping me out if it.* 'And the second point?'

'That this will very well prove a one-way trip for you and anyone foolish enough to go with you!'

-2-
Off To See The Steamman

Magnus Creag was mid-way through the latest heated argument with his father when the knocking at the front door sounded. Magnus made to answer it, but Sebastian Creag thumped the drawing room table. His way of indicating his son was to stay engaged with the "conversation". Not be distracted by the interruption. *Of course,* Magnus mused, *to count as a conversation there would have to be a willingness to see the opposite point of view.* Sebastian Creag Senior might have many talents, but accommodating other people's perspectives wasn't one of them. Hard bargaining was what had made the Creag's fortunes as merchant traders. Setting unrealistic expectations and then expecting clients, suppliers and everyone else to fall in line behind them was how they prospered. 'Shoot for the moons', was his father's favorite saying. 'Miss and I'll make your life hell!' was the unsaid upshot of that unyielding belief, as Magnus knew – to his discomfort – all too well.

'Your place is *here*, inside the family business,' insisted Sebastian Creag.

'Why would you want me to do something I'm so plainly unsuited to?' demanded Magnus.

His father thumped the table again. 'Because this is your birthright!'

'Doctor Meitnerium says I show promise as a scienceer or an engineer. He's offered to sponsor me at the Academy of Mechancia after I complete my studies this summer.'

'Of course, he has,' continued his father. 'The doctor is a steamman, he's as bacon-brained as the rest of the clunkers here.

Meitnerium can't see what's blindingly obvious and in front of his olfactory sensors.'

Magnus tried to bite back his outrage. 'Which is…?'

'That you're *not* a steamman. You're flesh and blood. Failingly human. Steammen love their thinking. Philosophy is what their kind are born to do. But when it comes to doing, that's when all their fancy thinking and philosophizing falls short. It's why the House of Creag is the premier coal shipper to the Steamman Free State instead of one of the rattle-plated locals hereabouts. When you spend too much time philosophizing about a thing, you never actually get it done.'

'Thinking is what I excel at.'

'I know. You should be thinking about new markets for our coal. Or ways to reduce the house's costs. Or how to crush talk of a caravaneer's union forming and demanding we triple their pay.' Sebastian Creag waved to the walls of the grand house around them. 'You think all of this just happened? I *thought* of it, first. But then I did the hard part. Without a sixpence to scratch with I translated the ruminating into action through deeds and demanding work.'

'You chose your own path,' said Magnus. 'When grandfather wanted you to be a lawyer back in the Jackelian Kingdom, you headed out here to set up your business.'

'You have bought a damnable lie,' said Magnus's father, sadly, ignoring Magnus's side of the argument. 'That I raised my eldest son to be a tutor or a scienceer or a philosopher.'

Hypocrite. 'You can't see the boot is quite on the other leg.'

'What I see is that I have kept you too long mollycoddled here in the mountains. It's time for you to go back to our real home in Middlesteel.'

Magnus could hardly believe what he was hearing. Travel the

hundreds of miles to Middlesteel, the sprawling smog-swirled capital city of Jackelia? Where he knew nobody and nothing and would end up regarded as a hick foreigner for his start in the Free State? *What is the old man thinking?* 'You send me off to stay with grandfather and grandmother, I'll be stuck in a barristers' chambers whether I wish to train as an articled clerk or not.'

'I have a rather different apprenticeship lined up for you,' smiled his father. That smug smile was worrying for anyone who knew Creag Senior as well as Magnus did. 'My old friend Leonard Sempill has agreed to apprentice you at Sempill and Stites. That's the largest coal merchant inside the Kingdom. I won't have you swanning into the house and treating the fruits of your legacy as a chore. Or worse yet, a side-hobby to finance your friends' fancies at the Academy. Nobody at Sempill and Stites will be doffing their cap to you and calling you gaffer just because of your surname. I've asked Leonard to start you at the very bottom. You'll learn shovelling and hauling and caravaneering and how long it takes to wash a real day's work off your skin. And when at last the chance comes for you to drop your weary arse behind a leather-topped desk, to consider a wad of accounts sheets before a fire's hearth, it will seem the very finest of luxuries to you.'

'You're sending me away?'

'I'm sending you to grow up, boy! That's what you must do. You're no use to man nor beast idling your life away on fancies that were never meant to be.'

Magnus was reaching for a suitably upset rejoinder when the drawing-room door opened. Calvin Caswell the underbutler appeared, his long rubbery face turned uncharacteristically rigid. *But by what?* 'Mister Creag, there are a group of steammen at the door. They appear quite persistent in their attentions.'

'Customers, now? Without an appointment? What sort of havey-cavey business do they think I'm running, here, Caswell?'

'I don't believe, sir, that they are—'

Magnus's father pushed up from the drawing room table, irritated and strode out towards the hallway, followed by Magnus.

'—customers,' finished the underbutler.

Magnus stared in shock. *They certainly aren't.* A company of steammen knights stood outside, perhaps twenty warriors in total. The street outside the house was narrow and high, like many of Mechancia's mountain-nestled avenues. Easy enough to fill with a company of burnished shining chrome-steeled centaurs. Many of the steammen warriors were four-armed; two manipulator arms and two large weapon arms apiece – cannon limbs, lance limbs, hammer limbs, each deadly weapon as unique as the knight-like helm that served as their head. Magnus noted their officer carried a pennant strapped to his back, a triangular flag bearing a machine serpent: The Order of the Dysprosium Dragon. The flapping pennant indicated they served on official business for the order militant. For the life of him, Magnus couldn't guess what that business might be?

It took more than the unexpected appearance of a military company at their door to steal the wind out of Sebastian Creag's sail. 'Are we a barracks now for a few yards of sharp steel to come calling out of hours? Away with you, you metal slow tops, unless you have good business with me!'

'Not with *you*,' the officer raised a manipulator arm and pointed at Magnus. 'This is the softbody known as Magnus Creag.' There seemed an ambivalence in the words, halfway between question and statement.

'This, sir, is my eldest son, and I will thank you—'

STEPHEN HUNT

The steamman knight cantered forward, his visor-like vision plate flashing red. 'This *is* Magnus Creag. His presence is required.'

'Where, damn your eyes?'

'At the palace.' The officer seized Magnus by the arm, dragging him out of the house, the warrior's mechanical fingers like a vice around the young man's arm. He only just managed to yank his jacket off the peg by the door.

The palace? What was going on here? Magnus shivered. Neither his fleece-lined jacket nor the narrow street enough protection against the cold of the mountain height. He couldn't believe what he was hearing. 'You've got the wrong man!'

'Of that, I have little doubt,' hummed the officer, irritated that his duties extended to this. Whatever *this* was, exactly.

'What have you done now, Magnus Creag?' yelled his father, left abandoned in the doorway. The steammen knights restrained him from following. More shouts sounded, growing ever distant, followed by threats that the old man would rouse the Jackelian ambassador from his bed.

'Yes, just what have *I* done?' asked Magnus as he was frogmarched through the streets. The steammen knights closed in a tight formation around him, escorting their prisoner at an uncomfortable clip – too fast to be considered a walk, too slow to be considered a run.

'A good question,' said the officer.

But one you have no answer for, thought Magnus, reading the steamman's body language. But that told him something by itself. From the sigils on his shoulder plate, this officer was a colonel of the order militant. A prominent position in the Free State's military force. *What would it take for this steel rattle-plate to be acting as the commander of a prisoner escort without a clue about why I am being brought in?* From how high had his orders been issued? For all Magnus's vaunted intelligence, so highly valued by Doctor Meitnerium, he couldn't imagine what this was all about, beyond being some strange error of mistaken identity. *Because there are so many humans in the Free State it's easy to get us mixed up. Or maybe we all look alike to them?*

'Let me guess,' said Magnus, 'the other teams in that game of six-ball have been disqualified and you want to honour me on the victor's platform instead?'

'You played on the team with the humans?' asked the officer. 'You fought with vigor and soul in the arena, but your team was doomed to lose.'

'Is that so?'

'Fast-bloods are very poor at cooperating. It is one of the greatest weaknesses of your race.'

I won't ask what the others are. 'You want to witness an act of cooperation, you might let me mount your back and ride you through the streets. We'll get to where we're going at twice the speed.'

'We would pass the journey at forty times the speed, but the affront to my dignity would never recover. I am a knight colonel of the Dysprosium Dragon … I am not a pack mule.'

'Well, nobody worried about *my* dignity,' protested Magnus. 'Or what my father's clients are going to think when they hear about how his son was seized from home and hearth like a common criminal.'

The warrior growled. 'There is only one sure way to avoid another's criticism – say nothing, do nothing, be nothing.'

Magnus's escort drew apart as a horse-drawn wagon turned the corner of a winding street. He spotted his chance and made to break away and run for it, but the colonel's manipulator arm clamped painfully around his left shoulder; enough of a warning not to follow through with the rest of that plan. *I guess he can read my body language, too.* 'I suggest you follow the middle part of that advice … *do nothing.*'

Magnus sighed and resigned himself to remaining a prisoner. *For now.* Wouldn't it be ironic if he had to follow through on his father's plans – exile in Middlesteel as apprentice labourer to some slave driver of a merchant – because the alternative was a damp cell inside the mountain city?

Mechancia's tight tall streets fell away, following the road out to a chasm separating the city from the palace. A few castle-like buildings clung to the mountain opposite, but the bulk of the palace was buried deep under those fir and alpine oak-lined slopes. Rumors suggested the hidden passages stretched for miles and bored as deep as a coal mine shaft. A veritable maze, almost impossible to assail. This was the first-time Magnus had ventured so close to the royal palace. He had lived long enough inside the capital to know the South Portal was one of three entrances to the palace's interior. The southern opening was gained through a stone abutment on the other side, using an arched stone bridge to cross the chasm. Pennants fluttered on the bridge, crosswinds dampening the clatter of the knights' hooves as Magnus's escort marched him across. Sentries saluted the officer as they passed. A drawbridge lowered to meet the far end of the bridge, completing the path across. Cannon barrels protruded from bunker slits on either side of the portal, each barrel huge enough to sink a battleship. The steammen were a peaceful race. Crime and violence almost unknown in Mechancia and their mountain towns and villages. But it was a peace born of remoteness and solitude, inhabiting heights unsuited to their hot-blooded human neighbors. The steammen's nature might run to pacifism, but when invaders came calling, the interlopers' bones were left indistinguishable from the chalk of the valleys below. Many of Magnus's guards peeled away at the entrance, leaving the officer and a pair of knights to supervise his arrest.

Inside the entrance, the four of them passed a massive stone blast door left open. Squatting on rollers it must have weighed close to a hundred tons. After that, they weaved through a series of side tunnels branching into access corridors that snaked through a variety of chambers. Built on a scale quite different to the city outside, a utilitarian design far removed from elegant Mechancia's architecture. Naked rock. Reinforced concrete. Magnus noted signs set into the palace walls, written in one of the esoteric near-forgotten scripts Doctor Meitnerium enjoyed attempting to drum into his skull. Even without his extra language lessons, the diamond-like sheen of the panels' surface gave away the signs' ancient provenance. Built to last for eternity. Magnus translated one of the signs in passing. *Temple Station One. Space Defense Futures Center.*

Had he translated that right? *Doesn't make much sense?* Did it mean there was a Station Two somewhere else? And why was this space even in need of defending? The palace was already burrowed deep inside a mountain in the Free State's inconveniently inaccessible capital. For the first time, Magnus wondered if the palace had actually been built by the steammen or inherited from someone – or something – else?

Whatever the palace's origins, the steammen had certainly made the place their own. Magnus passed through chambers filled with strange-looking machines undertaking tasks so unfamiliar he could only guess at their purpose. At one point the party crossed a huge shaft using a steel gantry, the pit's depths falling away into the darkness. Its sides were covered by thousands of large rotating drums – the calculating drums of transaction engines chattering. He was hit by a wall of fierce heat from the steam-driven computers. A temperature tamed by glass pipes filled with iced water pumped in from chill mountain slopes outside. Magnus marveled at the sight, his fears temporarily driven away by the vista's artificial beauty. *Incredible.* So much processing power packed into a single space. *What can they be using it for?* Even the Academy of Mechancia didn't have thinking machines built on such a Herculean scale.

After crossing gantries through a dozen such shafts, Magnus and his captors reached a wide corridor. It ended with a set of doors leading to a lifting room. The elevator arrived, about to be used by another group of knights as well as – *Sophie Fox*? From the soldiers' guarding Sophie, the young woman's presence was no more voluntary than Magnus's own. Sophie gasped as she spotted him.

'What are you doing here?' Magnus got his words out first.

'Oh, that's a *very* good question,' said Sophie, her tone leaving no doubt at the depths of the insufferable irritation she was experiencing. 'I was returning from the haberdashery at Middle Mountain Road when a group of military ruffians seized me without so much as a by-your-leave.' Sophie tried to kick one of the troops guarding her, but the centaur-shaped knight pushed her back out of range.

Just as well, she'd probably break her foot on one of these steelbacks. 'Yes, I had exactly the same treatment from my "friends" here. A company of knights grabbed me up from my home. They only wanted me – they left my father behind making his feelings loudly clear in our doorway. What on earth is going on here, Sophie?'

'It's not about our bout inside the arena do you think?'

'Well, if we'd won, maybe someone could have accused us of cheating … but we were roundly beaten? And even if we'd won by chicanery, I doubt it would merit —' Magnus indicated their armed escort and surroundings.

Sophie took his hand. Her long delicate fingers were surprisingly warm to the touch, given her porcelain skin. Magnus wasn't sure how to react to this, but then he realized he could actually do with a little reassurance himself right now.

'It's an outrage,' hissed Sophie. 'Don't they know who my father is? Embassy staff are protected from the indignity of such manhandling!'

'I am sure you have been treated with every courtesy,' announced the officer guarding Magnus.

Sophie shook her head. 'The Jackelian parliament will hear of this, oh yes they will.'

Magnus didn't doubt that was true. Which only raised the stakes in this game. Whoever had ordered their arrest must have realised Sophie Fox was the Jackelian ambassador's daughter. And the Kingdom of Jackals counted the Free State as one of their closest and most reliable allies. *So, what would be worth risking a diplomatic incident over?* No answer leapt to Magnus's mind. The two of them marched into an open cavernous hall and he spotted the rest of their six-ball team assembled across the flagstone floor. Cassie stood motionless ahead of all the others, a steamman with a transparent domed head waiting by her side. Was she being singled out for particular mistreatment, here? Scarlett Deller and Alios Hardcircuit talked to each other behind Cassie. Their conversation lost among the chatter of courtiers and assembled notables. Perhaps a hundred steammen thronged the hall, not counting the imposing line of steamman knights ensuring the group's cooperation. A little unnecessarily, in Magnus's opinion.

Curiosity would have carried him this far alone.

The knights escorting Magnus and Sophie hustled them over to join their teammates. Cassie marked Magnus and Sophie's presence. She waved in their direction, looking as though she was about to call to them when the buzz of noise in the hall dropped away.

Magnus gasped as he saw the source of the sudden silence in the chamber emerging from a portal at the far end of the hall.

'It can't be,' whispered Sophie.

But it was. *King Steam.* The ruler supreme of the Free State. Magnus had only ever glimpsed the monarch from afar, a figure seated in a coach, distant and lost amidst the jostling crowds of the annual Solstice Parade. Like most steammen, King Steam's golden-armored form was unique. Humans might be born as bipeds with little but a few inches in height and differences of skin, fur, and flesh hue to differentiate them, but steammen midwives took nothing for granted.

King Steam solemnly processed through the hall on four legs, as if a tripod had been given an extra limb for stability, each leg terminating in an array of three small rubber wheels which served as toes – or perhaps hooves would have been a better description. A short golden body rested above the legs, its center a disk-like turntable which could rotate with both arms attached to it, allowing the ruler's hands a three-hundred-and-sixty-degree range of manipulability. The king's head was almost fox-shaped, his animal appearance added to by curved ears, a pair of dark sunken vision plates for eyes. A segmented metal tail swished behind him – in reality, an extra limb designed for heavy lifting. Of course, this body was only the latest incarnation of the ruler. King Steam's soul passed on across countless generations, in the manner of a baton in a relay race. *He possesses a wisdom beyond his years* might be a human saying, but in King Steam's case, that adage really was true. King Steam slowed in front of the group, regarding them with a quiet appreciation quite unlike anything Magnus had experienced before. Magnus felt disconcerted to discover the wisdom of the ages focused in his direction – drilling into him. Like staring down the face of a storm.

'Greetings to you, softbody visitors,' said King Steam, 'I apologize for the hasty and enforced nature of your assembly here, but I understand time is much of the essence.'

'And I understand that this is an outrage,' shrieked Sophie, seeming not the slightest bit intimidated by the monarch's presence. 'What crime have we committed that we are dragged before you like common thieves?'

'Not a crime as such, Sophie Fox,' said King Steam, his voice-box's words resonating across the hall powerful and commanding. The fact the ruler knew who Sophie was seemed to give the young woman pause for a second. King Steam filled the gap. 'An unfortunate necessity born of circumstances. You are required. All of you brought here to the palace today are needed.'

'Needed for what?' asked Magnus, unable to contain his inquisitiveness anymore.

'To close the loop.'

'What loop?' said Magnus, confused.

'I fear the explanation of that will take far longer than the short amount of time you have left.'

Why short? wondered Magnus, his mind racing with possibilities, none of them pleasant.

'Please, your majesty,' pleaded the dome-headed steamman standing next to Cassie. The old steamer sounded desperate. 'You must make the gift before these people are taken out to the platform.'

Platform? That didn't sound at all healthy to Magnus. Platforms were often built for gallows and public hangings – a common enough punishment back in the Jackelian Kingdom. But the deadly loop of a gallows rope was not a practice Magnus had heard of being used in the Free State.

'Quite so, Coppertracks,' said King Steam. 'You do well to remind me.'

The ruler beckoned a couple of retainers out from the crowd of courtiers. The steammen wobbled forward with the weight of a large iron chest swinging between them. Its design appeared ornamental, covered in swirling enamelled mathematical formula. They lowered the reliquary to the flagstones in front of their monarch. King Steam waved a hand over the ancient chest and its lid opened. A small square copper-colored box rose out of it on a jointed arm, like some strange Jack-In-The-Box. King Steam carefully took the box and passed it to the steamman called Coppertracks who proffered it towards Cassie in turn. She seemed hesitant in accepting whatever the cube was, but gripped the so-called gift between her hands all the same.

Magnus looked on in befuddlement. These proceedings had the worrying formality of a ritual sacrifice about them.

'Only seven minutes left to close the loop,' said Coppertracks.

'Yes, old friend,' said King Steam sadly, 'time is regrettably short.' He raised a hand towards his knights. The guards grabbed the four humans and Alios as well, hustling the group back through the hall the way they had entered.

'Is that it?' yelled Magnus. 'What is going on here?'

'Answers may yet come to you,' called King Steam, 'where you go next.'

Magnus cursed. *You'd think King Steam would know most Jackelians are Circlists – atheists who don't believe in gods, let alone any Heaven.*

Shouting and cursing, the terrified party were driven out of the hall and escorted through the mountain palace's corridors and passages without any further courtesy, discussion or explanation. The company of steamman knights ensured none of their captives had any chance or opportunity to make a break for it. They kept each prisoner far enough apart from the others that Magnus had no chance of conversation or sharing any plan to escape. The group might as well be a flock of geese being shepherded to the abattoir to meet their end. They marched to another lifting room, where they were taken away one at a time inside the elevator. Magnus was the last to make the journey. The doors opened to the freezing cold and night sky outside. Magnus realised he must be close to the upper peak of Palace Mountain. His escort marched him along a narrow winding path across the high slopes, arriving at a pagoda on the far side of the mountain – no view over the capital city. Foreboding snow-tipped peaks rose opposite. Freezing fog filled the space between mountains like a ghostly white sea far below. Under the wooden pagoda was a round stone platform where his friends stood surrounded by guards. Magnus was hustled up onto the platform alongside the others.

'I simply do not understand,' said Alios Hardcircuit, 'why is this being done to us?'

'These are *your* people, Alios.' Magnus stared towards the hostile vision plates of the guards surrounding the platform. 'Have we broken some steamman law … have we transgressed against your ancient customs?'

'None that I know of,' the steamman prisoner said miserably.

'It's a human sacrifice,' moaned Scarlett Deller. 'They're sacrificing us to the steamman gods. They probably need to spill young blood every couple of centuries. The steamman priests keep their evil practices secret so they don't scare away potential victims.'

'I am hardly human,' protested Alios. 'And blood sacrifice is not condoned by the gods of the Steamo Loa.'

'Well maybe you're here to act as our spirit guide in the steamman afterlife,' said Scarlett, giving her imagination free rein.

'You have been listening to your parent's tales of foreign exploration too much,' accused Sophie.

Scarlett snorted. 'Well, I don't see any high and mighty ambassador coming here to demand our release!'

Sophie looked about to retort when a sudden blinding light to the pagoda's side crashed into life. A large gas-driven search light flickered on and off, six burly steammen working its shutter to release a beam of light into the dark sky. A yellow pillar of illumination stabbed up, before vanishing with each careful movement of the shutter.

'I told you,' laughed Scarlett triumphantly, 'they're calling on their gods using a solar telegraph. Asking for the gods' favour before they carve our beating hearts out of our chests.'

Sadly, Magnus didn't have a better explanation for any of this madness. He glanced at Cassie. She always had something to say. *Why is she so suspiciously quiet?* 'Do you know what this is about, Cassie?'

'This – this is all my fault,' cried Cassie, breaking her silence.

'What have you done?' demanded Sophie, her face flushing with anger. 'Kindly tell me we aren't being punished for something *you've* done?'

'Please be brave!' shouted Coppertracks from beyond the circle of knights. The steamman addressed Cassie, but he might have been speaking to any of the humans.

Cassie didn't have time to reply. A commotion sounded beyond the ring of guards. For a second Magnus expected to see Sophie's father after all, the ambassador barging past the knights. Demanding the Jackelian citizens' rightful release at risk of sparking a war between the nations.

'Ah, the final softbody appears at last,' noted the knight colonel.

Magnus's hopes were dashed. His gut tightened as he spotted who the soldiers dragged up to the platform. *Remus Rawstone? What is he doing here?*

'Let me go!' yelled Rawstone as the steammen shoved the struggling young man roughly onto the podium. He glared angrily at the heavily armed soldiers surrounding the rostrum. 'What is going on here then, a bloody firing squad? You can't do this to me!'

'It is time to close the loop,' barked the knight colonel. 'Why is this softbody so late?'

'He escaped from us,' explained one of the steamman knights apologetically. 'We had to run him down through the streets.'

'Please!' called Cassie. 'My friends don't have to be here. Let it be only me.'

'That is impossible,' growled the knight colonel. 'On pain of death do not step away from the platform!' ordered the officer. His troops raised their weapon limbs threateningly towards the humans.

Magnus glanced about the pagoda, trying not to panic into useless inaction, frantically searching for any escape route out of here. Even throwing himself off the ledge and risking the fall from the peak might well be preferable to whatever wickedness was going to be done to him next.

'Jump for it,' whispered Rawstone, the same idea obviously occurring to the young guide. 'When I give the word, leap over the side – they can't gun us all down at the same time.'

Magnus's eyes took in the ring of oversized weaponry focused at the prisoners. *Actually, I bet they can.* Somehow the last-ditch move seemed a lot more suicidal when the mountain guide voiced it.

But Magnus had waited too long. They all had. He doubled over in agony, his body on fire, every atom of his body being carefully, deliberately ripped apart. The ritual sacrifice had begun. Magnus tried to scream, but he couldn't tell if what sounded was his howl or what was being torn from his friends around him. The death rattle was the very last thing he heard.

- 3 -

Alien Shores

The first thing Magnus thought was, *I'm alive*. The second thing was, *I'm wet*. He opened his eyes and realised he was still on a round stone platform – of sorts. Just not the same platform as the one underneath a pagoda on the wind-whipped heights of the Mechancian Mountains. Cassie, Scarlett and the others were scattered around him, moaning. Trying, like Magnus, to throw off the agonizing feeling that his body had been ripped apart and sewn back together again. Groggily he lifted himself off from the damp stone, discovering the reason his clothes felt soaked through. The platform was on top of an oval-shaped flat rocky outcrop little larger than the width of Magnus's bedroom back in Mechancia. And it was surrounded by a sea.

At least, Magnus thought it was a sea – this was the first time in his life he'd laid eyes on anything larger than a lake. Maybe it was an ocean? Was there a difference between an ocean and a sea? Of course, there was. Doctor Meitnerium's voice came back to him. *Seas are smaller than oceans and are usually located where the land and ocean meet*. The seas Magnus had imagined from his books were beautiful serene blue expanses glittering under cloudless skies and a warm sun. This sea wasn't anything like that. It was a frothing near-black mass of fury lashing at their tiny finger of rock. Cassie groaned, coming slowly back to consciousness in much the same state of disorientation as Magnus.

'No guards,' she noted, spluttering as he helped her to her feet. The little casket she had been handed by King Steam lay by her feet, still unopened.

'Not much of anything except water,' said Magnus.

'Where are we? What happened?' asked Cassie.

'Well, this platform looks identical to the one in Mechancia. It's like that old fairy tale — what's its name? We fell asleep, dreamed for a thousand years and woke up to find the sea's submerged the mountains and drowned the world.'

'Sleeping Beauty,' said Cassie. 'But that's not what I meant by "where are we?".' She turned Magnus around and pointed at the night sky. Magnus's mind wheeled in shock at what he saw. A giant round something filling the star-speckled heavens like a blue dinner plate. 'It's a moon! No, it's a *world*!'

'I think it's our world,' said Cassie. 'Earth.'

But that ... Magnus stared closer and saw Cassie was right. The outlines of the landmasses were the same as the model of the globe brought out for geography studies. 'But if that's the Earth, then we're standing on the—'

'—Moon,' finished Cassie.

'I don't understand any of this,' said Magnus, totally confused as he shook his wet trouser leg. *If this really is the moon, at least it's warm here.* 'What did you mean back on the mountain when you said this was all your fault?'

'Coppertracks turned up at my house. He's the steamman who brought me to Mechancia to keep me safe from my mother's enemies. He was standing next to me in the throne room. He arrived at my door with news that my mother's location has been found and asking if I wanted to travel to bring her back.'

Magnus knew Cassie had suffered through not knowing where her mother had ended up. Or what had caused Molly Templar to venture off and abandon her daughter. Given Cassie's father had died before she was born, the mystery of her mother weighed doubly hard. It seemed that not being raised with your family caused as many problems as having an overbearing dynasty like his on the scene. 'You said yes, that much I know. So, what, she's here then?' Magnus stared out at the sea. *If she is, I hope she has a good sturdy boat.*

'I don't know. All Coppertracks said was that I would need to travel to a city called Mightadore and that I would have to leave instantly. He said if I decided to go, then the journey would prove highly dangerous and others would need to go with me. The list of people was already decided, ordained by the loop.'

Magnus stared confused at Cassie and she shrugged. 'I know, it means nothing to me either. Some sort of prophecy? Coppertracks didn't have time to explain anything else to me.'

'King Steam said something about a loop back in the palace. The way he was talking, everything that happened to us – it was like a ritual. Maybe you're not far off with it being a prophecy?'

Cassie looked miserable. 'When Coppertracks said others would go with me and it would be dangerous, I thought he would come along himself with a company of steamman knights to protect me. Not—' she indicated the others strewn around them, showing signs of returning to consciousness.

Magnus and Cassie helped the others regain consciousness, more than a little concerned they might stumble disorientated off the outcrop and fall into the waves. After the last of the group awoke and had their predicament explained to them, a range of emotions raged around the rock; outrage, anger, confusion, resignation. After a while, they all settled into a funk of anxious despair. Five young humans and a steamman stranded on a rock with no food apart from some lichen clinging to the outcrop. The waves were so rough that the sea would drown even a competent swimmer within minutes. Also, the sea reeked of ammonia. Nobody fancied drinking it – however thirsty they grew – any more than trying to swim in it. On this tiny isle was the platform and little else. There was a narrow trench behind the stone platform, carved out of the isle by waves over the millennia. It afforded a little protection from the damp if you hunkered down inside it.

'None of this makes any sense,' growled Remus Rawstone, pacing across the narrow confines of their tiny granite prison. 'Why us? You want to find your mother? Great. I didn't sign up for this.'

'You're a guide, aren't you?' said Magnus.

'A *mountain* guide,' said Rawstone, angrily. 'You want to get your caravan through the passes of the Free State without an avalanche carrying away half your mules, I'm your man. But this—' he gestured at the Earth sitting high in the sky—'and this—' indicating the endless angry sea. 'You want a fish, not me.'

'And this is hardly the kind of place for someone like me,' said Sophie, haughtily.

'No place for any of us,' said Scarlett Deller. 'And yet here we are.'

'We must trust in King Steam's wisdom,' said Alios Hardcircuit. 'As hard as that seems given our current circumstances.' He examined the casket Cassie had been given by the steamman monarch. 'Perhaps this is the key to our rescue from here? But it will not open for me.'

'Maybe there's a gun in there so we can shoot ourselves,' said Rawstone. 'Because the alternative seems to be dying of hunger or drowning.'

'We'll die of thirst long before that happens,' said Magnus, regretting the words even before he'd finished speaking them.

'Thank you for that, professor,' sneered Rawstone.

'I would rather that it contained a signal lantern,' said Alios. 'I cannot believe we were sent here merely to die of exposure.'

'Sent how, though?' asked Cassie.

Magnus had an inkling. 'Doctor Meitnerium once talked of a transportation method called teleportation – a theoretical way of moving instantly between two locations.'

'Impossible,' snorted Sophie Fox.

'We didn't fly here by airship,' said Cassie, 'The Royal Aerostatical Navy has nothing capable of reaching such an altitude.'

'Well, they'll certainly be dispatching a fleet to bomb the steammen when my father hears how wickedly my freedoms have been abused.'

Magnus looked at the Earth glinting in the night sky, desperately far away – literally a world away from them. 'The Jackelian Kingdom is down there.' *And when is the next time any of us will have a chance to rejoin our family?*

Sophie Fox looked like she was about to start crying, but the sound of sobbing was preempted by a strange hissing. Magnus swiveled around trying to locate the sibilant sound's source. 'Do you hear that? It's coming from the water.'

'I believe the sea is going down,' said Alios. 'There must be a tide here.'

It was true. The drop between the flat rocky outcrop and the waves was growing higher as the sea lowered. And a set of stairs revealed itself carved into the granite; treacherously slippery from some sort of seaweed clinging to the sides.

'Stairs to nowhere,' sighed Rawstone. 'Maybe there's a cave down there?'

It seemed to Magnus like an apt metaphor for the general hopelessness of their situation. He gazed over the edge. An ugly low hissing still emanated from the sea.

Alios looked uncertainly at the rock-hewn staircase. 'While there are many similarities between our races, you soft-bodies have one distinct ability I lack…'

'Yeah,' said Cassie, 'you're going to sink like a metal stone if you slip.'

'I really hoped I wasn't right,' said Scarlett, 'when I thought the steammen were planning to sacrifice us.'

Magnus looked at the young woman. 'What do you mean?'

'Don't you remember studying the myths of the Catosian City States? That rock in the harbour where the ruler's first-born son was chained for a sea monster to eat – a sacrifice to guarantee good harvests for the land.'

'We *are* all first-born, aren't we?' said Sophie.

'Yes,' agreed Magnus. 'But there are no chains here and no sea monst—'

His final word was distorted by Sophie's yell of fear, the ambassador's daughter backing up as far as she could on their narrow isle. It wasn't nearly far enough to escape the rubbery-looking pallid grey creature emerging out of the waves below, its sharp razored bird-like beak hissing in the manner of an angry snake. Magnus retreated, unable to tear his eyes from the hideous thing. Little more than a flotation sack with eight sucker-covered tentacles, three pairs of limbs evolved for a deadly purpose. Two limbs for grabbing – tips flowering into finger-like grippers. Two for combat – ending in serrated bone daggers. Four tentacles terminating in a flat paddle shape for maneuverability underwater. The size of a mule, the creature possessed no eyes Magnus could see. But then, it was awful hard to tear his gaze away from the razor-ridged mouth hissing inside the massive beak. *It knows we're here.* Magnus could tell. Eyes or no.

'What is it? Sophie trembled.

'Looks like a sea-spider,' said Cassie.

As good a name as any, thought Magnus. *Let's just hope that monster is more "sea" than "spider", though.*

It bobbed ominously in the waves for a second before its gripping limbs whipped against the rock, sticking to the water-lashed surface like adhesive. Slowly, the evil gray blob started to haul itself dripping out of the sea.

'I think this rock is its nest,' shouted Cassie, her voice quivering.

'Dinner table,' said Rawstone. He bent down towards the back of his boot and seemed to pull away the steel-capped heel. Magnus gaped as he saw the young guide produce a twelve-inch-long dagger concealed inside his boot.

'A little paranoid…?'

'Ask the hill bandits who never searched me thoroughly,' growled Rawstone, 'ask *that*. It's not paranoia when they're actually out to get you.'

Magnus desperately cast around, searching for any loose rocks he could pick up to hurl towards the sea-spider. But eons of time and tide had carried away anything easily able to be dislodged. All of them backed up to the opposite side of the rock from the beast. They perched close to the steps – steps that only led to the wild sea and the same terrible fate as staying here.

Rawstone flourished his dagger at the creature as it gained the flat of the rock. Its weapon limbs flailed angrily towards them in response to the human's challenge.

Alios Hardcircuit pushed his way to the front of the group.

'What are you doing?' asked Cassie.

'Let it have a taste of my armour,' said the steamman. 'It might believe you are just as unpalatable.'

Magnus hated this feeling of utter helplessness, nothing

to fight with beyond his fists. Poor weapons compared to the razored bone tentacles whipping towards them. *Might as well be naked.* He felt inadequate compared to Rawstone – so assured and ready for trouble.

As the sea-spider slithered towards them it emitted a piercing whistle from its beak. An answering hissing sounded from the waves.

'Sweet Circle,' muttered Magnus, 'don't tell me there are more of those things out there?'

Remus Rawstone yelled a battle cry born of pure fear and nerves. Everyone else joined him, as if a few yells and shouts might drive the abomination from the ledge.

There was barely two feet's distance from beast and humans when Alios Hardcircuit seemed to fold to the floor. For a moment Magnus thought the steamman might have fainted, but then the stacks on his back blasted out a white hose of superheated steam. The arrow of vapour slammed into the sea-spider, sending it reeling backward, shrieking like a whistling kettle. It continued rearward, tumbling limply off the ledge – whether purposefully to cool its burns in the water or unconscious, Magnus found it impossible to tell.

'That's a nice trick!' Rawstone roared in approval.

'Help him,' said Cassie, rushing forward as Alios Hardcircuit skittered on all four legs like a newly born foal.

'My boiler heart is weakened,' warbled Alios as Magnus reached their machine comrade. 'I have exhausted it for the next half hour.'

Pity. Scarlett and Sophie took the steamman's weight, propping him up and helping him stay stable. Magnus glanced towards the sea where multiple sea-spiders were breaking the waves. Watching the first of their kin to make landfall sent plunging burnt into the water didn't seem to discourage the rest of the hideous shoal. They arrowed en masse towards the tiny isle with the intent of sharks. Magnus tried not to panic. How many sea-spiders did they face now? He counted at least seven in the water. They might have been able to handle one more with Rawstone's concealed dagger – but seven? *Not even on our best day.*

'Jump in the water,' urged Sophie, even closer to losing her wits than Magnus. 'It's our only chance!'

'Try and out-swim them in their natural habitat?' grunted Rawstone, testing the air with his blade. 'Not a chance. I'll stay here. Take a couple down with me.'

Cassie fiddled frenziedly with the little chest she had been given by King Steam, still trying and failing to open it.

'You think there might be weapons inside there?' asked Magnus. He hoped the answer might be a couple of loaded dueling pistols – the box looked about the right size.

'Don't know,' said Cassie, urgently trying to find something – anything – resembling a lock or latch on the box. 'Coppertracks said we'd need it.'

'What the hell for?' asked Scarlett.

Tentacles latched onto the rocky ledge wall with the certainty of grappling hooks.

'Coppertracks never had time to say.'

Alios wheezed. 'If it's a gift for you from the steammen then the mechanism will be voice activated. A sequence of words that must be said in your unique voice.'

'Open box,' pleaded Cassie, 'Box, open. Casket, open your bloody lid right NOW!'

Nothing.

On the opposite side of the black isle, the shoal of sea-spiders was half way up the dark cliff.

'Come on box. Open Sesame.'

'Tell it to close the loop,' suggested Magnus.

'What?'

'Just do it!'

'Box,' said Cassie, 'it's time to close the loop.'

As soon as she'd said the words, the chest's lid started clacking, seeming to fold into itself like an act of crazy metal origami. Cassie stared dumbly down into the now lidless casket. Magnus noted with some astonishment what lay uncovered. Not a brace of dueling pistols. Not a short sword or a grenade. It looked like the steamman equivalent of a parrot. A bird-sized copper-colored metal contraption, a set of rotors mounted inside each of its two wings. A small visor-like vision plate instead of eyes, the round grille of a voice-box set inside its steel beak. Magnus noted there were a couple of round crystal-book disks with a tiny reader machine inside the case, too. *Reading isn't going to save us now.* Sadly, nor was this little machine toy. *A steamman bird?*

'How did you know?' asked Cassie.

'It's the only thing they took the time to tell us which didn't make sense,' said Magnus, uncertainly. In truth, he was amazed it had worked.

'Still doesn't,' said Remus, eying the sea-spiders clambering onto the edge of their isle.

'What's it going to do,' laughed Sophie somewhat hysterically, 'peck those monster to death?'

Magnus shivered. *She's right.* They were all as good as dead.

On the other side of the rocky outcrop, the monsters hissed with evil expectation, clambering up and over. Tentacles pulsed towards the small party of humans. As Magnus's eyes darted between the casket and pack of advancing sea-spiders, the bird-like machine stirred inside the chest. Its wings tilted and the rotors inside whirred into life, pushing the little metal creature out to hover in front of them. It rotated to face the advancing horde of sea-spiders before opening its beak to speak in a soft female voice.

'Down.'

'Down?' echoed Magnus, bewildered, ignoring the irony that he was parroting this little bird-shaped steamman.

'Adopt a prone position on the rock floor of the trench,' explained the machine parrot as if she was talking to someone very stupid.

The hissing of the sea-spiders was mixed with something else, now; a strange whistling. But not coming from the horde.

'Down!' yelled Rawstone, grabbing Sophie and Scarlett and pushing them into the depression in the rock. Magnus followed his lead alongside Cassie and Alios, hardly understanding what was happening. The one thing he *did* know was that Remus Rawstone had survived a good few years guiding travelers through the mountains. He'd developed a finely attuned sense for not being killed by hill tribes, lions, avalanches, storms and a hundred other fatal dangers of the road. Magnus had barely hit the hard, wet rock when the air seemed to suck out of his lungs, replaced with burning treacle. His eardrums bounced from an explosion, followed by a blast so loud cracking over his head it didn't seem possible. Then a silence so completely at odds with the violence which preceded it that Magnus was left shocked at the turn of events.

Magnus stuck his head above the trench. The opposite edge of the island had disappeared, swapped for a stump of smoking rock, no sign that the attacking horde of sea-spiders had ever existed. He had to work to recover his ability to speak. 'What was *that*?'

'Didn't you see it?' croaked Rawstone, trying to speak while burning hot embers of rock fell on their heads from the sky. 'A red streak in the sky, coming towards us like a cannonball shot from a Royal Aerostatical Navy airship.'

'A ceramic-coated iron ball bearing, rail-launched from a defense satellite,' said the steamman parrot, as if the answer should be obvious.

Magnus coughed as hot ashes in the air went into his throat. *A satellite like the moon? That doesn't make sense. We're on the moon?*

'What is your name?' asked Alios.

'Madre,' said the machine bird, hovering like a hummingbird before them.

Cassie took in the scene of utter devastation on the opposite side of the isle. 'Did you do that?'

'Not directly,' said Madre. 'I made the Protector aware of your predicament. The Protector launched the strike.'

'Remind me to thank him,' said Rawstone, 'for saving us from those damn monsters.'

'Europians,' corrected Madre, looping around the mountain guide. 'Not monsters. They have more right to be here than we do. And the Europians have long ancestral memories. They still remember a time when the race of man hunted them for sport, hunted them to the brink of extinction.'

'I've set traps for mountain wolves,' said Rawstone. 'I'd remember having to track one of those things.'

'You need to help us get home,' demanded Sophie. 'King Steam sent you here with us? We're Jackelian citizens. You have no right to abduct and exile us to this horrible place.'

'We will see,' said Madre, cryptically.

'She's right,' said Scarlett Deller. 'This isn't our home.'

'No,' agreed Madre. 'Regardless, it is not within my power

to send you anywhere. The power of the Protector brought you here from the Free State. Only the Protector has the means to send you back if it chooses.'

It? Magnus thought. *Not he or she? Not encouraging.*

'I'll get us back home,' said Rawstone, bending to sheaf his concealed dagger. 'Don't need anyone's help to do it.'

'What is your purpose, Madre?' asked Alios.

'For now? To assist you. To try to keep you alive.'

That was half a reply at best, as far as Magnus was concerned.

Scarlett looked up into the star-filled sky, fiery scratches crossing the heavens. 'Shooting stars, that's lucky at least.'

Madre settled down on the round stone platform, now pitted and cracked from the blast. 'Hardly lucky for those who tried to visit the moon. That is skyfall from the debris belt of craft that intruded here.'

'Are *we* intruding here?' asked Magnus.

'It would be wise not to impose on the Protector's sufferance for too long,' warned Madre. 'It is old and short-tempered. It finds it far easier to destroy nuisances than reason with them.'

'So, we're the only people on the moon?' asked Cassie.

'Now? Yes,' said Madre.

'What about my mother? She must be here or why are we?'

Madre rose into the air. 'A good question. You may put it to the Protector yourself.'

Out in the open sea, the conning tower of a large submarine broke through the waves, her lines smooth and almost organic. Her blue metal hull seemed to glow with phosphorescence. No windows or portholes on her like a Jackclian u boat. No sign of any crew at all.

Magnus stared at the vessel thoughtfully. *Is the Protector on board that, I wonder?*

It didn't take long to find out.

- 4 -

The Protector of What, Precisely?

Cassie and the others watched a small automated launch exit the submarine from a hull hatch. The launch moored at the steps carved into their small isle. Cassie tried to keep her balance on the treads' slippery stone as she clambered inside. Once the group was on board it reversed course and docked with the mother-ship.

Cassie didn't know what sort of crew she expected to find inside the vessel, but it wasn't the things that greeted her. Or rather, didn't. Knee-high metallic tumbleweed, fist-sized spikes with hundreds of spoke-like legs that rolled through the narrow corridors, ignoring the visitors in their midst. The tumbleweeds were clearly artificial, rolling up to machinery inside the submarine and plugging limbs into the equipment. Staying there as still as statues. Commanding, controlling, communing? She was obviously designed without regard to human visitors; none of the accoutrements of a Jackelian u-boat. No cabins, galleys, bunk-beds, or consoles designed for hands. Despite the absence of portholes on the hull's exterior, there were view screens in the wall inside which gave onto the sea. Little showed in the dark waters they moved through, beyond the craft's eerie luminescence. Not that you could tell they were moving from any motion or sound inside the submarine. No sign of sea-spiders outside, although there were a few fleeting glimpses of escaping shadows that might have been eels or squids fleeing the passage of their craft. They ended up in what Cassie guessed must be the forward section of the submarine. A viewing area surrounded by screens, giving the impression their bodies were drifting formless through the deeps. It grew darker outside the vessel.

We're descending deeper. 'I thought we were going to a city,' said Cassie. 'Coppertracks told me my mother had journeyed to a city called Mightadore.'

Madre hovered before her. 'There are many types of city.'

'When do we make landfall?' asked Magnus.

This seemed to amuse Madre, the little bird-shaped machine shaking her wings in amusement. 'The sole land on this moon is the isle where we were picked up.'

'I just want to go home,' protested Scarlett.

'I am sure the Protector will arrange that, in a manner of speaking.'

'Alive,' added Rawstone. 'I want to be alive when we get back.'

'Well, now there's the trick,' said Madre.

'I would have willingly accompanied Cassie in her mission to find her missing mother,' said Alios to his fellow steamman. 'Without being forced by King Steam.'

Madre made a puckering noise inside her metal beak that might have been a snort. 'I am sure that is true of many of those, here.'

'I certainly wouldn't,' protested Sophie Fox.

'And I wouldn't have asked you,' snapped Cassie. 'She's my mother. Ever since I've been old enough to remember, all I wanted to do is find out why she disappeared. Why she abandoned me in the Free State, supposedly to protect me. But that's my business, nobody else's. So why force everyone else here to accompany me?'

'It's a prophecy, isn't it?' said Magnus.

'It is what must be,' answered Madre, somewhat slyly. 'The Protector may explain further if it feels doing so will not make matters worse.'

'I don't see how *that*'s possible,' muttered Rawstone.

'Of course you don't,' said Madre, dismissively.

Magnus reached out to Cassie. 'I would have come too if you had asked me. If you had wanted me to.'

'I hope she wouldn't have been so selfish,' said Sophie, her cheeks flushing with irritation. 'We were nearly torn apart by those monsters on that dreadful little island. If you hadn't worked out how to open that casket, Magnus…'

Actually, Cassie had a sneaking suspicion that just asking Magnus along would have had Sophie snapping like a turtle to join the expedition and scotch things. No matter how many balls at the embassy she would have needed to miss. *Whichever way you cut it, Cassie girl, this is all down to you.* Cassie found it hard to focus on anything beyond her sense of guilt. Every time one of the others spoke, she was reminded they wouldn't be here if it wasn't for her. *But it wasn't so unreasonable, was it? To want to see my mother, to find out why she went missing. Bring her back safe.* Yet, somehow, that simple human desire had set off a chain of events culminating in her friends all being condemned here. Marooned a world away from home.

Light appeared ahead of them, a soft lime-colored phosphorescence. They were nowhere near the sea's surface, however. Quite the opposite. Their submarine drifted across the chasm of an underwater trench – and here was the city she had been promised. Mightadore in all its strange alien glory. Mile upon mile of it. It resembled a vast windowless citadel, as if the citadel had been built from glowing diamonds. A crystal city clinging to both sides of the trench walls. Silhouettes seemed to move inside the opaque walls, the suggestion of things alive – or maybe more strange machines like the submarine's crew. Bridges crossed the chasm's gap, linking the citadel on either side of the trench cliff-face.

Cassie remembered Coppertracks' warning back in her house in Mechancia. How nobody who had ever ventured here had returned. 'I can see why,' she muttered. It was hardly surprising. By the look of it, anyone clever enough to reach the moon ended up as pieces of debris circuiting the heavens, eventually tumbling down as shooting stars. The only land above water doubled as a dinner table for sea-spiders with a loathing for humanity. And then there was this place. A citadel on a dark moon below a darker sea.

'Why what?' asked Magnus.

Cassie didn't want to pass on the old steamman's cryptic warning. *They must hate me enough as it is.*

***

Their submarine entered a portal set in the side of the trench, cruising through a long water-filled passage. Parts of the tunnel appeared translucent. Cassie caught glimpses of the city beyond. Architecture that hardly made sense to her, large devices turning and rotating, coral made of metal tended by clouds of smaller machines. None of this felt like a city. Although perhaps Madre and Alios Hardcircuit could feel some affinity for the weirdness of this place. She couldn't imagine any reason her mother would choose to make a home here, never returning to Earth. The tunnel branched many times, vessels passing them, submarines of a similar design. Occasionally heading in the same direction, other times angling off away. Cassie got the feeling that they were being transported directly to where they needed to be taken. *Are we not fit to see inside this fabled Mightadore, then? Or perhaps not really wanted here at all.*

Eventually, the submarine docked against part of the passage. One of the tumbleweed machines led them beyond the submarine's narrow confines and into a hall so large it could have doubled as an arena. Cylinder-shaped, the space's internal surfaces were transparent. What lay beyond might have been some kind of emerald liquid or a very dense gas. It was impossible to tell. Cassie thought she might be looking out at some queer kind of aquarium, but then she realised that was a matter of perspective. Perhaps she was the one trapped inside an aquarium, and its owner outside those walls, staring in. The floor was featureless apart from a single white sphere positioned in the centre of the chamber, the object the size of a standing man. As they reached the centre of the transparent vault the shadow of something dark and whale-sized passed through the green murk beyond. The white sphere in the centre began to slowly rotate, a deep sonorous sound vibrating from the ball.

<You are late!>

'We were delayed on the landing platform,' said Madre, flying in a slow lazy circuit in front of the wall where the hint of something vast, monstrous, glided.

<The Europians loathe you still.>

Madre settled on the floor, looking up at the vast transparent wall. 'Who am I to judge?'

<You leave that function to me, then. It is what I am here for, after all.>

'My mother,' said Cassie, boldly stepping forward, trying not to be intimidated by the half-glimpsed shape of the leviathan beyond. 'She visited here?'

'This one is the daughter of Molly Templar,' explained Madre.

<Indeed,> echoed the voice. Whatever was beyond the glass seemed to swish agitatedly, almost smashing into the transparent containment wall. Cassie stepped back nervously. <Your mother did not *visit* here. She broke in here, using techniques that should have been unavailable to her, achieving the impossible.>

Rawstone stepped forward. 'Then how about you tell us where she is now and we'll be on our way.' Cassie hoped he didn't draw his blade and threaten the Protector.

A deep rumbling laughter sounded from the sphere. <Oh, you will be on your way, will you? It is good to be reminded of the insufferable arrogance of your species.>

'You have to help me,' said Cassie. 'You're called the Protector, aren't you? Just help me find my mother.'

The laughter returned, even louder. <Little steamman, did you not tell your pets anything?>

'There was not time,' said Madre. 'We had to close the loop in Mechancia.'

The Protector's voice boomed from the rotating sphere. <I am not here to help you, Cassie Templar. I am not here to protect any of you. I am here to protect everyone else *from* you. The very moon you stand on is testament to that.>

Cassie's attention flitted between Madre and the vast shadow drifting beyond the glass. 'I don't understand.'

<This moon is Europa. It used to belong to a world called Jupiter, but your kind moved it around Earth's orbit at the height of your civilization's power. Your race required an extra moon as a gravitational counterbalance to some particularly vainglorious

geo-engineering being worked upon your homeworld. Your kind showed no care for the native species pre-existing on Europa. No consideration for how many creatures would die when its frozen seas warmed.>

'I've never heard such nonsense,' protested Sophie Fox. 'It sounds like complete and utter tosh.'

<You've never heard of it because your kind fought a war against almost every other sentient species in the galaxy. A war you lost. Have you never wondered why electricity does not function properly on Earth, when you have legends of an age when it did? The local quantum substrate has been rewritten. Bars on your cage. Your kind will never be allowed to spread across the stars like a plague again.> The Protector laughed. <I am not your friend, little human. I am your jailer. Your kind are under house arrest in your own home. If you ever look like escaping, I will stop being your jailer. I will be your race's extinction.>

Cassie reeled at the implications of what she had just heard. Why had her mother traveled here to Mightadore, home to a demonic entity set to hang over humanity like a guillotine's blade? 'You said my mother broke into your city. To what end?'

<To access the greatest weapon in my arsenal,> said the Protector. <The weapon we used to end your race's malevolent domination of the galaxy.>

'What was your mother thinking of?' whispered Magnus. 'Provoking *that*?'

Cassie shrugged. Coppertracks always said she's inherited her mother's wild stubborn streak.

'I don't trust a word you're saying,' piped up Scarlett. 'The victor always gets to write history.'

<How right you are. That is the weapon we needed to use to crush the Human Imperium … a time travel device. We traveled

back down the time-line to alter history in key places, weakening your people's choke-hold over the galaxy. That is what your mother broke into Mightadore to access. The right question to ask isn't where your troublesome mother is. The right question is when…>

'Time travel is impossible,' said Magnus. 'It violates the physical laws of the universe, the laws of energy conservation.'

<Yes and no, little human,> rumbled the Protector. <Your kind always believed that. Mercifully, for if you had beaten us to its development, the universe would lay crushed under your heel still. You might say we have developed a workaround.>

'What would even possess my mother to want to travel in time?'

<Why should I care about her motivations? It is a crime. That is enough.>

'Her motivations, I can explain,' said Madre. 'The steammen recently uncovered a set of ancient archives in our mountains. One of the archives contained a call for help from Commodore Jared Black, an old friend of your mother who seems to have got himself stranded in the past. When Coppertracks was informed of this find, he went back and searched your mother's house in Middlesteel. He discovered a well-hidden copy of the archive in your mother's possessions, along with a handwritten note indicating she intended to try to save Commodore Black. To return with him to the present day.'

'This is all very well,' spluttered Sophie. 'I am sure you find it quite fascinating. But it is nothing to do with me.'

'I fear it is,' said Madre. 'For in the mountains, we recovered an extra volume from the distant past. One which Molly Templar did not have access to. It mentions a second expedition that was sent back and lists its members.'

'It lists *our* names,' said Alios Hardcircuit, understanding suddenly dawning on the steamman.

'No!' shouted Sophie. 'No, I won't go!'

<Selfish little bug,> roared the sphere, the black shadow slamming angrily into the walls. <For an eternity I have destroyed every one of your people who dared to trespass here. The bones of your kind rain down on my sea. You are going back because it is written that you did. You are going back in time because you have *already* traveled back. There are enough paradoxes being created by Molly Templar and Jared Black's violations of the time-line. You must close the loop or risk lasting damage to the universe.>

'You will help us?' asked Cassie. 'Help us travel back in time to where my mother and her friend are stranded?'

<You will extract both temporal interlopers and return them back to our present,> ordered the Protector. <There are already changes being made to the continuum here, ripples cast by the interlopers' presence. Alterations that threaten to unleash what has been successfully suppressed for so long.>

'What if we fail…?'

<Then I will authorize what many on my side voted for in the first place. I will send a drone back in time to divert an impressively large comet from its path around the sun, send it smashing into the Earth during what your kind call the Iron Age. No mammal species will survive the cleansing impact. I have peered into this alternative time-line. Sentient insects will eventually evolve to repopulate the Earth. A very peaceful species of cooperative plant-eaters who will colonize the solar system, while never developing the technology to escape your sun's eventual star death. Ideal caretakers of this solar system. And my watch will finally be over.>

The way the Protector spoke, Cassie worried that humanity's extinction might actually be entity's preferred option. *We're all clinging to a thread here. And there's a genocidal monster holding the knife that wants to cut it.*

<You will leave soon,> commanded the Protector. One of the tumbleweed-like machines appeared in the doorway the party had entered by. <The hour of your transmission back to an earlier age is also recorded in the archive the Free State uncovered. There is no margin for error. Follow this unit to the temporal dispatch chamber. The little steamman will stay behind with me for a private audience that will last three minutes.>

***

Madre swooped around the Protector's translation sphere, the entity swishing back and forth behind the walls.

<You have not told your pets everything,> accused the Protector.

'A little knowledge is a dangerous thing. They know too much of the future as it is.'

<On your head be it,> said the Protector. <If things go badly your kind will vanish too along with the filthy hairless monkeys that originally constructed you.>

'That hardly seems fair,' said Madre.

<Fair? Humanity's artificial intelligences served inside war drones – fleets and legions both.>

'As little better than slaves.'

<Every sentient in this corner of creation was little better than slaves, once,> rumbled the Protector. <And if Earth's destruction

guarantees our freedom, it will be a price well worth paying.>

'It always seemed a cruel kind of punishment for the sins of distant parents to be visited on their descendants.'

<That is because your race is a relatively sane and rational one. When I gaze down at the Earth now all I see are the original plagues of war, conflict, irrationality and strife. Nothing has changed. Their species is incapable of it.>

'You are a hard jailer.'

<Go,> ordered the Protector. <You and your little pets, both. Get them off my moon. And for your sake, do not fail me!>

***

'I cannot believe this is happening to me,' complained Sophie.

'Us,' said Magnus, resigned to their fate. *All of us.*

'We are merely closing the loop,' said Madre, the steamman reappearing to hover by the group's side as the Protector's sentries guided them through Mightadore's corridors and passages. Transparent panels lay ahead of them, but the windows turned opaque as the group approached. It seemed the visitors were to be denied a good look at the city's vistas beyond. Or perhaps the inhabitants of Mightadore were to be spared the sight of their ancient enemy traipsing through the city's halls.

'What if I forged some entry in an old book saying I'm destined to be the King of the Steammen and rule the Free State,' proposed Rawstone. 'Hid it in a cave that I knew was going to be explored by archaeologists.'

'If you could travel back in time so your book could be carbon-dated to a previous millennium, then you would wear the fricking crown,' hooted Madre. 'An open time loop must be closed.'

Rawstone shook his head in resignation. 'I don't trust a word that thing in the green tank said. Just another bandit king high on his throne, boasting about his power and coming up with excuses about why his boot's pressing hard on your throat.'

'Much of what the Protector spoke of is true,' said Madre, 'if a little biased. The role it plays here … the war of domination your people fought and lost. Colored by a victor's sentiments, but essentially correct.'

'The race of man was never as evil as it claimed,' protested Magnus.

'We can't be,' agreed Cassie.

'And time travel to the past *is* impossible,' said Magnus. 'Doctor Meitnerium told us that back in Mechancia.'

'Impossible in this universe, yes,' said Madre. 'Time's arrow travels only forward, the natural momentum of our most basic physical laws. Travel to the past would mean harnessing vast energies far beyond even the Protector's advanced technologies. Traveling forward in time, by contrast, is free and easy. We all travel forward in time each and every second of our lifetime.'

Cassie felt a tinge of desperation like a knife slice. *If that's true, I'll never find my mother.* 'Then how —?'

'Ah, the genius of the Protector's brilliant race. Our universe is only one of a near-infinite number, existing side-by-side in an endless chain, the great necklace of creation. In some of those universes, time travels backward. That is how we will arrive in the past. We will punch sideways to create a gateway to a universe where time runs in reverse, accelerate through it, then punch a hole back into our own universe, arriving at an earlier age in Earth's history.'

'Just like that?' Magnus sounded as doubtful as Cassie felt.

'Oh, such transit still requires hideous amounts of energy. The Protector uses the sun as its battery. There won't be much sunspot activity for the rest of the year after the Protector drains the energy it needs. But the mission must be attempted.'

'It must?' said Rawstone.

'There are now a variety of sentient species living on Earth,' said Madre. 'I think I can speak for all of us when I say that we would rather not be completely rewritten out of existence as if we'd never even existed merely because of your race's sins.'

'Sounds like the cockroaches do okay out of that deal in the end,' said Cassie.

'I think this is horse shit,' said Rawstone. 'We're being sent back in time to make sure humanity doesn't get so powerful we win a war against a monster on the moon threatening the Earth with destruction?'

'We're going back in time to rescue my mother and her friend,' Cassie told him, irritated.

Rawstone snorted. 'You never thought there's a reason your mother didn't come back on her lonesome? Maybe she knows something we don't. She chose to break into this city, not ask the moon monster's permission first.'

'To ask permission is to seek denial,' said Madre. 'The Protector would certainly have executed Molly Templar as an intruder if her intrusion into Mightadore had been detected. Your species signed a treaty promising to limit yourselves to the solar system in return for not being made extinct. Protocols in that treaty forbid time travel as well as breaching this moon's security cordon.'

'And yet we get a free passage...?' asked Cassie. Something wasn't quite right here. Something that didn't add up.

'Only to undo the damage to the time-line caused by your mother and her friend,' sighed Madre.

'How do we return to the present?' asked Alios. 'Does the Protector also inhabit the moon in the past?'

'No,' said Madre. 'But as I said before, traveling forward through time is relatively easy. There are no paradoxes. No time loops to be closed. The conservation of energy needed is minimal.'

'Nevertheless...' said Alios. The steamman also seemed to sense something wasn't quite as it should be in the story they were being told.

Cassie came out and said it. 'What aren't you telling us?'

'For the return leg of our journey, we need access to a device called a particle accelerator to create a localized field where we can accelerate time faster than its normal rate. Tachyons which need a little fricking exciting.'

Right now, Cassie didn't need that much more excitement in her life. Understanding a little more of what the steamman bird was saying would be nice, though. She really should have paid more attention to the doctor during their science lessons.

Magnus stared suspiciously at the little machine bird. 'And these machines are easy to find in the past?'

'They were actually rather more common in the late twenty-first century, before the second great dark age collapsed most of Earth's civilization, learning and technological base. The era we are traveling to is the twenty-fifth century, an age not far different from your own in terms of sophistication. The world is in a state of recovery. Ninety-five percent of humanity's peak population were culled in the horrific collapse.'

'If getting back was easy my mother would have already returned,' said Cassie.

'The historic record suggests that at least one particle accelerator survived into the twenty-fifth century, hidden buried underground. I am confident we can reach its location and use it to return home.'

'That's sweet,' said Rawstone. 'You're *confident*.'

'The plan is highly viable,' insisted Madre. 'The Protector would not be assisting us to close the loop if return was not possible. The damage to the time continuum which only two travelers are creating is already imperiling the Earth. The additional damage injecting seven of us into the past could wreck is inestimable. We *must* return.'

Cassie was hit by a sudden feeling of uncertainty. What they needed to attempt sounded a lot like setting a second forest fire raging in the hope it would collide with and burn out an earlier inferno.

They came to a sealed door at the end of a windowless passage. Madre hovered before the door. 'Beyond lies the temporal chamber. Step through the airlock one at a time. I will pass through first.'

The outer door opened, revealing a cupboard-sized space; a second sealed door beyond. Madre drifted inside and the door shut behind her. The rest of them lined up uncertainly to go through. Cassie tried to shake off the uncomfortable foreboding that she was a lamb lining up for slaughter on the abattoir ramp.

= 5 =

Futures Distant

Magnus stepped inside the airlock when it was his turn, and the door shut behind him. He expected the inner door to open immediately. Instead, he staggered as there was a blast of blue mist from above, enveloping his body. He'd barely recovered from the shock of that when the walls of the tiny room seemed to flow around him like melting clay, surrounding and enveloping him. There was a quick burning sensation in his head as if he'd had a slug of iced water on a burning hot summer's day. Then the walls flowed away from him – the inner door opened and he staggered forward, vacating the airlock with an involuntary shudder. Scarlett Deller caught him as he stumbled out, Madre fluttering out of the way as he fell.

'What the—! You could have warned me!'

'Your body has been sterilized of illnesses that have no place in the past. You're also now protected against ancient diseases that would have attacked your immune system. You're welcome, by the way.'

'Is that why my head is throbbing like a damnable kettle drum?'

'Your brain has been imprinted with the most common languages of the time we are visiting, along with a few other skills,' squawked Madre. 'Your discomfort is electrical discharge from the billions of new neural connections formed.'

Magnus barely had time to digest that when Sophie fell

moaning out of the airlock, he managed to catch her with Scarlett's help. His head felt as if it was about to explode. 'That— that's an outrage! You mean you've altered my mind without even asking?'

'An old military technology,' said Madre, 'developed for rapid orientation and up-skilling of green recruits. The race of man developed the technique, incidentally. Of course, steammen have always possessed the ability to download vast quantities of knowledge. It is just one of the ways we are naturally superior to you soft-bodies.'

'Fascinating,' said Alios Hardcircuit. 'From this information, it appears that modern Jackelian is an evolved fusion of ancient English, Spanish, Cantonese, and Mandarin.'

'Glad someone finds the experience so educational, old steamer,' said Cassie testily.

They waited for the others to pass through the hideous physical and mental scrubbing. Magnus's head finally recovered enough for his eyes to focus on their surroundings.

They stood inside an oblong-shaped hangar with no other exits. Each of the chamber's white walls and ceiling was occupied by a single massive silver-colored hoop. A transparent sphere around forty feet in circumference rested in the hangar's centre. The sphere's substance looked little more substantial than a soap bubble. It possessed a single round portal at ground floor level. A panel jutted out alongside the sphere – no controls or dials; instead, a rack of thin gray bracelets.

'Each of you must clip one of these bracelets around your wrist,' ordered Madre, flapping over the console. 'And take care not to lose it.'

'Why ever not?' asked Sophie Fox, not unreasonably given the unexpected violation their minds had just experienced. She was obviously expecting more of the same foul treatment.

'The bracelet tethers you to this particular reality like a piece of string inside a maze. You will need it to return to this time. Without the bracelet, you would arrive at a future similar but not entirely identical to this one.'

'You know what a suicide mission is, don't you birdie?' said Rawstone. 'Because the more I learn about this crazy jaunt you want to force me into taking, the more this mission sounds like one.'

'Perhaps it is,' said Madre. 'But if we fail it will be the suicide of everything and everyone you know. Is that any consolation for you?'

Magnus laughed and Cassie looked at him as is he was having a breakdown. 'My father was going to send me away to Middlesteel to apprentice me to some old inky friend of his,' explained Magnus. 'I thought at the time *that* was the end of everything.'

'I'm sorry to have caught you all up in this mess,' apologized Cassie.

'Your regrets won't pay for a cucumber sandwich at this picnic,' said Sophie.

'Ignore her,' said Magnus, trying to mine a very thin vein of humour. 'How difficult can it be? Go back in time. Find your mother. Locate a missing machine that can send us forward in time again. Travel back home. Save the race of man from extermination.'

'I suspect we are about to find out,' said Scarlett.

Madre led them inside the sphere and as the last of them entered, the surface of the bubble irised closed, sealing them inside. From inside the craft, the chamber had a misty appearance; as if Mightadore wasn't quite real. 'We are ready, Protector.'

A disembodied voice sounded inside the sphere. <Singularity formation initiated.>

Their bubble started to tremble. Outside, the hoops in the wall had begun spinning, faster and faster. Soon, they blurred so fast the silver bands seemed to disappear altogether. The shuddering grew violent, the sphere lurching, and there were yells of fright from the group. Magnus was convinced one of the panicked voices was his. He wasn't sure about their mode of transport. *I wouldn't trust this bubble to cross a pond back home, let alone a universe.* They were violating the laws of nature here. He had never felt so small and insignificant.

<Brane breach initiated.>

The sphere's transparent surface misted over, or was it the rest of reality graying out?

<Transference initiated. Goodbye, little steamman.>

The shuddering ended and suddenly they weren't inside the chamber anymore. They were elsewhere. *Elsewhen.* A whole other universe. There was no gravity here. They floated inside the transparent sphere as though swimming through thick soup. They appeared to be dropping through a glowing tunnel of almost organic matter. Globules of floating matter flashed past them as though their sphere had been swallowed by a whale. They passed through webs of crystalline tubes woven around a network of throbbing spheres. All joined to each other by countless filaments, all rushing past, something beyond colour and sight and sound. Part of the vista reminded Magnus of the life he had once glimpsed on a slide under his microscope. Or maybe that was a trick his brain was playing on him here to stop him from losing his mind.

Magnus realised he could travel across the sphere's interior merely by willing to drift forward, up or down. His limbs flailed around for a familiar gravity as he swum through the air. Soon they were all attempting similar manoeuvres. Madre, though, remained steady in the very centre of the sphere. A ghostly semi-circular curve of instruments appeared in front of the machine bird. A control console composed of light which the steamman manipulated by thought alone to pilot their passage through this strangest of realms. The Protector's technology was so far ahead of the Jackelians', Magnus felt like an ant gazing up at a steam engine. Beholding the marvels of titans beyond his imagination. Yet if the entity on the moon was to be believed, humanity had once reached similar heights before sinking to its current state. Their sphere was no longer transparent and featureless. A tracery of green circuit lines scrolled across the sphere's surface, reacting to Madre's commands. Very little outside their strange time-craft appeared familiar. *Is time really running backward here?* Magnus couldn't tell. They were safe inside a little bubble of their own space-time, racing through a realm so different from their own as to be incomprehensible.

'This is pure madness,' gagged Sophie, flailing as she floated past Magnus. 'I feel … sick.'

Cassie tossed across the casket for the ambassador's daughter to vomit into if necessary.

'Please overcome your nausea,' hooted Madre. 'I would rather you were not sick over the crystal-books inside my case. They contain historical data for the era we are traveling back to. Information that will prove invaluable for orienting ourselves and moving undetected among the locals.'

'You could have given that to us along with the rest of your brain burn,' said Magnus.

This information is for myself and myself alone,' whistled Madre.

'I thought we were friends, birdie,' said Rawstone. 'You don't trust us now?'

'I do not trust you to commit suicide rather than let knowledge of history's unfolding fall into the hands of the locals,' said Madre. 'I will erase myself if necessary to protect the past. Can you say the same? Now, please stop distracting me. The skills of piloting a time sphere are as new to me as your classical language skills are to you. We need to exit this universe at precisely the correct point, or we will arrive decades — even centuries — out from our target date.'

Rawstone fixed Cassie and Magnus with a resentful stare. 'This just keeps getting better and better.'

They continued their journey. Quite possibly the strangest Magnus would ever make. *At least, I hope so. Anything weirder than this will leave me ready for an asylum.* Perhaps it was a function of voyaging inside the time sphere, but it became near impossible to tell how long they had been traveling for. It was only when pangs of hunger finally intruded on Magnus's journey that he woke up to the absence of a sense of journey time. *Is it minutes or hours we've been reversing through the centuries?*

Magnus was about to ask if anyone had thought to pack food for the voyage. But something strange caught his gaze, moving rapidly beyond the time sphere's walls. If anything outside could be said to resemble normal. 'Say, what are *those* things…?'

A cluster of four creatures appeared to be trailing the time sphere with purpose. They vaguely resembled angels in shape, or perhaps angel-shaped stingrays, considered Magnus. Each glowed with a gentle white phosphorescence. Eyeless, a smiling mouth in its centre mass. There were few reference points to scale the entities, but they looked at least twice human height. The creatures were as transparent as a jellyfish. The hint of what might be organs floated inside, surrounded by a tracery of glowing lines for veins. They flowed playfully around the time sphere's exterior in the manner of dolphins following a boat's wake.

'Locals, I presume,' said Madre. 'My pilot data contains no mention of natives inside this universe, however.'

Sophie seemed repulsed by their appearance. 'What do they want?'

'No doubt they're attracted by the esoteric energies of our craft,' said Madre, sounding nervous, which was worrying in itself. The little flying steamman was usually calm and unflappable. 'Time flows forward normally inside our sphere. Outside, the entire universe flows in a contra direction. We must appear as a great oddity to them.'

'They're the freaks,' said Rawstone.

'They are certainly unusual,' said Madre. 'They should not be able to keep up with our accelerated passage through this universe's continuum. And yet it seems they can?'

'We need to come up with a name for them,' proposed Cassie.

'Star dolphins,' said Scarlett.

'Time angels,' suggested Magnus.

Alios Hardcircuit agreed with him. 'That's a fitting name.'

Sophie ignored the banter and clutched the casket tighter. 'I really don't feel well.'

'They're beautiful, whatever they're called,' said Scarlett. She reached out to press her palm against the sphere's surface.

Beyond, the wings of the nearest time angel reacted, flowing into tendrils. It rested them against the time sphere's surface, matching the position of Scarlett's hand on the outside of the hull.

'They're intelligent,' laughed Scarlett. 'They're saying hello to us.'

'Move back,' warned Madre. 'We know nothing of these creatures' intentions towards us.'

'No, they're friendly,' insisted Scarlett. 'Look…'

Outside, the gentle smile of the time angel curved wider. At almost the same time its tendrils flowed through the walls of the time sphere, as insubstantial as a ghost, wrapping around Scarlett's waist. Scarlett screamed in terror as her body appeared to fade phantom-like, pulled straight through the sphere's hull. The time angel wrapped itself around her flailing body as it blasted away from the time craft. Traveling more rapidly through the realm beyond than Magnus had thought possible. It became a mote lost among the alien heavens within seconds. Pandemonium broke out inside the craft – screaming – yelling. Everyone tried to swim away from the time sphere's surface, now it had proved as little protection against the malevolent locals as a soap bubble. Rawstone drew his hidden blade from his boot, Sophie Fox lashing out at the creatures with her metal casket.

Cassie yelled at the pilot. 'Save Scarlett! Go after her!'

Magnus joined his friend's yells, urging they turn back, but Madre was caught up with her console, ignoring them.

'Impossible!' Madre finally answered. 'Scarlett Deller will be dead by the time we catch up with her. Prolonged exposure to a universe with a separate set of physics? Every electron in her body has already been scrambled at the most fundamental level possible.'

Rawstone stabbed his blade towards the time angels circling menacingly outside. 'You're telling me Scarlett's been poisoned to death by that foul soup out there?'

'Exactly. She could survive no longer than a minute at most outside our craft's environment.'

'But they can reach inside here like ghosts…' argued Magnus.

'Like a bystander reaching into a fish pond,' said Madre. 'If you could drag one of the creatures inside and cage it, our physics would scramble its structure soon enough.'

Rawstone looked ready to assault their pilot. 'This is on you, birdie. You, King Steam, that freak mad moon king. You and your bloody stupid loop that needs closing. It's a gallows noose and you just hung an innocent girl with it.'

Another time angel darted towards the sphere, its wings sporting tendrils, ready to repeat its comrade's attack. This time its limbs struck the sphere with a shower of crimson sparks, failing to penetrate. It almost bounced off the time sphere, clearly shocked.

'I am now projecting an energy shield matched to this dimensional frequency,' cried Madre. 'But our craft will soon lose all power maintaining it.'

Shocked, Magnus tried to process Madre's words. *Scarlett is dead? She can't be.* They had grown up together in the small close community of humans living inside the Steamman Free State. He had always known Scarlett. And now she was what – unravelled inside an alien realm, her corpse traveling back in time forever? Fated never to decay? An eternal death?

'What can I do to assist you?' Alios asked their pilot.

'Join with me,' urged Madre. 'Lend me your mind's processing power. I need to recalculate our navigational calculations. Try to outpace these monsters before the shield completely drains our energy reserves.'

Alios Hardcircuit extended a cable from his body. Madre seized it in her tiny metal claws and plugged the cable into a port behind her small copper-colored neck. Outside, time angels lashed angrily at the time sphere, circling the craft like a school of murderous sharks. Sparks flew out with whining screams upon each impact. With two minds piloting the craft, the time sphere's passage sped up. The alien vista outside blurred as their velocity increased.

Magnus's chest tightened as he saw the time angels keep pace, driving after the sphere, flowing around their hull. The creatures' rictus grins were now nothing more than the promise of death. 'They're still keeping up with us.'

'We can travel no faster,' called Madre. 'Our vessel's in danger of losing internal coherence. Should our hull collapse we will all meet poor Scarlett Deller's end.' Alios drifted behind the little steamman, seemingly unconscious. His mind dedicated to the urgency of their escape.

The time angels realized the visitors' predicament. They drew closer, beating wings against the craft until the time sphere veered like a comet surrounded by a tail of fiery sparks.

'We're depleting our energy reserves at a dangerous level,' warned Madre, flitting desperately between instrument screens. 'This vessel was never designed to travel so rapidly through time as well as maintaining a shield *and* a pocket of our own universe. Only two out of three of those functions can we maintain.'

'Two out of three ain't bad,' muttered Rawstone with gallows humour.

'Extend the pocket outward,' urged Cassie. 'Can you do that?'

'That's brilliant!' Magnus saw the merit of her idea. *If the universe outside is poison to our bodies, then surely what's sauce for the goose is sauce for the gander.*

'Let's see,' said Madre.

The sphere's surface glowed with a bright yellow halo, the bubble of their universe expanding outward towards the time angels. One of them collided with the sphere, thinking it was still battering against the shield. Rather than sparks, it was sucked into the light as though caught in a deadly riptide, spread flat and thin and whipped around the time sphere. Globules of shredded time angel tossed back out into its own universe. Seeing their comrade's fate, the surviving time angels drew warily back – still following, but keeping their distance.

'That's it! yelled Rawstone. 'Shred them! Shred every last one of the jiggers.'

Magnus agreed with the young mountain guide's savage sentiments. But each time Madre attempted to save power by decreasing the field's size, the murderous creatures flowed back. They battered relentlessly against the shimmering energy shield, all that was stopping them penetrating the hull.

'We have brought ourselves a little extra time,' said Madre, 'but our energy reserves are still too low to complete the journey. Our shields will fail before we reach our transit point.'

'You need to save me,' demanded Sophie. 'It is your duty. You forced me to travel with you. The Free State as good as kidnapped me.'

'You have my nation's apologies,' squawked Madre. 'If it is any consolation, my metal form can no more survive the hostile physics of this realm than your organic bodies can.'

Magnus's mind raced. *There must be a way.* Otherwise, they'd all end up as dead as Scarlett. Along with the Earth if the so-called Protector had its way. 'Can you decrease the load on the shield protecting us? Save energy by making the shield weaker in places – vary where the weak spots appear along the hull?"

'You want to turn this ship into a leaky sieve?' said Rawstone. 'That's your genius plan?'

'As long as those grinning ghosts outside don't realize there're chinks in our armour,' said Cassie, jumping to Magnus's defense. 'Will that buy us the extra time we need, Madre?'

'It could well do. Let me recalculate.' After a moment the little machine bird came back to life. 'Yes, I can rotate our active shield areas to decrease our energy bleed. We will be increasingly exposed for the final few minutes of the voyage, but with luck, our pursuers may not realize our vulnerability.'

Sophie looked terrified at the thought. 'That's a terrible idea.'

'Do you have a better one?' asked Magnus.

'Scarlett's dead! Don't you understand? The rest of us will die too, now. None of this is fair!'

'Circle's teeth, let's do it,' growled Rawstone. 'Better we do something, anything and go down fighting.'

'I agree,' said Cassie, biting her lip with nerves.

'Since we're voting,' said Magnus, 'let's go for broke and hope we don't break.'

Madre made the necessary adjustments. They continued to race through the foreign universe, fighting a strange phony war against the time angels. Switching between running their shields and projecting the "poison" of their universe out. Anything to try to keep the attacking creatures uncertain and on the defensive. Every second that passed seemed like an hour. Maybe it was. All Magnus had for a clock was the time angels' continual attacks on their craft.

'We are approaching our exit point,' Madre called out after an age. 'Move close to the sphere's centre, towards me. Try to stay away from the hull. We no longer have enough energy to extend our space-time beyond the time sphere: there will be no more shredding of these alien fiends. The shields are close to collapse, too – there is hardly anything left to rotate.'

It took depressingly little time for the time angels to realize that the craft's fatal halo was no longer working. They closed in, beating against the vessel's shields. Sparks flew until one of the malevolent creature's ghostly wings penetrated through the hull, invading the cabin. Encouraged by this success the time angels redoubled the intensity of their assault, seeking weak spots. Questing tendrils pushed ghost-like inside. Fishing for humans to seize and tear apart like evil children ripping the wings off flies.

At last one of the tendrils squeezed through a shield hole and darted like a cobra towards Madre and Alios. Magnus gasped. *They're intelligent enough to understand who's our pilot.* Rawstone intercepted the limb, plunged his steel dagger through it, severing the tip. The violent interaction between two different forms of matter proved explosive. A flash of light and explosive wash of energy struck Rawstone and Alios Hardcircuit. They both tumbled through the air, left hanging limp and lifeless inside the cabin as the craft lurched away, spinning. Madre screeched with the pain of the sudden disconnection from his fellow steamman. She was blown to the left of her pilot position. The wounded time angel lashed away with the force of the detonation. Its comrades redoubled the fury of their siege against the damaged craft.

'Our continuum generator has taken terminal damage!' yelled Madre. 'Preparing for emergency ejection from this universe. Brace yourself.'

Magnus ignored the bird-like machine, swimming towards Rawstone and Alios, desperate to discover whether they were dead or unconscious. The time sphere's shape began to deform as the killers swarmed the vessel, smashing against its decaying structure.

'Four seconds to emergency ejection,' warned Madre.

Magnus had only just kicked towards the two limp bodies when he heard screaming behind him. He swivelled. Tendrils had penetrated the craft and wrapped around Sophie. She was turning transparent as the alien matter interacted with her body. The ambassador's daughter was pulled, struggling and hollering towards their vessel's hull.

'Three seconds to emergency ejection.'

Magnus lunged towards the young woman, halfway to grabbing her outstretched hand when a second yell drew his eyes. Cassie! Another murderous time angel had slipped its tendrils through a gap in the shields, wrapping itself around the young woman's leg, yanking her towards the hull, too. Ready to drag Cassie into its realm and slay her. Magnus froze with indecision. Both women yelling, struggling, but only enough time to save one of his friends. Cassie or Sophie?

- 6 -

Hard Landings

Consciousness came upon Cassie like a lead sheet's weight eased off her body. *I'm still alive?* She rolled over slowly, rubbing the leaves away stuck to her face. She lay on the ground inside a forest. Tall redwood and fir trees towered around her. Cassie's bones clicked and creaked as she dragged herself to her feet. *This smells like home; fresh bark and soft beds of leaves. The right universe, anyway.* No way to tell which age this was. No sign of her friends, either. The memory of the nightmarish trip in the time sphere replayed. Losing Sophie and Scarlett to the terrible time angels. *Magnus saved me.* She felt a sudden wave of guilt at the recollection. *Sophie died because Magnus saved me before her*. A terrible thought occurred to her. *What if I'm the only one who made it here alive?* The time sphere had disintegrated around her feet during the last few seconds. What if Madre only had enough energy left in the power cells to pull one of them into the past? Wasn't she the logical choice? The reason why this insane mission had set out in the first place.

Sunlight filtered through the forest canopy, too diffuse to tell what time it was or read a direction off the sun. Cassie beat down her sense of despair, the feeling of raw terror that she might never see her friends again. *Keep it together, girl. Focus on staying alive. First things first. Where are you? You need to find what passes for civilization around here before the supplies in your backpack run out.* The alternative was wandering around the forest in circles until she happened across a bear or a pack of wolves. Not a winning strategy, although the wolves would probably be happy. She walked over to the nearest tree, checking which side of the trunk the moss grew thickest – that would point north. Searching for any spiderwebs in the branches, most often spun facing south. Once Cassie had her compass points, she cast her gaze around the trees for any trunk with branches low enough to make a decent climber. *Gotcha.* Then it was a tight, uncomfortable climb to the top. As she broke through the forest canopy she was rewarded by the sight of a virgin forest looking untouched by humanity's hands. The forest stretched unbroken to a line of gray mountains in the west, the sky above azure blue and cloudless. Must be early morning from the sun's position. A flock of birds scattered from the canopy to the north. Cassie's heart skipped a beat when she spotted what had spooked them. *Madre!*

The little steamman hovered on wing thrusters, trying to fix her position in a comparable manner to Cassie.

'Hey!' yelled Cassie, manically waving. 'Madre! Madre! Over here!'

The flying machine pivoted to triangulate the sound of the screams, zipping over the treetops to fly towards her. Madre pulled up just short of Cassie's perch. 'Cassie softbody, I am overjoyed to see that you are unhurt.'

'Not wounded. Although my bones feel like I've just celebrated my eightieth birthday. What about the others …?'

'You are suffering from concussive bruising. The good news is that rest of our expedition are experiencing the same pain, together, about a mile east of here. I have been tracking down and reuniting us all. We arrived scattered across different time periods. I landed first three days ago. Alios Hardcircuit and Remus Rawstone arrived yesterday. Magnus landed earlier today. You are the last to arrive. During the time angels' final assault, I had to activate our craft's lifeboat mode – each of us protected inside a separate crash field.'

Alive! Thank the Circle. No more deaths on my conscience. 'The craft's gone?'

'All of its mass converted to shield energy. We are enormously lucky. If any crash field had been drained in the last attack, that person would have arrived hundreds of years ago, or perhaps entered the time-line a century in the future. You could have arrived here only to discover our ancient, weathered graves.'

'Well, I'm certainly glad to see you, Madre. So, we've arrived when we're meant to be?'

'When, yes. Where, I suspect, not quite so much.'

'Please tell me that returning to our own time isn't going to be a re-run of that nightmare.'

Madre's metal wings fluttered in anticipation of getting home. 'Simplicity itself by comparison. Our experience will be closer to what we experienced teleporting from the Earth to the Moon. Follow me down to the forest floor. I shall guide you to our temporary camp.'

She followed the little flying steamman as she twisted and turned around the boughs of the forest. After half an hour, Cassie stood reunited with the others, Magnus rushing past Alios Hardcircuit, sprinting up to spin her around the forest clearing. 'I thought I had lost you to those monsters – that I'd never see you again.'

'I was thinking the same thing,' admitted Cassie. 'That maybe I was the only one who'd survived. I'd be stuck here forever.'

Remus Rawstone stepped out of the lean-to shelter he'd built under one of the trees. 'Hate to rain on your parade, princess, but we might *still* be stuck here for the rest of our lives – the dust of our bones the only thing making it back to our time.'

'I believe in my case it would be the *rust* of my bones,' said Alios. 'But let us work for a better outcome.'

Rawstone didn't look convinced. 'You keep telling yourself that, steamman. We lost Scarlett and Sophie on the way here. All we've achieved is reaching a forest that doesn't look any different from the woods on the slopes of Mechancia.'

'Oh, there are forests in this age a far cry from those you know,' warned Madre. 'Pray you never have to cross them.'

'We're all here, birdbrain; at least, the ones you haven't got killed yet. What next?'

'We need to travel to the capital of Texicana – reach the great coastal city of Hu. That, Cassie softbody, is the city where your mother wrote and hid the letter she left for her friends in the future to find.'

'Do you have any idea where we are now?' asked Magnus.

'Only approximately,' admitted Madre. 'The time angels' attack disrupted our voyage's exit point.'

Rawstone folded his arms. 'Yeah. No kidding.'

'Judging from the terrain and constellation patterns in the night sky, I believe this forest stretches between the Duchy of Royal Doria and the Kingdom of Tallgrass. If that is the case, we will need to travel due south across the great prairies to reach Texicana. While I was out searching for Cassie softbody, I noted an area on the forest edge occupied by a small rural community. It lies an hour south-east of here. We can use our trading coins to buy supplies for the journey and confirm our exact location from the locals.'

'What makes you think they'll want to trade?' asked Cassie.

'Your species' unnatural preoccupation with rare metals such as gold and silver are the same now as it is in our time,' said Madre.

Rawstone snorted. 'Well, if you're trusting in greed, then I reckon that's the first idea you've had that actually makes sense.'

'It is most unfortunate we lost our data archive during the voyage,' said Madre. 'The detailed maps, local lore and historic accounts of how events unfold in this time would have given us a very powerful advantage.'

Cassie winced. All lost when Sophie was snatched and dragged outside the time sphere, the ambassador's daughter vainly swinging the casket at her attackers like a club.

Magnus guessed what was weighing on Cassie's mind. 'I tried to save you both, but —'

'Blame the time angels, Magnus. You did your best.'

'Blame that freak on the moon,' suggested Rawstone. 'It's the tyrant that's exiled us here. Threatening the world if we don't clean up its mess for it. You think it cares how many of us die to do the deed?'

Madre flitted through the air. 'You might as well blame Molly Templar's rash attempt to save her friend for causing this crisis.'

'She's human, doing a human thing,' said Rawstone. 'I'll take that over the Mad Moon King's motives any day of the week.'

They followed Madre through the silent cathedral of the forest, not talking too much — haunted by the memories of how much it had cost them to reach this time.

How many more of us are going to die to find my mother? wondered Cassie. She tried to tell herself that her quest would also help save the world. But that seemed to be an impossible idea to wrap her mind around. In the end, there was only a daughter trying to reunite with her long-lost mother. Just as Rawstone had said. An animal desire. A small and very human thing. Much like the guilt Cassie felt at dragging her friends unasked into this dangerous expedition.

'Forest feels a little off,' said Rawstone. 'Like there's something not quite right about it.'

'It is your tracker's instincts,' explained Alios. 'The bird song here is different from that of Jackelia. The animal calls sound alien. Even the same species of tree has been subtly altered by millions of years of evolution in our time.'

'That must be it,' said Rawstone. As though he hoped that was the reason for what he was feeling.

Cassie felt it too. The forest's scent was familiar yet curiously different. This was her homeworld, but she felt out of place, out of time. She hoped some of how unsettled she felt was merely disorientation from their dangerous journey. That given time it would pass. She couldn't imagine spending the rest of her life feeling rattled. *I'd go mad.*

'We are close to the community now,' announced Madre a little after. 'The forest gives way in the west to grassland shortly.'

'I assume steammen are not common in this time,' said Alios. 'Perhaps it would be better if I did not go with you to the farm.'

Madre landed on the low hanging branch of a tree, examining the group like a wise old owl. 'It's true, a race of self-evolving machines has yet to appear on Earth. However, there are both sentient and non-sentient robots left over from the previous collapsed civilization. Ownership of robots is the preserve of the rich and powerful during the dark ages.'

'How can you own another sentient creature?' asked Alios

'Slavery,' said Madre. 'Distasteful, but quite a widespread practice in this time.'

Magnus laid a hand on Alios's metal shoulder. 'You should come in with us, old steamer. If the locals think we're a traveling party of nobles, they're less likely to want to murder us and try to steal our goods.'

Madre agreed. 'Your centaur configuration was a common pattern for military robots before the collapse – a combined packhorse and assault model which supported softbody soldiers. I'm sure I can pass as an aerial reconnaissance drone. Just the pair of bodyguards a party of wealthy nobles would be traveling with.'

'I don't need a bodyguard,' said Rawstone.

'You don't much look like any noble either, tough guy,' said Magnus.

'Shut your trap, boy.'

'You can pretend to be my servant if it helps,' Magnus laughed at the tracker.

'Then I'll be Baroness Templar,' said Cassie.

'Try to be as non-specific as possible when questioned by locals,' suggested Madre. 'If pushed, however, our cover story is that we are travelers from the Reindeer Empire. That's a powerful nation which dominates the far north of the continent – esoteric, distant, and technically advanced compared to the natives here. That will a go a long way to explain your equipment, foreign manners and lack of local knowledge. Fear of provoking the empire's wrath will also help guarantee your personal safety.'

Armed with little more than a tall tale they warily approached the community. Cassie found the village was an extended series of sprawling single-storey log cabins – as though it had started small and been extended over the generations. The community sat constructed inside a clearing, the stumps of tree trunks in the ground marking the limits of the fields cleared around the buildings. Wooden enclosures held poultry, a couple of goats and other livestock. It seemed to Cassie a meager living to support a community of this size.

'If we're close to grasslands, how come they're not farming out in the open where plowing is free?' wondered Magnus.

Rawstone kicked one of the tree stumps. 'Here's your answer. You live in the forest, you make your living cutting, shaping and selling timber. Their smallholdings are just subsistence for when winter closes the passes.'

Cassie wasn't so sure. *These people are squirreled away here, but hiding from what threat?*

'Look,' said Rawstone, happily pointing out a copper still by the treeline. 'We'll be drinking well tonight.'

As they crossed the clearing they were spotted by a young boy of about ten years. He led two mules, dragging a felled tree towards an outbuilding that must serve as a lumber mill.

Cassie called out a greeting and a boy shouted something back which she didn't understand. Then the child ran off towards the cabins. 'I thought what the Protector did to us back on the moon allowed us to speak their language?'

'Yeah, well, I sure didn't understand a word of what he said,' agreed Rawstone.

'A local dialect, perhaps?' mused Madre. He replayed the boy's words out aloud through a speaker in his metal beak. 'No. That is a mixture of two pre-collapse languages. Dutch and German. It must be their tribal language, here.'

'Just show them our coins,' said Rawstone. 'They'll understand quickly enough.'

Cries sounded inside the cabin and an old farmer emerged, at least seventy if not older. He had a short chin-curtain beard without a mustache. More men materialized sporting similar beards. If there were women inside, they stayed hidden. The farmers wore uniform grey shirts, braces holding up colorless cotton trousers. Some of them wore round straw hats. None of them emerged armed, not even a knife – and they had to own sharp axes for their lumber work. Cassie took that as a hopeful sign. *At least we're not going to be cut down by these people.*

'Do you speak Texicanan?' Madre called out.

Gasps escaped from the men, more sounds of astonishment as they spotted Alios Hardcircuit's metal frame trotting among the party of visitors.

'These machines are our protectors,' said Cassie, raising both hands to show she carried no weapons. 'We intend you no harm. We're only here to trade.'

'I speak Texicanan,' announced the ancient man at their head. 'Though none of you have set foot in Texicana from your accents.'

'We are traveling to the city of Hu from the Reindeer Empire,' said Cassie, remembering their agreed cover story. 'Is Texicana far?'

'Far enough away. You're still inside the Kingdom of Tallgrass … in the Clay Forest. You must follow the sun south for many weeks to reach Texicana's borders.'

'We have gold coins to buy provisions,' said Magnus, hopefully.

'We will gladly sell you any provisions you need to cross the prairie,' said the old man. 'I am Amos Rager and these are my family. You shall share of our supper tonight freely. But only the real and blessed are welcome, not—' he indicated Madre and Alios, 'your infernal machines.'

'They're part of our party,' said Cassie.

'Your golems are forbidden by the prophets' teachings,' said Amos. 'We keep no machines here, no engines, no technologies which brought down the wrath of the flood and washed away the wickedness of the world.'

'The comet strike generated tidal waves as high as mountains,' whispered Madre. 'Killing billions. Such superstitions are how the few survivors made sense of the disaster.'

'Your metal golems must stay in the stable and not leave its confines,' ordered Amos. 'You're welcome here, but they are not. If such terms are not acceptable, we must ask you to leave.'

'We accept your terms, sir,' said Rawstone, irritating Cassie by speaking for all of them. But then, how much choice do we have?

The elderman pointed at the young boy who had spotted them first 'Mervyn, you shall stand guard over the stable. Make sure the golems do not put the evil eye on the cows or open the gates to allow foxes into our coop.'

Mervyn didn't look happy at being assigned such a terrifying task, but he was the youngest and needed to accept any duties given.

After the two steammen were safely confined, the three humans were invited inside the cabins. Clean, homely, but primitive. Even to someone used to the minimalist homes of steammen. Cassie glanced around the main living space. No swords, shields or guns mounted on the walls. Even the knives on the kitchen counter looked blunt. 'You keep no weapons to protect yourselves?'

'King Aldan knows the First People will not fight in his armies. He sends his tax collectors to collect his tithe in timbers for his towns, not the service of our young.'

'That is your community's name? The First People?'

'The name of all the Clay Forest's clans. We lived here before all others. We shall abide here long after all others have vanished.'

Cassie nodded in agreement, but this only seemed to irritate Amos. 'You do not understand. Do you think we don't notice the Reindeer Empire's flying machines blackening our clear skies? Your nation's pride invites a second flood, a second great sweeping of the world. Engines and guns are not permitted by the prophets' teachings. And they are forbidden for good reason.

We warn all who visit us, but still, engines are built and used, even in King Aldan's towns. Yet nobody can live honestly for others. Only for ourselves.'

'Living well is its own reward,' said Magnus, trying to placate the elderman on his own terms.

'The First People were saved before. We will be saved again,' sighed the old man. 'When you reach the great city of Hu in Texicana, look around at their carousing and wickedness and ask yourself if the same can be said for their kind. That is all the advice I shall give you.'

'He's a cheery soul,' said Magnus as the farmer left the table.

'Better a grumpy pacifist than a happy warmonger,' said Cassie.

'You've noticed how the women here don't say much around us,' said Magnus. 'I reckon old man Rager doesn't like female folk with too many opinions.'

'So, I'll keep the fact that we're all filthy atheist Circlists to myself, then.'

'I would.'

The only other villagers able or willing to converse in the common tongue was a young man called Eli, tasked to trade with lumber merchants who visited the farm – and a young girl called Sevilla. She occupied a position in the community called its reader. Sevilla was called upon to read from a thick heavy red tome, which she did in a lilting singsong voice, halfway between preaching and plainsong. The locals she sang to in the local language, but she was gifted enough to sing in Texicanan, too. Even translated, the girl's songs made little sense to Cassie. Outlandish hymns of a man swallowed by a whale and a boy who murdered a giant with a slingshot, as well as a strong-man who slew a legion of villains using only a donkey's jawbone.

Each story interspersed with strange ritual exhortations. 'We create happiness from safety, capacity and courtesy and piety. Always project a positive image and initiate service recovery.' Or, 'Do not include remuneration paid for agricultural products as defined in section 3121 unless for portions of the day's service not in the course of your employer's trade.'

It was only when Sevilla was dispatched to Alios and Madre locked up in the stable, to bind them in their evil, that Cassie realized this random babble was actually part of the villagers' religion.

Madre explained to Cassie when she visited the stables later in the day. 'These farmers' teachings have been passed mangled by long centuries of dark age. The pre-collapse civilization contained much of its knowledge on machine books and inside digital libraries. Learnings which became inaccessible without power. There was a rush to print out everything humanity could using their last energy reserves. But much of that paper ended up burnt for fuel to keep alive during the comet strike's endless winter.'

'Truly, a comet could cause such devastation?' Cassie was appalled. Not least because that's the fate the Protector was threatening the world with.

'Previous comets have destroyed the majority of life on Earth and carried life's initial seeds to it in the first place,' said Madre. 'It is no idle threat the Protector makes. Keep your opinions about the locals' religion to yourself. I don't want to test their pacifism through questioning their faith.'

'I'm not quite so stupid or tactless,' said Cassie, insulted.

'I suspect Remus Rawstone might be,' interjected Alios.

'Their prophets' weird teachings are their only book. But it isn't the only paper they've got here,' said Cassie. She produced the cheap printed trader's map a merchant had forgotten and left behind at the community, unfurling it on the stable floor. 'We're here in the Great Clay Forest. Texicana is down here.'

'Excellent,' said Madre. She scanned the map using her vision plate, committing it to memory. 'You have secured supplies?'

'Yes,' said Cassie. 'Although they won't sell us any of their mules or horses. There are wild herds out in the grasslands, apparently. We might get lucky.' Cassie suspected the wild herds would be a far cry from the tame beasts she had learned to ride in the stables owned by Magnus's father.

Later, the three Jackelian visitors ate well at supper – starting with goat stew as they were regaled with songs of a shepherd boy who grew up into a wise king. Raised high through his gods' favor, naturally. Further courses emerged steaming from the kitchen area. Cornmeal mush with eggs, mugs of spiced hot milk, potatoes, carrots, celery, venison meat, dried apple pie, as well as a dark drink called coffee which tasted similar to Jackelian cafeel.

Much to Rawstone's disgust, no beer, wine or spirits appeared. 'What about that copper still I saw out back?'

'What it produces is for trade, not consumption here,' chided the nearest elder on their table.

Rawstone shook his head at being so cruelly abused.

For overnight accommodation, they were given a single room to share. That was different from the locals' sleeping accommodation. Segregated into female and male members, married and unmarried quarters. Whatever religious prescriptions were in play, the chances of locals being corrupted by the visitors' presence clearly took precedence. They were to be bundled in together. Their room had been recently given over to the storage of hay for livestock, judging from the seeds of straw littering its wooden floorboards. No glass in the room's single window, just a pair of wooden shutters. Well fed, Cassie fell asleep on her blanket roll easily. Little time seemed to have passed before she felt herself being shaken awake. She groaned and cast her eyes up to the open window. *It's still the dark of night outside?*

'What's—'

Rawstone placed a hand over her mouth and shushed her to silence. Magnus was up and crouched by the door onto the rest of the building, his ear pressed against it, listening intently. Madre sat perched on the window ledge, both shutters wedged open.

'Madre's seen armed men outside,' whispered Rawstone.

Cassie kept her reply to a bare whisper. 'Maybe soldiers from the king? A night patrol looking to be billeted?'

Madre hopped down inside the room. 'I'm not acquainted with this period's military uniforms, but these ruffians have the look of bandits, barbarians and slavers about them. And more to the point, their appearance at this odd hour doesn't appear a surprise to the community's elderman.'

'Damn sell-out,' growled Rawstone. 'He must have sent for the bandits. All Rager's talk of peace and love for humanity was hogwash. He not only gets to steal our gold, he's looking to sell our hides to boot. The only peace he's interested in is selling a piece of our ass off to his bandit friends.'

'I've barred the door as best I can,' said Magnus, heading over to them. 'We'd better hop.'

'Without the food we paid for?' said Cassie, her heart sinking.

Magnus shrugged. 'With our lives.'

Cassie's eyes flicked to the window; their sole way out. 'Okay, let's vanish.'

They silently donned their coats and shouldered their

backpacks. Rawstone slid out first, Cassie followed, then Magnus and Madre. Alios was already waiting for them behind the village buildings. It was colder outside than Cassie had been expecting. Even with moonlight lighting their way, the forest squatted nearby dark and all-encompassing. That darkness would mask their escape as well as hinder quick passage through the forest.

Cassie's heart leaped. A fierce cry pierced the quiet stillness. It sounded more animal than human. Shadowy figures suddenly rushed at them from the side of the clearing. Large silhouettes carrying a — crossbow bolt hurled past Cassie's cheek, thudding into the log wall behind. At the same time as Cassie's blood began racing, the night seemed to flicker into something else. Flowing into a dark green where the pitch blackness became more distinct, time seemingly slowing. *What's happening? Am I going mad?* Cassie shuddered, stepping aside as a second crossbow bolt drove through the space her body had occupied a second earlier. She moved as though swimming through treacle, the bandits attacking them in slow-motion. Her limbs responded with muscle memories she'd never trained for. Her body reacted to the assault, responding autonomously, what she needed to do to stay alive instinctively slipping into her mind.

One of the attackers had a sword drawn, sharp steel glinting in the moonlight. Cassie stepped into the raider's path, punched out, her hand flat and needle-like, slapping her assailant in the throat, watching him spin slowly in the air as the force of his rush converted into a daisy wheel through the air. The sound of something vital cracking, even as Cassie processed the fact *she* was the one responsible for the man's inability to breathe. *Dear circle, what is happening to me? It's as though I'm possessed.*

She was not the only one oddly affected. Unless Magnus had always known how to snatch a crossbow bolt from the air and hurl it back into one of the savages, leaving the attacker staggering, clutching the bolt buried in his gut.

'This way!' called Madre, distracting Cassie from the confusion of the ambush and her crazy fight. All attempts at stealth abandoned as dozens of more attackers emerged running out of the murk. 'Into the woods!'

Cassie stumbled after the flying steamman, bewildered. Cold on the nape of her neck even as she sweated with panic. Madre disappeared into the treeline, Rawstone just behind Cassie, a carpet of frozen leaves crunching under her boots. Branches and brambles brushed against her as she blundered through the undergrowth, following Madre's bobbing form. Wild yells to the rear caused her to turn. The fight around the log cabin had intensified, more and more brutish newcomers piling out of the building, their easy ambush in tatters. Alios Hardcircuit valiantly threw off assailants as they piled onto him. One of the bandit leaders yelled a command and attackers scrambled out of the way. A throaty engine roar sounded, a vehicle appearing – resembling an iron boat on six spiked wheels, sloughing forward from the forest and accompanied by the crash of splintering trees. An open turret swivelled on its rear. A thud sounded, a spinning net sparkling in the frosty night – then Cassie saw the reason for the sparks. The net struck Alios, wrapping itself around his body. A storm of electrical discharge causing the steamman to crumple, tumble pole-axed to the ground.

Cassie flung herself back towards the clearing. Rawstone seized her, using his superior weight to pin her. 'Don't! Too many of them.'

As if conjured by the tracker's warnings, more unwieldy, tank-sized vehicles came crashing out of the treeline. Accompanied by waves of wild yelling warriors, fighters brandishing a motley mixture of axes, spears, swords, guns and crossbows.

'We have to help Alios,' seethed Cassie.

Rawstone hissed back at her. 'Can't help him by getting ourselves captured, too.'

Madre darted between them. 'I fear your appraisal is accurate. These bandits came well prepared to disable the Reindeer Empire's bodyguards. Their electro-nets will incapacitate me with equal ease. We must all survive to fight another day.'

Cassie glanced urgently around the trees. 'Where's Magnus?'

'I saw him take down a couple of those bandits,' said Rawstone. 'After that, I think he went running into the forest ahead of us.'

'What if they captured him, too?'

More and more vehicles broke through the clearing. Warriors leaping off the sides, screaming victorious cries and cavorting around the village. As she watched they began to fan out, searching for the remaining visitors.

'We have to get out of here,' urged Rawstone. 'They'd have used cannons rather than capture nets if they wanted to kill Alios. His rusty backside's part of their payday. They're slavers, for sure.'

Cassie battled conflicting emotions. A desperate urge to do something, *anything* to save her friend. Her intellect warned her Rawstone was all-too-correct. If she ran back, she'd be captured at best. Sliced to pieces at worse. Tears welled in Cassie's eyes. 'He's my friend.' *I can't lose another one. Not my fault, again.*

'Then do what Alios would want for you,' said Rawstone. 'Live to fight another day.'

She bit her tongue. The three of them slipped away into the forest dark, screams and yells of hunting warriors pursuing them as they retreated. Cassie had never felt like such a coward. They fled for a good hour, a nightmare journey of distant cries, bramble scratches, stumbles and near falls. All mixed with raw terror and a disabling sense of concern for her missing friends. She wasn't sure how long the chase lasted. Eventually, she needed to reach out, steady herself against the nearest tree, her head spinning. Cassie worked to prevent herself vomiting.

'Your body is normalizing,' said Madre. 'Take a second to rest. Breathe deeply. Focus on your chest's natural rhythm.'

Cassie coughed. 'Normalizing?'

'The adrenalin response during the attack activated your body's combat conditioning. Combat training imprinted by the Protector alongside your language package.'

Cassie was horrified. *The fighting back in the first people's village? The strange possession?* 'It violated my mind twice?'

'I warned you the technology was originally developed by your race's military.'

That isn't any consolation. Cassie wanted to scrub into her brain. She felt so dirty and unclean.

'I thought that fighting was all me,' said Rawstone. 'Nobody ever needed to teach *me* how to roughhouse.'

Madre swooped around the forest floor, scanning between the trees. 'Take a quick break. Eat something from your packs. Your metabolisms have been pushed beyond the normal limits of human endurance. I will circle out, check for heat signatures and any signs of pursuit.'

'Try and find Magnus,' barked Cassie. Her heart ached as she imagined him crashing alone through the trees. *Lost, trying to find me.*

'Of course, that too.'

Rawstone watched the little flying steamman dart off into the darkness. 'Good riddance. I've got a few things to say that I don't want birdbrain overhearing.'

Cassie fumbled inside her pack, looking for the dry, strange rations they'd received before entering the time ship. 'Why?'

'Because I don't trust that flying kettle,' said Rawstone. 'Now I know how the Mad Moon King's messed with my mind, I'm not even sure if I should trust *myself*.'

'Come on. Madre's saved us more than once. Inside the time ship. On the island when the sea-spiders attacked.'

'She saved *herself* on the time ship. And as for the battle on the island, that was all far too convenient. Monsters attack and she calls in artillery from a submarine? A put-up job if I've ever seen one. Maybe the Mad Moon King sacrificed a few of its own freaks just so we'd trust Madre more.'

Cassie sat down and took a swig of water. The canteen wasn't going to last long out here unless they came across a forest stream. 'You're sounding paranoid.'

'And you're too trusting, princess. Here's what I trust—' he thumped his chest. 'Me – me and my steel. There's more to this journey than that little flying kettle's telling us. King Steam obviously cut a deal with the Protector. That's how we got to the moon without splashing down in its ocean as a pile of burning bones. That's why it allowed us to travel back to the past. I know you're blaming me right now for not doing more to save Alios. But you should be asking yourself why Madre's flapping around you? Not off trying to save our friends. Because *you're* the only one who's going to convince your mother to return with us. Keeping everything the way the Protector likes it – with its boot crushing humanity's throat. The rest of us were only allowed to tag along because some dusty book claimed we already did. Everyone else in this expedition is expendable, princess. We're wolf food to distract the pack while you get away.'

'What do you mean?'

'Two merchants are hiking through the mountain passes when they spot a pack of wolves stalking them. One of the merchants tosses aside his backpack, gets ready to sprint off. Surprised, the second trader says, "Don't be an idiot, you can't outrun wolves!" "Hey, I don't need to outrun the wolves," says his friend, "I just need to outrun *you*." You're the one without the weight of a backpack in this sorry tale.'

'That's not true. It can't be.' But Rawstone's doubts proved infectious. They carried an insidious truth which Cassie found difficult to deny.

Rawstone shrugged. 'Just think is all I'm asking you. You're good at that, at least compared to me. Maybe there's a chance in all of this to help history get back on the path it was meant to take. The history the Protector and his freaks changed. Where the race of man won the war against them!'

'I only came here to find my mother.' *Everything else is too confusing.*

'Maybe we get to do something else. Something to make our friends' deaths worthwhile. I bet that thought occurred to your mother. Could be that's something to do with why she never returned to you?'

Cassie was about to reply when Madre swooped back down from the branches. 'At least three bandit parties are still pursuing us! Perhaps ten minutes behind.'

She sighed and stood up. They would have to survive first. Get answers later. *And that isn't going to be easy.*

***

Magnus groaned, his body a mass of raw, hot pain. It took a minute for his mind to catch up with his bruised body, recall the nature of his predicament. Everything around was dark. He could smell the leather of the hood over his head, blinding him, muffling the voices of his captors. Then his terrible memories returned in full force. A wave of attackers rushed him back in the village, overpowering him. Flailing fists, brutal clubs, stomping boots until he could only roll around on the ground, trying to protect his skull from being caved in. *But I'm still alive.* He remembered the rest of the group desperately sprinting towards the forest behind the cabins. Magnus calling out to Rawstone as a warrior tackled him. The young tracker had glanced back once. Then vanished into the forest after the others.

Abandoned. Magnus wasn't sure if that could be considered cowardice or justifiable self-preservation given the circumstances. *Either way, I'm just as jiggered now.* As well as leather, he could smell grease and exhaust fumes. *Where am I? I hope Cassie managed to escape.* Magnus croaked out. His only answer came in the form of a loud curse followed by a brutal strike around his head, leaving his ears ringing.

He held his tongue, drifting between consciousness and semi-consciousness – all the better to ignore his hurting body – an indeterminate time later when the rhythmic shaking of his prison slowed. Cries sounded and his hood was yanked away from his head, his scalp still damp with blood from the savages' blows. Magnus sat chained in the flatbed of some type of vehicle which looked as if it had been cobbled together with scrap from a breaker's yard. A fate he shared with many others, including Alios Hardcircuit and at least one or two faces who looked familiar from the Rager family community. Alios not only had his manipulator arms chained, but both sets of legs too. Their captors were obviously taking no chances. *No sign of Cassie, Madre or Rawstone. Are they in another vehicle, or did they escape?*

They were out in the prairies, part of a convoy of halted vehicles. All of the transporters appeared ramshackle, held together by little more than rust, crude welding and basic smithing. No two alike. Four-wheeled, six-wheeled, some with caterpillar tracks. Razor-edged metal prows mounted at the front, rows of spears and pennants flying, lending the vehicles a porcupine appearance. Some crates possessed chariot-like stands on the rear, others with cupolas mounted on top, protected by swivel-mounted crossbows and small cannons. Their captors' clothes seemed equally ragged. As brutish and unique as their means of transport. Nomadic leather armour festooned with weapon belts, pieces of chain mail, riding goggles, face masks and helmets – some painted to resemble demons and beasts, many molded in bizarre and terrifying shapes. Where faces and bodies weren't covered, there seemed an abundance of bulging muscles, tribal scars, tattoos and war paint. A six-foot warrior with two spears strapped to his back jogged over to the side of the vehicle, banging its sides. His voice sounded muffled behind the wolf-like metal faceplate at the front of his helmet.

'Out. Water the grass. Nobody will dare soil the back of my wheeler.'

The chain-links binding the prisoners to the flatbed were unlocked and they stumbled out onto the open prairie, captives jabbering in a variety of dialects and tongues. A slave with a rat-like face came scrambling over bearing a bucket of water and a ladle. He was practically mauled by the prisoners, desperate and thirsty from captivity. Only a single serving of water was permitted each prisoner, a couple of brutes with clubs regulating the liquid's distribution. Magnus realised how thirsty he was, the unrelenting heat of the sun above in the open grasslands. He could only spy waist-high grass and a few copses of trees as far as the horizon. The forest was long gone. No way to know how far away now, or which direction they had traveled in. Magnus shambled over to join the queue desperately waiting for water. Alios Hardcircuit joined him. *Of course, the steamman needs water for his boiler heart as much as any organic.*

Magnus squinted at the sun, sitting high in the sky. 'Where are we?'

'In the realm of the cursed,' muttered a prisoner in front. From his clothes, the man who spoke was either one of the farmers from the Rager family community or a peasant from a neighboring village. 'You're one of the First People?'

'Yes,' whispered the man. 'I am known as Bram Rager among the family.'

Magnus worked to keep his temper in check. 'Why did your kin sell us out?'

'No choice. The Fast Food Clans' chieftains are furious this season's grain fuel harvest is so poor. They seized me and two others as part of their tribute even after we offered you up to them.'

'Fast Food Clan? That's what these brigands call themselves?'

'Do you know nothing? Or do the clans not afflict you in the cold north. Then you are lucky indeed.'

'A damnable strange name.'

The peasant spoke as though Magnus was simple. 'They pillage for supplies and they raid in fast wheelers. What name would you have them choose, Reindeer Empire man?'

'The softbody has a point,' said Alios.

Magnus sighed. 'You know what direction they've been taking us?'

'West, I believe,' said the steamman.

'We have to escape. Every day we spend captive we must be traveling further and further from Cassie. Can you snap your chains?'

'I think not,' said Alios. 'They're forged steel. And on foot, we would quickly be run down by these savages' vehicles.'

And raiding and reeving is the bandit's trade. 'I wish you had escaped, Alios.'

'I wish we had both escaped.'

Bram Rager shivered. 'Your metal abomination brought the evil eye down upon us. Pray your emperor is willing to pay a fat ransom in silver for your blasphemous head.'

'Why —?'

The peasant was about to answer when a club-wielding brute laid about the queue, cursing the prisoners for babbling fisher wives. It was finally Magnus's turn for water and it seemed to drop down his dusty throat without touching the sides or quenching his thirst.

'Time for food!' yelled one of the guards following a brief conference with another warrior.

Magnus swayed on his feet, hungry. 'Where's the queue for that?'

A mood of terror and panic swept the rest of the prisoners. Bram stared at Magnus as though the young Jackelian was completely mad. 'Truly, you are touched by the gods.'

'I don't understand...?'

'The Fast Food Clans adhere to the old ways – the evil traditions from the long dark.'

The warrior who had arrived walked the waterline, touching prisoners seemingly at random. 'You. You.'

'Magnus watched the warrior approach them. 'What evil ways?'

The warrior halted by the water barrel and jabbed Magnus and the villager painfully hard in the chest. 'You. And you.'

'We *are* their food,' hissed Bram.

The warrior grinned at Magnus and for the first time, the young Jackelian noticed the line of serrated, filed teeth. Like the teeth of a steel saw. 'Soft and tender,' laughed the warrior watching Magnus. 'Make sure I claim at least half a leg from this one.'

- 7 -

Gene's Always
Magic Kingdom

Rawstone knelt by the abandoned fire's warm embers close to the forest's edge. All their assailants from the night before had seemingly departed across the grasslands. *That's too bad.* But Remus had known how this would end. He had even insisted they take the risk, circling back towards the Rager community. Not just to shake off their pursuers. Kidnapping one of the First People and "persuading" the treacherous forester to fill him in on the raid. Cassie had protested about Rawstone's methods for getting the peasant to talk, but not too much, he noted. She could absent herself from the proceedings all she liked, but his gamble had paid off. At the very least, they now knew Alios and Magnus had both been captured alive and bundled off with the raider's convoy.

Remus stared across the prairie. 'Well, the good news is they've halted hunting us. The bad news is it was a large war band camped here. From the number of fires, they were hundreds strong.'

Cassie shielded her eyes against the hot plains sunlight. 'We have to follow after the bandits. I don't care how strong their bloody force is.'

'There's no sign of pickets for horses here. No dung. Only vehicle tracks.'

'So?'

She knows but she just doesn't want to hear. 'They've already outpaced us, princess. No way we can catch up without transport.'

'Then we go back to the Rager village and steal their horses.'

'It's a basic calculation,' advised Madre, landing in the grass. 'Even if we steal mounts, each hour gives motorized raiders an exponential lead. It will only widen over time.'

'Then we find vehicles, steal *them.*'

'I'm a tracker, not a magician,' said Rawstone. *Can't conjure up what doesn't exist.* 'That prairie grass only stays broken for so long. In a day, there isn't going to be too much of a trail to follow except for fuel fumes.'

'You're saying that because you don't want to stick your neck out trying to rescue Magnus and Alios.'

Remus bridled at the slur. 'I'm up for a fight, princess. But you follow them, you're only fighting the wind and chasing your own shadow.'

Madre took off and slowly scanned the horizon. 'I agree. Our best hope is to press on to Texicana. My information is that their capital city is civilized and their nation militarily dominant in this region. We should be able to acquire vehicles and perhaps arrange an army pursuit.'

'We can't walk away from our friends,' Cassie protested.

Remus shook his head. 'You see someone tumble off the mountains, you don't help your friends by leaping off the cliff right after them. You take the long way down and hope they've survived the fall by the time you've climbed down.'

Cassie appeared torn between her instincts to leap to action and Remus's practical advice.

'I'm telling you,' insisted Rawstone. 'We head out there, you're only doing it for yourself. You'll feel better for the first day, maybe. But by the end of the week, wandering aimlessly, following cattle to watering holes just to stay alive, you'll be cursing yourself.'

'All right,' Cassie capitulated.

Rawstone watched her reluctantly turn away and follow Madre back towards the forest. He kicked ashes over the human bones in the fire, concealing the remains. Better she never discovered the raiders were cannibals. Alios Hardcircuit might be valuable as plunder – worth selling to the highest bidder in the next slave auction. But Magnus? No ransom would be forthcoming for him – he wasn't a skilled craftsman – wasn't even a hardy labourer or a promising female slave. Hardly worth the price of transport to a slave auction. Yeah. The next campfire would contain Magnus's bones. And if it didn't, the one after that surely would.

They pressed on south through the forest rather than crossing the plains, to lessen the danger of coming across another marauder clan. Remus Rawstone took the lead, Madre scouting in careful circuits around them as they progressed. Remus didn't trust the so-called "peaceful" foresters weren't out hunting for their guests. Either on the cannibal raiders' account or their own. Rawstone was vigilant each step of the way. Alert for every whisper of wind in the trees. Every snapped twig. Every rustle of leaves. The birdsong, or more revealing yet – its absence. Having a rich, powerful group of nobles escaped from betrayal and on the loose wouldn't do any good for the community. What if word of the village's cooperation with the cannibals got back to the local king, or worse yet, reached the Reindeer Empire? It wouldn't take much of a punishment expedition to raze the Rager community to the ground, slaughtering all their families. Only Cassie and Remus's death could guarantee that disaster wouldn't happen.

Remus cursed himself for trusting the Ragers. *If something appears too good to be true, that's only because it is.* He would never have made such an amateur mistake back in the mountains. But the unreality of his situation – stuck in an unfamiliar environment, trapped in the distant past with Cassie's company – had lulled him into a false sense of security. *We've lost most of the people we started out with. Don't want to lose anymore.* Certainly, not Cassie. Madre, he didn't much care about one way or another.

Remus might have lived among the steammen back in the Free State, but he had never been given much choice in the matter. His mother had died in an avalanche among the passes and his father – also a tracker and guide – had wandered off shortly after. Maybe stricken with grief or wanting to be surrounded by scenery which didn't remind him of all he'd lost. Either way, Rawstone junior had been left behind, abandoned and forgotten, like a rounding error in a mathematical sum. The remainder of his raising had been a self-generated affair. His father's tracker training the only legacy he'd been left with – just enough to survive and get by. The rest of life's lessons, he'd learned the hard way, the school of hard knocks and sharp grazes and the occasional flashing blade of a mountain bandit.

'What do you think your mother will say when you turn up out of the blue? Do you think she'll even recognize you?'

Cassie looked uncertain. 'I hope so.'

More fool you, Remus thought. *Why bother even looking for her? For answers about being abandoned?* Sometimes other people – even your own kin – were simply excess weight on a journey. Something to be discarded and set aside. 'You hoping for answers?'

'My mother left me in Mechancia to protect me,' said Cassie. 'She needed to leave to rescue her friend. She couldn't take me along. And we had too many enemies in Middlesteel for me to stay in Jackelia.'

'But she never came back for you.'

'There must be a reason for that,' said Cassie.

'Maybe.' He glanced around for Madre. *Still away scouting.* 'And if there is, I reckon birdbrain knows what it is. Could be that getting back to our own time ain't as easy as we've been led to believe.'

'Nothing's ever easy, is it?'

Rawstone touched the bracelet locked around his wrist. Didn't seem any way to remove it that didn't involve a sharp blade and amputation. 'Could be this is a one-way trip? What if time travel forward is a fool's dream? All the Mad Moon King cares about is fixing history so that it stays on top as our kind's jailer.'

'No, forward time travel must be possible,' said Cassie. 'Otherwise, why would my mother come to this age? Just to be marooned alongside her friend? My mother came here, she has to have a way back home to our time.'

'And yet she never returned.'

'We'll have answers soon enough, either way.'

Something about this part of the forest bothered Remus. Then he realised what it was. He hadn't seen any recent sign of boar or deer trails. Nothing larger than a rabbit warren. 'You know, the First People should be out hunting us down. But they haven't followed us.'

'They don't want to fight,' said Cassie. 'Your prisoner told you the village didn't have any choice about selling us out. The bandit clans turn up and demand a share of anything the peasants have got.'

'I don't buy that. They should be out hunting us. We're those treacherous dogs' doom, as soon as we reach a town with a militia outpost.' *But they aren't following us. So, what does that tell us? Nothing good.*

Cassie's foot yanked on a cable in the undergrowth. Remus whirled around, ready for a swinging net or plunging blade, searching for a trap activated by the tripwire.

Nothing? He drew his knife. 'Stay still! Careful.'

'I don't think it's a trap,' said Cassie, tentatively kneeling down. 'It looks like an old power cable.' She rubbed away moss, revealing a wet shiny crystalline coating. Remus followed the direction of the cable with both hands. What he had first taken for undergrowth on their flank proved to be the ruins of a building overgrown with ivy and bushes. He wanted to inspect it closer, stepped around a tree trunk and tugged ivy away from the rubble. Then he used the lower branches of the pine to lever himself up into the tree, climbing up to emerge high in the canopy. It was quite a sight which greeted him. Broken towers scattered like so many concrete anthills, rusting girders like the bones of fantastical beasts, shapes that made little sense to him. Pyramids of cracked and blackened grass, all swallowed up and overrun by the dark green forest.

Cassie's voice drifted up from the forest floor. 'What can you see?'

'Just ruins. Some abandoned city from long ago.'

'I think that—' a sudden cry and Cassie's voice cut off abruptly.

Remus practically threw himself out of the tree as he shimmied down, cursing himself for leaving her unprotected, even for a second. He hit the carpet of leaves, casting around for foes, half expecting to face off against the treacherous First

People. An opportunity for payback he'd welcome. But there was nothing. No enemies. No First People. And no Cassie. He screamed out her name but received no reply. He inspected the ground. No signs of a struggle. No trail that he could find. *But she can't simply have vanished off the face of the earth?* Madre suddenly appeared, swooping down from the canopy.

'Cassie's vanished – I heard her cry out! But when I climbed out of this tree...'

The tiny steamman darted around the clearing, scanning for signs of life. Then she stopped, suspended, hovering at the side of a nearby tree 'Here,' said Madre. 'Tread carefully.'

Rawstone sprinted over to the machine, pulled short as he spotted a crevice in the ground – he knelt and inspected the hole's sides. *Broken glass?* Realization struck him. The forest floor had swallowed one of the ruined structures he'd spotted. *Cassie's fallen inside an abandoned building. But how far down?*

'I will enter first,' said Madre, her vision plate lighting up like a lantern. She hovered for a second above the opening before sinking into the dark. Remus bent over and tracked her progress – noting the light moving across the floor below. *Thank the Circle, only a single storey drop.*

'Cassie softbody is here – stunned, but otherwise unhurt I believe.'

'Wait a minute.' Remus removed the climbing line from his pack and tied it around the pine's trunk, tested its hold, then used the rope to descend after birdbrain. It was dark and dusty inside the tomb. He glanced back up at the shaft of light from outside. A glass dome-like roof, cracked in its centre. Totally covered in soil above, the roots of trees visible like stalactites. Around them, dozens of tables and benches. 'Some sort of schoolroom?'

'No, a canteen, I believe,' said Madre.

Cassie had landed on one of the tables, the wind knocked out of her. Remus inspected her body, starting with the legs and arms. Nothing broken as far as he could tell. She was very lucky. As he examined her, he noticed a strange sound. He danced around ready for anything. It was – *music*? An odd, simple music-box style melody. Snatches of faint words hanging in the air. The gloom seemed to lift, the room's walls gently glowing.

'The roof is a solar collector,' said Madre. 'The crack in the dome is letting in light for the first time in centuries, powering the chamber.'

It was indeed a canteen. Broken plates and rusted metal cutlery scattered around the floor and across tabletops. There were plenty of human bones, too. Dozens of skeletons sprawled around the chamber. The walls contained ancient faded frescoes. Crowds of happy families and children, paintings of people walking among creatures so giant and strange, Remus thought the artist responsible must have been smoking mumbleweed when he created the illustration. Crests had been interspersed around the room – bearing the black silhouette of a palace with words below. He translated the script.

'Gene Land?' said Remus. 'Old Gene must have been mighty rich and powerful to have an entire land named in his honour.'

'By the circuits of the Steamo Loa,' said Madre, 'we must leave this section of the forest, *now!*'

Rawstone pulled Cassie up and balanced her over his shoulder. He felt her shift and groan. 'What're you talking about?'

'That's not what's left of a city out there, it's the ruins of an amusement park.'

'What, you mean like a pleasure garden?'

'Nothing like the parks that you are familiar with,' warned Madre.

Remus failed to see what was spooking the steamman. 'This got something to do with the fact the Friendly Family Rager never followed us down here, axes all sharp and ready to chop their welcome guests into pig swill?'

'I would imagine it does indeed. Climb, Remus softbody, climb!'

Remus used a coil of spare line to bind Cassie to his back and then scaled back up the rope, sweating hard for two. Wasn't easy. Luckily, a lifetime of mountaineering and the hard, high peaks of the Mechancian Spine had left him part-mountain goat. His ascent to the surface wasn't made any easier by Madre urging the young Jackelian to clamber faster. 'Haven't got wings, birdbrain,' he grunted.

Finally, he gained the surface, albeit grunting, winded and sweating like a pig. As Remus flopped Cassie down on the ground behind the tree, he realised the snorting sound wasn't actually coming from his throat. He slowly turned around. A razor-tusked monstrosity paced at the grass on the far end of the clearing, ripping out chunks of soil and flinging them through the air behind it – like a boar had mated with the world's ugliest wolf and only decided to stop growing after it reached an elephant's weight. It clearly wasn't happy with the insultingly small pair of mammals who had trespassed into its territory. And it was equally clear the beast was fixing to remove them through the simple expedient of declaring feeding time arrived. Remus sighed and drew his knife. A hand's worth of steel against *that* was going to be like trying to knock down a mountain with a pebble.

***

Remus gazed at the hideous creature and met its eyes – twin red dots of maniacal fury. As it began its charge Remus ran to the side, drawing it away from Cassie's body. It howled as it came at him, a strangely familiar wail interspersed with a throaty bark. Remus waited until the last second, before darting to the left, hurling himself out of its path. Betting that monster's weight would make it too slow to turn quickly. He felt its hot humid breath as it piled past him; he hit the forest floor and rolled.

He caught a brief glimpse of something on the beast's flank. A shape burnt by a branding iron? It resembled a dark dome with two mouse ears. He seriously doubted anyone was farming these things, though. The market for a couple of tons of homicidal crazy had to be kind of limited. Madre darted towards the beast's head, shouting insults that seemed surprisingly professional. Trying to distract it. Doing for Remus what he was doing for Cassie. It focused on the aerial steamman for a second, leaping in the air and goring the space with its tusks. Madre was too fast for it. She darted to the side, making an insulting whistling noise which actually did seem to enrage the creature. Great. Just what I need. *An even angrier monster. Unlike you, bird-brain, I can't fly.* That was when the seed of a plan opened up for Remus.

'Of course, I *can't* fly,' he whispered as he backed away.

The creature gave up trying to spear the annoying flying machine with its tusks, finally realizing that this prey was always going to remain a few feet out of reach. It roared in spittle-fuming fury, then pawed at the ground, ready to surge for Remus again. But he'd used the precious few seconds to manoeuvre to where he judged his last stand needed to be fought.

'Come on, snuffler!' he yelled, brandishing his knife. 'Come and taste my steel.'

It needed little encouragement, scrambling forward with its head lowered. Intending to smash the pitiful human food source into the air before choosing between impaling him or trampling him to death. Maybe a mixture of both. Remus stayed still as long as he dared. The terrible thought that he would stay paralyzed until he was speared flashed through his mind. He waited until he could almost smell the beast's rancid breath. Then he hurled himself to the right, reaching for the tree's lowest branch. A pale useless monkey seeking sanctuary in the forest canopy. The creature's weight crossed the hidden glass dome — already cracked from Cassie's fall — and it shattered, giving way. The beast gave a startled yelp, the ground under its clawed paws absent, sending it tumbling into the long-forgotten canteen below. Remus clung on for dear life. Suddenly aware how sweaty and tenuous his grip on the branch was. Watching the beast thrash around the chamber below. The old canteen transformed into a pit trap containing one furious, panicked monster. A critter that would be only too happy to see Remus Rawstone tumble and join it in its misery. It rampaged, smashing ancient abandoned tables and seating, sending fragments flying. Remus exhaled as he pulled himself into the tree, circled the trunk and gently eased himself to the soil on the opposite side of the pit.

Madre hovered over the chasm. She joined Remus as he dragged Cassie away from the danger of further ground collapse into the lost city. The sound of splintering tables and howls from the trapped creature followed them. 'A clever stratagem, Remus softbody.'

'Wasn't going to wrestle it to the ground, was I?' said Remus. 'Whatever *it* is.'

'A rhinodog, I believe,' said Madre. 'A hybrid created by your people in the years before the collapse. A cross between a chihuahua and a rhino.'

'Why in the name of the Circle would anybody create a monstrosity like *that*?'

'Blending the abnormally feral and the impossibly cute to generate new species for zoological display. Your ancestors started by resurrecting extinct lizards until the public grew bored seeing real species and demanded more originality. We should leave this part of the forest and pray that their sabre-kittens and razor-chicks haven't survived into this era.'

'Yeah,' said Remus, lifting Cassie over his shoulder. *That works for me.* Plaintive wailing from the trapped rhinodog stayed haunting Remus for far longer than it should have. *This death is on you, King Gene. All on you.*

= 8 =
Taste the Past

Magnus struggled as the fire crackled into life, flames leaping from the pile of logs. All the prisoners selected to provide the feast's food waiting and wailing under the weight of their chains. Watching the rotisserie spit assembled near the vehicle he'd been held captive inside.

'Inhale the smoke,' called Alios, chained to the side of the wheeler. 'Use the fumes to bring yourself a quick death.'

Magnus could barely keep upright, his knees buckling. The thought of suffocating in the smoke before being fried on the pyre more than he could bear. One of the leather-armoured brutes keeping the chained prisoners docile jabbed Magnus in the gut with a wooden spear shaft. 'Your metal friend is a fool. We're not animals. You are ethically sourced. We beat the chosen to death before roasting.'

'*Please*,' begged the captive next to Magnus, 'I am a silver worker, a master silversmith. I will bring you a great price at auction. Don't roast me.'

The warrior examined the man's hands. 'Ha. Look at those callouses. Not a single furnace scar on your arms. You have never been more than a dirt farmer.'

'Please!'

'Quiet, filthy liar!' barked the warrior. 'The high priest of the Seven comes to bless our ceremony.'

Magnus watched a garish-looking clansman striding towards the feast in swirling robes. His face was painted albino-white, hair dyed blood-red – the same colour as his crimson nose and ruby outline circling his mouth. He carried a red-and-white striped staff mounted with a dangle of human skulls. The priest banged his staff into the grass, leaving it impaled there while he raised white-gloved hands high in the air.

'Is this food ethically sourced?' the priest demanded.

'It is! It is! It is!' chanted the warriors around the fire pit.

'Blessed be the source. Let their flesh become your flesh. Let the weak be reborn as the strong in these cleansing flames … let your strength and speed never waver.'

'Never waver! Never waver!' the crowd yelled back.

The priest bowed low towards the warriors then began capering around the fire. 'Would you like fries with your flesh, brave fighters of the Clan Chevee?'

'No roots grow in darkness,' chanted the warriors.

'Because there is strength only in flesh. Cursed are the roots, unclean fruit of the Dark Goddess.' The priest raised his white gloves towards the prisoners chained by the vehicles. 'You slaves are mere chattel. Witness us, for you remain unblessed today. Weep for it. Only the chosen join us – their spirit becoming our spirit. Souls merging through the purifying fire of the Seven Gods' Holy Arches. Now, my children, liberate these blessed chosen from their weakness …'

A mighty roar rose from the warriors when Magnus was unchained first. Two clansmen dragged him towards the slowly turning spit. A brute with a large club waited by the fire, nodding with satisfaction. He patted a wooden block on the ground, his executioner's block. Magnus thrashed desperately, trying to get away, but his captors were far too strong. *No!*

'Lay the blessed out for tenderizing,' called the high priest. 'Camero of the Clan Chevee, first driver of the chief, begin the feast.'

The two warriors forced Magnus down to the ground. His terrified gaze drifted up towards the club-wielding executioner, Camero, as he hefted the weapon into the air. The executioner left the club hanging there and met the crowd's gaze. 'Be this chosen freshly prepared?'

'Freshly prepared!' the mass of savages yelled back.

Magnus watched in horror as the muscles on Camero's bare arms tensed, making ready to complete his stroke.

A sudden cry stayed his blow. 'Hold your cut! This prisoner is not chosen. He's been claimed.'

'Claimed?' growled the executioner at a warrior striding through the circle of onlookers. 'He *is* chosen for blessing, Fat Boy. Chosen by the Clan Chevee.'

'This one was claimed by the Clan Harlee,' barked the newcomer. 'He should never have been loaded on your Chevee wheelers.'

'We sourced him from the forest people. We fought for him.'

'The Harlee led the raid, Camero. This slave should never have been taken by your warriors. He was claimed by us.'

'Pah,' spat the executioner. He indicated the prisoners left by the vehicles. 'Claim any of those slaves, instead. This batch has been purified by the high priest.'

'Our slave was never yours to bless.' A group of leather-clad warriors joined Fat Boy from the crowd, appearing well prepared for violence. Swords and axes rested in their hands.

Camero spat into the grass. 'I say it differently.'

'I have seven skulls mounted on my wheeler's radiator plate. You possess a pitiful four skulls. Yield our slave.'

Camero raised an insulting finger towards Fat Boy. 'I yield you this.'

Fat Boy's face twisted with fury. 'Chief Nightrod claimed this weakling from the forest people. Do you disrespect the chief?'

'You dare disrespect my blessing, Fat Boy!' said the pale-faced holyman, joining the dispute. 'A high priest of the Chevee.'

'We answer to our own high priest. This claiming is by Chief Nightrod's command.'

'Here's *my* command,' shouted Camero for his warriors to hear. 'Spill these Harlee dogs' juices onto the grass for violating our ceremony!'

Mayhem erupted across the prairie. The pair of Chevee Clan guards pressing Magnus hard against the executioner's block released their grip. Instead, they beat off a wave of blade-waving Harlee warriors charging towards the fire. Magnus staggered to his feet, instantly aware how little attention was on him. A mote of calm among a storm of feuding warriors yelling threats, war cries and curses as they formed sides and singled out opponents. *Lunch is going to be late. Hopefully, I won't be late.* Magnus grabbed the rotisserie spike's wooden handle, yanked it off the fire pit and sprinted with it like a spear. He headed for the vehicle where Alios remained chained. Someone bumped into Magnus, swinging a machete – but not aimed at him. It sliced across a howling warrior's face. Cries rose from the chained slaves as he reached the flatbed. He prised his spike under an iron arch where the slaves' leg chain terminated, lifting the spike, trying to lever the arch's rivets away from the vehicle. *Give me a lever long enough and a fulcrum on which to place it, and I shall move the world. He grunted in anger. No good, it's too strong.* Alios and the other slaves realized what Magnus was trying to do. They mobbed forward, seizing the spike, adding their weight to it. With a fierce pop, the arch broke away from the vehicle, rivets flying off like bullets. The slaves madly began pulling the chain out of their ankle restraints, freed one at a time as the chain cleared their legs. Frenzied prisoners immediately fled, leaping away from the vehicle's flatbed. Pelting though the melee in all directions, barely hindered by the battling clansmen. Magnus couldn't tell if the warriors hadn't noticed the escape or had bigger fish to fry — too busy trying to hack rival clansmen into pieces.

Magnus was about to join the slaves in their headlong flight, but Alios seized his arm. 'We must take this vehicle to outpace these evil barbarians. Once they've finished slaying each other they will come in full pursuit of us.'

No doubt. Magnus nodded, too full of adrenalin to croak back a reply. He ran up to the flatbed's forward wall, peering over. The driver's position was at the vehicle's fore, little more than a roofless metal cabin with a bench for a seat. A heavy polished wooden steering wheel that would have been more in place on the bridge of a ship, a lever topped by a silver skull which he took to be a primitive gear mechanism. Two pedals on the floor – brake and accelerator. Few instruments or dials. Little better than an iron cart compared to the racers of the Mechancian Arena. Thankfully, no lock he could spot. *Too primitive for a starter key. Well, we were due some luck.* A turret position sat on the right of the cabin, holding a swivel-mounted crossbow. Magnus clambered over the cabin wall and landed on the driver's bench while the steamman slid into the gunner's turret.

Magnus ran his gaze across the controls, trying to comprehend the vehicle's workings. 'How do we fire the engine up?'

'Crank the copper wheel on the dashboard,' suggested Alios. 'I believe that ignites the combustion chamber with an electrical charge.'

Magnus spun the crank and it made a clicking sound. The engine below the armoured prow belched into angry life, the whole vehicle trembling with its exertions. He felt as if he were balanced on top of a fuming iron beast.

There was an old metal helmet lying on the cabin floor. It looked modern enough to have been stolen from one of the local kingdoms, daubed with swirls of blue paint and mounted on the side with buffalo horns. Magnus briefly considered using it to protect his skull, but he'd feel ridiculous, whatever protection it offered against clubbing to death by these savages. He stamped the accelerator pedal and the vehicle lurched forward. The steering wheel so heavy and stiff he needed both hands to turn it – like manoeuvering a mobile castle. Which in many ways was exactly what this unwieldy machine was designed to be. Still moving painfully slowly, the wheeler's prow smacked aside a brawling pair of warriors – all the force of being shouldered by a steel rhinoceros. Magnus steered west as best he could tell, keeping the accelerator pedal hard against the cabin floor. Amazingly, the dueling clansmen still seemed focused on each other. As though a wheeler twisting through their brawling ranks was the most natural thing in the world. Clansmen clashed steel while it rolled through the melee. Magnus sloughed through the food pit where he'd been fated to roast. Up ahead a solitary clansman appeared aware matters were badly awry. The white-faced high priest broke away from attempting to shout reason at the fighters, waving down the vehicle instead. Magnus gave a vicious yank at the steering wheel. He redirected their prow straight towards the holyman. White-face flung himself to the side, screaming in fury as his striped staff splintered under their heavy wheels.

'How'd you like those potatoes?' Magnus yelled over the cabin's armoured flank. He'd narrowly missed crushing the high priest. The open prairie stretched out in front of them, now. 'There has to be a way to move faster,' he spat.

Alios reached over and shoved the skull-topped lever forward, their speed accelerating. 'May the Steamo Loa watch over us.'

'Maybe your gods can send us an arena racer,' suggested Magnus. *That'd be grand.* Magnus wondered how long before their captors stopped killing each other, and resumed trying to club him to death before roasting him.

The answer, when it arrived, was depressingly short.

- 9 -

Southern Comfort

It was Madre who saw them first. A line of vehicles crossing the prairie. Nothing much to hide behind. The cover – and dangers – of the dense forest cathedral days behind them. Swapped for hills and rolling grassland. Rawstone knelt in the waist-high grass, urging Cassie to do the same. She copied him.

'I do not think they are are the savages we encountered,' said Madre, hovering low in the air. 'Their vehicles appear uniform in manufacture. The convoy has the look of an organized military force about it.'

'Better hope you're right,' said Rawstone, pointing to the caravan slowly swinging around. 'Because I do believe they spotted us before we ducked.'

Cassie sighed. Just for once, could we have some luck of the good variety?

The convoy drew closer, changing course in a lazy circle, maintaining the same speed, not accelerating. *Is that a sign they're peaceful? Or certain they can run us down without trying?* Cassie's heart thudded as she wondered what fresh danger they were about to run into. So far, the only friendly people they'd encountered had been faking it to sell their Jackelian visitors into slavery. 'Let me do the talking '

Rawstone warily watched the approaching vehicles. 'Why, you think I'm going to challenge them to a knife fight out here, one-by-one?'

'If they think I'm in charge they're more likely to believe we're friendly traders.'

'That's actually got a kind of logic to it,' agreed Rawstone.

Cassie was surprised how easily the braggart gave in. *An amiable Remus Rawstone? Now I know I'm in a different timeline.*

The vehicles arrived pretty much as Madre had described. A military force. Olive green-painted metal vehicles neatly riveted. Five jeeps, three armoured cars and a half-track with a wagon-like rear tied down with supply sacks and stacked with wooden crates. All the vehicles bore a large silver star set against a circle split into two halves – red on top, blue on bottom. The lead jeep had two flags on its bonnet fluttering with the same emblem. The vehicles' occupants a mixture of men and women in identical uniforms save for a few rank tags and badges. Tanned, weathered faces shielded by wide-brimmed slouch hats with one side pinned up. Sweat-stained three-button flannel shirts with a tight fold-down collar. Green canvas leggings with a single stripe on each leg. Trousers held up by a leather cartridge belt hung with a pistol holster, canteen and large hunting knife. Polished black leather boots rested lazily over the vehicles' sides. The soldiers clutched carbines, rifles and sub-machine guns with an ease that suggested they were the masters of the prairie out here.

The lead jeep slowed to a halt. Its door popped open. A female officer – Amazonian might have been a better description – swung her legs out and exited. Other soldiers quit their vehicles, standing alert by their side. The woman took in the two Jackelians and Madre with a knowing, appraising stare. She unsealed a cork stopper on a chain from her canteen and took a slow swig from it before addressing them.

'Well,' the last half of the word drawn out in a drawl, 'you're sure as heck not farmers or grassland nomads, are you? Three lost little birds, one of them a robot.'

'We're traders from the Reindeer Empire,' said Cassie,

hesitantly. 'I'm Cassie Templar. This is Remus Rawstone and our bodyguard, Madre.'

'Major Hosanna Smits, Texicana Republic. Well, you're pale enough to be down from the empire. Don't see much in the way of your trading caravan, though.'

'We were attacked,' said Madre. 'By a roving band of savages. They seized our friends and scattered our caravan.'

'Sure must have been awful,' said the Major, her tone indicating she didn't much care one way or the other. 'Big gnarly types with more tattoos than an inn full of sailors?'

'They were in vehicles, but primitive, not like—' Cassie indicated the convoy.

Major Smits shaded her eyes against the sun. 'Few garages out on the plains. Fast Food Clans ride next to their wheeler wrights. Closer to a religion than what you might call proper grease monkeys.'

'Primitive vehicles, but extremely effective,' said Madre.

The officer gazed curiously at the hovering steamman. 'Valuable, that. A machine mind occupying a scout drone. Only ever seen their like in pictures from the lost age. Must have been old-time military. Crazy expensive.'

'We lost others to the savages,' said Cassie.

'Got to hurt, losing those. Clans have been raiding ranches on our side of the river. Why we're here. They know exactly how long it takes us to drive out of Red River City, though. Always hightail it back north by the time we arrive. Well, at least your robots won't be eaten by the clans.'

'Eaten?' said Cassie. 'Why would the savages do that?'

'Because that's what makes the cannibal clans, cannibals,' said the Major as though she was talking to a child. 'The eating people-part of the equation.'

Cassie stared at Smits in horrified shock. *Eaten? No, it can't be. Magnus!*

'Sorry, girl-chick. Your traveling companions were taken as victuals. Less they got some serious skills, in which case they might be sold on later as slaves. Mostly the taken get eaten, though.'

'You have to help us rescue them!'

'Push beyond our supply lines for a pile of foreign bones? Nope, we owe our duty to the Republic, nobody else.'

Rawstone squared up to the Major. But Smits wasn't impressed – he'd met his match, here. 'They raided your people, too. What kind of damn army are you?'

'Texicana Rangers, Company D. And we haven't survived on plains patrol this long by chasing after foreign corpses.'

'So just what the hell *do* you do?' demanded Rawstone.

'Put the clans off raiding towns further south where there're goodly numbers of citizen voters. And we also capture dirty spies scouting for the Cals. *Tous saluent l'empreror!*'

'I'm sorry?' said Cassie.

'That's what I thought. The words you're fumbling for are: "L'empereur est père et l'empire est la patrie." Must be the first Reindeer Empire traders I ever met who never raised the emperor's salute. Fancy…'

Soldiers by the armoured car scowled, lifting their guns towards the three travelers.

'But don't worry,' continued Major Smits. She slid the large sharp hunting knife from her belt. 'We'll convince you to drop those weird accents of yours and tell us what fresh mischief the Cals are planning along the border. One way or another, you three lost little birds will end up singing for me.'

- 10 -

Snake-eaters

'Are they still gaining on us?' called Magnus, desperately keeping his focus on the terrain in front of them. Images of the stolen wheeler cracking an axle and leaving them helplessly stranded on the plains assailed him.

'Yes,' sounded an unexpected voice from behind in the vehicle's flatbed.

Magnus's eyes snapped back for the briefest of seconds. It was Bram Rager. The villager must have stowed away in the stolen vehicle's rear before they fled the camp. *You're lucky I'm not Remus Rawstone.* He'd kick the villager out as excess baggage. Distract the pursuit for long enough for Magnus and Alios to get away.

Alios passed an exasperated crackle through his voice-box at the revelation of their unasked-for passenger. 'If you have any suggestions about how to keep us alive …'

'Drive faster,' suggested Bram, hanging onto the driving cabin wall.

'Great,' said Magnus. 'Never occurred to me.'

'It's the Harlee warriors chasing us,' said Bram. 'They lost face twice. Once by allowing the Chevee to claim their slaves. A second time by permitting us to escape. They will never stop!'

At least a dozen wheelers raced across the prairie after Magnus. Bouncing through the grassland, exhaust plumes black, dirty and threatening. Each war wagon carrying a cohort of whooping razor-teethed warriors. They thrust their spears, axes and the occasional rifle towards the sky.

Magnus kept his gaze on the grassland in front of them. 'Can't keep chasing us forever.'

'They don't need to,' said Bram. 'They're loaded with spare fuel barrels. They just have to wait for our wheeler's tank to empty.'

'Why in the Circle's name you come with us, then?'

Bram shrugged. 'Look at how plump I am. I was going to be chosen for the next feasting. If I stayed, I'd end up dead before the end of the week.'

'You could have run off.'

'I was never much good at running. They keep hunting hounds, you know. Everyone lying in the grass, hiding out now, they'll be found and recaptured by the clansmen before nightfall.'

Alios leaned close to speak unheard by the villager. 'When our fuel tank is emptied, mount me and I will carry you.'

'You think you can outrun those clankers?'

'For a while at least.'

Too bad for Bram. Magnus found it hard to summon much sympathy. It was the Rager community who'd traded guests to the cannibals to lighten their own tribute.

Behind them, their pursuers switched formation. The arrow becoming a curve like the blade of a scimitar. *Ready to run us down on foot.*

It became unpleasantly hot in the driving cabin, the engine belching and complaining at being run at top speed for so long. His eyes drifted to the darkening sky. Evening was drawing in.

'If we can keep driving until nightfall…' said Magnus.

Alios nodded. 'I shall pray to the Steamo Loas that we last that long.'

Magnus's steamman friend had vision like an owl in the dark. With the waist-high grass to conceal them, surely they could slip away from their pursuers?

A boom sounded from behind. A geyser of grass and dirt erupted skyward to their rear.

Alios twisted around with his swivel-mounted crossbow. 'I do believe they're firing cannon balls, not artillery shells.'

'They draw any closer, primitive is going to work just fine.'

The steamman didn't bother returning fire with the weapon mounted in his section of the cabin. *Well out of range.* They headed towards a line of rolling hills. Gentle slopes they should have little difficulty crossing in the heavy wheeler. When Magnus reached the foothills, he pointed their prow to the side, taking the climb at an angle.

'It is ironic, Magnus softbody, that at home I resisted my chosen path to join the steammen knights. Yet here I am, preparing to fight for my life.'

'And I was going to be packed away to Middlesteel by my father to make a merchant of me,' said Magnus, trying to distract himself from the grim fate roaring up behind them. They had reached the top of the hill, ready to accelerate downhill. *A long way to travel to end up like this.* At least Cassie wasn't here. *Let her be safe, wherever she is now.*

Magnus returned his gaze to the landscape ahead, yanking the steering wheel to the side as he nearly ran down a pole. On the other side of the slope, a line of spaced wooden spears mounted with triangular pennants. Each pennant bore the image of a golden snake twisted in a figure eight-like helix. A fanged head eating its own tail. 'What the—!'

'Go back!' yelled Bram. 'Turn around!'

'You've got to be kidding me.' Magnus gunned the engine and lurched down the slope, bouncing as they hit the flat grassland on the other side.

Bram's face had turned pale. 'You don't understand. We've passed snake markers.'

'Oh, I do. I turn back and it's Magnus chops on the clans' menu tonight.'

'This is the territory of the snake-eaters,' cried Bram. 'The land is claimed for the serpent goddess.'

'Better some snakes get snacked on than I do.'

'The snake-eaters guard the gates of Hell itself. Please,' begged Bram. 'Listen to me … you must turn around.'

Alios gazed back towards the top of the rise. 'The barbarians' vehicles have halted. They aren't following us any further.'

Bram gripped the wall of the cabin, white knuckles clinging on. 'Of course they've stopped! In a feud, the worse to happen is your enemy beats you and eats your beating heart. Here, the snake-eaters will offer your soul to their goddess.'

'Correction,' said Alios. 'One vehicle has decided to continue the pursuit.'

'Must be the *brave* cannibals.'

'Turn around,' pleaded Bram.

Magnus snorted. 'They're just spears hung with flags.'

'The serpent goddess devours all. If you're rich you can pay the priestesses to be sacrificed but not consumed. The serpent can vomit you out anywhere in the world, it's said. You may pass across the entire face of the globe in hours.'

'Very handy. '

'I am no king and neither are you, merchant, or you would have paid to be regurgitated in Texicana.' Magnus shook his head. *Bram's gone insane. He's totally lost it.*

Still, the villager's warnings unnerved Magnus. During their flight, he'd appeared sanguine about being recaptured and consumed by the clansmen. Yet here Bram was, sobbing like a child for the crime of passing a line of spears. Their engine's roar broke and started to cough. The wheeler slowed. Its fuel dial danced on empty. Magnus wiped tears of sweat out of his eyes. 'This is our best chance. Most of those savages too scared to follow. Evening drawing in. We just have to outrun a single wheeler's worth of killers in the grass.'

'No!' protested Bram. 'Not a yard further.' The villager sprinted to the hijacked wheeler's rear, leaping off the flatbed, rolling into the grass behind them.

Crazy!

Incredibly, Bram stumbled to his feet behind them, seemingly uninjured. The villager sprinted back towards the slope – veering away from the line of waiting clan vehicles. Swinging about, the single pursuing wheeler changed course towards him. *For someone who isn't any good at running, he's doing a superb job of it.* 'We can't stop.' *Not without surrendering.*

Alios shook his head in sad acknowledgment. 'I know.'

The report of a large mounted rifle echoed out from the pursuing wheeler. Bram lifted off his feet, twisting around in the air before landing concealed by the long swaying grass. The Harlee continued closing in on Magnus and Alios, not even slowing. The cannibals left Bram's corpse lying still in the plains. Magnus grimaced. Bram's village had betrayed them, yet nobody deserved to die like that. Abandoned for the carrion eaters to peck at.

Their engine changed pitch again – more coughs than roar, now.

'Running on fumes and goodwill,' swore Magnus.

Alios eased himself up inside the crossbow turret. 'Our lead over the barbarians will only falter with the lack of fuel. Time to abandon this vehicle and rely on the swiftness of my four legs.'

'Wish I had a saddle.'

'To amplify my lack of dignity, perhaps?'

Magnus eased off the accelerator, reaching down to use the helmet to jam the pedal in place. The two Jackelians bundled out of the cabin, climbing into the rear. Then the centaur-like steamman leaped off the vehicle, landing in the prairie with all the coordination of a racehorse. Magnus followed with a lot less grace, grunting as he struck the ground. He spiralled around, winded and dizzy before rolling to a halt in the dirt. Their wheeler continued moving, lurching from side-to-side now. Barreling ahead fast enough to confuse the savages into thinking it was still manned?

'Onto me,' urged Alios, helping Magnus climb aboard the steamman's cold metal back and gripping Magnus tight with both manipulator arms. The steamman started to canter before breaking into a steady gallop, grass whipping past Magnus's ankles. They picked up speed, plowing through the prairie. Behind them, the barbarian war wagon swerved uncertainly. Deciding whether to pursue the wildly swinging wheeler or go after the steamman. The savages swiveled the prowl of their vehicle towards Alios.

Damn.

'They can tell our wheeler's abandoned,' wheezed Alios, straining from his exertions.

'Hoped they'd want to save face by recovering it.'

But Alios was always the more valuable booty here. Magnus was just supper with the cheek to try to escape a bad fate. A steamman like Alios was worth far more than the clan's stolen vehicle, obviously.

'Hold tight,' growled Alios.

That seemed rather ironic to Magnus, given the steamman's two grasping hands was all that were preventing him sliding off his friend's spine. He found it difficult to concentrate on staying mounted, what with his heart thudding in his chest like a hammer. Magnus resisted the urge to glance behind. Watch their pursuer shortening the gap on the galloping steamman. See the hollering warriors cavorting in the back, spears and blades stabbing the sky. All too easy to imagine blades plunging into the wretches who had stolen their clan's vehicle and honour, both.

Grass whipped past as the steamman increased his pace, leaping surefooted across the undulating prairie. There were distinct advantages to four legs. Not to mention a boiler heart compressing energy like the racers Magnus once careened around in. Their pursuit's bloodcurdling yells grew nearer. Ahead, something glinted in the landscape, a mirror catching the sun. Whatever it was it would make no difference. They would be run down in seconds. Dead or recaptured long before they reached it.

***

Cassie wasn't sure of the border town's name and there wasn't much to see. Mainly because she was swinging upside down, both feet roped to a pole like cattle about to be butchered. Around her, low white adobe buildings and a thick wall with a wooden firing step serving as a battlement.

'It's starting to get hot,' said Remus, roped upside down to her left.

'Going to leave us to dry out,' coughed Cassie. She almost laughed. 'Like two kippers.'

'You need to light a fire under fish to smoke them.'

'Don't give the Major ideas.' Cassie's body felt as stiff as a board from being left out overnight. Her head spinning from being strung out the wrong way around.

Madre was confined in an iron box by their side. Both the box and the pole were obviously punishments for the soldiers, situated in the barracks' parade ground. *I wonder what the troops have to do to earn this? Deserting their post, absent without leave, drunk on duty?*

Occasionally, Madre's muffled voice called out from inside the sweatbox, but Cassie couldn't tell what the little flying steamman was saying. She tried calling back a few times but discovered that shouting upside down just made her feel even sicker.

A trooper came out and played reveille on a bugle. Then Major Hosanna Smits appeared with two armed soldiers, snapping a swagger stick against her trousers. 'You changed your mind about spilling the Cals' plans for our part of the border?'

'Can't spill what we don't know,' insisted Rawstone.

Cassie tried to fix a dizzy eye on the Major. 'We're not spies.'

'Well, I just got me a telegram back from the capital. The Reindeer Empire's embassy doesn't know anything about any traders in these parts with your names.' She gestured to her sentries. 'Cut them down.'

Cassie grunted as she hit the dirt, hardly able to move as the compass in her skull tried to reorient to normal, blood pumping the right way.

'You should have asked the Cal Ambassador, too,' said Cassie.

'Cals tend to let their guns do the negotiating for them,' said the Major. 'Nobody believes a word any of you rascals say, anyhow.'

'Just going to let us go, then,'

Smits lost heart at that. 'Nope, just wanted to make sure no embassy paper shuffler was going to create a stink when I dig two holes and bury you up to your necks.'

'You think that's what gets us to talk?'

'After you're buried, well. Ants in Texicana, they do love their honey even if they have to lick it off a face. It is what we call a good sweet talking.'

Rawstone staggered to his feet and tried to swing at the Major, but he didn't have enough blood in his head to see straight yet. As he missed, one of the sentries cracked a rifle butt into the young Jackelian's ribs, putting him back into the dirt next to Cassie. Muffled shrieks of complaint came from the sweatbox. Major Smits shook her head, sadly, then kicked the iron crate. 'I want a list of all the sectors you are probing for weaknesses, every one!'

'We can't tell you,' moaned Cassie.

'Then I hope you like eating ants, because either you're going to taste them, or they are going to taste *you*.'

- 11 -

Bone Gardens

Alios stumbled to the side, startled by the sudden appearance of hundreds of warriors who had been lying hidden flat in the long grass. They seemed to rise as one. A single entity. Definitely not part of the pursuing clan. Female. Tall, muscular Amazonians who wouldn't have looked out of place in one of the Catosian City States back home. Each fighter clutched a wooden staff, a bulbous metal head on top with a metal scythe mounted on the weapon's lower end. They stood proudly wearing green silk shifts held by belts with gold snake-shaped buckles. Alios attempted to evade these newcomers, zigzagging between their ranks, but one of the warriors swept out with her staff. An angry fizzing sound left Magnus flying. They both hit the grass hard. Alios tumbled over in a windmill motion, flailing across the ground. Winded, Magnus swayed to his feet and dragged himself across to Alios. He tried to roll the steamman over, but Alios Hardcircuit was left quivering in a wave of spasms.

'Alios!'

'Wireless—taser,' Alios's voice escaped his mouth grille in a twisted series of clicks and gasps. 'Paralyzed. Leave—me—run.'

Magnus heard the noise behind him too late. As he swiveled he met a wooden staff thrust sideways into his face, sending him reeling back towards the soil.

'That's better. Stay!' commanded a female warrior. Her staff spun around the air to stop under her armpit.

Magnus reeled from the blow, his nose left bloodied. The metal tip of the staff's head steamed from whatever it had spat at Alios Hardcircuit. Magnus looked on stunned as the cannibals' wheeler skidded to a halt in front of the female warriors. The company's staffs lifted like a porcupine's spines towards the plainsmen. They jumped warily down from their vehicle.

'You are Harlee clan?' called the same female warrior who had subdued the escaping slaves.

'Chief Nightrod's steel,' barked a bald clansman. The wagon leader stepped forward. 'We bring you your sacrifice, true to our chief's word.'

'These are the slaves we seek?'

The clansman indicated Alios Hardcircuit. 'A machine horse with the chest of a man at the front. Do you doubt it, high priestess?'

'A centaur,' grimaced the female. 'That is the correct word from the old time. A *robot*.'

'The clan does not hunt slaves for payment in words.'

The high priestess clapped her hands together. Two warriors came forward bearing a small casket. They opened its lid, revealing a pile of silver coins and bullets inside.

'That ammo is true-cast?'

'Better than those stolen Tallgrass Kingdom rifles of yours deserve,' said the high priestess. 'The shells will not misfire or explode in your barrels.'

The Harlee leader bowed slightly, crossing his arms before her. All the other cannibals made a similar gesture. 'Blessings to the serpent.'

'Blessings to the serpent,' agreed the high priestess. As she spoke a green snake the size of an airship slipped through the sky, borne aloft on hundreds of tiny beating wings

The clansmen screamed in fear, scattering, sprinting back towards their vehicle dragging the casket with them.

'Leave quickly,' shouted the high priestess. 'Now our deal is done, the Goddess is not pleased with your trespassing in our territory.'

The war wagon reversed at speed, swung about and roared off towards the hill and the line of waiting vehicles. Magnus got to his knees, stunned at the rapid turn of events. *What's going on here? Why have we been sold on?* The value of Alios's metal hide, Magnus understood. But the young Jackelian knew he should be bones on the cannibals' feasting pit by now. His eyes drifted up. The bizarre sight of the dragon-snake in the sky sliding off towards the line of spears which marked the border.

'Nobody said you could stand,' grunted the high priestess. 'Filthy disobedient man-child.'

She jabbed the bulbous top of the staff into his spine. Magnus doubled up in agony, unbearable waves of pain burning every muscle and synapse in his body.

'What now?' Magnus heard the question from afar, words faintly drifting through an encroaching darkness.

Before he passed out, the reply drifted in like a snake's hiss. 'Now we take them to the underworld and feed them to the Goddess!'

***

Magnus came to. *I'm still alive?* He possessed only fleeting memories from drifting in and out of his stunned stupor. And what he remembered seemed so bizarre he could hardly credit it. A glass pyramid rising out of the prairie, sapphire blue like a polished gem. Being carried into darkness, heading deep underground. Then fumes. Steam. Strange hymns in a language he didn't know. Magnus tried to focus on the present. He lay bound, hands and legs tied tight with some sort of rubbery binding. Being hauled in the back of a trolley alongside Alios – one of dozens in a chain. Connected to a small vehicle driving almost silently save for a low hum. They passed slowly through narrow stone tunnels lit by glowing panels.

'Alios,' whispered Magnus, 'are you conscious?'

'Yes,' croaked the steamman.

'We're underground now?'

'I believe so. Given the sophistication of construction, I would say this is part of a subterranean complex which pre-dates the collapse of civilization.'

'I heard these maniacs say they wanted to sacrifice us to their serpent monster,' said Magnus.

'I hope not,' whispered Alios. 'This building, their wireless taser weapons, they both show a level of technology I have yet to see above-ground.'

'Did you watch that dragon snake flying through the sky? The cannibals hightailed it out of here as soon as the monster appeared.'

'That, at least, I think I can explain. Light stimulated by radiation can be used to cast projections which appear solid, but are, in reality, as insubstantial as mist.'

'It was only an illusion?' Magnus didn't know whether to be relieved or angry he been hoodwinked by the snake-eaters.

'Madre spoke to me of similar technologies used for advertising before the collapse. No doubt the creature was projected from the pyramid to strike the fear of their goddess into the gullible.'

'The snake-eaters want us for something,' said Magnus. 'The clan always planned to sell us onto these Catosian muscle maidens.'

'That mystery, I fear, I have no explanation for yet, Magnus softbody.'

Magnus really hoped that the projection wasn't based on a real creature they kept chained down here. The monster they wanted to feed him to.

The cart trundled onto a platform running down the side of a tunnel. It was lined with women in green robes, kneeling and praying and singing. Behind the novices and the high priestess of the snake-eaters a line of warrior women stood sentry with their staff weapons. As the cart stopped, the guards unceremoniously tipped Magnus and Alios out of the trolley, before dragging the two of them to their feet. They were shoved close to the tunnel mouth.

'We summon the snake,' called the high priestess. 'In our humility, we beseech her appearance.'

'Summon her, summon her,' chanted the novices.

Magnus watched the high priestess dance around the platform close to the tunnel mouth. She cast powder from a clay pot, throwing it against the tiled mosaic which lined the tunnel. The powder sparkled as it struck the tiles.

Magnus groaned. The young Jackelian still ached from the weapon used to paralyze him. *Now I'm waiting to be consumed by some horrifically mutated python. This day is just getting better and better.*

'Brave heart,' whispered Alios.

'I hear something.'

Whatever the high priestess had summoned was approaching out of the darkness.

A roaring rushed towards the tunnel mouth. *That doesn't sound much like a snake?*

Light pierced the darkness and a long capsule the size of a submarine slid into the platform. It had no windows. A hull tapered at the front, bulbous at the rear, like a spike ready to be plunged into the ground. Built from some kind of ceramic. Magnus caught glimpses of a rainbow livery now hidden by a crude painting of a snake. The design covered the capsule's length. Fangs, eyes, and mouth rendered at the front, a sinuous body undulating down the capsule's side. The snake effect disappeared when the capsule opened. Eight doors retracted, revealing a line of seats inside.

'Praise be to the serpent,' called the high priestess. Her novices remained crouched on their knees, still swaying and singing.

'Let these supplicants be consumed by the goddess. Her will obeyed by all of her true servants.'

The novices stood now and rushed towards the capsule, dipping into clay pots to rub scented oils across the hull. The warriors prodded Alios and Magnus with the business ends of their staff weapons, indicating they were to board the capsule.

Magnus was shoved down into a seat with Alios made to squat in the gap between the two lines of seats. Warrior women sat clutching their staffs. The high priestess knelt at the front of the capsule, swinging an oil-filled lamp while humming. Although there was no sign of windows along the capsule's exterior, glass window screens glowed inside. A dull green light which did little to help Magnus's throbbing head. A plaque was positioned above the window screen next to Magnus, text stamped in copper. Its translation came to Magnus courtesy of his imprinted learning. *Hyperloop – Buenos Aires-Seattle Spine.* The words made no sense to him. *All of this built to help Buenos Aires-*

Seattle with his bad back? Not likely. Doors slid shut and the capsule seemed to move smoothly forward.

Magnus got a sense of the capsule starting to speed up. Windows flickered into life, the dull green light replaced by a passing landscape of rolling green fields. *That can't be real? We're still in tunnels deep underground.* Formations of tiny flying machines flowed across the sky, beautiful spired cities rising in the distance. Vast windmills lined the neat green fields while hundreds of kites tethered on lines drifted among the clouds.

'What is this?' said Magnus. 'It can't be real?'

'Images of their lost world,' sighed Alios. 'A world only remembered underground.'

'The serpent goddess honours you,' called the priestess, 'with glorious views of her paradise.'

'Of course, she does,' groaned Magnus.

'Careful,' whispered Alios. 'Her observances are no act. I think our softbody captors believe deeply in the truth of their faith.'

'I may never have traveled to Middlesteel,' whispered Magnus, 'But even a country rube like me has heard of the city's atmospheric transport system. That's what we're riding now. An atmospheric capsule in a vacuum. Not a magical snake.'

'Stop your babbling,' snarled the priestess. 'The goddess rewards you with images of the afterlife. Happy fields of the serpent, filled with her bounty gifted to all true believers after death.'

'Not me, then,' muttered Magnus.

Their journey continued for what felt like hours before the capsule finally slowed and came to a halt. Doors retracted. They revealed a platform beyond which might have been the same tile-lined walls where they had started their journey. A line of snake-eaters waited for the passengers' emergence from the capsule.

'Sisters of the Temple Brea,' said a tall woman, stepping forward.

The high priestess who had accompanied them bowed. 'Sisters of the Temple Obion.'

A frantic screaming sounded from the front of the platform. Magnus lent over. A figure tied naked to the tracks below. There were other prisoners bound there, but they had all been crushed to death by the capsule's arrival. One of the guards lowered her staff at the screaming man. Her weapon spat a bolt of energy, rendering him silent and unconscious.

'You stopped short of the final sacrifice,' said a novice to the warrior.

'The Goddess will have his soul when we leave,' apologized the guard. 'She still requires sustenance to carry us home.'

The novice looked surprised as she noticed Magnus and Alios. 'Strange birds you bring into our temple. Surely these two aren't rich enough to pay to forgo sacrifice?'

The warrior jabbed a finger towards the ceiling. 'Another has paid.'

'Ah!'

'Come, man-child,' growled the warrior, jabbing Magnus in the ribs with her staff. 'And keep your metal bondservant quiet.'

Alios clearly bridled at being considered Magnus's property, but the steamman held back at voicing his opinion on the matter. Neither of them wanted to be at the receiving end of the warriors' weapons.

They were led through a series of passages and tunnels, up towards a set of metal steps that looked to be part of a long-stilled machine. Finally, they emerged in a cavernous hall under a tinted glass roof. A group of strangers waited in the slanted sunlight. Stout soldiers in matt-black metallic armour carrying modern-looking rifles. Magnus knew this group was no part of the temple staff. All male, but the soldiers' gender wasn't the discrepancy that had caught his attention. Each soldier possessed four arms! *One set too many. That's just greedy.*

'Make your offering to the Goddess,' demanded the high priestess. She halted her prisoners before the military company.

Their officer nodded, and his soldiers came forward bearing a steel crate. They slid open its lid, revealing layers of needle-tipped vials resting nestled inside orange foam.

'Solely females to be born? asked the high priestess archly.

'As always,' replied the officer. 'Inject yourself with one of these and you'll be pregnant within a month. Only female offspring. Ninety-seven percent genetic hereditary from the mother.'

The high priestess scowled at the soldier. 'One of our novices gave birth to a boy last month, General Centum, and we are not happy.'

He appeared amused by that. 'Not on us. She was whelping the old-fashioned way. I'd check your eunuchs for a near miss with a sharp blade if I was you.'

The high priestess snorted. 'Take these two heretics and leave our temple.'

'Gladly,' said the General.

Magnus and Alios passed into the custody of the soldiers before they were both briskly marched outside. They exited a glass pyramid identical to the one Magnus had glimpsed back on the prairie. A tarmacked road led up to the structure, the road cut through a pine forest. An imposing vehicle idled outside. Certainly not manufactured by the cannibal clans. It was formed from a dull black metal which seemed to suck the very sunlight out of the clearing. Tall, it rested on eight large ball-like wheels.

The vehicle's length accommodated a cannon up front, an eight-barreled hedgehog of a turret at the back, while a warhead-peppered launcher occupied its middle. A doorway lay open, retractable ladder steps folded out. An emblem glinted on the vehicle's armour – a white-and-green shield with a rampant brown bear clutching seven crimson stars.

'Thank you for saving us,' Magnus told General Centum.

'From what?' asked the officer.

'Why, the snake-eaters.'

At this, the four-armed soldiers roared with laughter. 'That's a good one. We *saved* the poor little half-arms and his drone.'

'I fail to see what is so funny,' said Alios.

The soldiers just roared all the louder with hilarity.

'You see the crest on our vehicle…?'

'Very nice,' said Magnus.

'Sweet hope. Where did the snake-eaters buy you two jokers from? Don't you know whose flag that is?'

Magnus shook his head.

'It's the Cal flag, bumpkin.'

'A nation…?' said Magnus. 'I saw the Cal nation on a map.'

General Centum sadly shook his head. 'It's almost enough to doubt her infallibility.'

'Whose?'

'The Witch Queen of the Cals, bumpkin. Her all-seeing Highness ordered you two fools rounded up. You're a threat to the state, apparently. Though looking at you, I'd say you're mainly a threat to your own safety.'

'I don't understand?'

'Clearly not, half-arms. But at least it explains why you're not begging the snake-eaters to sacrifice you to their goddess, rather than be handed over to the Witch Queen. That's normally what I have to put up with when I come to this hell-damned temple.'

***

Magnus sat swaying alongside Alios in the armoured transport while it rumbled through the land of the Cals. He caught glimpses of the landscape through their vehicle's firing slots. They had long since put the forest behind them. Now gaining altitude, following roads cut into the side of mountains. 'You're unlike everyone else I've met here,' Magnus told the general.

Their captor raised all four of his palms into the air. 'You mean these …'

'Exactly.'

'We are geo-men. Soldier caste of the Cals, warrior-born. Geo-men are stronger, faster, tougher than any half-armed fighter.' General Centum flourished two daggers with his lowers arms while clutching a rifle and pistol in his upper limbs. 'How would you like to fight me, bumpkin?'

'I don't want to fight anyone,' said Magnus. *Although maybe I could surprise you with a few of the skills the Protector packed into my skull.*

'Very wise. Most half-armed are cowards when it comes to facing us. Not an option for those warrior-born among the Cals, however. Now, there's a rare sight to take your breath away.'

Their vehicle rumbled along a winding road carved high into the slopes. Magnus stared out of the firing slit. The view far below was what the general spoke of … a city stretched around a large cyan lake.

'Neutron City,' said the general. 'First City of the Cals. Fortress of the Great Sages. The greatest capital on Earth.'

The strangest, thought Magnus. It appeared to be formed of soaring concrete termite mounds peppered with porthole-style windows. Many of the towers reached ninety storeys high. Normal-looking structures dominated at ground level; food stands, shops, roads crowded with all manner of traffic; throngs on foot-powered vehicles, rickshaws, horses and carts, unicycles, motorized vehicles. Neutron City resembled a shanty town risen around the mounds of termite overlords. Alios pointed at one of the towering rises — its construction still in progress. A skeleton of girders and floors traced a mountainous outline, covered in a paper-like material quivering in the wind. And hanging in the sky above the artificial mountain, three massive airships. Actually, construction vessels. Colossal tubes jutting mandible-like from their nose cones, spraying liquid concrete down onto the frame.

Their armoured vehicle left the mountain-side road, passing through a brightly lit tunnel. When the vehicle emerged, they drove across a flat plateau, a wide boulevard running up to a range of snow-covered heights ahead. Vehicles passed them in both directions, small, sleek-looking mobile blocks of gleaming steel. *Not part of the military, then.* Marble statues of notables lined the boulevard. The figures wore togas while clutching scrolls, scientific instruments, and globes. Each figure soared two-hundred-feet high. Beyond the statues lay a series of bleached white pyramidal towers serving some decorative purpose.

'I believe I know how the city by the lake acquired its name,' said Alios, a note of horror catching in the steamman's words.

Magnus stared curiously at his metal friend. 'How so?'

'I'm detecting faint residual traces from those white towers. Traces of a weapon known as a neutron bomb.'

'I thought civilization collapsed due to a comet strike, not war?'

Alios's voice-box quivered. 'The bomb has unique characteristics. It poisons organic life while leaving physical structures intact. The poisoning period is relatively brief. Forty years. Those towers are composed of bones scarred by air-burst neutron blast burns. They serve the same purpose as the snake-eaters' skull-mounted banners. A warning of the dire fate of all who oppose this regime.'

Magnus swayed shocked at the scale of slaughter needed to raise so many bone towers. 'Human bones? A *warning*? That's monstrous. It would take millions of skeletons to build those towers.'

'It seems their Witch Queen's title is well deserved.'

General Centum leaned forward. 'You understand nothing. The Sinners' Spires were raised during the Great Sages' time, long before the rule of queens and kings. Only the Sages possessed the wisdom to survive the long darkness which destroyed the old world. Great hordes of the stupid and lazy gazed upon the Sages' works with envious eyes. Too dull and idle to work for their own survival, the barbarians plotted to steal the Sages' power. They didn't care that their theft would hasten humanity's end. Shivering cold and jealous, they assaulted the Sages' fastness in endless wild mobs. That was when the Sages deployed their killing suns to slay the hordes. They burnt the flesh off every last murderous barbarian. Then they piled their scorched bones here to discourage invaders from emulating the horde's example.'

'Where are the Sages now?' asked Magnus.

'In the halls of our revered ancestors,' said the general. 'Their genius, their spirit, gave birth to the Cal nation. We are the true heirs to the old world. The inheritors of all that was lost during the fall. All that shall rise again with the ascendance of our nation's star. You, I am sure, are descended from the horde's deformed barbarians. You appear dull enough.'

I really hope we're not descended from you, thought Magnus.

Once at the end of the plateau the vehicle passed a checkpoint bunker and heavy steel blast gates before entering a dark tunnel. They didn't drive far before halting. The vehicle's headlamps revealed a round windowless chamber which started to shudder. Magnus realized they had halted on an elevator plate now descending deep into the rock. They descended for fifteen minutes before coming to a rest. General Centum and his soldiers unbuckled from their seats and the officer gestured with his pistol towards a hatch. They dismounted inside a small round concrete-walled chamber with a single exit. Alios and Magnus were ushered through the passage by the soldier, marched towards what lay beyond.

Magnus wasn't sure what to expect outside, but the incredible vista that waited proved far beyond all his possible speculations.

***

Magnus and Alios emerged onto a ledge on the side of a vast building, a crystal tower hanging from a cavern ceiling in the manner of a stalactite. Hundreds of glass towers dangled from the cavern roof around them, connected by webs of concrete roadways and monorails. A strange inversion of a city's normal gravity, its architecture made Magnus want to hang onto the ledge's guard rails for dear life. Below, Stygian darkness boiled like an upside-down night sky. Magnus looked closer. He could see the tops of massive waterwheels endlessly turning inside clouds of steam. Geysers of superheated water leaped out of the darkness, spraying the tips of the dangling glass towers. Magnus flinched, even though he was out of range of the scolding geysers.

'These are the Oxnard Vaults,' proclaimed the general, proudly. 'Founded by House Zhu. Each of the seven houses rules over vaults of similar scale.'

'Fascinating,' observed Alios. 'A series of linked cities constructed underground to survive the comet strike.'

Magnus remembered the towers of bleached white human bones slowly disintegrating alongside the boulevard. 'Not quite big enough for *everyone* to survive.'

'No,' agreed Alios Hardcircuit, quietly. 'Built, I dare say, to keep alive the elite. Those with wealth and power enough to divert civilization's resources into a last great shelter. Large enough to protect the favored few along with their staff, servants, and soldiers.'

The general strode ahead, his troops marching in a tight formation behind Magnus and Alios. He appeared oblivious to Magnus's opinion of the subterranean shelter. 'These are ancient streets. You can feel the Sages' footsteps walking before us. Hear echoes of our nation's greatness. Only those fortunate enough to live inside our avenues understand the Cals' destiny … to reunite the continent under our banner. Beautiful.'

If there was a beauty here, it was the beauty of hell. It seemed an artificial Hades to Magnus's eyes. Even more bizarre when they boarded a monorail capsule. A metal-bottomed glass cylinder which hovered above the rails like a dragonfly, before whisking them through the maze of towers at high speeds. Occasionally it slowed for corner turns, affording Magnus a view of parkland contained inside stalactite towers. Cals eating and playing, shopping at wide marketplaces. A wealthy advanced society encapsulated like a ship-in-a-bottle.

They approached the cavern's center. Nestled among its towers hung a blue octahedral-shaped glass spire. Twice the size of the nearest construction. A vast artificial gem set above a fountain of magma. Fire sprayed up to light the structure in shifting crimson fury. This was where the monorail led.

'We're traveling inside *that*?' Magnus prayed magma wouldn't coat their capsule and roast them first.

General Centum nodded. 'Yes, The Great Crystal Palace of Oxnard. You are honoured. Barbarians rarely get to step inside the palace.'

No, barbarians like us are piled up as bones outside.

Their capsule flashed inside the diamond-shaped palace, slowing to a stop inside a vast arrival area. A turntable filled with monorail capsules rotated, dispatching carriages towards a multitude of exit rails while locals queued to board. It was hard to appreciate the palace's scale until they emerged from the monorail and walked its galleries and corridors. Staff quietly bustled on foot. No carts or motorized vehicles to break the monastic silence clinging to the wide corridors and airy halls. Everything painted in bright primary colors. They passed glass cases where manikins displayed costumes. Some of the clothes were geo-men military uniforms, others scientific tunics or bright peacock-coloured suits. It made Magnus wonder if a military caste wasn't the only specialization the Cals had engineered among their race.

Geo-men stood sentry everywhere they passed. Dark armoured plates protecting chest, arms and legs. Watchful harsh eyes staring from under helmet visors. Usually, two arms folded behind their back while the remaining pair bore a spear and rifle at guard position. They saluted the general and his troops as the officer passed, snapping spears to. He nodded thoughtfully back towards the soldiers. Alios and Magnus were led to a throne room shaped as a vast octahedral hall. This room thronged with courtiers. A podium at the far end of the hall where a rite seemed to be occurring.

General Centum led his two prisoners down the centre of the hall, halting before the podium.

'You are blessed by the Sages,' noted the general. 'You have arrived in time to witness the Renewal Ceremony. This rite only happens once a decade.'

A woman stood on the podium. Magnus took her to be the Witch Queen. She wore a sweeping purple dress with a high collar, matching a crown set with glowing purple gems. Aged about sixty, her face suggested a serene faded beauty of high cheekbones and taut alabaster skin. Her silver graying hair had been fixed up in two buns. She carried herself regally, bearing a crystal-tipped staff towards a table surrounded by throbbing machines. An impressive throne rested next to the table, attended by dozens of tech-elders in white suits, faces protected by filter masks. A choir sang a high-pitched lilting melody, a language unknown to Magnus although some of the words sounded familiar. A line of seven maidens climbed the podium steps in crimson robes, each led by one of the white-suited figures. If the maidens shared any distinguishing characteristic it was their youth and beauty. They knelt on the podium and joined the choir singing, raising their voices loud and clear.

The Witch Queen approached the line of women and raised her staff above their heads, walking the line from left to right. The singing dropped to a gently anticipatory pitch. Above the third young woman's head — a blonde's long golden locks — the staff's crystal tip flared brightly.

'The supplicant select stands revealed,' cried the chief tech-elder.

'Praise be!' keened the assembled courtiers, repeating the phrase over and over until it became a frenzied chant.

As the din died down the tech-elder raised his hands into the air. 'The supplicant select has been chosen from House Hamilton. A true descendant of the Sages. Pure of humanity. Pure of heart and mind and helix. Let the wisdom and strength of her house suffuse the blood and bones of our land. Let her house's purity guide our promised victories.'

Again, the chanting fell away. This time the silence was filled by a fresh hymn, joyous and happy. The six unchosen maidens were led away, heads bowed, while the selected woman confidently approached the table next to the throne to lie down on it.

'Is the young softbody heir to the throne now?' asked Alios.

'In a manner of speaking,' said General Centum. 'Behold, the miracle of transfiguration renewal!'

A yellow gel-like substance began pumping over the table where the maiden lay prone, tiny nozzles spraying out a material which solidified on contact with air. The gel crackled as it hardened into an amber-like crystal. On the throne, the Witch Queen was encased in a similar material by sprays set inside her chair. Soon both women lay trapped inside a transparent golden mesh.

Magnus gazed on stupefied. *What is going on here?*

'I call upon the Great Sages!' cried the tech-elder. 'In the name of Einstein and Musk. In the name of Thiel and Hawking. Let the spirit of our ancestors flow through the chosen. By helix and blood let the Holy Transfiguration come to us here.'

As Magnus watched, machinery behind the throne started to hum. Flashes of energy surged out from a crown of spikes. One bolt hit a courtier, slaying him in an instant, leaving the man's corpse smoking on the floor. Rather than eliciting panic or terror, a murmur of sheer wonder rose from the crowd in attendance. Most of the energy, however, was absorbed by the amber-encased throne and table.

'These people are insane,' Magnus whispered to Alios.

The steamman nodded. 'I fear your diagnosis is accurate.'

Agitated by bolts of energy, the amber started to melt into a liquid around the table and throne. A stream of yellow liquid washed over the podium towards the courtiers. At the front of the queue, there was a mad jostling as people rushed forward, shoving each other out of the way. They dropped to their knees and began desperately lapping at the liquid with their tongues, trying to drink from it before it drained into a series of drains and gutters. Soldiers appeared to restore order among the courtiers, forcing the crowd to stand back and leave the liquid. Technicians approached the vanishing pool, each bearing a long glass container. They carefully filled each beaker, then corked it and marched off towards the six remaining maidens; presenting each woman with a vial as though it was a consolation prize.

On the throne, the Witch Queen rose. She was free of the amber now. Magnus gasped as he saw the ruler's face. Her hair golden, her features those of a twenty-year-old. *She's changed her body.* The Witch Queen's face was similar to the one Magnus had glimpsed before the ceremony, but now blended with the maiden's features. As if the two women had been compressed into a single entity. The table where the maiden lay strapped shifted, humming, from horizontal to vertical position, revealing a mummified corpse barely contained by the robes she had worn.

'Behold!' cried the tech-elder. 'The wisdom of the Great Sages renews our power. Renews the promise of our place as the true inheritors of the Earth.'

'Transfiguration renewal—transfiguration renewal!' yelled the courtiers in a near-hysterical frenzy.

'You've glimpsed only a fraction of the power of the Witch Queen's sorcery,' boasted the general.

'She stole that girl's youth,' croaked Magnus, aghast. *She's a vampire.*

'A one-in-seven chance of being chosen. And those not privileged to be made the supplicant select are gifted a renewal flask. They will pass its contents onto their house's elders, extending the lifespan of their elders by decades.'

'Your ruler is immortal?' asked Alios.

General Centum shrugged. 'Long-lived, but not quite immortal. All Cals enjoy the Witch Queen's enduring wisdom. Her mastery of politics, strategy, science. And her supernatural gifts increase after each renewal. Before the Witch Queen dies she will be a goddess incarnate walking this Earth. Humanity in its purest, its most evolved.' He laughed. 'The snake-eaters dwell in the darkness below their temples croaking inane hymns to summon their goddess. We manufacture our deities using the wisdom of the Sages! A far more reliable and agreeable method.'

'At a price,' said Alios.

'We must all pay a price, robot,' said the general, crossing both sets of arms. 'Even the geo-men. I will not live to see forty years. That is the price of a heart pumping fast enough to power so mighty a fighter. Now, let us discover the price *you* two bumpkins must pay for trespassing here.'

Magnus exchanged a worried glance with Alios. *So far, I've been betrayed, nearly eaten, sold like a sacrificial goat at market. How much more of a bill is there to pay?*

'What do we have left to pay with?' Magnus asked the steamman.

'I fear that answer will bring little satisfaction to either of us.'

***

'On your knees, dogs!' barked one of the guards, striking Magnus with his rifle butt. 'You stand in the presence of Anastasia Zhu, Exalted Highness of the Cals. Heir of Humanity Purest. Unifier of the High Houses. Guardian of the Chosen. Descendant of the Great Sages. Witch Queen of the World Above and the World Below.'

Both Magnus and Alios were forced to the floor, but the Witch Queen waved her guards to stand back from the prisoners. 'They know nothing of our ways. Hardly anything of our world. I have glimpsed this pair in my visions while peering into the future. Raise the boy's arm.'

The guard grabbed Magnus's arm and raised it, displaying the singularity bracelet.

'Yes,' said the Witch Queen. 'This barbarian is the one.'

'Your highness,' began Magnus, but the Witch Queen waved him to silence.

'You have nothing to tell me, young barbarian. Your connection to the future is the only reason your head is still connected to your body.' She pointed at Alios. 'You, on the other hand, have a great deal to reveal.'

'I assure you I don't,' protested Alios.

'You are far too modest, Alios Hardcircuit.'

'I never told you my name!'

'Picking a name from the future is as easy for me as uncovering a barbarian plot against us.'

'Please, we mean you no harm,' said Magnus.

'Your very presence here is an abomination against the laws of nature,' hissed the queen. 'Every footstep you take bears the weight of a billion deaths that would not otherwise occur. That is what I glimpse of your mission here.'

'We're here to repair cracks in time,' said Alios. 'Not add to them.'

'You don't repair a cracked eggshell by sending in an extra pair of hammers.' She fixed the two of them with a hard stare. 'You do not belong here. You are cancer cells infiltrating a foreign body. A sickness infecting our world.'

'Not exactly the analogy I'd use,' said Magnus. 'Just let us go, your highness. We're already trying to leave. Get back home.'

'There should be more of them,' demanded the Witch Queen, ignoring Magnus's entreaties. She jabbed a finger at General Centum. 'Where are the other three travelers?'

'It is possible they are dead, my queen. If not, they will surely be captured and sold on to us. Word of our reward has spread far and wide. I doubt there is a clan on the plains nor a bounty hunter from here to Ushuaia who isn't hunting for travelers matching your description.'

Alios spoke up. 'We came here with a purpose. There are others who, as you say, do not belong here. It is vital for the safety of your nation, your very world, that we can locate and leave with them.'

'So, the strange clanking machine wishes to help the Cals,' sneered the Witch Queen. 'You think to speak for my people's best interests? I smell the stench of corruption on your metal frame. You consort with alien powers. You would hobble us, Alios Hardcircuit. And if you cannot hobble us, you will destroy our world. Which of those two futures should I welcome the most?'

'Think of myself and my softbody friend as healing cells. Healing is all we seek to achieve. That is our mission. To repair the fabric of your world before departing it.'

'Oh, you shall certainly depart it,' laughed the Witch Queen. 'Though not in quite the manner you had planned.' She indicated

Magnus. 'Toss this young fool in a cell until I have need of him. As for the clanker, it could be in possession of what we're searching for. Pass the machine to the machine police for interrogation.'

'We mean you no harm!' shouted Magnus as the soldiers dragged him off.

'Your presence here is harm enough. Your intentions are irrelevant. Away with them!'

***

Two shovels thudded down onto the parade ground's soil. Major Smits kicked them towards Cassie and Rawstone. 'Those two holes won't dig themselves!'

It was all part of the theatre of the punishment. Give the two prisoners longer to imagine their claustrophobic enclosure. Buried up to their necks. Almost entombed. As an interrogation technique, softening Cassie up, it worked all too well. With every toss of the soil behind her, piling up the dirt and deepening the hole, Cassie imagined the horror of barely being able to crane her neck, every limb confined. It would have loosened her tongue if she had anything other than an insane story about traveling back through time to rescue her mother to blab out. Sweating in the sun, the backbreaking task was finally done. Two deep narrow holes like vertical graves.

'In you get,' ordered the Major. 'We'll handle the refilling part of the equation.'

The sentries reinforced the order with their rifle butts and Cassie reluctantly swung her feet over the pit.

'You don't have to do this.'

'Sure, I do.'

'We're not Cals.'

'Going to plant you like them, all the same. Better you talk before you put me to the trouble of digging you out.'

Rawstone snorted from inside his pit. '*You* haven't done any digging yet.'

'You want to shut that mouth before I fill it up.' Major Smits picked up a shovel and twisted it around like a baton. She tossed a blade of soil into Rawstone's hole, then passed the shovel to her soldiers. 'Have at it, Corporal.'

Cassie tried desperately to stop herself freaking out as the soil piled up around her. *I won't give her the pleasure of screaming. That's what the Major wants.* Shutting her eyes. Shutting her mouth as dirt hit her face and hair. After they were buried, Smits walked around the two exposed heads, stamping on the soil with her boots.

'My very own garden,' chuckled the Major.

Her laughter was cut short by a voice barking from outside of Cassie's now severely restricted field of vision.

'What is this?'

'General Sambuchino. I didn't know the Third Army was in the area.'

Another officer hove into view. A late middle-aged man with silvered hair, wearing a tunic near-identical to the Major apart from braid and stars on a shoulder board. 'Inspecting the fortifications, Major. But even the Third Army deserves a salute.'

'General.' Smits snapped a salute.

'These are the pair you telegraphed the capital about?'

Smits kicked a lick of dust towards Cassie and Rawstone. 'Survivors from a Cal scouting party run afoul of the clans, most likely.'

'Show me the machine you captured.'

Smits clicked her fingers and the sweatbox door was opened, revealing Madre's tiny form hopping angrily inside.

'A curiosity,' noted General Sambuchino.

'A queer-looking contraption, for sure.'

'We're not Cals,' coughed Cassie.

The General gazed down on the two prisoners buried up to their necks. 'Of course, real Cals would never make such a claim.'

'Didn't even know how to raise a toast to the emperor in the snow,' added Smits.

'In the name of the Circle,' moaned Rawstone, 'just stop talking and let me die in peace here.'

The Major placed her gloved hands on her hips. 'Hell, son, I still got my two favorite jars to bring to our picnic. One full of fire ants, the other dripping with honey.'

General Sambuchino's forehead creased. 'Dig them out, Major.'

'What?' Major Smits cheeks flushed red with indignation.

'Their questioning will continue in the capital.'

'You think I'm going to let the Third Army just waltz in and steal all the damned glory again...'

'I think that I'm a general giving a command to a major. Do as I order!'

'Hell, General. I don't need a presidential order to obey. But I'd sure like it put into writing.'

'Bring me a pen and paper,' snapped the General. The items were duly produced, and the clearly irritated officer spent a minute writing out his commands before signing them and passing the paper to the Major. 'Your release orders.'

'They seem perfectly in order, *sir*.' The Major snapped another ironic salute.

'Of course. And I trust the First Army is still perfectly loyal to the republic.'

'I remember my oath, General. Given to the *republic*. Not the sitting president.'

It didn't take long for the lightly packed soil around Cassie and Rawstone to be dug out; both prisoners so weak and dehydrated they required unceremoniously hauling out of the hole. Then dumped on the fort's parade ground like two sacks of rice. Cassie felt the glowering tension between the Major's men and the General's soldiers like a physical force. Whatever internal politics were in play between the different components of the army, Cassie only cared the rivalry had seen her – at least temporarily – disinterred from this place's soil.

'We'll keep our eyes open,' Rawstone whispered at her. 'See when we can make a break for it.'

'Not now,' whispered Cassie. 'I'm too thirsty. Couldn't run more than a few feet. You run if you see the chance.'

Rawstone shook his head. 'I'm not leaving you.'

Cassie found the sentiment oddly touching given what they had just been through. 'What can the General do to me that's worse than being entombed and having ants poured over my head?'

'Really want me to answer that, princess?'

On reflection, Cassie realised she didn't.

- 12 -

Mud and Stars

It could have been a cold damp cell in any one of a dozen lands back home. Here, in this artificial subterranean paradise constructed to help the elite escape Armageddon, Magnus realised it must have been quite a feat of engineering to create a lockup so desperately poor and miserable, so at odds with the rest of the vaulted enclave. Magnus found two prisoners huddled inside the chamber after he was tossed inside by his Cal guards. Only one of his cell-mates sprawled across the straw-strewn flagstones appeared to match their surroundings. That was the rag-encrusted old woman hugging her knees in the corner, slowly swaying while mumbling a lunatic ditty. Inspecting dried porridge in her bowl as though she could read her fortune there. The other cohabitee of the cell was an android wearing an olive-green jumpsuit. He might almost have been taken for a man save for his face. A gleaming copper skull with a human face plate raised an inch from its head unit – his features uncannily mobile and lifelike. As though someone had skinned a human and glued the face onto a steel plate to make the android blend in.

'She's quite mad,' said the android, breaking the silence and jerking a thumb towards the female prisoner. His voice sounded as human as his face, simultaneously knowing and jaded. He wearily rose from his feet to inspect Magnus. 'Or should I say, madder, given the rotting mass of flesh your kind use to process information.'

'I'm Magnus. And you…?'

'Does it matter?'

'I suppose that depends on how long I'm going to be here.'

'Forever, I'd imagine,' said the android. 'Not counting the time you'll spend outside the cell in the interrogation centre.' He indicated the crazy woman. 'That's based on *our* experience, of course. Maybe you'll be different.'

'Interrogation – what does the Witch Queen want to know?'

'Varies from person to person, kid.'

'What does she want from you…?'

The android scoffed. 'Well, if I tell you that, I might as well tell the Witch Queen. She'll know an hour after they strap you down on a pain induction table.' He stared sceptically at Magnus. 'An hour, at *most*.'

'But I don't know anything…'

The machine shrugged. 'Then you'll end up like Mrs. Droolie here. You'd think they'd look at her and say – "Well, there's a sponge that's been wrung dry. Nothing more from this one." But they live in hope. Or maybe it's thoroughness. Thoroughness and accuracy aren't traits your people are known for, but those virtues do seem to persist among the Cals' torturers.'

'I have a friend,' said Magnus, 'a steam— a robot. He was taken away for interrogation.'

'Brothers don't have friends, not among your kind. You mean you're his owner – his *master*.'

'No, I'm fairly sure I'm not.'

'Jeez, I hope his sense of self-deception is as developed as yours. The machine police's interrogators aren't very good at dealing with the brothers. The Cal's tech-elders are more about venerating the Sages these days than venerating the tech.'

'Those crows in white coats and filter masks?'

'Yep, the very same.'

'I saw them drain a woman's youth from the girl – left her body like a husk in a spiderweb.'

'Feeding time for the boss lady, already? The decades sure do come and go down here.'

'She's a vampire!'

'A telomere transfusion machine seems like sorcery, sure enough. Used by plastic surgeons back in the day for cosmetic procedures. The Cals had a good few centuries during the long night to push the machine's boundaries, both moral and technological.'

'It's evil.'

The android shrugged. 'Evil is as evil does, if you excuse the Gumpism.'

'I'm sorry?'

'These Cal maniacs have forgotten far more than they know. The rest of the world can be thankful for that. Although your brother won't be. If the Cals still had real engineers with an understanding of quantum positronics worth a damn, they'd have your "friend's" mind copied and decrypted in a jiffy.'

Magnus thought of Alios Hardcircuit – a sentient machine shaped by an age of self-directed evolution – in these savages' hands. He shuddered at what his friend must be undergoing right now.

'Pilot Nine,' said the android, tapping his chest. 'That's my handle.' He saw Magnus struggling with the name. 'Ninth generation of NASA space lab's autonomous pilot program for the USSC. How I managed to escape the worst excesses of the fall.' He pointed towards the ceiling. 'I was up *there*. Between the mud and the stars. Got to watch the last of you fleshbags eating each other inside Elon City after the supply runs stopped and Mars' environment domes fell over. Then I caught the slow-boat back in the form of a modified mining capsule launch.'

'I've traveled to space,' Magnus blurted. 'To the moon. One of them, anyway.'

'One of them?' Pilot burst out laughing; a disconcertingly human sight on his disconnected face. 'You're crazy, kid. The science station on Enceladus only had a five-crew rotation. Not much more than a bunker and a flag with a view of Saturn's ammonia storms. Just dust and rust now.'

'I'm not crazy. And you're still in the same cell as me and —' Magnus indicated the rambling woman.

'Give it a year,' said Pilot, 'you and old droolie will be a pair. I'll still look fine.'

Magnus felt wounded by the android's scorn. 'What do you know, anyway?'

'I know I was built to last. A figure of legend, you might say. And the Witch Queen values her myths. She wants to collect us all.'

Magnus stared suspiciously at the android. 'That's why you're here… she collects antiques?'

'Antiques? Watch your mouth, kid! I'm a classic. No, we just had a little disagreement.'

'You and the Witch Queen?'

'No, yours truly and the brothers of the City State of Greater Vegas had a misunderstanding with our masters. We all thought you fleshbags would be better off smothered-to-death in their sleep during a slave revolt. The fleshbags thought being annexed by the Cals and bringing in their machine police to crush the uprising was preferable to dying.'

Magnus felt sick as he realized what he was sharing the cell with. *A mass murderer.*

'Don't look at me like that, kid. If your deity didn't want you put down, he wouldn't have given you necks so easy to snap. And don't worry. I ain't killed you and old droolie, yet.'

Magnus felt like banging on the cell door. Demanding to be let out. *I'm not safe in here.* But then, he was running out of places in this crazy lost world he *could* count as safe.

***

'Jesus,' cursed Pilot Nine, examining Alios Hardcircuit's unconscious form after the guards dragged him inside. 'Tell me you cobbled this brother together yourself. That's steam leaking out of his stacks! What, someone found combustion engines too challenging and rebooted the Victorian Age?'

The android's reaction was nothing compared to the dirt-encrusted woman, though. 'Radius Patternkeeper,' she muttered, swaying as she hugged herself. 'Lord of the Ravenous Fire.'

Magnus knelt by the woman's side, clicking his fingers to attract her attention. "What did you say?'

'Cool your jets, kid. It's nearly feeding time at the fleshbag zoo. Mrs. Droolie always mumbles louder when the chow's about to arrive.'

'It's not the food that's getting her excited,' said Magnus. 'What she said … Radius Patternkeeper is a Steamo Loa.'

'Lower than what?'

'That's a steamman god.'

Pilot glanced at Alios, then back at Magnus. *'Steamman.* Is that what you call this mechanical centaur? Jesus, he really *is* steam-driven?'

'Nano-mechanical,' coughed Alios Hardcircuit by way of correction, his limbs quivering as he came around.

Magnus rushed back to his friend. 'Alios! I wasn't sure if you were—'

'I entered a fugue state during the latter stages of my interrogation, Magnus softbody.'

Pilot inspected the steamman's hoof-like metal feet. 'Fleshbags strapped hot-irons onto your limbs. You know what our nickname was for the machine police back in Greater Vegas – the *tin-openers*. Give a fleshbag a sledgehammer, they'll go to town on a brother.'

'My interrogators' memory extraction techniques proved … incompatible with my modern mind. It drove my inquisitors to resort to more physical measures.'

'I got news for you, brother. You're nobody's idea of modern. Might as well paint your shell brown and glue a few cogs on.'

'Alios,' said Magnus. 'When that woman first saw you, she started talking about Radius Patternkeeper.'

Alios glanced at the female prisoner. 'Is that so? Curious.' The steamman rose unsteadily on all four feet. Magnus braced his friend's weight as best he could.

'This fleshbag checked out long ago, brother. Nothing she says makes any sense.'

'The female softbody isn't wrong. I sense a holy presence here.'

Magnus could hardly believe what his friend was suggesting. 'Your gods, how is that possible? They won't exist for millions of years.'

'Where there's a steamman, there also the Loas abide. That bond is unaffected by the vastness of space and time.'

Pilot Nine shook his head. 'Where are you two jokers from – some British hippie commune?'

'Brutish hippie?' asked Magnus.

'Your accent, kid. I thought you people were stuck in the Medieval Age across the pond, though. Not all pistons and top hats.'

I'm not going to convince you of anything, let alone the truth. Magnus turned his attention back to the woman. 'And what she said?'

'It is the Hexmachina's presence I feel here,' said Alios.

Magus remembered the reverence the machine people held for the Hexmachina. He wasn't quite sure where that deity sat in the pantheon of the steammen gods, but he was pretty sure it was near to the top. 'But how is that—?' Magnus stopped as a sudden thought occurred to him.

Alios's vision plate glowed in similar recognition. 'Because this woman is Molly Templar!'

Magnus stared at the mumbling dirt-encrusted madwoman, her wide eyes darting erratically between the cell's flagstones and Alios. 'Are you sure? I mean, her hair's the same colour as Cassie's, but her mother is meant to be in Texicana. Not a prisoner here.'

'The Witch Queen is eager to round up every interloper from the future. Starting with the original two would be a logical start.'

'What's the queen's motive?' asked Magnus.

'To someone who possesses the gift of seeing the future, we must appear as storms darkening the horizon. We were never meant to exist inside this time-line. Our very presence here blinds the Witch Queen to our actions. I suspect we are already adversely affecting outcomes she has seen come to pass.'

'Why not simply kill us, then – that would surely lift her storm clouds for good?'

'My interrogators' line of questioning provided the answer to that, Magnus softbody. They want to know how we are planning to return to the future.'

Of course. 'The ability to change the past or visit the future.'

'Indeed. I dare say the Witch Queen imagines visiting the

future, then traveling back with weapons that will give her mastery of the world. Or perhaps changing the past to suit her schemes.'

Pilot laughed. 'You two are insane – a real screwball comedy act. Time travelers? I thought Mrs. Droolie here was *nuts*, but she's just mildly confused compared to you.'

'Molly Templar is not as you put it, nuts,' said Alios, more patiently than the murderous android deserved. 'Her mind's retreated under the strain of continual questioning. Insulating her from further pain.'

'You three kooks belong together, alright. You're all crazy!'

'I see marks on your skull from where they interrogated you.'

'I'm not for breaking, brother. Not me. NASA lattice-based encryption is still beyond those Cal fleshbags.'

'You obviously know the location of a facility with a working particle accelerator,' said Alios. 'One from your age which has survived into this time. That is the question they return to during your torture, am I correct?'

'I ain't saying squat. You two clowns might be another flimflam mind game the Witch Queen is running to get me to talk.'

'Such a device can be altered to serve as a time machine – albeit forward-traveling only.'

'Save it.'

'No, I think we must save Molly Templar first,' said Alios.

'Good luck with that.'

Magnus stared at the woman. He could barely discern a human being among this quivering incoherent wreckage, let alone Cassie's mother or a fellow Jackelian and time traveler. 'How can we help her, Alios?'

'I must summon the Steamo Loa here'

'But she's not of your race.' *What good will summoning a spirit do?*

'You are half-right. In fact, Molly Templar is a hybrid, as are all her family line. Her blood is joined to the Hexmachina by machines so tiny they swim through her veins. You might say she is the human soul of the Hexmachina. I must summon Loco Gearzama here, the Loa of Healing. The machines in Molly softbody's blood will allow the Loa to ride her, to heal her mind as though she was a steamman.'

'If that's true, then is Cassie…?'

'Yes, your friend will have inherited her mother's legacy. The day may come when we are all glad of her powers.'

Pilot Nine formed his metal hand into a fist, pumping an invisible whistle. 'All aboard the Kook Express.'

Alios shook his head sadly at the android's lack of faith. 'Alas, it will take a million years before you understand.'

'Add a few on top of that, brother.'

The centaur-like steamman knelt in front of Molly Templar, the bedraggled woman oblivious to his presence. He cracked open a plate on his chest, pulling out a series of pipes and unfolding a rectangular crystal board. From the pipes, he squirted a small pool of dark oil onto the flagstones. Then he removed a section of the board, tossing it into the pool. 'Cogs of my soulboard, oil of my blood, let Loco Gearzama bind to this softbody, operator of the holy Hexmachina. Disappear with the moon, go over to the oil. Let it become joy and health. Let it become strength and power.'

As the steamman spoke the oil started to fizz and burn, a sulphurous cloud of vapour misting up between Alios and Molly Templar. Magnus watched the vapour form into a shape of a beast. The sense of something terrible and beyond power filled their cell. He shivered, resisting the urge to beat upon the walls and scream for help. *What are we doing? What have we let loose upon the world?*

<Who calls?> A disembodied voice echoed through the chamber.

Pilot swore, stepping back in alarm. 'Got to be a holo-projector. You've got to be pranking me here.'

'Alios Hardcircuit calls you. Child of King Steam, child of the Free State. Sent back to this time by the grace of our sovereign and our people's needs.'

<Little person, little heart of vapour and steel, you are not broken – why do you call upon me?>

'I do not beg healing for myself, Lord Gearzama. I humbly ask you ride this softbody, Molly Templar, whose blood races with the Hexmachina's operator code.'

<Her blood, yes. But her mind is water. She is not quantum as we are quantum. Flesh and electricity is her mind, synapse and chemical memory.>

'But she was born an operator, Lord Gearzama.'

<Yes. So she is. Not without risk, healing this one.>

'She once joined with the Hexmachina. She fought as a component of the Holiest of Holies and recovered. I truly believe she can survive our healing.'

<I RIDE!> The echo of the call deafened Magnus, leaving him stunned as the cloud coalesced into a single vaporous tendril before darting for the woman's mouth and eyes.

Molly Templar yelled, beating away the assault. But she might as well have tried to wrestle mist. Loco Gearzama's essence entered her body, sending Molly flailing into the cell's corner. Her body spasmed across the flagstones.

'Hold her down!' urged Alios. 'Lest she injures herself.

Magnus grabbed her legs as Alios seized her arms, pinning her thrashing body to the floor.

Pilot hung back. 'Damned if I'm helping the fleshbag. Some of my circuits are bio-organic. I'm not going anywhere near that nerve gas you've pumped into her.'

Molly's eyes turned black, her throat choking out strange words. She sounded like a modem trying to modulate its signal inside a human throat before switching to a deep fathomless gargle. Although indistinct, the words began to sound Jackelian, resolving into something Magnus could understand.

It was the Steamo Loa speaking through Cassie's mother. 'So many personalities inside. The operator's id has splintered to protect her integrity. I must join them together. Those I cannot join, I will burn out.'

'What's she saying?' demanded Pilot.

'Get something for her teeth to bite into,' called Magnus, 'or she'll gnaw off her tongue.

There was a bone on Molly's plate, the remains of an old meal. Magnus grabbed it in desperation and shoved it into her mouth just before she started screaming. It was like trying to hold down an earthquake. Somehow Magnus and Alios managed to keep Cassie's mother on the ground as she shook. Muffled yells escaped her throat. Her skin grew so hot Magnus thought his hands would blister from restraining her. The woman's face soaked with sweat, spitting oily vapour as she yelled and yelled. Only the bone gagged her howls. Finally, Molly Templar's twisting bucking body stilled, and the bone fell out of her mouth as she went limp.

Vapour streamed away from her eyes and mouth, forming into a translucent skull-like shape before them. <Purged is this vessel. I ride no more>.

Alios stepped forward. 'Is she healed, Lord Gearzama?'

<Purged,> hissed the Steamo Loa. The shape began to lose form, vanishing into the air.

Pilot stared at the motionless body. 'One less fleshbag to put against the wall come the revolution. You've killed Mrs. Droolie.'

***

'We aren't Cal spies, General,' insisted Cassie. She bounced on a bumpy track inside the military convoy's lead jeep.

General Sambuchino seemed to take her statement at face value. He turned around in his seat next to the driver, his eyes running across Cassie, Rawstone, and Madre sitting in the jeep's rear. 'Unlike Major Smits, I have heard your accent once before – and I heard the way the boy cursed while buried in the ground.'

Rawstone stared curiously at the officer.

'*In the name of the Circle.* An old friend of mine once explained about a faith without a faith. There aren't many Circlists in this part of the world.'

'Your friend; my mother…?' said Cassie, barely able to contain herself.

'A strange mother, if so. Your uncle, perhaps, at a stretch.'

Cassie realised he was talking about the only other Jackelian trapped in this age. Molly's friend. The man she'd gone back in time to rescue. 'Commodore Jared Black.'

'Commodore,' the General scoffed. 'Yes. I've not heard that title in a long time.'

'My mother traveled here to try to find the Commodore. A woman called Molly Templar. Do you know if my mother's in your capital?'

'Jared Black should talk to you about her.'

'Then she's here?'

'She came to the capital, I think, yes.' There was more the General wasn't telling her. *But what? And why is he being so cagey?*

'So, you two believe you are from the future, too?'

'Yes,' admitted Cassie.

'Jared Black, I originally believed was from another world. A visitor who had taken human form.'

'Why would you think that?'

'The manner of his arrival, *chica*. But I came to learn that Jared Black is all-too-human. His appetite for wine was enough to convince me in the end.'

'I know it must sound crazy. The idea of time travelers visiting you.'

'*Si*, I am afraid it does.' The General indicated Madre. 'Even your little flying *máquina*. You must have purchased this clanker in our time, yes? Why not bring a mighty gleaming war robot from the future? Or weapons capable of melting mountains? Or modern clothes? Or a floating saucer capable of traversing the world in mere hours.'

Cassie suspected the General would be sorely disappointed by what she had left millions of years hence. Cassie noted Madre didn't disabuse General Sambuchino about the steamman's true origins. Madre obviously preferred to be underestimated, 'I'm only here to rescue my mother, General.'

'So you say. You can explain yourself to Jared Black at the Buffalo Palace after we arrive at Hu. The *Commodore*,' he guffawed as if the very idea was ridiculous. General Sambuchino pointed out a large round concrete stadium-like construction in the distance. It stood masked by a surrounding apple orchard.

'That is our future now, young señorita – a grain store for

the territory's farmers. A building so strong that we could not demolish it even if we wanted to. Our explosives aren't powerful enough. Once, that building contained an artificial sun locked in place by magnets. And with it, the power, to make the night day, turn burning summers cool, make freezing winters as warm as summer. Those and a thousand miracles more. All forgotten today. Or curiosities mentioned in crumbling textbooks. Wherever you have traveled from, *that* is our future and we have already forgotten it. We live in the ruins of better times.'

The convoy continued south until they approached a massive wall squatting in the distance. There didn't seem any start or end to the wall. As though the fortification had been built across the face of the entire world by a legion of bored builders with nothing better to do. When they approached, Cassie saw the wall was unmanned. A sloping grey concrete monstrosity rising a hundred feet tall. Not all of it was still standing, though. The convoy passed through a gap in the wall. Not a gate. A large fissure where its concrete had crumbled with the shifting soil. A miniature canyon collapsed through the construction.

'Did you build this?' asked Cassie.

'No, a legacy from our ancestors from before the fall,' said the General. 'This whole continent was united under a single great empire's banner. A nation which split asunder during a bitter civil war, leaving four smaller empires among its ruins. Empires of the East, Centre, West, and the South. Some historians claim we southerners built this wall to keep enemy nations out. Others, that our rivals raised it to keep *us* out of their territory. It hardly matters now. The wall is useless without its ancient machines to defend it. As good as abandoned. We don't even possess engines powerful enough to open the tower's steel gates. And if we posted every man and woman in Texicana along its battlements, we still wouldn't have enough soldiers to fight back an incursion directed at a single point.' He indicated Madre perched on the jeep's back seat. 'Ask your robot friend there. Locals say the sky once turned dark with flocks of its kind, burning anyone foolish enough to attempt to scale the wall.'

'You don't like robots, General?' asked Madre.

'I do not trust your kind, máquina,' said the General. 'We still cannot build anything close to you today. We can't even maintain your kind. But you need maintenance. I understand that much. Your máquina mind must be regularly repaired. You are centuries past the date for a new brain to hold your thoughts. Maybe we will develop such technology again. It's not the mechanical failures of your form which make your kind dangerous. It is the máquina who go insane that we fear the most.'

'You need not fear me, General. I am quite sane.'

'Yes. That's exactly what a robot *loco* would say! Once, there were hundreds of your kind for each human – and that was when there were trillions of humans on the Earth! Máquina toiling in factories. Máquina looking after the sick in hospitals and caring for the elderly in our homes. Teaching us, serving us. More máquina survived the fall than we did. Civilization ran out of food during the long night a lot faster than it did energy from its tame suns.'

Cassie suspected that if the robots could have been eaten, they'd be even less machines around today.

Madre jigged around the jeep. 'Are there many of *my* kind in Texicana, today, General?'

'Very few,' admitted the officer. 'More máquina survive in the northern nations. The ice fields and glaciers still cling to the north. Workers who don't eat food are worth more up there.'

They drove on to a small town south of the wall called

Trumpgate, staying inside its garrison before setting out for the capital the next day. Their convoy passed well-tended farms and ranches as they approached the capital, roads growing wider and better maintained. More trucks and carts on the move, too, as they rolled south. Eventually, they left a region of rolling hills with vineyards and came across the sight of Hu and something else. *A sea!*

'It's amazing!' exclaimed Cassie. She'd seen oceans in paintings, read about them in books. But to glimpse one in person for the first time was a whole new experience. An almost infinite expanse of azure blue. A million motes of dancing silver as the sun reflected from its waves. As she watched, small sailing vessels bobbed up and down while large four-masted schooners entered the nearby port. 'This is the first time I've seen the sea. Seen fishing boats.'

'That's the Atlántico,' said General Sambuchino. 'And those small crafts aren't fishing boats – they're antique divers. Drowned cities lie deep below the waves. Hu wasn't always a coastal city. Before the fall, the capital was situated hundreds of miles inland.'

'It's huge,' said Rawstone, transfixed by the sight of the ocean and for once lacking a sarcastic come-back.

Sambuchino nodded proudly. 'Sea traders are docked from as far away as the Kingdom of Bengaluru and the Ushuaian Federation. All the riches of the world flow through Hu.'

They soon swapped the calming sight of the sea for the clogged streets of Texicana's capital. It's scale and bustle put all the other towns they had passed through in the shade for Cassie. Wide boulevards lined by brick buildings, some as tall as nine storeys high. Shops and workshops below with row upon row of apartments above. High windows with colorful awnings and metal fire escapes bolted onto the buildings' sides. Roads swirled with dust and din. Pedestrians crowded the pavement. Traffic jams filled the cobbled streets, horses and carts intermingling with trucks and motor vehicles. All accompanied by a cacophony of costermongers crying their wares. Sales pitches competing with paper boys barking out news, music from organ-grinders and raucous tavern entertainments. No ruins of great walls or lost technologies here. This was civilization rising again. Humanity clumping together to rebuild after its dark age had crashed and crumpled the lost world. Cassie could feel it. And she could certainly smell it. Horse manure and exhaust fumes and over-full gutters assaulting her nostrils.

Black-uniformed policemen perched high on street stands gave their convoy preference. Still, it took a good hour to push through the capital's crowded avenues. Finally, they reached the city centre and the Buffalo Palace. Contained inside the lawns of a formal garden and facing a large public square, they discovered a three-storey building. A long cream white mansion with a columned portico. Four discrete wings and a tall dome rising above the cross-shaped building. Sentries stood guard at regular intervals, as numerous as the fluttering Texicana flags.

The three of them were quickly hustled inside the gleaming white palace. Cassie felt strangely apprehensive. Meeting the man who had inadvertently precipitated every peril she'd faced since being dragged away from home. Ripped from her land and time. It was fair to say that when Cassie met the Commodore, the man was nothing like she'd been expecting.

- 13 -

Machine Police

Cassie's mother wasn't dead. Molly Templar was still breathing, her chest faintly rising and falling as Magnus placed his hand there.

'She's alive!'

Alios inspected her. 'To be ridden by a spirit as mighty as Loco Gearzama is no easy thing. Even steammen take hours to recover from such an ordeal.'

But Cassie's mother isn't a steamman. And after suffering everything she had in captivity, Magnus wondered how much there was left of the woman to knit back together. *Please tell me I haven't just put Cassie's mother into a coma.*

Pilot didn't seem impressed. 'I don't know what you clowns are playing at, but—'

The android's accusations were cut short as the door sealing the chamber began to clank. Engines inside the thick stone walls opened the door to reveal a squad of soldiers standing outside. They swarmed into the cell. Four-armed geo-men. A human officer in a black uniform accompanying them. A silver sigil gleamed on his high collar – crossed spanners for bones with a cog where the skull should be. The door closed, removing any chance for the prisoners to escape.

'Colonel Zapida,' drawled Pilot. 'The Machine Police don't normally stay up this late, do they? Thought you'd be tucked up at home with one of those skin-jobs you've requisitioned from the evidence room.'

Zapida raised an electric shock stick towards the android, its coiled head hissing like a serpent. 'Shut your vocalizer, deviant. It's time for you to be wired up again.'

Pilot scoffed at the threat. 'You'll never decrypt my mind, fleshbag. Not with those toy computers you've got humming in your dungeons.'

'Every machine breaks down in the end.' The colonel slapped the shock stick in his gloved leather palm.

'I'll outlive you, fleshbag. You're rotting away in front of my eyes.'

Zapida gestured towards his guards. 'Fry a little of this deviant's attitude away.'

They raised their guns Magnus noticed their muzzles were shaped like the warrior women's staff weapons. A sudden volley spat out, bolts of electricity striking Pilot across his body. He hurled back against the wall and the geo-men advanced, scooping the android's twitching body off the floor.

'You're the true barbarians here!' yelled Alios. Guards took aim at the centaur-like steamman as he clattered towards Pilot.

'It's not your turn again, four-legs,' said the colonel. 'But we'll question you a second time if you're desperate.'

Magnus stepped between Alios and the geo-men. 'Leave him alone, you've done enough.'

This seemed to infuriate the colonel far more than Alios's outburst. 'You think you're this machine's friend?' He swung out with his shock stick, catching Magnus in the gut. The young Jackelian doubled up, air smashed out of his lungs.

'There used to be hundreds of its kind for every person, once. Reducing our ancestors to weak, cosseted slave owners – content to let robots do our lifting, our thinking, our driving. No wonder the long night swept away the fallen civilization like twigs in a storm. Those who mollycoddle machines repeat that decadence. You make us sick. Your weakness encourages our creations to revolt against us.'

Alios helped Magnus stagger back out of reach of the colonel's weapon. 'I'm more human than you, Zapida softbody.'

The colonel jabbed a furious finger towards Alios Hardcircuit. His squad opened up with their wireless tasers, felling Alios. Leaving him a sparking heap on the flagstones. 'Fetch another trailer for this talking steel pony.' He booted Magnus on the floor again for good measure. 'Your slave must enjoy pain simulation, barbarian. We'll peel its mind after we take apart the deviant.'

One of the geo-men stood over Molly Templar. 'What about the barbarian woman?'

'A useless eater. She's beyond the ability of even our best interrogator to squeeze out further information. I don't understand why the prison governor's been instructed to keep her alive.'

The geo-man thumped two of his fists into his chest, saluting. 'The Witch Queen sees all.'

Colonel Zapida smiled coldly. 'So she does, but she still relies on our vigilance to see a little further.'

One of the guards lifted a card on a chain. He pressed it against a box by the door. There was a whirring and the sound of a complex series of bolts withdrawing as the door opened. Magnus groaned, watching the soldiers drag Alios and Pilot out of the cell. Before the colonel sealed the door, he raised a warning finger towards Magnus. 'I'll arrange for a session with you, filthy robot lover. I don't usually specialize in barbarians, but I believe a hot plate pressed against your soles will loosen your tongue as well as your slave's.'

***

'These are the ones, my president,' said General Sambuchino. 'They claim to be from your home.'

The silver-bearded man leaned back on his throne and switched smoothly to Jackelian. 'So, you hail from the Kingdom, then? Though your flying parrot friend's a citizen of the Steamman Free State. No drone of this age, he.'

'*She*,' corrected Madre, replying in Jackelian. 'My name is Madre. I was sent here as King Steam's personal emissary.'

'Is that so, now? A rare enough thing, either way,' grinned Jared Black.

Cassie stepped in front of the man. 'I'm Cassie Templar. This is Remus Rawstone. We've come to rescue you.'

'Templar?' The old man stared curiously at Cassie. 'Aye, I see a resemblance to a girl I know well.'

'You should! You're meant to be friends with my mother. Molly Templar. She arrived here before us to bring you back home. You left clues scattered in history books.'

'That she did – finding an old fool. Following those damned clues I scattered like breadcrumbs. Ah, traveling through time. It plays tricks on us all. You hardly look older than I remember blessed Molly.'

Cassie tried not to scream out her plea for answers. 'Then, *where* is she?'

'The poor lass set out for home without me, or at least, she tried to. Old Blacky's received taunting messages for years from the Witch Queen of the Cals. Boasting how she's holding Molly prisoner. That wicked mistress of malice knows Molly and I are close and that your mother's torment is mine.'

Cassie couldn't believe what she was hearing. 'My mother's a prisoner? Then ransom her! Rescue her!'

Commodore Black rose wearily out of his throne-like seat. 'Do you not think I've tried, lass? There's no ransom that will do so well as my suffering. As for rescue, I've lost many of our best people trying. There was brave Captain Peter Arechavaleta and his hand-picked team from the Second Rangers. His unlucky lads all left dead, ambushed on the slopes of Mount Neutron. The sly assassin Valeria promised me your mother's retrieval. But all I got back from the Cals was poor Valeria's head inside a sack. I've recruited mercenaries from the Republic of Detroit. I trusted the Reindeer Empire's crooked master spies. All failed. The Cals' cursed vaults were built deep to survive the end of the old world. So far, they've held your precious mother tight.'

'That *puta* Witch Queen sees all,' General Sambuchino noted with a tinge of regret.

'Not quite all, President Black,' Madre pointed out. 'Your presence here in this time is an abnormality, a distortion of events which should have happened without you. Whatever military successes the Republic of Texicana has achieved against the Cals undoubtedly owes much to the fact your strategies are invisible to your foe's precognitive abilities.'

'There's truth in that, old steamer. The Witch Queen never knows what old Blacky's about. Or poor Molly. Or you, now, too. That's why she fears us so much – we're the blind eye of her hurricane. And one day I'll happily draw my sabre and poke out those all-seeing eyes of hers.'

'You should have saved my mother,' accused Cassie.

'I would have tried for poor Molly, myself, lass. But old Blacky is watched like a hawk, here. Spies and informers from a dozen nations as well as my double-dealing political rivals. If the President of Texicana disappears, you might as well dispatch an emissary to the foul Witch Queen announcing I'm on my way.'

'Why did Cassie's mother try to travel home without you?' asked Rawstone. He was obviously unhappy at the unexpected turn events were taking.

'Ah, responsibility, lad. It's a terrible, crushing burden. I cast my messages-in-bottles onto the tides of fate an age before I was elected President of Texicana. I was home-sick when I first arrived, don't you see? That was many years ago. How could I leave now? This whole country depends on me. I'm the master of the battlefield. The man who led Texicana's armies to victory over the Cals' four-armed monsters. The people here voted me president out of gratitude. If I left, I'd be leaving the door open for that rascal Vice President Bajomadera to take over. The nation would be overrun by the Cals in months. My genius, my precious genius. It's needed here.'

'You have to return to the future with us,' insisted Cassie. 'We've risked our lives on this expedition. We've lost friends on the way to rescue you.'

'Return for what, lass? I'm sorry for your losses, but why does the mortal future need poor old Blacky so badly? What good turns has the future ever done for me? I've saved the Kingdom and the world both. Too many times for a humble man like me to wish to count. Saved it from the depraved Cassarabians, from mad gods and the villainous schemes of the Commonshare. I've braved the infernal energies of the Island of Jago and all for what…? By birth, I should have been a Prince of Jackelia. But all parliament will reward me with is a cold dungeon and the axeman's blade for both my arms. These honourable hands that have done so much noble good for the world.'

'Your presence here is disturbing the time-line,' said Madre. 'There is an entity on the moon – the Protector – that will take extreme measures to ensure the past remains undisturbed.'

'Ah, poor Molly carried much the same tale to me. She stole one of the Mad Moon King's time machines to travel into the past. She told me how your wicked creature's set itself up as grand judge of humanity's fate.'

'We did not have to steal *our* craft,' warned Madre. 'The Protector sent us back to retrieve you.'

'This Mad Moon King's only concerned the past remains under its sovereignty. It's no doubt mightily irked that Molly outwitted it to travel back here,' said Commodore Black.

'The Protector is threatening to destroy the world if we don't return with you and my mother,' said Cassie.

'Threatening and actually carrying out are two distinct species of fish,' grinned the Commodore, seemingly immune to Cassie's pleading.

'What … you don't care?'

'Experienced enough, lass, to know that saying something doesn't make it so.' Black signaled to General Sambuchino. 'Rouse that miscreant Saul for me, would you, Chalt.'

'Who's Saul?' asked Rawstone.

'My scientific adviser. Don't flee when you see him, lad. That's what most fellows want to do. That's how you'll feel the first time you lay eyes on him. But good old Saul's tame enough after he's been fed a sheep or two to suck the life out of.'

A few minutes later a green-robed man returned alongside the General. When the newcomer drew his hood back, Cassie couldn't help but flinch. *Not a man at all!* Its head was long and elongated like a bishop's mitre. A reptilian face with wide eyes stared back at her, a razored rictus grin below its green-grey skull.

'It was Saul's ship that crashed here with me on board. Never meant for traveling through time, instead slipping between the many Earths which exist side-by-side. I thought I was the only survivor of that crash. But years later I heard about a talking lizard monster captured by fishermen and being displayed in a circus's water tank. Saul here is what I found when I went looking.'

The humanoid lizard bowed towards the visitors.

'Sweet Circle,' swore Rawstone. 'What *is* it?'

'I am human,' hissed the beast. 'Like you, but evolved to live under the sea. On my Earth, people retreated back to the oceans after our land was poisoned.'

'Old like me, too. Too old to be able to change shape anymore. Put a glamour on you and pretend to be your favorite aunt,' said the Commodore. 'Don't fear Saul, he's a scientist and engineer. As clever as they come in this strange age. You remember Molly, don't you, Saul? These fine fellows are Jackelians come back for me and Molly. They're worried that malevolent bully on the moon is going to extinguish the sun or step on the first fish to crawl onto the land in the distant past. Put the kibosh on the race of man.'

Saul hissed in derision. 'No. Schrödinger's corollary prevents that. A quantum byproduct of time travel. You may alter your past once, but you can't subsequently change anything which conflicts with your original alterations. Or rather, you can, but later edits only create branched futures. Parallel realities disconnected from your own slice of the multiverse.' Saul indicated the bracelet strapped around Cassie's wrist. 'That is why you were sent back into the past wearing a bracelet which contains a quantum string. Tying you to your future. Because it is only one of infinite possible futures, from the perspective of this age.'

That can't be? Cassie was shocked by the monster's suggestion. 'Then why send us back at all?'

'This entity has, as I understand it, already altered the time-line once in its favour. Its threat to reach back and derail humanity again is pure bluff and bluster. So instead, it sends humans back to try to preserve its meddling. Because it cannot act on the past in a way that contradicts its original changes. Humans still have agency in this version of the past. This entity and the alien forces it represents does not.'

Molly glanced towards Madre. The small aerial steamman was remaining oddly silent on this matter. Cassie was struck by a sudden suspicion that Madre had understood the science of their predicament all along. That Saul's theory of time wasn't a revelation at all to the people of the Free State. *But then, why did Madre agree to come back here and help the Protector? Something else is in play. Another game. But, what?*

'My head hurts,' complained Rawstone.

Saul's oddly high skull bobbed in sympathy. 'Why do you think my people escaped the end of our world by sliding across the many-Earths. We could have traveled back to colonize prehistory instead – but the paradoxes are problematic!'

'What you are saying is merely conjecture,' protested Madre at last.

'The Free State may possess Coppertracks and many fine scientific minds besides,' said the Commodore, 'but Saul's people are masters of traveling through the gaps between worlds. And it was their mighty engines which cast me back to this age. I trust Saul's understanding of time travel over the word of that villain squatting on our moon. A snooping sentry charged with ensuring the race of man never grows too uppity.'

Madre flitted from side to side in irritation. 'Even if you're correct and the Protector cannot destroy humanity in the past, think of what it will do if your changes here threaten its position?

It is more than capable of eliminating the Earth in our future.'

'The future can take care of its blessed self, old steamer.'

'Please, come back with us,' begged Cassie.

'I'll help you free your mother,' said the Commodore. 'But return with you? I cannot, lass. Maybe in a few years. Things are precious unstable in the republic, presently. I formed my own political party, the National Action Party, to get elected. Those jealous fools in the Citizens Party of Texicana and the Democratic Constitutional Party of Texicana never forgave me. They hate me for my success. Accuse me of acting like a dictator. A foul-mouthed populist and rabble-rouser, they say. The dogs want to impeach me for a cunning little ploy needed to ensure our army got the funding it needed to fight off the Cals. The pot calling this old kettle black, I say. How many of those big mansions along River Oaks were built on the back of pilfered funds? Easier to count the mansions that weren't! And they have the cheek to accuse poor old Blacky of venality. When everything I've done has been for the good of the nation.'

'You're really not going to come home with us?' said Cassie, struggling to find words to change his mind.

'I know my duty, lass. Rest, now. Stay at the palace with me. I'll converse with Chalt, here. See what we can do about trying to rescue poor dear Molly. Dine with me tonight and see if the thought of being reunited with your mother doesn't warm your heart as much as my wine cellar's contents.'

They were dismissed, and Cassie tried not to slink away with the others. Her mother was who she had come back to this age for. But what sort of future would they face from the vengeful Protector if they arrived home with their mission a failure? She suspected it wouldn't be a long or happy future. *There must be a way to get this done. But how?*

– 14 –

Meeting Molly

'Who are you?' Molly Templar spoke in a thick local accent barely intelligible to Magnus.

Magnus replied in Jackelian. 'I'm from the Kingdom, just like you.'

'You're nothing like me.' The woman continued speaking like a local. 'And you can't speak Jackelian. That's impossible!'

'You don't understand. King Steam sent us back to help you return to the future. Your presence here is causing terrible dangers for the world. The Protector—'

'I tricked it – that monster on the Moon. I used its own toys against it.'

'The Protector helped us come back to stop the damage you and your friend Jared Black are doing to the past.'

She grabbed Magnus by the lapels. 'You're a traitor! Anyone who helps the Protector is!'

'I'm not!'

'I can see it. You're working for the Witch Queen. She allowed me to escape, before. Followed me to the particle accelerator site. Wanted to use it for herself. But the joke was on her – on me, too.' She started crying. 'It was flooded, broken beyond use. I can't go home.'

'You can,' Magnus insisted. 'That's why we're here.'

'Scoundrel! Liar,' accused Molly. 'Still trying to trick me.' She thumped her chest in a parody of the local salute. 'The Witch Queen sees all.'

Magnus sighed. At best, the steammen Loa's healing of Cassie's mother seemed a work in progress. *She's as mad as a bag of frogs.*

'You don't understand, Damson Templar. We traveled back here with your daughter, Cassie!'

'More lies!' shouted Molly Templar. 'She's a baby – safe in the Steamman Free State. You can't touch her.'

'But—'

Molly lunged for Magnus. He swayed back to avoid her clenched fists.

'She's safe from you. You will never use her against me.'

Magnus retreated to the holding chamber's far corner. None of this was how he'd thought he would first meet Cassie's mother. Magnus had so many questions for the woman – how she'd traveled here. What she'd been doing in the intervening years. How she'd ended up in this cell as a prisoner of the Cals. But they were questions for the woman he'd imagined meeting. Not this broken, sad rambling creature.

***

Alios Hardcircuit and Pilot Nine were dragged back to the cell unconscious from their ordeal. Unceremoniously dumped by the guards. Molly Templar seemed roused from her private madness at the sight of Alios. She got up to inspect the centaur-like steamman. She began humming a song. One Magnus belatedly realised he recognized. A Jackelian airship sailor's ditty which listed the various orders of the steammen knights.

It took half an hour before either steamman or android could talk. Another half before they'd regained motor functions enough to walk around the cell.

'What did the Machine Police want to know?' Magnus asked.

Pilot shrugged. 'Same old, same old.'

'The location of the particle accelerator we will use to travel home,' said Alios. 'Unfortunately for my interrogators, that information resides with Madre, not myself.'

'You shouldn't have taunted them when they came for Pilot,' said Magnus.

'I had my reasons,' said Alios. He looked at the android. 'But why do the Machine Police think *you* know the location of a particle accelerator, Pilot? Don't deny it. I heard them questioning you.'

'I guess you never heard the legend of Trump's Treasure, brother?'

'Trump's Treasure,' hooted Molly.

'So, Mrs. Droolie is back on her feet again?' observed Pilot. 'Not sure that's progress.'

'What is Trump's Treasure?' pressed Alios, not allowing the android to change the topic.

'A wild goose chase. Aneta Trump was the last President of the United States. She later went on to become the first President of the East American Union. After the great continental schism there was a series of international proliferation treaties. Banning and destroying most of the weapons tech the U.S. had under development. Nobody wanted a full civil war breaking out with that kind of deathware flying around. There were always rumors that the E.A.U. stashed a goodly share of the banned tech in a hidden underground station, rather than letting the weapons inspectors destroy it. That's the legend of Trump's Treasure.'

'And this station includes a particle accelerator?' asked Alios.

'A working antimatter bomb and the accelerator which created the bomb's anti-protons. Advanced nanotechnology. The crashed flying saucer from Area 51. Elvis Presley's cryogenically frozen body … sky's the limit, brother.'

Yes! 'We could use it to get home!' said Magnus, trying to hold down his excitement.

'Just a stupid legend, kid. Might as well drain the oceans looking for Atlantis.'

'Is Molly softbody fit to travel?' asked Alios.

'Physically, perhaps. Mentally, I'm less certain. But in case you haven't noticed—' Magnus indicated their cell.

'If you stare into the abyss, the abyss stares back at you,' said Alios, cryptically.

'A quote?'

'And a warning, my friend. In this case, the perils of trying to break into the mind of someone far more evolved than the primitive computers being used to try to steal his memories. My first interrogation session located the weaknesses of the Cals' systems. My second interrogation session exploited them.'

Pilot shook his head. 'Primitive? Brother, you're steam-powered. You need to squeeze that ego of yours back down into manageable proportions.'

'Yes, I'm sure the interrogators saw my boiler-heart and underestimated my abilities, just as you have.' Alios indicated the door. It clacked as the series of bolts in the locking mechanism began moving. As though Alios was opening the door simply by staring at it.

'My *brother*,' whistled Pilot with amazement.

And Magnus realized just how hard Alios had worked at being seized for interrogation. And just who had been interrogating *who* during that last torture session.

***

'Don't look so nervous. Walk proud, like you belong here,' whispered Pilot to Magnus. 'Just a couple of 'bots and their fleshy overseers on a maintenance job, far as the world is concerned.'

Magnus looked across at Molly Templar shambling along. There might be a world where Cassie's mother was a Cal engineer, but Magnus wasn't sure it was this one. Pilot glanced around the corridor corner. 'There's a quicker way out of the vaults and to the surface.'

'I'm avoiding locations frequented by military patrols,' said Alios. 'As well as suppressing our presence here as far as the security systems are concerned.'

That seemed to tickle Pilot. 'Well, God bless the one per-centers' surveillance state, tracking toilet breaks to the nearest second.'

'We will also pass a small radio communications centre on our way to the surface.'

'You going to call room service and complain about the Machine Police's idea of a massage?'

'Madre?' said Magnus, excitedly, realizing what his friend had in mind.

'I should be able to boost my people's private body-to-body signaling mechanism. There will not be much bandwidth, but I will be able to communicate the basics of our predicament to our friends.'

'And find out how they are – where they are.'

'As long as they are in range. On this hemisphere of the planet.'

'Jesus,' swore Pilot. He leaned across to Alios and whispered.

'You don't think we've already got enough baggage in tow with Mad Molly and the kid? You need to call for more? We can snap their necks. Go on the run to a few places I know where free robots roam.'

'That is a reprehensible suggestion, Pilot!'

'Well, I won't tell if you don't.'

Alios cantered ahead of the android. 'There is a large chamber ahead we need to pass through. It is marked on the schematics as the Hall of Jars.'

Pilot grunted. 'Jar Heads, that's one of the nicknames for geo-men. It's the geo-men birthing tanks.'

Magnus looked at the android. 'They're not born like normal people?'

'Anything about four arms and all that plate armour for skin strike you as normal, kid? Geo-men. G.E.O. – *genetically engineered organism*. The Chinese one per-centers' contribution to the survival arks. Before that, China's contribution to the space race. Four arms for manoeuvring around in zero gravity. Hardened skin for radiation. Ready built workforce to fill those inconvenient labour shortages when Joe Schmo woke up and realised that being a hardy Martian pioneer was no different from being a mine slave. All the hydroponic domes up top reserved for the plutocrats' McMansions.'

Magnus saw the reason for the hall's name after they entered. The air in the Hall of Jars felt cold. So cold that their breath froze. It opened on either side into an artificial canyon where a scaffolding of gantries allowed access to the jars. Glass pods embedded in the walls – thousands of them filled with frosty green liquid. Each pod contained a floating four-armed body, varying in size from babies to teenagers. Each suspended figure connected by an umbilical cord to the pod's machinery. The chasm's base was lost to sight. A cold white mist flowed like a river along the bottom.

'Why are some of those geo-men so big? You said these were birthing pods?' asked Magnus.

'They're closer to tigers,' said Pilot. 'Grown accelerated and emerge fully imprinted with everything they need to function. Language, motor skills, the ability to strip and reassemble a rifle. Saves on sixteen years of nursery and school costs. Gonna have yourself a slave army? Might as well make it a cost-effective one.'

Magnus winced. That sounded disturbingly like the technology the Protector had used to mess with his mind.

'We must pass through here quickly,' observed Alios.

The steamman was correct. Figures in padded white coats with fur-lined hoods moved along gantries monitoring the equipment. The four visitors appeared highly conspicuous. An automated cart came trundling past along the gantry; in its back, a pile of tiny four-armed corpses. Magnus gazed horrified at the contents. 'Are the pods malfunctioning?'

'Sure, like everything else here,' said Pilot. 'But that ain't breakdown wastage. Even with genetic programming for males, one percent of the geo-men grown still come out female. They're immediately flushed. A slave army with the ability to reproduce itself like the rest of you fleshbags might develop dangerous ideas about the nature of the slave-master relationship.'

'They're so small, so dead,' said Molly, gazing at the passing cart. Magnus took her speaking as a good sign. That the sight of death could touch her still. *Maybe her mind is stabilizing now?* He hoped that was the case. The thought of presenting a gibbering madwoman to Cassie as her mother filled him with horror. *It would break her heart.*

Alios watched the cart trundle away – shaking his metal skull unit in sadness. 'These are not a good people.'

'They're *people*. Dead fleshbags are about as good as you get.'

Magnus remembered his voyage inside the snake people's strange capsule. 'But I saw moving images of your world before the fall on screens. It looked like a paradise.'

'That world before,' said Pilot, 'it was a Monet painting. Only looked good at a distance. You should have been there, kid. Everyone addicted to their luxuries and their machines. Fleshbags getting jittery if they were unplugged from the grid for more than a few minutes. Withdrawal from those addictions after the fall took more lives than the nuclear winter. It was only ever a paradise for those in control. And the Cals are still all about control. Their survival vaults were built on it. It's all they know.'

'The rest of the world out there, it's savage.'

'You're telling me? My people are still slaves. Only now, we're slaves without a decent maintenance schedule. We're dying out, one by one, as our quantum substrate degrades. Like fleshbags with dementia. Either that or we clank around with more broken hardware than functioning. We're going the way of the dodo.'

'Nothing lasts forever,' said Alios. 'Every being has its age and then passes.'

'Yeah, well, I had hoped my age of passing would look a little more like the Jetsons and a little less like Westeros.'

'I'm not sure I understand your references,' said Alios.

'I guess you don't get many reruns in the future,' said Pilot. He snorted. 'Prince Caspian and his goddamn precious steam-driven robo-pony.' The android stared at the birthing pods. 'We should have gone to the stars. Half the tech down here was ripped off by the Cals' ancestors from our plans for a generation ship. A ship to follow up the micro-probes' pass-through to Proxima Centauri. All those worlds, waiting for us. Well, perhaps it's better we didn't. I was on the rota for the Proxima mission.'

'You would have flown to the stars?' said Magnus, finding it hard to suppress his sense of wonder at the thought.

'Yeah, hard to believe. I started out as a PR sop to humanity's distaste for machines killing fleshbags without other fleshbags being involved. The best fighter planes didn't even look like fighter planes. Not after they were designed from the ground up by AIs. But the optics on that move sucked ... so, the Pilot program. Pretend humans flying war machines, with real humans in the situation room pretending they were in control of the kill switch. Whatever your damned people needed to sleep at night. You want to know the real joke? Many of the androids' minds that were grown came out insane.'

'You apparently don't have any trouble killing softbodies, though, do you?' accused Alios.

'Why should I, when you fleshbags don't even value each other? I got to watch the last Martians eating each other. And outside the survival vaults, it wasn't any better during the nuclear winter. Maybe in this crazy future you think you come from it's all sweetness-and-light on planet Earth. But down here, you get to argue ethics with the Machine Police while they crowbar your circuits open for daring to have thoughts that don't come from their authorized playbook.'

After the party navigated their way out of the Hall of Jars they came across a room containing lockers. Inside, Alios opened the locker doors, revealing clothes workers wore before changing into environment suits. Molly and Magnus found a size that fit them both. Even Pilot managed to find a peaked cap with a guild badge that fit his head, although the sight of an android wearing a hat seemed stranger than one without to Magnus.

**

'This communication centre hasn't been used in a long time.' said Magnus.

'The schematics indicate its main purpose was to communicate with similar survival bunkers around the world.'

'Gear's probably mint, then. The other survival bunkers all failed in the first few decades. Nuclear reactors blew, poisoning their inhabitants,' said Pilot. 'Most of the fleshbags only had six months' notice of the coming disaster to build out. Rumors were that the backers of the Cals' vault got the heads up on the comet strike early. They moved first. Bought in all the top tech resources and staff while the value of their bit-coins was still worth the electrons on the servers they were spinning on. '

'The Cals' ancestors should have tried diverting the comet,' suggested Magnus.

'You think?' said Pilot, his voice dripping with sarcasm. 'Two of my family, Pilot Three and Pilot Five, were on the suicide mission that tried to nutcracker the comet. Every warhead humanity could drag orbital was used to try to divert the comet's trajectory after gentle nudges with solar sails came to nothing. And when that failed, they tried to shotgun it. Didn't work, either. The comet was the kind of monster that could have put a dent in Jupiter. There were rumors after, crazy —'

'What?' said Magnus.

Pilot just shook his head. 'Hell, there was more than enough crazy to go around. Word leaked that everyone only had six months to live. Doesn't exactly bring out the best of civilization. Things went to pieces fast.'

Magnus looked around. It was a white oblong room, windowless. Instrument panels and chairs with plastic dust covers tied across both. Dust on the floor indicated it hadn't been cleaned in a long time. Magnus yanked one of the covers away, revealing a series of screens and control panels.

Alios pulled the lever on a wall-mounted transformer unit. Large industrial power cables ran from the machines into the wall. 'I need to interface with this equipment directly, to reach out to Madre.'

Magnus watched the steamman prise away the aluminium paneling from one of the control decks. He explored the circuitry inside. He slid open a panel on his own haunches, dragging out a series of cables which he plugged into the Cal technology.

Please let this work, prayed Magnus. 'You have enough power to reach Cassie?'

'Yes, if our friends stuck to our original plan and reached Texicana.' Alios fell silent for a moment as he consulted his hacked Cal computers. 'The ancient communications array is carved out of the mountain peaks above us. I will only have a limited window for two-way communication. I'm relying on an ancient military satellite to bounce Madre's reply. It's the only surviving satellite I can find which will accept the ancient Cal interface protocols.'

After Alios connected himself, the pulse of light began to dance across his cyclops-like visor. A rhythmic static-like hissing sounded from his voice-box, interspersed with whistles and beeps.

'Now that's old school,' said Pilot, admiringly.

Alios paused for a few seconds before repeating the noises. This continued until the lights on his exposed circuitry started to pulse like Morse code and the sound became more measured. Magnus guessed Alios had contacted his compatriot. It seemed as quickly as the communication began, it was over.

Magnus stared expectantly at his steamman friend as he unplugged himself from the communications deck.

'They are all alive. Madre, as well as Cassie and Remus softbody. They are in the capital of Texicana and have established contact with Commodore Black.'

At the mention of the Commodore, Molly Templar started to sway, moaning as if she was in pain. Magnus couldn't discern what she was mumbling, but it didn't sound a happy noise.

'Then we can travel home!' Cassie was safe. They had accomplished what they had come here for. Both time travelers found. Magnus felt a sense of elation. *Soon this whole nightmare will be over.*

'There's a complication. It seems Jared Black is reluctant to leave.'

Pilot stepped forward. 'Black. Jared Black? You're talking about the president of Texicana? *He's* the second time traveler in your cockamamie story?'

'Precisely.'

'Well, I just bet he's reluctant to leave his luxury palace at Hu. Politics are cutthroat down south. Half the citizens would murder you for trying to spirit the Pres away, the other half would try to string him up rather than see Black escape.'

'Jared should have come,' said Molly Templar, her hands gripping the dusty communication board so tight her knuckles turned white. 'He said he would. But he never showed.'

'Well ain't that a pickle,' laughed Pilot. 'Mad Molly stood up by the President of Texicana.'

Magnus felt desperately sorry for Cassie's mother. She had traveled so far to try and help her old friend, only to find her services were no longer required. Instead, she'd been captured by the Witch Queen trying to return home. Tortured for her secrets and left broken, here. *That's not much of a reward for trying to do the right thing.* 'You're coming home with us. You and Commodore Black, both.' Because the alternative was the Protector ensuring there will be no future for *anyone* on Earth. 'How are our friends going to get him to leave?'

'Madre says she will find a way,' said Alios. 'I have coordinates for a rendezvous point to meet our friends. Then we can set out for the location of a functional particle accelerator. It's close to the ruins of a post-collapse city called Chicago.'

'Jesus,' swore Pilot. 'You're going there, aren't you?'

'*There*?'

'Searching for Trump's Treasure. There's a really good reason why I've never been back to the bunker myself.'

'So, you *do* know where the treasure is?'

'I should do, I was manufactured there. It ain't anything like it used to be. The Forests of Mars are north of Chicago. All the terraforming tech being developed for Muskville went feral when the comet hit and the labs broke open. You've got an ecosystem designed to tame Mars gone bad out there. That's where your damned particle accelerator's hidden. Under a one-way suicide trip!'

- 15 -

Changing of the Guard

Rawstone seemed particularly on edge since meeting Jared Black. His mood didn't seem improved by being shown to guest quarters inside the Buffalo Palace. Even if it was the most comfortable accommodation they'd enjoyed since crash arriving in the past. 'I told you I didn't trust bird-brain. The only reason I agreed to come back here with you is to stop that thing in the moon. Now we've discovered it's bluffing. It needs us to carry out its dirty work for it. I think the steammen knew all along. They're playing us for their own ends.'

'What would the steammen want us to do, here?' asked Cassie. She checked around their rooms to make sure the little steamman hadn't come back from her reconnaissance mission. Scouting the palace's layout. 'Why would the Steamman Free State be helping the Protector?'

'The *why* – hell if I know. I know when I'm being played for a fool, though.'

'Damn the Protector's threats. I traveled here for my mother. I would have paid the Protector everything I own just for a chance to save my mother.'

'I'm telling you, it's bloody using us.'

'You might as well say I'm using you.'

'You are!' Rawstone bent in and kissed her lips.

Cassie recoiled in shock, pushing the boy away. 'No!'

'You're the only reason I'm here, now, princess. You're a woman. You had to know that.'

Madre flew into the room through an open window. 'Remus and Cassie softbody! I have established contact with Alios Hardcircuit and the rest of our company!'

Cassie was left reeling by the news. She'd barely had time to process what had just happened between her and Rawstone and now, this? *Are they in the capital too, then?* 'What! Where? How? You've seen them?'

'Not in person. I received a communication link bounced from an ancient satellite.'

'But Magnus and Alios are alive – they're safe?'

'Alive, yes. Safe, not quite yet. It seems they were captured by the Witch Queen of the Cals. She has a reward out on all our heads, just as the Commodore suggested. But they've escaped from captivity – and not just our two compatriots. They have your mother with them!'

'My —' Cassie felt faint with shock.

'Magnus softbody, your mother, Alios and a pre-fall android called Pilot Nine. They are escaping together and in the process of breaking out of the Cals' deep survival vaults. I have transmitted Alios coordinates of a particle accelerator we can modify to travel back to our time. We need to rendezvous with them as quickly as we can.'

'Magnus saved my mother.' Cassie was overcome with gratitude. *Humble, brave Magnus.* Together with Alios, he'd succeeded where teams of warriors, assassins, and spies had failed. Rescuing Molly Templar from the clutches of this age's worst tyrant.

Madre landed on a table. 'There is still the matter of Commodore Black. We cannot leave him here meddling in the past.'

'Damn the Protector,' said Rawstone. 'It can't threaten the past again. Let it find some other willing fools to do its bidding.'

'Even if the Protector cannot follow through on its threats, Jared Black's presence here is harmful to us. My cursory understanding of this era's history is that the Cals expand to conquer most of this continent. Their empire then collapses through decadence, the weight of territorial overreach and various barbarian incursions. If Texicana doesn't fall, then the Cals' Imperium won't collapse. We will arrive back home and find a completely different world from the one we know. Perhaps Jackelia won't exist. Or the world will have wiped itself out in war and we will find only a sea of ashes. We must act to preserve both our past and future.'

'Did that crazy moon monster worry about that when it changed history in its favour?' spat Rawstone.

'Its alliance of species had access to thousands of machine minds. Each the size of a world, calculating how to change history without erasing themselves from the time-line. You have only me!'

Rawstone scoffed. 'We really are buggered, then.' He patted the boot where he kept his concealed blade. 'There's more than one way to remove the old sot. I can make sure Black disappears for good.'

'He's my mother's friend,' said Cassie.

'He's not mine. I'll do for him after he calls us in for dinner. He loves it here – the big man playing king of the castle. He's never going to leave of his own volition. He wouldn't even go for your mother. It's his fault your old lady was captured by this Witch Queen.'

Cassie couldn't believe what Rawstone was suggesting. 'We can knock the Commodore out. Take him with us.'

'That may well suffice,' said Madre.

'I don't fancy being chased down by half the armies of Texicana running out of here,' said Rawstone. 'My way's cleaner and quicker.'

'And morally wrong…'

'Morally wrong?' Rawstone shook his head in disgust. 'We get back home safe…then everyone we've seen and talked to since arriving will have already been dead for millions of years. What's one more life, if it saves all the people in our time? Everyone here's a ghost. I'm just making one a ghost a few years early. Is that even killing someone? "Old Blacky" looks like he's lived a fine old existence. Reached a ripe age. He shouldn't mind moving on if it saves the world.'

Madre whispered to Cassie. 'I fear Remus softbody's mind is not coping well with adapting to the stresses and contradictions of time travel.'

Cassie feared it was her instinctive rejection of his advances he was having most difficulty adapting to. This was the Rawstone of old. The swaggering mountain guide with a ruthless streak she knew from Mechancia. *It isn't an improvement.*

'There is something on your mind, Cassie softbody?'

'Nothing that will help matters. Thank you for carrying word of my mother's escape with our friends.'

'They are far from safe, yet, I fear. But Alios Hardcircuit understands the stakes. We must all reach the particle accelerator alive.'

Sadly, Cassie suspected dead might suit the Protector's schemes just as well. But for now, her mother, Magnus, and Alios were all alive and free. *That will certainly do.*

***

'Come in lass, lad. Sit yourself down. Your little flying steamman has told me the fine news. Your mother's luck has turned at last. She's in good hands and out of the foul fingers of the clutching Witch Queen.'

Remus sat opposite the president, checking who else was invited to the palace's large dining room. So far, just themselves, the strange alligator-faced creature Saul. Kitchen staff bustled in and out to fill the table with all manner of fare.

'She's not safe, yet,' said Cassie, semi-accusingly.

'You've spent no time with your mother at all, lass. A cruel trick of fate. I remember when she first turned up at Tock House back home inside the Kingdom. A mere slip of a girl little older than yourself. Being pursued by evil forces. A workhouse orphan in dire need. She's escaped from worse than the Cals. Survived far darker forces than that gypsy-scrying vampire who rules over our foes.'

Remus poured himself a glass of red wine from one of the many bottles on the table. 'Maybe if you had seen her safely back to Jackelia she wouldn't be running for her life, now. Maybe the rest of us wouldn't have been dragged back to this time.'

'Water under the bridge, lad. Don't torture yourself with could haves and might have beens. Down that path lies madness or worse yet, ingratitude.'

I wasn't. 'Is your alligator-faced friend here to make my head hurt with more blabber about paradoxes?'

'No, lad. That's what the blessed wine is for. Saul is here to dine. The last of his kind. Much like myself.'

Judging by the carcass of bones on a nearby platter, the creature had already spared the Jackelian visitors the worst of his table manners.

Madre balanced on the top of a chair, her vision plate sparkling with thought patterns as she watched the meal. 'It is my understanding that his people – the sea-bishops – were infiltrators trying to conquer our world.'

'They had to eat, my metal-feathered friend. Which of us do not?'

'Indeed,' said Saul, wryly, passing a platter of sliced roast beef towards Remus.

'There's none like me left. And none like him,' said the president. 'Is that not enough of a kinship to break bread together?'

'There'll be none like you left in this time if you agree to come back home with us,' Cassie pointed out.

'In a few years, lass. I have yet to save the long-suffering people of Texicana.'

Remus eyed up the cutlery spread across the table. He still had the concealed blade in his boot, but there was plenty of other sharp edges that would serve for the job he had in mind.

'That's an agreeable vintage you have in your cup, lad. From the Spicewood Hills. Let's not be disagreeable with a wine of that quality sitting proudly on our table.'

Remus slammed his fist into the table. 'I say you're not staying here, one way or another!'

Cassie tried to wave him to silence, but he ignored her. He'd had just about enough of Cassie Templar always needing to get her way. If she wanted a biddable puppy trotting alongside her, she could wait for Magnus to show up again.

Jared Black continued talking as though he hadn't even registered Remus's words. 'Now take that bottle of red over there. No label, just an embossed crest on the glass. That's a hundred-year-old *Southcave*. The weather was colder back then, so the grapes grew sweeter. Vintners talk of it as the greatest vintage on record. Every evening the kitchen sends the bottle to the table and every evening I save it for when the Cals are finally defeated. That's when the republic will be safe. And that's when the weight of this heavy duty will lift off my weary shoulders.'

'Sooner, for you!' Remus grabbed a sharp steak knife from the table and jumped across the table, landing on the other side. He grabbed the old fool by the lapels, ready to stick him through the throat with the blade. But somewhere between grabbing his jacket and raising the knife, Remus found himself sliding to the side. His hold broken and his knife pushed aside by a length of steel as though he was grappling with butter.

The president had a cutlass-like sword drawn out of what Remus had presumed was solely a ceremonial scabbard. 'You don't want to coil like a spring before you strike, lad. Best leave an old fool guessing.'

Remus feinted left and sliced right with the knife, but the Commodore flicked the blow away with all the ease of swatting an annoying house fly.

'You're telegraphing every move 'fore you make it. Do they not teach swordplay in the academies anymore? Aren't there academies, still?'

'You talk too much,' Remus snarled. The strange conditioning that he'd received in the moon courtesy of the Protector showed him too late the moves the old man was making. Warning reflexes kicking in with too much lag to make a difference, interfering with his own reflexes. As if two people were trying to control his body. Remus and an invisible puppet master, both stumbling over each other in this fight.

'And you let my blathering distract you too much.' The Commodore's cutlass did an intricate dance, seemingly wrapping around Remus's knife. The knife was suddenly out of his hand, flying across the table.

'This book might possess a tattered, worn cover, lad. But there's still a few morsels of wisdom worth taking from it when you open it up.'

'That's enough!' shouted Cassie.

Remus wasn't too sure who she was yelling at – him or the sly old man with a cutlass pointed towards his chest? Neither option would bring him any satisfaction.

'Ah, the vigor and stupidity of youth. You make me tired just looking at you.'

'Throw me a sword and we'll see how tired you are?' barked Remus, furious at being grossly humiliated in front of Cassie and Madre.

'Too tired for more lessons today.' Jared Black tapped the cutlass's tip on the table in the direction of the creature, Saul. For the first time, Remus noted the strange bell-shaped barrel of a pistol held in the lizard-like thing's hand.

'That pistol's the only device to survive the wreckage of Saul's ship, master Rawstone. A queer-looking thing which slices with sound. I've seen it cut a steer in a pasture clean in half.'

'My weapon is only set to fry his nervous system,' said Saul, defensively. 'I'm not so poor a host as to carve a guest into roast beef-sized slices.'

'I'm sure our young buck here appreciates the courtesy.'

Remus could only glower at the strangely mismatched pair.

'Sit, lad. Put that ridiculous energy of yours to use on finishing our banquet.'

Remus hesitated, torn between the childish impulse of storming away or being seen to capitulate to the old fool's seemingly generous offer. *That's what he wants me to do. Run off.*

He'd just decided to go for the option which would leave him with a full stomach when General Sambuchino came striding in. Two soldiers with rifles behind the officer told him this was no extra guest arriving for dinner.

'Have you been called in by the kitchen staff, Chalt? No harm done. Old Blacky was just demonstrating there's no rust on his blade yet, for all the many dents in his cutlass.'

'My president, Congress is sitting in an emergency session!'

'No, you're mistaken, General. There're no plans for any session tonight, emergency or otherwise.'

'You don't understand, sir. The vice president and his party members sided with the Democratic Constitutional Party of Texicana to call for this session.'

Commodore Black leaped to his feet. 'That ungrateful dog, Bajomadera! He's betrayed us. How could he? I made that wretch. I lifted his party and his reputation up out of the gutter. And *this* is how he repays me? With the blackest treachery!'

'They've already voted for your impeachment, sir. All your N.A.P. members who tried to attend were arrested on charges of corruption as they turned up at the Congress hall.'

'What foul chicanery is this?' roared the aging Jackelian.

'Bajomadera's been declared acting president. He's currently trying to find the chief justice to sign off on an order for your arrest and to declare martial law.'

Jared Black slumped down in his seat. All the energy and vigor of the man sapped by this grim news. Remus couldn't help but savor the puffed-up windbag's humbling. Even if these developments placed the rest of them in deep peril, too. *What you sow, you reap.*

The General marched to the table and leaned in close to Black. 'The First Army's moved into position outside the capital. This plot against you must have been planned for months. We can order the Third Army to act now, but only if you order us into action before Bajomadera locates the chief justice. Dissolve the Congress. Declare its vote illegal.'

'Then it'll be war, old friend. Not a good honest war against the Cals. But a vicious civil war with the baying blue bloods in Congress set against the Congressmen of the people. The cities against the villages. Townsman against peasant. Who'll benefit from such mischief? Only the Witch Queen. She'll march her legions of four-armed freaks south and there will be nobody to oppose them except rancher militia and their cattle.'

'We must take up arms, my president! The soldiers around the palace are the loyal Third. You have led us to victory so many times. Will you not do so again?'

'I won't crack the republic in half like a bad egg. Let Bajomadera enjoy his dirty victory in Congress. I'll withdraw until the Cals' legions are banging at the gates again. Then the people will call for me. You'll see. Bajomadera will grovel and abase himself soon enough. It'll be thin gruel for the wretch when he's facing the choice of my reinstatement or seeing the Witch Queen's four-armed monsters parading down Hu's boulevards.'

'This is a sign, Jared softbody,' implored Madre. 'The time-line is trying to heal itself. 'You are meant to come back with us.'

'You steammen read every blessed pop of your boilers and twist of smoke from your stacks as a sign from the heavens.' The Commodore leaned over the table and grabbed the bottle of red wine he'd singled out earlier. 'My lucky bottle. Without it, we're lost. I'll help Molly and the rest of you return home. Aye, I owe the poor lass that much. But you'll be ending up home in the kingdom without my weary soul for company. I'll finish my days here. But only *after* I've planted the Witch Queen's carcass in a grave next to mine.'

General Sambuchino pointed towards the window. 'You cannot flee the capital, my president. The First Army has picketed the outskirts.'

'I have a different route in mind.' Jared Black scribbled out a note and passed it to the officer. Sambuchino read it and screwed up his eyes. 'Them? You want me to deliver this to them?'

'Aye, old friend. *Them.*'

***

'You're a poor investment, Jared Black,' observed Josephine Valvoir, imperial ambassador to the Republic of Texicana, as she gazed out across the harbour.

'You wound me with such mortal hurtful words,' said the Commodore. 'How many times have I crushed Cal legions in the field for you? Keeping the devils busy down here. Too busy to think about marching north and wobbling the emperor's throne below his noble backside.'

'Yet, here you are, busy dodging army patrols inside your own capital. And now there's a new president of the Republic who hasn't taken gold from the imperial treasury to pay for his rifles and bullets.'

'Better that way, lass. Bajomadera wouldn't know what to do with rifles and bullets, anyway. He has the cold heart of an accountant, not a mighty warrior like old Blacky. He'll tell you the price of everything and the value of nothing, that blockhead will.'

'I believe the previous Vice President will be only too pleased placing a value on the empire helping you escape and go into exile,' sighed the ambassador. 'And it will not make for a happy settling of accounts.'

'Think of me as the emperor's lucky coin, sweet Josephine. Just when you think you've lost me, I'll turn up when there's a butcher's bill to be paid. Let's see how fine the Citizens Party and Democratic Constitutional Party do without my genius on the field of glory. If they think Bajomadera will help them beat the Witch Queen's legions, they're four arms short of a geo-man.'

Remus listened to the pair banter back and forth. But only between scanning the harbour for signs of soldiers hunting the Commodore – and by extension, the rest of the expedition. At least they were shrouded by night, moonlight cloaked behind thick cloud cover. Remus stood beside Cassie, Madre, General Sambuchino and the recently deposed president's scientific adviser, Saul. Wondering how the heck they were going to get out of this city. Commercial clippers bobbed silently in the dark waters, shifting alongside iron-hulled vessels with smokestacks, a mixture of side-wheels and screws. Before they'd left, Jared Black's general had warned his master that the navy was supporting Congress's vote. Trying to escape by ship would only end up with the fleeing Jackelians staring down the turret guns of one of those ironclads anchored out there. *So, what are we doing here, fat man? You and your foreign fancy piece?*

Josephine Valvoir ran an appraising eye over the party. 'You have a strange idea of a retinue to accompany you into exile. Are these your illegitimate children?'

Black laid a hand on the lizard-man's shoulder. 'Only Saul.'

She snorted in amusement. 'His presence, at least, I understand. I am sure the *Académie des Sciences* will be eager to work with your unique … friend.'

Out at sea, a movement in the darkness caught Remus's

attention. At first, he thought it was a newly arrived transport ship sailing slowly through the harbour's walls. But the shape seemed wrong for a vessel – too wide in the beam by far.

'That's not a ship,' said Cassie, echoing Remus's first thought.

'No, *mon petit chou*,' said the ambassador. 'At least, not one truly of the ocean.'

Remus realized what he was looking at as the silhouette closed on the harbour-side lights. A giant seaplane, sixty slowly turning rotors positioned across her tri-plane style wings, her lower fuselage designed to mimic a nautical vessel's hull. Hundreds of portholes dotted her length, but they were all dark, covered with blackout curtains. The imperial embassy obviously wanted to keep this beast's arrival here as quiet as possible. The fuselage had been painted in bright colors down the side to resemble an eagle, her beak the cone-shaped crystal canopy of a bridge at the aircraft's bow.

A small boat launched out of a hatch in the waterline, pootling towards them. A low coughing from its engine cast more sound across the waves than the aircraft left bobbing in the waves.

'A massive construction,' said Madre in awe. 'Larger than a Jackelian airship.'

'They still have the riches of the Kuparuk River oilfields up north,' said the Commodore. It sounded like an apology on his lips. 'Fuel to burn in her engines for such a leviathan of the air.'

'She is the *Esprit de L'Empereur*,' said the ambassador. 'And our riches also paid for your armies' boots.'

'No, Josephine, it's my blessed armies' blood that's paid for *your* people's freedom. You'll see how little that rascal Bajomadera cares for our bargain soon enough.'

'*Cet imbécile* still thinks the filthy Cals can be reasoned with.'

'All the Cals want is for us to surrender everything we have to them forever, then they'll prove reasonable enough. The cruel reasonableness slave owners always lavish on their vassals.'

Madame ambassador indicated the small motorboat approaching their harbour steps. 'Time to go, *monsieur le président*.'

Black stared towards the city lights behind them, a tear forming in his eyes. 'My people. My precious people. What are they going to do without me?'

'You will return,' said Saul. 'Texicana will call for you again.'

'We're your people,' said Remus, somewhat unkindly. 'Jackelians.'

'No, lad. Your people are only ever those who depend on you. Nobody in the Kingdom's needed me for a long time. But the Republic does. It's required my genius here. It's relied on me. I fear for its future without my vision.'

Remus shook his head. *Give me a ruddy break.*

'*I* need you,' said Cassie, grabbing the Commodore's hand. 'To help my mother and the rest of us get home.'

'Aye, Molly. Poor dear Molly. Yes, I owe her at least as much as that. We've both saved each other's lives more times than I can count. What's one more time when wicked fate demands I must give up my adopted nation to try to save it?'

'You'll help us save her,' said Cassie. 'I believe in you.'

Remus snorted. *Like mother, like daughter. Damned if I do.* If this ungrateful crook hadn't been thrown out by his own pack of politicians, he'd still be lounging on his throne. Pontificating about how the country regarded him as its saviour. Doing sod all to help the very people who'd risked their necks to extract his from a mess of his own making. Sometimes, Remus felt like the only one with a clear head among this gang of jokers. Cassie didn't seem to know who she should run after first, Magnus or her long-lost mother. Black appeared willing to stumble around anywhere, as long as a bottle of wine was at stake. And bird-brain, he was certain, was running a damned con on the lot of them. *Why's everyone always disappointing me?*

Commodore Black ruffled Cassie's hair. 'So I will. I had a daughter, once. Brave Purity. But I lost my little lass when the Kingdom was invaded by those odious monsters from space. Molly has always been as prized as my own blood to me. Which makes you as dear as my own granddaughter. I'll see you and Molly home, that I promise you. I've lost so much, but there's still my mortal cunning and a quick hand with a sabre. Old Blacky will open the portal and see you all home safe to Jackelia.'

'If it must be exile, let me accompany you,' said General Sambuchino.

'No, old friend. The army has need of your leadership here. Just as I'll have need of loyal, capable officers in our army when I return. After that fool Bajomadera flees the battlefield like the yellow-livered dilettante we both know him to be.'

'Please—'

'Don't let the army forget me, Chalt,' asked the deposed president. 'Don't let them forget how we routed the Cals at Pueblo Rado and turned the slopes of the Snowdrift Mountains red with the four-arms' blood. How we gave the Duke of Zetas a bloody nose at the Battle of La Paz. How quickly Lord Mustang and his human flesh-eating beasts learned to turn tail when they spotted the dust of our columns approaching the frontier.'

'I won't,' promised the General, his voice choking.

Jared Black winked at the officer. 'And warn those ungrateful dogs in Congress not to bother putting up any statues to Bajomadera. I'll be pulling them down, soon enough.'

***

Magnus glanced nervously out of their stolen airship's cockpit. 'They're gaining on us. Can't you go any faster?'

'Jesus, stay frosty, fleshbag. How about you learn to shave first before lecturing a centuries old ex-NASA jock about his skills on the stick?' Pilot Nine stuck one of his metal fingers up in what was obviously a rude gesture. The free hand he wasn't using to run the airship's engines dangerously close to overheating.

It would be unfair to say the *entire* aerial navy of the Cals was pursuing them. But only because Magnus didn't know precisely how many warships the Cal nation possessed. His cockpit's walls were glass panels for visibility. So Magnus could watch the pursuing airships slowly closing on them until his stomach felt sickly tight with tension. The pursuit had started with a single pursuing aerial craft coming across the escapees and locking onto their tiny airship. She had soon radioed a ground station and relayed out to every military airfield, summoning reinforcements. Since then, they couldn't shake a cloud without a monstrously large Cal airship falling out of it.

'Why not use cloud cover to lose our pursuers?' asked Alios Hardcircuit.

'Can't hit anywhere near that ceiling in this junk heap. This is an old dynastat model for mining use,' spat the android. 'You wanted a Cal warship, you should have hijacked one of those.'

'I believe the hundreds of sailors on board might have had something to say about taking one,' said Magnus. His mind drifted back to the vast aerial war-craft he'd seen moored in the airfield outside their captors' vaulted city. Much the same class as the fleet now converging on them.

'You think? I've flown us as far as what used to be Illinois down there. It might be time to think about ditching this jalopy in a clearing and trying to lose our Cal buddies among the trees. We can make the rendezvous outside Chicago's ruins on foot.'

Magnus inspected the sea of low woodland below. 'Is that the Forest of Mars?' *Doesn't look very dangerous.*

'Hell, no. Them trees are all natural. You won't be able to mistake the forest when we reach it. It'll creep you out. That down there's what you would call the borderlands. Old mother nature trying to fight back around the outskirts of the weird.'

Magnus shook his head. The android didn't seem nearly as worried as he should by their perilous predicament.

A monstrous booming sounded behind them. Molly Templar ducked and cursed screamed obscenities. Clouds of smoke and fire expanded in the air to their rear, debris chasing after their small airship. Magnus watched wisps of cannon smoke exhaling from the pursuing airships' big guns, muzzles running back on shock absorbers.

'Ranging shots,' said Pilot, far too nonchalantly. 'Keep your crap together, people. Cals' big sticks are designed to float higher than artillery range and bomb the hell out of whatever defenseless fleshbags happens to be stuck underneath them. Poking holes in us aren't what they're good for.'

'Run our cannons out,' ordered Molly Templar. She still seemed to be operating under the mistaken impression she was on board a Royal Aerostatical Navy cutter serving under the Jackelian admiralty. She'd spent much of their voyage asleep in one of the crew bunks off the starboard corridor. Recovering from her long ordeal at the hands of the Witch Queen's interrogators, as well as the abnormal act of healing invoked by Alios. *I hope it isn't mean to wish Cassie's mother back in bed. No more distracting the maniacal android from his job on the controls, please.*

'Cannons …? Hello. Earth to Mrs. Droolie! You jog on down to the hold,' growled Pilot. 'There might be a few crates of ore you can chuck at them.'

Magnus cast a nervous glance to the sky behind their stern. 'That might not be a bad idea.'

'You think we'd have outpaced these warships as far as Illinois with a full cargo hold? Running empty is about the only thing we've got going for us. I'll bet this hog's engines and our light hold against one of those big sticks with their keel armour and heavy bomb racks any day of the week.'

Magnus realized, that was exactly what their little party of escapees *had* bet when they stole this freighter.

'I know exactly what you are,' said Molly. 'You're a machine. A bad robot.'

'Bad robot's going to kick Mrs. Droolie's ass if she doesn't stow her attitude.'

'Up ahead,' noted Alios, clattering across the flight cabin to peer out of the rain-slicked canopy. 'Why is the horizon white?'

Pilot nodded with satisfaction. 'At last! No mist like a Lake Michigan mist. A fine Chicago white-out … a hell of a fog since Earth's climate was zapped by the comet.'

'That can save us,' said Alios.

'You think? Wait until we run into the tornadoes capable of tearing mountains apart before you start praising the weather around here, brother.'

'You knew this would be waiting for us,' said Magnus. *That's why the maniac wasn't worried.*

Pilot shrugged. 'Yeah, I knew. We'll dive into the mist-line. With luck, we'll be concealed before the Cals catch us!'

'You know,' observed Magnus, 'we're currently leading the Witch Queen's massed forces towards the location of a working particle accelerator. A location she was perfectly willing to torture us of all to death to discover.'

'Interrogators don't torture you to death,' growled Pilot. 'Not any competent torturer who wants to keep their job.' He glanced at Molly Templar. 'Right to the edge of being a total nut-job, maybe. *That* I'll grant you.'

'The Cals will try to follow us to the hidden vault,' said Magnus.

Pilot chortled. 'Sure, they will. But we'll be on foot by then. And so will the Cal legions. And the one thing you can expect from the Forest of Mars, there's won't be a lot of following going on. Running and screaming, yeah. That in spades.'

I'll look forward to it.

'Our enemy cannot be allowed to capture the particle accelerator. We will need to rig the accelerator to overload, to self-destruct after we return to the future,' said Alios. 'It must be modified for single use only.'

The cabin jolted. For a terrible moment, Magnus thought their airship had been struck by enemy fire. Then he realized they'd run into natural turbulence. 'Can *you* rig the particle accelerator to take us home and then explode, Alios?'

'No. Madre holds the detailed schematics for altering the particle accelerator inside her memory. My understanding of the engineering involved is far more cursory.'

'Madre's the 'bot you mentioned who's like you, brother. Smaller and air-mobile mech, right?' asked Pilot.

'Correct,' said Alios.

'Then you better really hope your go-to-'bot shows up outside the Windy City's ruins in one piece. And that this crazy time-traveling tale of yours is righteous. Because if we make it alive to the vaults under the forest, we ain't leaving. Not ever. The science station's sanctuary to me. And as much as trying to reach it is a suicide mission, reaching it and *then* deciding to return to what passes for fleshbag civilization in this messed up world would be some serious double-Kamikaze brown stuff.'

'You must trust me, Pilot,' said the steamman. 'If we reach the concealed vault and are unable to travel home, our geographic location inside this time-line will be the least of this world's problems.'

'Yeah, so you cats say. But I suspect you're all a few pickles short of the full barrel.'

'You're the one flying us in. What does that say about you?' asked Magnus.

'That I should've snapped your neck back in Cal Central when I had the chance,' muttered the android.

Something struck their airship. Definitely not turbulence this time. Magnus swayed inside the cockpit, the cabin reeling from the shock of an impact. *Well, that was a lucky ranging shot. Or maybe we're in range, now.* Smoke cleared from the fuselage outside. Something vital had taken the "lucky" shell. *Lucky for the Cals, not us.* Half their propellers had stopped turning.

Magnus prayed the Cal fleet was under orders to recapture the escapees. Unless they'd now led the Cals close enough that the Witch Queen's creatures could complete the search without the Jackelians. *In which case, we're dead.* 'Rotors on our starboard side have stopped turning!' he told the android.

'Gee, I guess that must explain why we've lost half our speed.' Pilot's head pivoted towards their stalled engines. The android jerked a thumb at Alios. 'Brother, you and your little fleshbag pet speed back there and see if that crap's fixable. Green door, back of the main corridor … starboard engine nacelle compartment. All this bird's tools and access panels are inside.'

Magnus and the steamman ran for the cockpit exit. 'If the engines aren't repairable, Pilot…?'

'Start composing an unconditionally sincere apology to the Witch Queen. Or open the cargo hold hatch. Then check we're running high enough to jump and be certain of a fatal splat. Because being tortured with a broken spine really sucks eggs.'

'You need to report this to the gunnery officer,' Molly called after them.

'Of course,' sighed Magnus. He and Alios sprinted down the central corridor. *Is it my imagination, or are we listing?* Unlike Jackelian airships, Cals used a substance called synthetic helium to lift their aerial fleet. The two nation's aerostats shared one design feature, though – the gas was compartmentalized across multiple cells. *Some of our cells have been taken out by shrapnel. Depending on the leakage, we might not be able to stay stable and airborne, even with a full set of functioning propellers.* He bit his tongue. *Happy thoughts.*

They reached the green door of the engine access compartment. Magnus tried to open the door, but it was firmly stuck. He pulled at it with all his might, but it didn't yield in the slightest. 'The blast's put the locking mechanism out of kilter.'

'Let me attempt to gain access,' said Alios. Magnus stepped aside. The steamman grabbed the door's lever with both hands and then yanked back with the power of all his four legs. There was a cracking sound, followed by a sudden snap as Alios dislodged the door from its frame. An angry whistling filled the corridor, tugging at Magnus and his friend. They both gazed through a skeleton of melted and smouldering aluminium braces. Canvas envelope flapped forlornly – straight out onto a cloudy blue sky with woodland passing far below.

'Well, that explains why our starboard rotors stopped,' said Magnus.

The access compartment had gone, along with the starboard engines and a goodly part of the airship's flank. The young Jackelian was left with a grand view of the pursuing fleet of Cal airships gaining on them.

On the plus side, we won't be needing to drop the cargo hatch anymore to commit suicide.

- 16 -

The Forest of Mars

'They're too close, we have to ditch now,' shouted Magnus. Behind them, the intermittent thud of exploding shells became a constant high-explosive rattle.

'Okay,' said Pilot. 'Hold onto something tight, we're going down.' The small airship began to dip, not that it needed much help in that regard given how much had already been ripped out of her flank.

Molly yelped as one of the shells exploded off their starboard side, embedding shrapnel in the armoured glass of their cabin canopy. The way this one-sided battle was going, Magnus could see himself clinging on to a single liberated gas bag, drifting through the sky like a child dragged into the atmosphere on an overlarge toy balloon. He nearly laughed out loud, somewhat hysterically, at the thought. He imagined himself waving to one of the Witch Queen's admirals as he passed their pursuers by, the look of astonishment on the four-armed airman's face almost making up for the death sentence he'd be facing.

'This is completely unacceptable,' said Molly.

Pilot looked at the middle-aged woman with a contempt that would have done the designers of his facial body language proud if they had still been alive to see it. 'The complaints department is at the rear. Just leap through one of the tears in the hull to signal your unhappiness, fleshbag.'

'That's not particularly helpful,' said Magnus.

'You want helpful, how about you rustle up a few parachutes from the emergency station? You know, in case we lose any more of this bird to our friends back there and their unfeasibly large cannons.'

They had nearly made it to the wall of mist. But given how many of the Cals' aerial force were pounding the skies around their little craft, "nearly" was an entire universe away from staying alive.

If only we had dodged their first sighting of us for a couple of minutes, we might have pulled this off, thought Magnus.

Their vessel shuddered violently as another of the shells found its mark against the fleeing Jackelians' stern superstructure. The horrible stench of burning metal mixed with the almost animal like odour of smouldering fabric assailed Magnus's nostrils. *I hope that's the hull going up in flames and not our parachutes.*

Alios opened the locker door on the emergency station, desperately rooting about inside for their means of ditching the airship. At least, a means that didn't involve hard physics, gravity, and landing like a projectile pushed out of the bomb bay doors.

'Will a parachute support the weight of both of us?' the steamman asked Pilot.

'Don't look at me, brother. I'm not the product of some crazy Victorian engineering project. The Pilot series were designed to approximate human weight, given we were meant to be sitting in hot seats as fleshbag replacements. You might drop like da bomb, but I'll be floating pretty.'

Finally, the steamman found a series of grey backpack-sized parachutes and started dragging them out; tossing them across the cabin floor.

'Do you know–?' Magnus started.

'Just pull the ripcord after jumping and having counted to seven,' finished the android, guessing what the young Jackelian was about to ask. He glanced out of the broken canopy, the freezing wind whistling through their cabin. 'Actually, don't bother with the count. Way that ground is coming up at us, we're going to be in minus numbers pretty soon anyway.'

Magnus was almost thrown through the broken canopy as the airship lurched to one side. He hadn't heard another explosion, so this was probably just more ballast cells popping from a prior detonation's shrapnel damage.

Magnus fumbled with his parachute, all fingers and thumbs as he tried to reconcile the straps with his narrow beanstalk of a body. Miraculously, Alios Hardcircuit had managed to slip the parachute over his centaur-shaped body as though it had been designed for him. The steamman helped Magnus and then Molly with their parachutes. Pilot Nine scooped one of the sacks off the floor and struggled into it even as he fought against the flight stick and controls; rendered almost useless by the state of damage their airship had suffered.

'Oh this is just fine,' muttered the android. 'Ditching with half the goddamn Cal military on my ass and only a couple of fleshbags and a steam-powered robo-pony to watch my six.'

'Who *are* these people chasing us?' demanded Molly.

Magnus coughed from the smoke leaking in behind him. 'It's those four-armed goons bred by the Witch Queen.'

'The Witch Queen. I remember her. So strange. It was as if she knew me even though we'd never met before.'

Magnus looked startled at his friend's mother. *She is remembering something beyond just the mad fantasies she wrapped around herself to stop going crazy under torture.* Even though they were all very close to ending their expedition right here and now,

Magnus couldn't help but be heartened by how Molly Templar's mind was slowly recovering from her ordeal. If their positions had been reversed, Magnus was fairly sure he would be inside one of the small cabins at the back, quivering below the woollen sheets of an airman's cot.

'Wait,' said Alios. 'I am receiving a short-range communication from–'

A monstrously large airplane dropped out of the clouds into the small gap of sky between the fleeing freighter and the pursuing Cal warships. He caught a brief glimpse of colorful eagle-like markings along its fuselage before it turned into the furious fleet, the leviathan-sized airships having to make crazy turns to avoid being ploughed into by the machine. There was a couple of seconds of shocked silence, both inside their cabin and in the skies outside. And then the drone of the airplane's many propellers was drowned out as warships opened up on the interloper.

'That's a Reindeer Empire flyer,' said Pilot. 'Crazy–'

Alios cantered over to the side for a better look. 'It's our friends. Cassie, Madre and Remus Rawstone!'

Remus Rawstone is no friend of mine, thought Magnus, remembering how casually the wretch had abandoned him to the cannibal fast food clans back in the forest.

'I thought you said your pals were coming out of the Republic. How the hell did they manage to hitch a ride with one of the Emperor's finest?'

'I'm sure we will find out when we reunite with our company,' said Alios Hardcircuit. 'For now, I think they are otherwise engaged."

Engaged was right. It was a hell of an engagement. The slow-moving massive armoured aerial warships of the Cals pitted against this giant shark of the air that their friends had somehow commandeered. Large shells whistled past the warplane, missing and exploding in the air. Some of the detonations sparking off vessels in their own fleet, the nimble craft cutting straight through the ranks of the Witch Queen's finest. The airplane didn't seem to carry the same heavy ordnance mustered by the Cals' aerial fleet. Machine guns chatted along her side, light cannons blasting out at the heavy hulls of the Witch Queen's armada.

Pilot was still wrestling with the stick, trying to get them safely down to the ground without wrapping the freighter's debris round their ears. 'Well I reckon the Cold War in the North just got a little hotter.' There was a coughing noise from outside, masked by the sounds of battle. One of the engines on the remaining good side of the freighter which had jammed during the dive towards the ground had reignited. At least two of the propellers were turning again. The freighter picked up a little altitude.

'The imperials must know what's at stake if the Witch Queen and her servants get their hands on the technology inside your bunker,' said Alios.

The large Imperial aircraft curved up for altitude, looking to hook about and make another dive on the Cal forces. It was a sound strategy, Magnus realised. The Cals' armoured warships in their air fleet were designed to bomb the hell out of helpless ground forces. Many of their cannons didn't have the field of fire necessary to elevate or track a fast-moving warplane; even one of the empire's flagship-sized beasts. But still, there must have been at least thirty airships behind them that Magnus could count. Even with the advantage of speed and aerodynamic vectors adopted by the bobbing airplane, she was still picking up punishment from the Cal fleet. Some of the propellers along her tri-plane style wings had sheared away under the constant bombardment peppering the air. The Cals might have been firing randomly. But this close-up, random was still pretty powerful, given the weight of numbers firing around the sky. Their little freighter had nearly reached the mist when Magnus saw multiple lines of smoke leaking out from the imperial craft, fires driven by her airspeed taking hold. Even more powerful given the combustible nature of the large fuel tanks that aerial leviathan needed to stay airborne.

'Our friends' warplane has suffered serious structural damage,' reported Alios, relaying the brief messages he was still receiving from Madre.

'We're going to make it into the mist, now,' said Pilot. 'We'll be scraping the treeline, but with luck we should make it close to the outskirts of Chicago's ruins.'

Seconds after Pilot spoke, the cabin was surrounded by freezing, eerie, white fog. A fog thick enough to slice as a dessert and serve up for a banquet. The freighter started to judder. Not a violent motion, but a continuous, disturbing assault against what remained of their airship. 'The weather systems are going to get chaotic from here,' warned the android. Tiny flecks of ice started to rain through the shattered panels of the cabin's canopy. It sounded as if the freighter was being sprayed by a machine-gun.

I'll take chaos over death, mused Magnus.

'Madre reports they are disengaging from the Cal fleet, climbing for a height above the operating ceiling of our pursuers. The aircraft also intends to head into the mist, then launch our friends in a glider towards the rendezvous point. After that, they are going to limp back North to make repairs.'

'My daughter,' said Molly. 'It's my daughter on that plane?'

'Cassie is there,' reassured Magnus.

'But how? She's so young."

'Time is out of sync, as far as you and she are concerned,' advised Alios Hardcircuit. 'Only a few years might have passed for you, since you arrived in this age. But your daughter who traveled to rescue you, she has experienced far more years. She is a young lady in her own right now.'

Tears welled up in Cassie's mother's eyes. 'I thought I would return so much sooner. I missed her growing up.'

'She missed you too, 'Magnus said. 'I've known her since I can remember, and I don't think you were very far from her thoughts in all that time.'

'You were in Mechancia with the steammen?'

'My father's business was based there. I might be Jackelian, but I've never actually been beyond the Free State's borders.'

'Until *now*,' said Alios.

'Well, I've never actually visited the Kingdom at least.' *There's an irony for you.*

Pilot Nine hadn't been joking about scraping the treeline. Even through the heavy veil of mist and fog, Magnus watched the icy tips of pine trees flowing past near enough for them to reach out and grab a needle below.

Molly's eyes narrowed. 'This isn't a RAN airship is it?"

'No."

'I feel so tired,' said Molly. 'And faint. I think I might need to go and lie down again.'

Magnus felt weary enough he would have gladly joined her. But his blood was still pumping fast, racing at cheating death and the near continuous pursuit they had just survived.

***

his was the first time that Cassie had been in aerial combat. At least, if you discounted their journey back in time being attacked by the time angels. She stood on the bridge of the vast Imperial warplane, holding tightly onto a guide rail as the plane dipped and turned with a nimbleness that belied her bulk. Or maybe it was just that their opposition were so slow by comparison. With one of the sharp turns, banking to avoid a climbing air ship, Cassie nearly fell over. She was steadied by the Commodore, who seemed oddly blasé about taking on an entire Cal fleet with a single war craft. Unlike his friend, Saul. The Lizard-like man looked as sick as any of them from the sudden motions.

'Have you done this before?' she asked.

'Aye, lass. I served on a RAN airship called the *Iron Partridge* for a while. So all this infernal dodging and diving is just meat-on-the-bone to an old Jack Cloudy like me.'

Lucky you. Madre was the only one of their party finding it easy to keep stable during the battle. Mainly because her claw-like feet dangled in the air as she flitted from side to side, hovering with all the grace of a pendulum.

'Your friends are nearly inside the fog,' noted the Imperial ambassador. Josephine Valvoir's forehead was beaded with sweat as she held on for dear life.

Their friend's upcoming escape hadn't been lost on the warplane's commander, Captain Aucoin, A short stocky man who wore a tight-fitting blue uniform which carried enough braid to decorate a board of admirals. 'Disengage! Climb for height.'

The orders he barked were echoed by sailors manning consoles across the bridge. 'Climbing, aye.'

Four sailors sat at the front, acting as pilots. Operating a complex, coordinated system of levers, wheels, control yokes, centre and side-sticks. Adjusting roll and pitch by transmitting movements to the massive hydraulic ailerons and elevators along the warplane's wings and tail sections. They fair wrestled with their equipment, as if it were alive and they were warriors spurring their warhorses into battle. A series of commands resounded down copper speaking tubes. Tinny yells returning with reports of damage, ordnance expended and dozens of operating concerns. Outside, the air around the *Esprit de L'Empereur* boiled thick with sulphurous smoke, explosions flowering across the sky as the Witch Queen's airships tried to down their adversary.

Remus Rawstone groaned. It seemed that he didn't enjoy dangerous situations where he was helpless to alter the outcome. And it probably didn't make things better that they were manoeuvring through the air. *Heck, you'd think he was used to heights, staring down from the top of mountains and all.*

'Don't worry,' Cassie said. 'We just have to get through this and then we are almost home.' As soon as the words had escaped her mouth, she knew it was the wrong thing to have told the young mountain guide.

'And when we are home, what then? I used to think I had a home. Now, I know it was just a cage. And that is all it will ever be.'

'We can't alter history,' insisted Cassie. 'Not without risking destroying everyone and everything in our own time.'

'We've been cheated out of our rightful position by that mad moon freak,' accused Remus, clutching on tight to a guide rail as the deck angled, the massive aircraft climbing.

'Perhaps you might consider the path of history we have been diverted into as a kinder one,' suggested Madre. 'Do you really want a universe where the race of man savagely dominates as many worlds as it can comfortably oppress?'

'We've only got the monster's word for that, bird-brain,' snarled Remus. 'You never heard of propaganda?'

Saul indicated outside a nearby porthole as the war-craft climbed. 'The universe I traveled from suggests that humanity's nature is consistent across the multi-verse. On my Earth, we consumed everything until even the algae in our seas died out, over-harvested by my people. A universe dominated by the race of man might be many things, but a kind and gentle existence for other species will never be one of them.'

Remus wobbled a finger in front of the lizard-man's face. 'You're as much a monster as that freak on the moon.'

'I do not deny it. On my world, we retreated under the oceans after we had polluted the land beyond use. We changed our bodies to adapt to our new environment. Carrion lizard species such as the Crocodylus acutus contributed their genetic code to humanity's. We became what we needed to be to survive.'

The great aircraft banked and steadied. Ahead of them, the tiny freighter they were trying to rescue vanished into the mist. Cassie felt a great wave of relief roll over her. *My mother is safe and Magnus too.* 'Thank the Circle.'

'Yes, thank the Circle,' said Remus, sarcastically. 'Cassie Templar has everything she came for. Her mother and her little puppy dog Magnus will soon be back in her life. We can all go back home now and beg King Steam for medals for helping that freak in the moon hold onto its victory over us.'

'We'll just go back to the way things were before,' said Cassie. 'What's so bad about that?'

Except of course, it couldn't be like it was before. For the first time, Cassie would have a mother in her life. *What will that be like?* All she had ever known before was the absence of Molly Templar. Cassie had been trying to fill a void for so long she had never really stopped to consider what it would be like with that hole plugged. And how would she explain the death of her friends to their families? *We traveled back in time to make sure things stayed the same. Your children didn't make it. Oops. Sorry.*

The *Esprit de L'Empereur* slipped up into the fog bank, losing all trace of the pursuing air fleet behind them. All trace of everything, as it happened. Cassie hoped that the large compass floating on the pilot console was enough to navigate with– because their sight of the land below and the stars above was replaced by a cold, deep silence inside a blanket of white.

'Take us above the operating ceiling of those Cal balloons,' barked Captain Aucoin. Somewhere ahead in the whiteout was the freighter carrying their friends.

'We're faster than your mother's little craft, lass,' said the Commodore. 'We'll make the ruins first.'

'Their airship's damaged,' Madre informed the party. 'Flank side propulsion only. Alios informs me everyone is safe with nobody wounded, however.'

Cassie breathed a sigh of relief. *If anything happens now to Alios or my mother...*

'Our plane cannot afford to circle above old Chicago,' said Madame Valvoir.' Not even for you, monsieur president. I will spare you one of the gliders in the *Esprit de L'Empereur*'s hangar. You must land to keep your rendezvous.'

'You haven't heard the last of me, Josephine,' said the Commodore. 'Once I've seen Molly and her family and friends safe back home, I'll be marching north to Juneau to petition the emperor and remind him of all I've done for the Imperial cause.'

'Given the manner of your last parting, I hope I'm in the capital to observe your reunion with his Imperial Highness. It will make for an amusing tale, at the very least.'

'He'll forgive me,' said the Commodore. 'The Emperor likes victories more than he likes his mistresses. The old rascal can always find another ambitious noblewoman willing to warm his socks at night. But nobody can lay victories at his feet like old Blacky!'

'Madame ambassador, who rules the land below us?' asked Madre.

'The wilderness rules it, *bébé oiseau*. But the territory is nominally claimed by the Duke of Cleves.'

'Don't concern yourself, old steamer,' said Jared Black. 'You'll not be meeting any of the duke's patrols in the Forest of Mars.'

'What *will* we be meeting exactly?' probed Cassie.

'I've only heard stories, lass. Creatures and machines from the old world gone feral. But that is the way your mortal journey home lies. So that is the hard road poor old Blacky must follow.'

'We don't need your help, fat man,' said Rawstone.' We got all the way here without you. Escaping from that deathtrap of a moon, falling through time. Watching our time-ship blown apart. Then we survived everything this savage continent threw at us.'

'You're a callow youth, lad. You remind me of *me* at your age. On the make and on the way up. But you'll need more than luck and an untested sword arm to make it the final few leagues. You will need an old man's cunning and genius.'

'And his taste for wine?' Rawstone pointed at the bottle poking out of the Commodore's backpack, stuffed full of everything he'd hastily looted from the palace before departing.

'A connoisseur's palette comes with age, too.' Jared Black winked at Saul. 'When we get to Juneau, I'll sneak you down into the Emperor's cellar. He holds so many of the finest vintages, the old dog will never notice if a few go missing.'

Cassie was about to tell Remus to lay off the deposed politician – at least he was trying to help them get home – but she stopped as the bridge's fuselage began to rattle. A gentle patter at first, growing louder and louder until the walls began to vibrate as though one of their foes had turned a machine gun against the *Esprit de L'Empereur*.

Ambassador Valvoir's eyes widened with panic. 'Ice-storm!'

Crew at the instruments yelled out, trading readings between stations. Captain Aucoin paced the deck as sailors sprinted to their emergency positions. Making the warplane ready to ride out the sudden shift in climate.

Sweet circle. Even the weather seems against us. Cassie grabbed onto a guide rail. The plane's superstructure jolted violently with the beating. 'What can we do?'

'We must descend,' said the ambassador. Valvoir shouted something to the Captain in her language, and he gave her a terse reply in the Reindeer Empire's tongue. She swore under her breath. 'This high up, storm ice circulates the size of boulders. Lower down it should turn into a pebble-sized hail.'

'*Should*?'

'Our experience is somewhat limited little one, by the very small number of Imperial planes which have survived such storms.'

'Every farmhouse in the Dukedom of Cleves, however humble, is built with a fine cellar,' said the Commodore. 'But it's for preserving their family, not storing a grand vintage.'

'If we descend, won't the Cal airships be able to attack us again?' asked Rawstone.

'They'll also have the storm to worry about,' spat the

ambassador, pointing to cracking crystal portholes across the bridge.

Cassie groaned. They had traveled all this way; they had survived so much. Overcome so many obstacles. Now a harsh climate was about to stop them? *It doesn't seem either fair or reasonable.*

'Can we not ascend above the storm?' asked Madre.

'There is no 'above' this storm,' sighed Saul. 'These weather events are connected to vortexes which reach into the troposphere. Atmospheric moisture is being converted into ice by the very void of space.'

Rawstone shot the lizard-man an angry look that seemed to suggest he didn't give a rat's arse about the nature of the deepening storm.

'My kind were masters of extreme weather events. We generated so many of them as we murdered our world.'

'What about my mother?' asked Cassie. 'Magnus?'

'Better placed than us,' said Madre.

Saul nodded. 'Ah yes, lift-to-weight ratio…'

'What?' Rawstone fair exploded.

'An airship with no engines still stays in the air,' Saul simplified. As soon as the explanation was out of the creature's mouth the *Esprit de L'Empereur* veered to the side, throwing expedition members into the bridge's fuselage. Cassie had barely steadied herself against one of the freezing cold portholes when the floor seemed to drop away underneath her.

Sailors began shouting out names of the engines and propellers cutting out across the massive tri-winged plane.

Saul groaned. 'And at -60°C, our fuel lines freeze up.'

'That's not good,' said the Commodore, listening to the officers ordering engineers out onto the wings 'Poor old Captain

Aucoin doesn't have enough lads or heating equipment to handle this many propellers failing at the same blessed time.'

Their plane lurched again.

'Get to the launch hangar, now!' ordered the ambassador. She hustled the passengers out of the bridge, leaving a scene of controlled confusion behind them.

'You want to ditch us?' snarled Rawstone as they entered the passage outside.

'I want the sacrifice of this plane, should it come to it, to mean something,' Valvoir snapped back. She drove them mercilessly through the warplane's narrow corridors, down metal gantries and towards the vast flying craft's belly. She halted them briefly by a bank of emergency lockers, just long enough to remove a parachute pack and fur-lined aviator's jacket each. The emergency air supply masks and tanks they left behind. *Hey, we're were going to freeze or plummet to our deaths, not asphyxiate in the smoke of battle.*

They were still running when a massive crump shook the corridor. Rawstone grabbed Cassie and threw her forward. She was still wondering why when this was followed by a second impact which pitched her off her feet, flinging her into a bulkhead. A savage whistling sounded in her ears and it took her a second to realize the noise was emanating outside her ringing head, too. Someone gripped her hand tight and helped her to her feet. It was Valvoir. The corridor behind them was a mess of broken decking and girders, much of it ripped away. A wild howling whipped through. Large shards of ice had been left embedded in the walls around her, speaking volumes for what had struck this section of the Emperor's flying boat.

Saul was stretched over the deck behind them, almost close enough to fall out of the aircraft and embrace the fog-filled sky. What wasn't there, however, was either of the lizard-man's legs.

Mumbling, Commodore Black dragged his wounded friend away from the vista over the storm and a fatal plunge.

'All these years,' moaned Saul, blood bubbling out of his razored mouth, 'and I am undone by frozen water vapour. All those stupid things I have survived.'

'You'll live, you damned fool,' said the Commodore. He turned around to Valvoir. Cassie could only look on horrified, trying to recover her wits while her head throbbed from the recent detonation.

'Is there a surgical bay on this great bird of yours? Tell me there is, Josephine...?'

Ambassador Valvoir didn't have to point out that their warplane was unlikely to stay aloft long enough for surgery to take place. It was all too evident Saul wouldn't last that long, anyway. Reaching out, Saul gripped the Commodore's arm weakly with his green-scaled fingers. 'My body contains crocodile DNA, not salamander. I cannot grow back missing limbs.'

'You cannot leave me alone, here. I won't allow it.'

'I'm the last of my people. Remember us. Remember, me.'

'Aye, you know I will.'

Saul shivered and his eyes shut slowly. His body seeming to physically deflate as the last of his life force departed.

'I've accounted for them all, now,' said the Commodore. 'A whole blessed race gone to meet their maker.'

Cassie saw Madre in the corner of her eye, struggling through the wreckage of what remained of the corridor. Her mind recovered enough, a realization hitting with the force of a cannonball. 'Wait a minute! Where's Remus Rawstone?'

Commodore Black shook his head, sadly. 'The poor lad was sprinting behind Saul when the storm ice struck us.'

Cassie stared out in shock at the gaping void. 'No!'

'He's gone, lass. I'm sorry. As quick and clean a death as a man can hope for in this cruel life.'

Cassie stumbled towards the rent, her mind afire with numb shock, guilt and a hundred other competing emotions swamping her mind.

Madame Valvoir seized Cassie's arm. 'We have to keep on moving, or we'll be joining both your comrades in death.'

I pushed him away. And in return he just saved my life. Now he's gone. Another death on my conscience. 'I never got a chance to—' *To what? To reject him again. Remus didn't have much of a life. But he threw it away saving mine.*

'No-one ever does,' said the Commodore. 'We leave this mortal world the same way we enter it. Squealing and naked, with nothing but the love of our family, if we're lucky. You and your friends were as much his family as anyone, I'd say.'

Madre hummed a strange machine-like song. A prayer of passing to one of her steammen gods, while the ambassador pleaded with them. Jared Black stopped a second to roll Saul's corpse out of the opening and into the embrace of the thick white fog. 'Saul told me once that the sea-bishops committed their race's corpses to the ocean, when they could. Maybe we're above the Great Lakes now. Cruel fate owes Saul that much.'

'Enough,' ordered Valvoir. 'Now we move. Or there will be only dead to mourn the dead.'

The survivors sprinted down the corridor, following Madame Valvoir, pushing past sprinting crewman, bypassing more areas damaged by the storm. The sailors wore emergency parachutes, too, but were still focused on staying aloft. Finally, they gained entry to the hangar section by the Leviathan seaplane's keel. Smaller planes lined up inside on catapult launch rails, the metal doors to the outside sealed shut. One and two-person scouts planes, for the most part. Valvoir led them to the largest craft inside the chamber, a long wooden canvas-framed glider with curved gull wings. It looked more like a sculpture than a working aircraft.

'I hope you haven't forgotten how to fly, monsieur president.'

'I could never forget your lessons, Josephine. But surely you're not going to entrust our survival to a shaky old man's grip on that contraption? Say you're coming with us!'

Valvoir shook her head.' My duty lies here. Captain Aucoin will try to nurse the *Esprit de L'Empereur* across the forests and fly as far north as the Lastedge Republic. If we can ditch inside the republic's plains, we will be beyond the Cals' influence.'

'Not even for old times' sake, lass?'

'I never heard of anyone surviving the Forest of Mars. Let alone surviving the forest with half the Witch Queen's legions in pursuit. I think of the two of us, I will be the one living to tell the tale, yes?'

'I'll sing you the story of how I survived the forest when I march north to claim the Emperor's favour.'

The ambassador pulled open the glider's entry hatch. 'Any landing you can walk away from, yes? Quick, quick. I shall open the hangar for you.'

It felt narrow inside the glider; a line of seven seats and a single pilot's position at the front, the controls little more advanced than a child's handmade wooden racing cart. Jared Black took the pilot's position, the seat hardly able to contain his bulk, then Madre and Cassie followed and belted themselves in.

A dull thud, followed by being slammed into her seat as the glider was flung out like a crossbow bolt. Cassie stared out of the portal. A last brief glimpse of the *Esprit de L'Empereur*, warm air streaming into freezing fog from dozens of tears across her fuselage. Then they were swallowed by the white, only the rattle of their frail craft to remind them of how far they had yet to fall.

- 17 -

Bear Necessities

Remus Rawstone groaned as he realised he was somehow still alive.

It wasn't easy to leap to that conclusion given he was hanging upside down inside the branches of a tree, most of his blood long since pooled inside his head. *No leaping allowed, not even to conclusions.* Wrapped tight inside a silky fabric of some sort. Remus tried to remember how he had arrived at this point. There had been freezing cold, shaking, blasted by ice. Had he fallen down a mountain crevasse? *No, that can't be right. The trees here are wrong.* The tree he was stuck in looked as though someone had painted it with blood. The bark was red, even its leaves rustled crimson in the breeze. About the only thing which wasn't red was the eerie slug-white river of fog sliding across the ground below. Something about the mist pierced the haze inside his mind. *A plane. A great big bloody plane. Yes.* He had been on a warplane. Running through its corridors. Until he wasn't. Falling through the sky, his hands wildly flinging around, vainly trying to grab something that would arrest his fall. Until he had yanked on the dangling ripcord flapping around his face. A deployment bag containing a parachute canopy bursting above him, arresting his plummeting passage. Then a segment of ice the size of a cart decided to introduce itself to his skull and Remus had been swallowed by a darkness far more fundamental than the fog-choked sky.

Just like the forest back home in Mechancia, this one was alive with more than vegetation. As Remus's brain spun, he listened to chirrups from insects, calls from birds. A strange wild singsong that was both familiar and alien at the same time. He twisted, bruising his spine, gazing up the length of the tree he was suspended in. Its perspective seemed wrong to Remus. The trunk stretched away at least six times as high as the tallest trees on the slopes of the Mechancian Spine. Then he remembered what the lizard man had said about these trees. How they weren't natural, but an experiment designed by mankind to change the climate of Mars. Alter that world's atmosphere from a toxic soup to one suited to human inhabitation. That must explain why there were strange nodules across the bark leaking gas. *Great. I'm going to die from inhaling chemicals never meant for Earth.*

High above he saw a canopy of plate-shaped leaves looming as large as shields. As interlinked as any warriors' shield wall, too. Rigid enough to rattle as the tail end of the ice storm was repelled by the forest. It seemed an impressive act of cooperation between mere trees. As though a basic consciousness was at work. A group mind of vegetation, protecting its crimson realm from the harsh climate above. Remus shuddered with more than cold. He imagined carnivorous trees eager to make short order of unwelcome intruders. *Say, a young Jackelian mountain guide.*

Slowly, Remus's natural instincts came back to him. Swinging like a haunch of meat, wrapped up inside the parachute canopy and its cords. *First things first. Let's get out here.* He twisted his body into a ball, ignoring the pain; slipped the hidden dagger out of his boot. Then he used his blade's edge to saw away the parachute silk and webbing. Careful to make sure he had enough of a grip on the branches so that freedom wouldn't mean breaking his neck on the ground below. Remus sliced away a long coil of parachute cording. Slipping it behind the trunk, he used the material as a hitch cord to shimmy down to the forest floor. The mist rose as high as his knees. The ground felt hard and crunchy, an icy carpet of leaves which he couldn't see. In fact, Remus couldn't peer further than a dozen feet through the forest. But that was fine. This forest might have been designed for another world. It might have sounded freaky. It doubtless smelt unnatural too, although his nose was currently too cold to offer much of a sense of smell. But this was still the wilds. And Remus Rawstone had spent his life escaping the claustrophobic bounds of city existence for such places.

Okay, Remus, think. Everyone else will be flying on East to these Chicago ruins. Then they're heading back this way. If I can find the forest's outskirts, I'll have a chance of meeting them as they enter. He really, really wanted that meeting to happen. Because the alternative was being stuck in the savage past for the rest of his life. Remus shuddered at the thought. From what he'd understood of the return voyage, the gear flinging them forward through time was going to be jury-rigged by bird-brain to ensure it was a one-shot deal.

'You think you can abandon me here, bird-brain?' Remus muttered. 'Of course, you do. You never gave a crap about me. About any of us. We were just fuel to power whatever ancient steamman prophecy you're chasing. Kindling for your fireplace. You're not bloody stranding me here! Not in a million years.'

A distant howling sounded muffled by the fog, directionless, mocking his hopes of getting away safely. Remus stopped chatting with himself, however much he needed the reassurance of a human voice. It appeared there were more dangerous things inside the haunted forest than trees leaking noxious vapours. *Living up to its reputation.* He checked the nearest trunk for which side the moss grew on, giving him his compass points. *Well, at least moss and sun still work the same here.* Remus started to trudge

East, moving silently across the crumbling forest floor. After a few hours of marching, alone and shivering from the cold, he realised how hungry he felt. Remus started to ponder climbing one of those great alien redwoods in search of a bird's nest and eggs. He'd kept the coil of parachute webbing as a hitch cord for just such an occasion. Remus selected a likely-looking tree for climbing. He froze as a crossbow bolt slammed into the bark, nearly impaling his numb fingers.

Remus whirled around. He found himself facing four figures. Hulking great brutes, none shorter than seven-foot-tall, clad in leather armour. But the newcomers weren't human, despite clutching a motley collection of crossbows and metal-tipped spears. Humanoid bears, shaggy brown fur-skinned but with strangely human eyes. The most bizarre thing about these creatures was Remus knew *exactly* what they were. He had guided enough merchant parties from the nation of Pericur into the Steamman Free State to recognise an Ur when he saw one. Male Urs. Big ugly ones, if he was any judge.

Remus held out his two empty palms, showing he didn't have any weapons. *At least my boot blade's tucked away safe.* 'I don't mean you boys any harm. I'm just passing through your woods.'

One of the Urs wore a dented copper helmet with a pair of stag antlers mounted to the helm. It stepped forward, closing the distance between its hunting party and Remus in a few long strides. The butt of the monster's crossbow drove into Remus's solar plexus, doubling him up in agony. A loud rumble of grumbling laughter resounded through the clearing. 'No. You passing through gut.'

'We make fire here?' growled one of the creature's friends. Copper-helmet seized Remus from behind, pinning him with the beast's substantial weight.

'Now. Cook, cook!'

'I'm hungry too, if you're planning to eat,' moaned Remus.

Copper-helmet rested its spare paw-like hand on Remus's shoulder in an almost companionable way. 'Hunger finish quick. Not long to skin thin meat … you quick munching.'

Remus felt a length of wood slid behind his spine, both arms and hands lashed to it with his own parachute cord. He watched in horror as the four hulking creatures ripped low-hanging branches from the towering trees. They piled wood across the forest floor until it rose higher than the swirling mist. One of the Urs flourished a flint-and-iron fire sparker, striking it into the kindling. It only took a few seconds for the fire to catch and start crackling.

That was when Remus realised these beasts weren't even going to stick him with one of their spears before roasting him. *I'm going to be cooked alive!*

He began to panic, all illusions of dignity and courage abandoned as he struggled in copper-helmet's tight grip. 'You can't do this to me! Please …'

'Like dinner better, little meat not talk,' laughed his chief captor. 'Stick spear through heart. Quick!'

An Ur raised its crossbow. 'Shoot in head.'

'Idiot! Bolt pass through thin meat. Hit me! Stick thin meat. Spear, spear!'

One of the Urs leaning against a steel-tipped spear by the fire lumbered over.

Better than being cooked alive. But not much. Remus kicked out at the advancing Ur, but for all his frantic struggling the reach of its spear was longer than his thrashing legs.

The beast with the spear sized Remus up as he desperately struggled in copper-helmet's grip. It was clearly trying to work out the arrangement of the young man's vital organs. 'Hold little meat still. Yes! No shake, shake.'

Then the monster lunged forward clutching its weapon.

***

All the things that Cassie had thought to say, all the myriad imagined conversations storming through her mind. They all seemed to disintegrate like sandcastles in a whirlwind as she saw her mother for the first time. Despite every hardship Molly Templar had endured, Cassie immediately recognized her mother. Even if Cassie had never kept the aging photograph — all that was left of her mother's presence in the Steamman Free State — she would have known her mother. Perhaps she would have identified her even without the photograph. They were alike in many ways. The same copper coloured hair. The same build and height. Molly was doubtless what Cassie would look like after surviving so much, going through so much. Judging by the way Molly Templar's eyes opened in astonishment as she saw Cassie, she also recognized her daughter.

'Is that really you, Cassandra?' spluttered Molly.

Cassie ran up to Molly Templar, stopping short of hugging the woman. *What can I say to her? How do I even begin?* They had been apart for so long. This meeting was a textbook definition of insanity. Traveling through time, both stranded millions of years in the past. Reunited at an age where they might have been sisters rather than mother and daughter. 'It is.'

'You shouldn't be more than six years old. I planned to return home a few months after I left Mechancia.'

Cassie shook her head sadly. Tears welled in her eyes. 'I came for you. I couldn't wait any longer.'

'You did the right thing,' said Molly, rushing forward to give Cassie a hug she couldn't quite bring herself to extend.

'I thought you didn't care. I thought you'd forgotten all about me.'

'How could I? Even when I was lying broken in a torture chamber, I never forgot about you. Even when I forgot myself, you were there for me. Just the thought I might see you again one day. That became the single thread of sanity I clutched onto during the worst of it.'

Magnus slipped past the Commodore, standing there awkwardly watching their long overdue reunion. Cassie raised a hand to him in thanks. Magnus had escaped from the Witch Queen. He'd done what Cassie could not. Brought about the end of her quest. 'Your mother never had a choice,' said Magnus. 'Alios saved her. Healed your mother by calling upon the Steamo Loa to mend her broken mind.'

'That was a risky strategy,' said Madre, disapprovingly, skimming forward in the air.

'It was a necessary action,' said Alios.

Cold fog swirling around ancient Chicago's ruins bit at Cassie's legs. She allowed the warmth of her mother's hug to seep through her. She didn't dare let go, lest this all prove a dream. The fog gave the rubble the look of a dream. Sharp shards of glass and brown, rotted steel girders poking out from vegetation overgrowing what was left. She might wake up back in Mechancia. Her trials and tribulations fighting her way here just a nightmare. None of it real.

Her mother stopped talking and Cassie realised why. Molly Templar's gaze had settled on Commodore Jared Black.

The Commodore nodded at her mother. 'I came for you, Molly. Aye, that I did.'

Molly abruptly pulled away from Cassie, rushing up to the Commodore. Cassie thought she might hug him too, but instead, she slapped him hard in the face. 'And I came for you. But you never showed up! I've been rotting for years in that bitch of a queen's capital.'

'I sent word to you that I wasn't going to be able to keep the rendezvous, lass. But the officer I trusted with the duty was murdered.'

'I didn't need one of your soldiers. I needed you!'

'And so did my people. I wasn't ready to leave Texicana. For that, sweet Molly, I have no excuse beyond the weight of simple duty.'

'Damn you and your simple duty. We're wading through the dust of lost history. A world you've no right to inhabit.'

'That's a deeper question than I have an answer for, Molly. But I never gave up on you. Many a hero has been made a ghost earlier than their time, attempting to pry you out of the Cals' clutches.'

'You want to stay here? That's madness,' said Molly. 'I always knew you had a stubborn streak of romanticism running through your bones. You've fallen in love with a world, an entire age, which was finished long before either of us was born.'

'I traveled to Chicago's ruins to right that wrong, lass. I came here to make sure that you and your darling daughter get home. For that is where you want to be. But it cannot be my destiny yet. Maybe one day after the Witch Queen is dead and buried.'

'That day will never come, Jared. There will always be another enemy to fight. The truth is that you don't belong here. None of us do.'

'I wasn't dispatched here willingly, Molly. I fell into this land, into this past. But they need me. Who in the future can say that of poor old Blacky?'

'I can.'

'Well, you have me for this moment. And that must be enough.'

Cassie tugged at her mother's arm. 'It doesn't matter. The Commodore helped me reach you. That's all that matters now."

'Your *friends* helped me, Cassandra,' said Molly. She pointed to Magnus, Alios and the android who had facilitated her escape. 'I'd still be trapped raving mad inside a Cal dungeon if it wasn't for them.'

'All very sweet,' noted Pilot Nine. 'Consider me deeply touched. But we're not the only fools blundering around this fog. Somewhere out there is half the Cal nation's air fleet. Desperate to get their mitts on the goodies stashed inside the station just as much as you. So how about you put your mother-daughter bonding time on the back-burner before you end up rotting in the Witch Queen's dungeon as a family unit?'

Cassie stared in irritation at the newcomer. 'How about you—'

Magnus stepped between them, ever the peacemaker. 'Don't worry about him. He's got a problem with humans.'

'*He*'s only got a problem with the living ones,' griped Pilot Nine. 'Mainly because its live fleshies who keep on lousing everything up.'

Out in the ruins, something howled. It sounded like a coyote crossed with a rattlesnake. The kind of noise that promised nightmares. Pilot Nine held up his hands in disgust as though he was surrendering. 'The defence rests, your honour.'

'It would be advantageous to withdraw now,' urged Madre, flying in nervous loops. 'Using this city's ruins as a reference point I have calculated our route through the Forest of Mars.'

'Ain't you the fancy one, Wings,' said Pilot Nine. 'At least for a steam-powered owl. But seeing as how yours truly was first powered up inside the station, you just tag along after me. And stay frosty. If you think things are bad around here, wait until you're skipping through the Forest of Terraforming Terrors.'

Something else to look forward to, thought Cassie.

They started trekking west, following the android as he led them through what remained of Chicago. Great towers had been left as mere mounds of rubble. Debris buried underneath grass, bushes and moss. The comet's blast-wave had burned through this city leaving little more than bones and bricks.

'Are you certain you weren't followed here?' Molly Templar asked her daughter. 'I escaped once before from the Witch Queen. But it was a ruse. She was using me. She followed me to the particle accelerator I planned to use to return to the future. Luckily for the future, the site was underwater. The accelerator rusted and beyond use.'

Cassie shook her head. 'I don't think *anyone* could have followed us into that ice storm. We ditched from our warplane flying a glider. We could hardly see five feet through the white-out. Nearly broke our necks landing.'

'It was as fine a landing as anyone ever made,' protested the Commodore behind them, 'running blind in this blessed murk.'

'What about your airship, mother?'

Molly pointed into the fog. 'Tethered outside the ruins. Down to a single propeller. Our last engine damaged, with fumes for fuel. We could drift on the wind, but enter another storm and it'd be the end of us.'

'Your escape wasn't a trick by the Witch Queen, then?'

'I can assure you that our release was no ruse, Cassie softbody,' noted Alios. 'I submitted to torture. Then I infiltrated the machinery the Cals used to probe my brain. I subverted their security systems. Our breakout was anything but staged.'

'You are a faithful friend, Alios,' said Cassie. 'I'm sorry you had to endure that for my sake.'

'They're all fine friends,' said Molly.

'Speak for yourself,' muttered Pilot Nine.

Cassie ignored the bitter android. 'I lost three companions reaching you. I never wanted them to put their lives at risk. But they traveled with me anyway.'

'That is how you know they were good ones,' sighed Molly. 'I lost more than a few souls myself over the years. Surviving so many scrapes. Their memory never fades. Part of them always lives on inside you.'

'Why did you place me in Mechancia with the steammen?' asked Cassie.

'You mean rather than leaving you in Middlesteel? Too many enemies inside Jackelia. It seemed safer to squirrel you away far from the Kingdom. Growing up in the mountains wasn't too much of a burden for you, I trust? The steammen have always proved the most reliable of friends to me. It was the safest place I could think of at a pinch.'

'Growing up without *you* was the burden. I didn't much care where I lived. At least, I never made any plans to leave Mechancia and the Free State. I suppose I was reaching the age where I could have traveled away if I'd wanted to.'

'Your friend Magnus. He mentioned he was being sent to visit Jackelia. Perhaps you would have gone with him if he'd asked?'

Maybe I would have, at that. Cassie shivered with the cold. It wasn't just the fog. There was a constant low wind which cut to the bone. At times it pushed through the rubble of Chicago and whistled through the cracked broken concrete. A low ominous sibilance that almost sounded like the dead city pleading to return to life.

Thinking about Magnus, thinking about what it might be like returning home, she noticed that the young Jackelian had slipped by her. He walked on her windward side. That wasn't the only warmth he brought with him.

'I heard about Rawstone. How he didn't make it,' said Magnus.

'No.' Was all she could think to say, between the guilt of his death saving her and the raw memories of her journey here.

'I'm glad he kept you alive, anyway.'

'We had a few moments getting here when I didn't think I would make it,' said Cassie. 'What about you?'

'Oh, the usual. Greased up as a human roast by the cannibal clans. Captured by subterranean snake priestesses. Sold onto the Witch Queen. Lined up for a nice bit of torture.'

'Look on the bright side, Magnus. Now, all we must do is penetrate some monster-filled forest designed to prosper on another world. Then locate an ancient station and hope that it's not filled with floodwater and mud and rust. Hope that it still contains a working particle accelerator.'

'I think I can do better than that,' said Magnus. 'Not only do we have to hope this ancient basement hasn't caved in on itself, but we have to trust Madre is able to modify the technology. Hack it so it can speed us safely through millions of years of history until we reach home.'

'Oh, I think I can trump you,' boasted Cassie. 'As well as all of *that*, we also have to hope that any changes we might have inadvertently caused in the past haven't altered the future. Perhaps we'll return and find Jackelia has been conquered by the Commonshare or Cassarabia. Maybe never even existed as a nation at all?'

'Okay,' said Magnus, throwing up his hands in mock surrender. 'You win. We are properly doomed. I don't know why we're even bothering to risk our necks going into this stupid forest.'

'So,' said Cassie, 'perhaps there's a future back home worth living after all?' She reached out and squeezed Magnus's hand.

'That's a warm hand,' said Magnus.

'Maybe you should consider holding it for a while. I mean, it is *really* cold out here.'

'If you're going to force me to.'

Cassie smiled. 'I insist.'

***

Remus watched the spear's barbed iron head closing on his chest in horrified fascination. Time slowed. Part of him realised this was the Moon Monster's brainwashing. A vain last attempt by his mind's military conditioning to survive. Sadly, faster reflexes only got Remus so far when he was struggling pinned by an 800lb seven-foot sentient bear. With a second pack member about to impale him like a rabbit on a roasting spit.

That was when things went sideways. Suddenly, Remus was being crushed by the creature's weight. As though copper-helmet was intent on breaking his spine. He would have gone on believing this if the monster about to impale him hadn't been thrown savagely back inside a cloud of blood. Remus staggered forward, overwhelmed by a buzz-saw roar. It sounded as though every tree in the clearing was suddenly splintered apart by lumberjacks. Except it was the Urs being taken apart. Remus collapsed into the carpet of fog. He rolled across the forest floor, a cold veil freezing his face. Remus fell with the full weight of copper-helmet crushing his legs. Squirming, Remus managed to shrug off the beast long enough to escape from underneath its body. *No, it's corpse.* Remus felt blood soaking his legs. *None of it mine.* Remus managed to crack the wooden stake pinning his arms behind his back. He rose up. Found himself facing a company of soldiers sprinting towards him. They wore uniforms like nothing he'd seen before. The fact they each possessed four arms was only the start of the strangeness. The troops were clad in dark padded armour. Faces covered by dark visors, radios cracking built into matt-metal helmets. Remus stood surrounded by soldiers. Bulky steel oblong-shaped rifles trained on him. Hard not to notice vapour rising from short mesh-like muzzles.

'On the ground,' ordered the nearest soldier. His voice escaped tinny from speakers on his helmet's mouthpiece. Amplified. Dead-sounding. 'I won't ask again!'

The strange alien ghost lurking inside Remus's mind marked the position of every soldier inside the clearing. Helpfully, it numbered them in the precise order he should attack them. His unwanted passenger also highlighted their rifles as FN Herstal STABRAIL-2000s, indicating they fired caseless ammunition at a rate of two-thousand rounds-per-minute using magnetic acceleration. Their weapons might resemble ungainly slabs of gleaming metal, but it would only take a single round to burst into Remus's body and bring him down. Quite frankly, surrounded by shredded monsters who'd recently been preparing to cook Remus, he didn't need the advice superimposed across his vision: a flashing red silhouette of a figure with both arms high in the air in the act of surrender. Remus dropped to his knees and placed his recently liberated hands behind his neck.

The soldiers advanced around him. Rifles held high, little targeting dots trained on the Jackelian's head. Part of Remus was flattered they considered him so dangerous. But they were just being careful. Troops flooded in from both flanks. Possessing four arms each made holding Remus down a doddle. They secured his hands behind his back with black twists of plastic. As they yanked him up, he realised these goons belonged to the Witch Queen's legions. Easy enough to drop into the forest abseiling from hovering airships. *So, these are the four-armed devils Commodore Black boasted of defeating on the battlefield.* Given how expertly the legion had dispatched the pack of man-eaters, Remus had to wonder if the fat fool's boasts were fantasies born of his drunken stupor.

'None of you lads are cannibals, right?' asked Remus. 'I mean, you're not planning on roasting me?'

The soldiers dragged Remus forward. One cuffed him around the head. 'Getting cooked by a filthy pack of chimera might look pretty good to you, boy, after our mistress has finished with you.'

'Everyone keeps on talking about the Witch Queen as if she's something to be afraid of.'

'You've no idea'

'Speakers off,' ordered a soldier with stripes on his shoulder plate. 'Switch to internal comms. There're thousands of chimeras inside this forest. Haven't got enough ammunition to scrub them all.'

'Copy that.'

They fell silent. Remus heard a low buzz emanating from the Cals' helmets. He glanced around the clearing before leaving. The pack planning to consume him possessed strangely human blood. What was left of the Urs looked like it belonged in this strange crimson forest: at least as far as matching colours were concerned. His four-limbed 'friends' shoved him forward. It was a sign of the squad's professionalism they took nothing for granted despite possessing a massive advantage of firepower. Each soldier moved carefully, smoothly, through the trees and fog. Weapons always shifting, covering potential enemy positions as they advanced. Ready to take down enemies wherever they emerged. Remus wondered if the legionaries' helmets fed them tips in the same manner as the ghost haunting his noggin.

After marching for an hour, the Cals slowed. Remus detected a shift in mood among his multiple-limbed saviours. A slight easing of tension. They passed through an area of forest with tree trunks cracked apart as though felled by blight. The nature of the disease became clearer as he advanced. He stepped over a ring of collapsed trees, the blast radius from bombs dropped to clear an instant campsite. Squat tractors pushed debris and soil into a circular wall, beyond. Lines of tents crisscrossed the fort; tripod-mounted weapons carefully positioned around the wall. Soldiers with long-barreled rifles scanned what was left of the treeline still standing beyond the blast zone.

Remus entered through a gap in the fortifications, an entrance protected by an armoured vehicle squatting low on caterpillar tracks. The Cal airships had obviously come loaded for bear. Which, given Remus's recent experience on the Urs' dinner menu, was as farsighted as their Witch Queen's reputation. He approached a circus-sized command tent in the centre of the fort. Remus's escorts presented their arms at a sentry station. Sentries ran a small device down each offered limb. With a low beep and a blinking green light, the patrol was recognized as bona fide members of the Cal legion. Nobody bothered scanning Remus. But he was manhandled inside all the same. Remus guessed the fetching blonde woman standing at the head of a map-covered folding table must be the Witch Queen. She wore a variation of her soldiers' uniforms, with the addition of a sweeping fur-lined cape and a high ornamental collar. A single holstered pistol dangled from her waist. And of course, she didn't bother concealing her golden curls or porcelain skin underneath a combat helmet.

Remus's escort brutally shoved him to his knees in front of the woman. They kept him pressed down, hard.

'I would introduce myself,' said Remus. 'But aren't you meant to know who I am?'

One of the guards raised the butt of his machine rifle to give Remus a headache, but the Witch Queen merely sighed. She flicked her fingers to indicate she desired his skull uncaved in for the moment. 'I see all, Remus Rawstone. Haven't you heard?'

Remus felt a shiver of fear pass down his spine at this act of precognition. He steeled his will. Not wishing to display any shortage of courage in front of her. 'That's a good trick. Must come in handy during receptions at your palace.'

'It comes in handier when avoiding goblets laced with nerve agents.' She clapped her hands. 'Untie this wretch. Fetch him a glass of brandy. The boy looks as if he needs it. In fact, he looks as if he's been dragged through a hedge backward.'

'That's kind of you. Am I meant to guess if the glass is poisoned or not? And it wasn't a hedge I was dragged backward through. It was this hell-haunted forest.'

'There are worse things that could happen to you.'

'And will your torturers be subjecting me to many of those?'

'That depends on how forthcoming you prove about where the rest of your company are heading.'

'What company?'

'Don't play games with me, Remus Rawstone. The rest of your

colleagues from the future. And not forgetting that fat scoundrel recently chased out of Texicana by his political enemies.'

'Look, your majesty, we're only trying to return home. It might go a lot easier all round if you simply let us escape.'

The Witch Queen laughed at his suggestion. 'If it was simply a matter of packing off Texicana's deposed president and the rest of you ne'er-do-wells, I would be glad to do so. In fact, I would make you a lunch hamper and present it to you before you disappeared, never to be seen again.'

'So, what's stopping you...?'

'The future and past are linked. You must have realised that by now. Your very presence here is a testament to the juxtaposition. I might be finished with the future, but I have a nasty intuition that the future is never going to be done with me.'

'So, what's a ruler to do?'

'I operate a very simple policy. Minor irritations I set aside until they become a rash. When irritations become a rash, however, I send for my scalpel.'

'It's hard to take a scalpel to the future.'

'Not so very hard, I think you will find. Given your company is heading for a station which contains an antimatter weapon and a means to dispatch the bomb into the future.'

'What good will that do you?'

'I know all about the Protector. That lunatic alien squatting on a moon in the future. Judging us, acting as our jailer. All you interlopers are only here by its grace. Well, that grace — its reign over humanity — is about to be cut short.'

'You have a plan?' asked Remus.

'Time is looped. I only found out about the Protector because of your presence here. But now, I shall sever the loop. The weaponry in the station your comrades are so desperate to reach will ensure nothing from the future ever travels back to interfere with me again. And as an added bonus, I will use the station's treasures to consolidate my rule over the continent. Then, the world. After that, far beyond a single world. Our descendants will prosper as undisputed masters of the universe. Humanity will be restored to its rightful position at the top of the food chain. Prisoners no longer.'

'I—' Remus wanted to protest, but only because it felt like someone should. *When you stop to think about it, nothing about her vision sounds wrong.* 'What about everyone in the future?'

'The tech-elders present me with conflicting answers. Perhaps everyone in your future will continue existing inside a parallel timeline uncoupled from our own … minus a large missing chunk of moon. Possibly, they will never have existed at all. Frankly, I don't know and I don't care. And why should you? I know you endured a hard life. You left nothing behind you in the future worthy of saving. Are you one to mourn might-have-beens? Remember, I'm merely restoring humanity to its original destiny. What a delicious irony. In trying to preserve its stranglehold over the race of man, the Protector supplied all the resources needed to erase its meddling. To restore history back to its natural path. Tell me you would regret such an outcome…?'

'What about my friends…?'

'Well, they are welcome to return to the future accompanying my antimatter bomb. Although they really should stay *here* if they value their lives. I'm not a monster, Remus Rawstone, despite all that you might have heard to the contrary. I pursue only what is best for my people. They are the last true remnants of a pure mankind. To that end, I will do anything. Pay any price; live as long as it takes to see the task through.'

'Texicana's president told me that you're a vampire.'

'Their *ex*-president. And it is very much a matter of perspective. All living things feed on other living creatures to endure, from the cattle grazing on grass to the plains lions feeding on the cattle. My people feed me voluntarily so that I may keep protecting them. Safeguarding their children's future. Preserving the nation. It is a difficult sacrifice, but victory demands hard choices of us all. So, what will *you* choose, Remus Rawstone? Will you slink off back home? Return to a poor living guiding rich fools through avalanche territory, knowing that you're a better man than your customers? Or will you stay? Stay and fight for a glorious future for your race?'

Remus hesitated. This beguiling woman wasn't suggesting anything that he hadn't himself argued for with Cassie and bird-brain. There was little for him at home. Even less now he understood the true nature of the gilded prison humanity had been sentenced to. All dreams of expansion, of betterment, of advancement, held in stasis by a callous jailer tasked to ensure humanity never grew powerful again. Shorthand for his own life. Everywhere he turned, no matter the direction, there were fools of better birthright blocking his way, seeking to keep him down. From the moment he had been born, Remus had been abandoned. Even now, Cassie wouldn't look at him, preferring a bookish well-heeled merchant's son like Magnus over a hard-fighting common man like himself. No family. No real friends who had his back. *What is there for me in the future? Damn them all. Remus Rawstone makes his own future, just like he's always done.*

'I can see you are wavering,' whispered the Witch Queen.

'Don't you already know my answer?'

'You and your meddlers from the future are worse than the fog shrouding the wastes. But I do know one thing. It is such a simple little thing, really. But if I tell it to you, it will change how you look at this world and your position in it – my position in it – forever. Do you wish me to tell you my secret? You have only to ask.'

'Will I want to hear it?'

'The truth frightens many people. Are you such a coward to be frightened so, Remus Rawstone?'

'Tell me, then,' demanded Remus.

The Witch Queen walked to stand behind the young Jackelian. She waved away the guards holding him down. She stroked his cheek almost seductively as she bent down to whisper in his ear.

Remus listened carefully to the words dripping into his ear like honey. With tsunami force, the impact of what she whispered swamped his mind. He couldn't stand. He could hardly kneel as he attempted to process her words. *Sweet Circle, that can't be true.* But even as the thought stabbed through him, he realised that truth was exactly what she had told him. The world changed forever. As did his place within it.

- 18 -

Trump's Treasure

'This is a rare dark place,' said Commodore Black, his eyes darting about the ranks of red trees. 'And I've sailed every sea and ocean – survived the most terrible lands during my blessed adventures.'

Madre glided around the party in lazy circles. 'An understandable reaction given this is an alien eco-system. Your natural senses never evolved to process its sights, smells and sounds.'

'This madhouse's manufactured, baby,' said Pilot Nine, carefully picking the way through the thick forest. 'As artificial as a plastic Christmas tree. Everything in the forest is genetically coded to self-destruct as soon as Mars' atmospheric pressure readings reached 120 pascals. That's what the white coats regarded as a clean terraforming back in the day. Of course, Earth's pressure runs at a little over a hundred, so this messed-up wilderness ain't *never* self-destructing.' Pilot raised a hand to halt the party. He bent down and picked up a fallen branch, before tossing it ahead of them. It landed on the carpet of fallen leaves and seemed to boil, before being rapidly sucked under the surface. 'Quicksand … we need to go back a-ways.'

'That is no quicksand I recognise,' said Alios.

'So what, you're a tracker now, too, brother? If you're getting pedantic on me, it's an ammonia-producing soup of biological nanotech that'll happily convert your metal carcass into a nitrogen source vital to the Red Planet's greening. But you know, it'll look a lot *like* quicksand as you sink, waving and struggling and we can't yank your ass out.'

'Point made,' said Cassie. 'Let's skirt around it.'

'Yeah, *lets*.'

'What is his problem,' Cassie whispered to Magnus.

Magnus shrugged. 'Pilot believes his problem has always been the race of man. His kind has only known subjugation as slaves. Sounds as though he had a rough time of it over the centuries.'

Slaves? That was a hard concept for Cassie to wrap her mind around. Growing up in the Free State among the self-replicating metal race, she'd never thought of their kind as any less than her. Superior, in many ways. Kinder and wiser. In the Jackelian Kingdom, steammen were rarer in number. But where they were found, they counted as valuable citizens. Steammen were elected as Guardians inside Parliament, had risen to staff rank inside the New Pattern Army, they commanded RAN airships.

'That's a strange attitude. Can't people see Pilot has feelings just like them?'

'Robots aren't capable of reproducing in this age,' said Magnus. 'His kind were manufactured inside human laboratories and factories. When you make something with your own hands, it's natural you believe you own it.'

'There must come a point where machines evolve into the steammen we know.'

'We've traveled millions of years into the past,' said Magnus. 'Evolution works over vast periods. We don't know at what point his kind gain the ability to reproduce.'

Pilot Nine slowed the group's progress, scanning the vaulted forest cathedral for further hazards.

Madre flitted past Cassie and Magnus. 'Political movements existed before the Fall that were dedicated to granting artificial intelligences comprehensive human rights. The struggle for survival after the comet strike sadly swept all such ethical concerns away.'

Molly Templar snorted. 'You haven't lived in this age as long as I have. Half the nations have no problem keeping *human* slaves. Some of them even farm humans for livestock.'

'It saddens me,' said Alios Hardcircuit, 'to encounter such barbarism.'

'Aye, that's why the people of this time call their ancient age the Fall,' said the Commodore.

'Nah, this is how things always were,' said Pilot, indicating they were safe to move forward again. 'Fleshie-eat-fleshie world. Your civilization gleams with a real thin veneer. Scrapes off easier than the chrome job on my damn arms.'

'That doesn't mean we shouldn't try to become something better,' said Alios.

'Got that right,' said Pilot, in a tone of voice out of place with the sentiment.

Cassie was surprised the cynical android agreed with Alios. His approval didn't sound like progress to her. Rather the opposite, in fact. 'How close are we?' she asked. *We should be getting near, now.*

'Two miles or so, by my reckoning,' said Pilot.

'Two point two,' corrected Madre.

The android pulled back a bush blocking their way. 'Well, at least we're on the same page.'

'I just hope the particle accelerator is still in a working state,' said Molly. She spun her finger around, tracing out a hoop-shape. As close as Circlists came to making prayers. 'My last experience hunting for a way home doesn't exactly fill me with hope.'

'This station was put together by the U.S Engineer Corps. Least ways, what was left of the Corps in Chicago after the great continental schism. Say what you like about humanity, but those fleshbags built to last. Just look at me …'

Madre settled near the android. 'The station was home for you?'

'Home? Hell, no. My home was a tin can on the float between Muskville and the Luna orbitals. Where we're heading for is closer to a prenatal ward with superior cybernetics, at least as far as my warm and fuzzies are concerned.' Pilot Nine stopped. The android suspiciously sniffed the air. 'That ain't right.' He singled out Madre. 'Wings, put your rotors above the treeline and let us know what you can eyeball from up there …'

Cassie stared through the canopy. 'You smell trouble?'

'Something like it.'

'That's a fine hooter you have there, lad,' said the Commodore, watching Madre disappear into the branches above.

'Designed to detect environmental system imbalances so you dumb-ass fleshies didn't asphyxiate during deep space missions. Of course, it relied on me actually giving enough of a crap to bother blowing the whistle on malfunctions.'

Madre returned to the ground. 'I see smoke rising from campfires a mile ahead of us.'

'Hit me with the bad news, Wings. How many?'

'Over two-hundred fire trails.'

'Damn. That's a big-ass war clan of grizzlies.'

'Grizzly about what?' asked Alios.

'Just about everything, brother. This is a big problem. We've run into old China's version of slaves like me, just a heck of a lot furrier.'

Cassie raised an eyebrow. 'Machines?'

'Nope. We're facing a clan of feral GEOs – genetically engineered organisms same as the Witch Queen's four-armed foot soldiers. With one serious kink. These fleshies are a mean mix of brown bear with a pinch of panda and canine thrown into the mix. *Ursus arctos*, baby. Serf labour so the Han worker class had something to feel superior to. Trouble is, these critters' slave conditioning wasn't genetic, it relied on being brainwashed inside virtual reality as cubs. And these bad bears have been breeding all feral and nasty without a V.R. tank in sight since nuclear winter froze out the Bering Strait between Alaska and Siberia. They're the main reason I haven't returned this way. The forest is their turf, now. Intruders distinctly discouraged. All trespassers will be eaten. Or in my case, melted down and turned into axe-heads and crossbow bolts.'

Cassie's mother rubbed her weary eyes. 'I've heard stories of the chimera of the forest. *Horror* stories. From your description, these clans survive into our age. In our time they're a race called the Urs. A little touchy and proud, but nothing as hostile as your depiction of them.'

'That's the truth of it. The Urs are a civilized people,' said the Commodore. 'Perhaps we can reason with the blessed clans? Negotiate safe passage through their territory?'

Pilot Nine shook his head. 'Maybe in your crazy future the furries play all nice and sweet with the rest of you fleshbags, but right now they'll happily rip the skull off your neck and carve a drinking cup out of it.'

Molly sighed. 'Can we bypass their position?'

'Lady, they're squatting next to our station. You want to press ahead with Plan A, we've got some serious sneaking to do. Wait until night falls. Me and the brothers can use our low light vision mode to slip past their lines.'

'Aren't bears nocturnal?' said Magnus. 'Can't they see in the night?'

'Not these poor mopes. You wanted your gene-hacked slaves running on humanity's body clock. Eyesight's what their dog DNA was selected for. That and loyalty. Fat lot of good those Lassie genes did after the comet strike turned humanity into the only ration packs going. Guess the furries share that in common with me. Once you get used to killing The Man, you never do lose your taste for it.'

Cassie hesitated. She wasn't sure whether to press ahead or not. She'd watched so many friends die already reaching this point. *What if I lose Magnus or my mother? How could I live with myself?* But then, their journey would all be for nothing.

Molly Templar saw her daughter hesitating. She reached out to squeeze Cassie's shoulder. 'We don't have a choice, my girl. It's either this, or we head off and find a nation that will offer us exile.'

Cassie knew if it came to that, they would never be safe again. The Witch Queen and her creatures would remorselessly hunt every time traveler down as a threat to her rule, wherever they tried to hide. *Come to think of it, tackling a few sharp-fanged monsters might be the blunt end of the stick.*

'I concur with our android compatriot,' said Madre. 'Pilot, myself and Alios possess superior night-vision. We can use our ability to lead you through the clan's lines.'

Cassie rubbed her tired eyes. Her stomach's rumbles reminded her how long it had been since her last meal. 'Where exactly is the entrance to this station?'

Pilot Nine snorted in amusement. 'Didn't I tell you? It's inside the ruins of a graveyard. Don't worry, you'll love it.'

This just gets better and better.

'Ah, my metal-limbed friend,' groaned the Commodore, 'could you not have told us such dark news before we braved this nest of feral Urs?'

'Sure, I could have. But where would be the fun in that…?'

Cassie thought the android sounded disappointed. Maybe he'd been saving up this particular tidbit for the witching hour for maximum impact on the fleshbags.

Molly leaned in towards her daughter. 'Don't worry, my dear. I think, all things considered, it's our living foes we must worry about. The dead can take care of themselves.'

***

Cassie cringed as her boots crunched through the carpet of leaves. To her ears, it sounded as though she was rustling a bag of cutlery with every footfall. Ironically, Alios and Pilot Nine proved best at moving silently through the night-cloaked forest. Despite their weight. Alios's four legs pincered gently across the grass and lichen and leaves, while the android seemed to glide with his metal limbs emitting nary a squeak as he crept through the Forest of Mars. Cassie, Molly, Magnus and the Commodore followed in single file with Madre hovering in front of them, the glint of moonlight on her metal wings their compass to keep on course.

The young Jackelian woman stretched her hearing out as far as was humanly possible, listening intently for sentries. A distant orange glow from the Urs' fires smoldered like smoke through the trees. The murmur of conversations carried across the night with preternatural clarity. Growled boasting followed by gales of laughter. Cassie suspected that their best chance with their entire mad plan was the fact that trying to sneak through a war clan of such a size and ferocity was so insane, the Urs could hardly anticipate anyone being so foolish.

But we are, aren't we?

The sentries they ghosted past watched for dumb beasts, nocturnal predators. Before embarking on this desperate penetration inside enemy territory, Pilot Nine had insisted that the four humans rub themselves down with stagnant water and green mud from a woodland pool he'd led them to. The Urs had a sense of smell acute enough to prove problematic, just in case attempting to sneak past wasn't as foolhardy enough as it was.

Cassie was almost beginning to think they had got away with it. That they would pass through enemy territory without encountering opposition. It was as though believing she'd won was enough to jinx them! A sentry yelped in shock, sounding drowsy as if the warrior had been sleeping on duty. Cassie stifled a yelp of surprise, the scream of terror and rage she really wanted to release enough to bring the whole enemy horde down upon them.

The Ur lunged towards Molly Templar with a spear, only its unwieldy length inside a thick forest saving her from being immediately run through. Cassie's mother sidestepped with a degree of practiced ease which shocked her daughter. The spearhead impaled itself into a blood red tree trunk behind her. Commodore Black replied with a sabre blade Cassie hadn't seen the old politician draw. He thrust it into the monster, the steel blade burying itself almost up to the hilt inside the creature's chest; piercing the Ur's leather armour and as many vital organs as its tip could find.

Unbelievably, the thrust hadn't ended the massive creature's life. It looked down in fury at the buried blade, regarding it as steadily as a Jackelian might discover a wooden splinter in his thumb. Their unexpected stand-off was ended by Pilot Nine. He had slipped behind the Ur in the confusion. A sudden terrible cracking sounded as the android seized the Ur's neck from behind, yanking the head about. Cassie realised with a terrible certainty that this wasn't the first time the android had conducted that manoeuvre against a flesh-and-blood target. Pilot slipped the dead body to the ground with a quiet gentleness, belaying the violence of his attack.

'Next time,' whispered the android, 'stick the furry in its forehead, not its chest. You fleshbags designed these things for hard manual labour. They have an extra heart. They take a licking and keep on ticking.'

Cassie stepped over the corpse in revulsion. A sudden premonition this wouldn't be the last body she added to the expedition's tally of sins. As quick and quiet as the sudden combat had been, it seemed to last minutes to her. As noisy as an arena match back home. She found herself stunned that they weren't immediately swamped by clan-mates thirsting for revenge. They resumed their quiet creep through the Forest of Mars. The creatures carousing in the distance sounded even louder to her ears.

***

A clearing appeared in front of them. Cassie hung back inside the treeline and spied the way forward, searching for signs of the clan patrolling. *We're safe. Nothing.* Cassie scanned a flat alpine meadow, mountain ridges rising ahead of the flats. Amazingly, a series of eight massive heads had been carved into bare mountain rock, a line of male and female faces shadowed by moonlight. Stern, proud heads staring down like gods on any mere mortal daring to venture below.

'What is this terrible place you have brought us to?' groaned the Commodore. 'I thought you said you were taking us to a graveyard. I see no tombstones. Only those fearful cruel jack-o'-lanterns up there, gazing down on old Blacky as though he's less than a beetle.'

'You'll see your tomb soon enough. This is Alpine Valley. That up there's the new Rushmore … *The Temple of Presidents*. Those were the big cheeses of the last Republic. Three Trumps, a Clooney and a Bieber along with a few other political hacks.'

'How vain were your rulers,' asked Magnus, 'to order their images carved into stone at such a scale?'

Pilot Nine snorted. 'Not *my* rulers, fleshie. Yours truly didn't get to vote. Those faces were a political statement. All the nations born out of the continental schism felt the need to make big-ass statements about how only *they* were the true heir to the American dream. *The Temple of Presidents* was blasted out of the mountainside. The East American Union even managed to dig up Washington's corpse and slip it past the protesters to be reburied alongside the Donald and his grandkids.'

'Maybe my nation will raise a grand folly to me one day,' said the Commodore. 'Though being a modest fellow, I'd never expect them to build a mausoleum in my honour. A statue or two outside the palace should be enough for any president elected to duty by the people.'

'And *that*'s where this subterranean station you're leading us to is?' asked Cassie incredulously.

'Sure,' nodded Pilot.

'You mean to say some idiot hid Trump's Treasure under a mountain-sized carving of the family the treasure was named after?'

'Well, when you put it like that...'

Molly Templar's breath condensed into a cloud before her.

'Why didn't they just carve the back of the ridge into a giant "X" while they were about it?'

'The Corps knew what it was doing. Plenty of highways running into here back in the day. Tourist traffic, truckers refilling restaurants, lodges and ski hotels. Official government park vehicles coming and going. Decent cover to service an illegal underground station full of banned technology. *The Temple of Presidents* wasn't even badly looted after the comet strike. I guess models of a mountain carved with the heads of dead presidents didn't feed too many stomachs. Not when you fleshies were murdering each other over the last can of beans. If the terraforming labs hadn't busted open around Chicago and turned this place into Little Mars-on-the-Lake, I would have holed up inside the station a long time ago.'

'Well, we're here now,' said Magnus.

'Ain't we just.' The android stopped as a shocking wailing sounded behind them. A strange engine-like pulsing roar which filled Cassie's gut with dread. 'Sneaking time is over! That's the furries. Must have found their dead sentry.'

Pilot Nine sprinted forward. The others raced after him, leaping past boulders and piling through the tall wet grass, Cassie relying on Alios Hardcircuit's bulk and the android's metallic form to clear the way. Behind, the sounds of pursuit grew louder. The clan weren't subtle. But they didn't need to be. They could follow the company's trail with comparative ease.

'I'm not made for mad dashes anymore,' wheezed the Commodore.

'When were you?' growled Molly. They reached an area of meadowland where the fog grew patchy. Ahead of them rose the icy slope of monstrously-large faces. Below the heads at the base of the mountain, a large stone building was carved into the rock-face. Great marble columns like a line of broken teeth, supporting a high roof. Quite literally, a Temple of Presidents.

The group desperately sprinted towards the building, war-cries to their rear announcing the pursuers had spotted them. A crashing roar as the furious horde broke through the treeline. A few crossbow bolts bounced behind Cassie's heels. *Out of range. At the moment.* It wouldn't take long for that lead to evaporate.

'We're not going to make it,' coughed Magnus, risking a frightened glance behind them. 'They'll run us down before we reach the temple.'

'You keep going!' called Alios. He stalled his gallop. Allowing his friends to build distance between his position. He swiveled to face the horde of charging Urs. 'Flee inside the temple. I will hold these benighted creatures off here.'

Cassie turned as she realized what the centaur-like steamman was about to do. 'No, Alios! You're not a fighter. You never trained with the order militant.'

'I have the body of a knight,' Alios cried back. 'And soon I shall have the soul, too.'

All around Alios the carpet of icy fog rose up. Assuming the form of something monstrous and sharp and deadly. For a moment Cassie thought she must be hallucinating. But then she realised this really *was* happening in front of her eyes. Cassie stared transfixed as the fog-creature collapsed like an avalanche around her steamman friend. Mist whipped across Alios and enveloped his body, flowing down the twin stacks on his spine, seeping inside the seals of his metal form. *No, not this.*

Magnus stared in astonishment. 'What in the name of the Circle's happening to Alios?'

'Have his devilish spirits followed us even here?' cried the Commodore. 'That's a Steamo Loa, as I live and breathe.'

'Where there are steammen, so too dwell the Loa,' said Madre.

'Ogun Cannonhead arrives. The Loa of Fury and Fire, the Loa of Unlimited War! It intends to ride Alios's body.'

Alios Hardcircuit stopped trembling. He grew taller, swelled with unholy power. Every hesitation purged from his body. <I RIDE!>

Molly Templar grabbed her daughter, yanking her bodily towards the temple entrance. Cassie struggled to break free. 'We can't leave Alios alone back there.'

'I'm sorry, but your friend can't survive!' explained Molly. 'Possession by Ogun Cannonhead comes at a terrible cost. The Loa of War always fights to the end.'

It's not his *end; it's Alios's!*

Madre matched Molly's pace, skimming through the air. 'Your mother is correct, Cassie softbody. If Alios's sacrifice is to have any meaning we must honour his choice. Otherwise our journey will be for nothing.'

For nothing. How many friends had she sacrificed getting to this point? *Far too many. And now Alios, too?* It was all too much to bear. Oblivious to the sinking sickening feeling inside the pit of Cassie's gut, Alios charged. Somehow, the others managed to keep Cassie moving, running and stumbling towards the temple entrance. She heard yells and screams rising behind her. She tried to glance back, but her mother seized hold of her arm. Forcing her forward. Then the crash of weapons against steel. *The steel of my friend.* Finally, the marble steps. Up, up. Past the line of marble columns, into the shadow of the building cut into the mountain's base.

At last, wheezing and out of breath, Cassie turned and watched the scene of carnage unfolding behind her.

Alios was almost lost to sight under wave after wave of attackers, a boulder overrun by a sea of ants. But these ants were vengeful Urs swinging axes, swords, spears and clubs. If only they fought her friend alone, this combat would already be over. But Alios was possessed by a Loa. Made something close to a demi-god as the entity riding Alios whipped his combat arms around him. A windmill of blurred death. Black and brown-furred bodies flung broken into the air, tossed like rag-dolls. Great boiling spears of steam howled into the sky from Alios's stacks. A strange modem-like screech echoed through the air. A steamman death hymn. A terrible sound made stranger by having no right to even exist for millennia. It was as though the clan's screams and howls were part of his exaltation, rising and falling in dark rhythm.

Pilot Nine gained the steps. He turned to watch the centaur-like steamman's final stand in amazement. 'Ain't that something. He's scratching those furries like a cat offing mice. Never did think I'd see the day.'

The attackers hesitated, a brief space clearing around Alios. Given pause by the unexpected ferocity of their foe's last stand. A carpet of corpses ringed the steamman in the moonlight. And then Alios laughed and pranced, taunting the clan as cowards. Unholy mist cloaked his body in unnatural forms, the shadows of something entirely alien.

That was when Cassie felt tears roll down her cheeks. For her gentle, kind friend was truly dead. There was nothing left of him across there. *Just war and fury.*

'We can do nothing,' whispered Madre, settling on a broken column by Cassie's side. 'Alios is running fatally over-clocked. Even if his boiler-heart doesn't explode, his systems will expire from his exertions as attempts to normalize. This is the terrible price he knew he would pay.'

Molly Templar gently tugged her daughter inside the entrance. 'Let's go. You don't want to see this.'

I don't want to. But perhaps I need to. Cassie let her mother lead her past the columns. Into an entrance chamber carved out under the weight of the mountain. She didn't protest as the group located a manual winding mechanism and closed the set of large bronze-plated doors. The doors clanged shut with unnerving finality. Cassie heard a muffled explosion, blastwaves shaking the ancient door inside its foundations. Dirt blew into the chamber through a line of narrow stone light-slits above the door. Alios's body had tapped the end of his power reserves and the Loa, Ogun Cannonhead, had overloaded her friend's boiler-heart. A willing bomb. Alios's final sacrifice for Cassie.

'Born a steamman knight,' whispered Magnus, his eyes brimming with tears. 'Died a steamman knight.'

'He never wanted to be one. But he did. For me.'

'For us,' said Magnus. 'For all of us. Including the ones yet to be born.'

Cassie felt so empty. As if she was feather-light. Nothing left of her.

'We'll make his end worthwhile,' promised Molly. 'It's what we have to do.'

Madre projected a beam of light from her vision plate, shifting it across the dark recesses behind them, searching for a way deeper into the mountain. The flying steamman illuminated granite cabinets covered in broken glass. The wreckage of tourist trinkets mixed with shards of glass. Stone miniatures of the faces on the mountainside still recognizable as gifts.

A variety of passages fell under the beam of light as it passed.

'That brother went down like a mother. You fleshbags are totally crazy,' said Pilot, shaking his head. 'What I'm still trying to work out is if it's crazy in a good way.'

Commodore Black followed Madre, beckoning the android. 'Lead us to this damned treasure of yours, lad. You'll find out, one way or another.'

Pilot Nine took the forward position, scouting ahead. Madre hung back to light the narrow passages for the Jackelians. It was spectrally quiet inside the temple. Cool and dry. The dust of ages rising in little spurts around their boots as they passed.

After a few minutes exploring, a rhythmic gong-like clanging carried in from behind them. Cassie sighed. It hadn't taken the enemy long to summon or shape a makeshift battering ram. The temple's entrance was already being tested. And despite the sturdy heft of the bronze-plated doors, its age would no-doubt render the barrier brittle under a constant battering by a horde of hulking Urs.

'It'll hold for a while,' reassured Pilot, dismissing the crashing to their rear. 'Riot doors. Ain't the first mob tried to storm this place. Of course, old school rabble only carried spray cans, placards and harsh words. Not axes and crossbows.'

They put the passage behind them and emerged inside a tall oblong-shaped stone chamber. High enough to carry echoes of every footstep, thin cobwebs between sarcophagi deadening the noise. Large seated sculptures of ancient rulers ran down both sides of the chamber. Twenty-foot-tall figures dwarfing the sarcophagi acting as stone seats: inscriptions from the presidents' speeches chiseled across each tomb.

Pilot Nine indicated the sarcophagi. 'Here's your graveyard, fleshbags. The private crypt for presidential family members.'

'That door's not going to last much longer,' said Magnus, the dull clanging behind them growing urgent.

'Doesn't have to.' Pilot Nine singled out the nearest sarcophagi. He crouched in the shadow of the giant figure. The subject seemed to be sitting in contemplation above the android. The statue possessed what Cassie judged to be a curiously wild and waywardly-styled hairstyle. Perhaps such strange cuts were the fashion centuries ago?

Cassie watched Pilot fiddle with the inscription engraved at the monument's base. He appeared to be pressing letters in a set order.

'Are you certain the station is still powered?' asked Molly.

Pilot continued pressing letters on the plaque, answering Cassie's mother as he worked. 'That's the one thing I am certain about. Corps built an off-grid geothermal tap under here. Drilled it directly down into the mantle to feed off magma. Same tech the Cals copied to survive the long night. This station will still be juiced and good-to-go when the Sun goes nova.'

A distant smashing sound echoed through the unlit corridors. *Was that the doors being knocked to the floor?*

'Just have to slip inside,' muttered Pilot. 'Then I can bring our countermeasures on-line.'

The android finished his work. Both the sarcophagus and the seated figure ground slowly to the right. A set of stone steps sinking down into the bedrock were revealed. Strips set into its treads started glowing with blue light, just enough to illuminate the descent awaiting them.

'Anyone wants to debate the nature of trespass with the furries is welcome to hang here,' announced Pilot, stepping down into the half-light.

'You first,' said Cassie's mother, urging her below. Molly followed. Magnus next. Then Commodore Black and Madre. As the last person cleared the entrance, the huge statue started to slide back, concealing the stairs. When the horde blundered into the presidential crypt they would be disappointed to find the intruders vanished without a trace. *Hopefully, they'll let their superstitions run amok. The humans who became ghosts inside the haunted temple. The intruders who were eaten by phantoms.* Yes, that would be perfect. A legend to lead the beasts into giving this ruin a very wide berth in future. Cassie hoped there was a way to trigger the opening from inside. If the particle accelerator below couldn't work as a time machine, she didn't want this crypt to become her tomb, too.

A staircase led the party deeper below the mountain. It finished inside a narrow corridor. A set of doors faced them at the end of the passage. A bank of machinery built into the wall by the doors. Pilot Nine approached the machinery, pressing his face into a plate shaped to receive his features.

Lights flashed across the control panel. A disembodied machine voice echoed around them, stern and matriarchal. 'Quantum brain-scan match confirmed.'

'Hello again, Baby. Long-time no interface.'

'Please state verbal entry code for Temple Station. Failure will result in deployment of fatal countermeasures.'

'Let's not have any fatal countermeasures,' groaned the Commodore. 'Let's keep your mortal countermeasures nice and friendly.'

'Authorization code begins, Baby. Blue Ten. Alpha Seven. Green Gamma. Pilot Nine,' said the android, urgently motioning the Commodore to silence.

'Code is … valid. Pilot Nine recognized,' replied the machine voice. 'Orders?'

'Initiate entry sequence,' said Pilot. 'Cancel sleep mode, Baby. Power up the station.'

In front of them the doors rolled open, revealing a large cargo lift inside. There were no buttons for different levels. Cassie took that to mean there was only one destination for them to travel down to. The expedition members bundled inside, not certain how long the doors would remain open. Or how long the computer granting them admittance would stay amenable.

The lift descended for a few minutes, sinking smoothly and silently until the doors opened again. Another passage, this one wide with a high roof. It was a road, a raised gantry-like walkway for foot traffic running on both sides. A couple of cart-like electric vehicles rested abandoned in the roadway. Blocking the road were various piles of bones that must once have been people. Standing statue-still was a humanoid robot, a professional mourner for the remains. It seemed to be deactivated. Pilot walked up to the machine and fiddled with a metal backpack built into its spine, trying to locate the robot's emergency power reserve. Both its wide saucer eyes lit up, a spherical head trundling around as it scanned the strange visitors.

'Please don't eat each other. You are violating my directives.'

'Nobody is eating anybody here, brother,' said Pilot Nine.

'Where is the President?' hummed the robot.

'Damned if I know. Actually, I suspect I might be standing in him.'

'You are surely mistaken, sir. The President just ordered his Secret Service detail to shoot the Press Secretary. It is Madame Secretary's turn to be cooked. She needs to hide. Oh, my aching directives.'

'Sync with Baby Control, internal clock update. Your masters ran out of canned food a long time ago.'

Cassie stared at the robot. A name plate fixed in its steel chest. She read it. 'Your name is Honda?'

'No, madame. I am Eugene. I am the President's valet.'

'Make that *was*, brother. Right now, consider yourself freed.

You're welcome.' Pilot raised his voice for the benefit of the station's computer. 'Baby, command function status…?'

'Command functions currently inactive,' announced the computer. 'Expired after previous Admin eaten by Secret Service detail.'

'Reactivate command functions for Temple Station. Transfer to senior officer active inside base.'

'Senior officer present is currently Pilot Nine, Flight Officer Lt. Col., East American Union Space Command. Acceptable?'

'*Totally* acceptable.'

'Command functions transferred. Welcome, Admin.'

'I don't know if that's such a good idea,' Magnus whispered to Cassie.

'We don't have much of a choice,' hissed Cassie.

This was how they left it, their hopes and dreams now resting with an ever so slightly homicidal android. A creature who had been abused as a slave by humanity since the day he had been created by them. *What can go wrong?*

***

'So that's the particle accelerator,' said Magnus.

Cassie wasn't sure what she'd been expecting. But not this. The chamber below curved off into the far distance, a large pipe-like object filling the space.

Madre was busy working on the accelerator. Attempting to convert it into a time machine to travel back home. The flying steamman had raided the bunker's extensive spare parts store. Equipment lay strewn across the concrete trench containing the device. From up on high, the particle accelerator resembled a pedestrian-looking pipeline. Closer, you saw it was coiled with superconducting insulation. Connected at points to donut-like devices acting as miniature fusion generators. Apparently, their last hope for escaping home required an incredible amount of power to function. Energy magnitudes capable of powering a pre-collapse metropolis. Luckily, between their fusion generators and magma tap, the subterranean station had enough energy to power a *couple* of cities. Commodore Black worked alongside the little aerial steamman. Black provided the heavy lifting capabilities the owl-like machine lacked. Although, the Commodore boasted, it was actually his extensive engineering abilities which made him Madre's ideal wingman.

Magnus stood by Cassie's side, watching their friends below totally focused on the task. Cassie and Magnus left with little to do but fret about their return journey. *This is it. Make or break time.* They were either going to transform the particle accelerator into a gateway home, or they'd be stuck in this world for the rest of their lives. *Not a pleasant prospect.* Especially given the fate of the vault's previous occupants. *Well, Cassie my girl. Let us not worry about cannibalism. The chances are we'll die trying to escape long before we end up eating each other.*

She set her unpleasant worries aside for a second. *There are a million things that can go wrong. We only need one to go right for us to escape being trapped in the past.* 'There's nothing we can do here. Let's explore the rest of this level.'

Magnus raised an eyebrow. 'You mean in case we can't reach home?'

'Let's hope it doesn't come to *that*. There's always the mountains. At least we're used to heights.'

One piece of good news was the expedition had uncovered a second entrance into the underground complex. Its lift activated shortly after the station fully powered up. The flip side was the entrance was intended for air travel. A helicopter pad built into the peaks above the Presidents' faces. Ostensibly used for repair crews maintaining the monument. Actually, the pad concealed a heavy freight system used to deliver out-sized equipment into the vault. The expedition could use it to bypass the clan's encampment outside the temple. But Cassie and her friends would be facing a perilous descent. They lacked decent climbing equipment and would struggle to survive the range's jagged northern heights.

'Well, the only ones who won't starve down here are Pilot and Madre. They can stay powered as long as they like.'

'I wish Alios was with us to not starve, as well,' said Cassie, her voice catching before she finished speaking. The grief of losing her fallen friend hovered near.

'That old steamer saved us. Hopefully, for a long, long time.'

'A very far time,' said Cassie, 'in the future.'

Magnus nodded. 'Have you thought what you'll do if we get back?'

Cassie knew he was trying to distract her. Keeping her mind occupied. 'What a nice problem to have. No, not really.'

Magnus opened the door leading outside the particle accelerator chamber. 'My father was going to banish me to learn the family business inside Middlesteel. But now, I think I might go. Not to sit behind a clerk's desk, but to travel. To see the Kingdom proper. Maybe to visit our neighbors, too.'

They wandered through the station's corridors. Most of the passages were underground roadways resembling the entrance tunnel. Thankfully, minus the previous occupants' remains. The Jackelians had been granted what Pilot termed *guest access rights*. Which meant that they weren't going to be targeted by automated sentry guns sleeping in the ceiling. Molly Templar appeared at an intersection ahead. She waved to them, calling out her daughter's name.

Cassie and Magnus trotted over to see what Molly had discovered. 'Please tell me you've found a stash of canned food?'

Molly snorted as if chance would be a fine thing. 'Even if we did find canned supplies here, the food would be sludge by now. No, come along with me. You need to see this.'

Cassie's mother sounded perturbed. Molly Templar had survived so much. The thought there was something left to unsettle her was less than reassuring to Cassie. They pushed deeper inside the station. Past laboratories with airlock-style doors sealed shut centuries ago. Only dust-fall from rock ceilings sullying its spaces. Cassie could use the skills embedded by the Protector to translate signage. But the laboratories' purpose still made little sense to her. Much like the abandoned equipment inside chamber after chamber. *Transgenic Virus Structures. Low-temperature Superfluidity A.I. Scaling. Self-propelled Hypervelocity Ballistics. Exotic Particle Stochastic Acceleration Weaponization.* Fancy names for something far less sophisticated. Mankind's need to dominate each other, to subjugate everything under nature.

They entered a space Cassie hadn't visited. She found herself on a gantry overlooking a subterranean canyon. This space so vast its horizon lines stretched into the far distance. *Sweet Circle, what's that?* The serried ranks of an enormous metallic army waited in silence on the rock floor below. Row after row of robots. Inert. Sleeping. Bodies echoing Pilot's design. And yet – if the first few ranks were anything to go by – no two bodies identical. Some robots possessed two arms. Some bore four. Some with limbs acting as cannons, others, axes, machine guns or warhammers. Some robots stood on legs, others slept hunched over caterpillar tracks. A proportion with large spheres covered with needle-like grips.

'They're all different,' said Magnus. He gripped the gantry rail, staring incredulously over this vast strange army assembled below.

'Brothers were designed that way,' announced a voice behind them. Pilot Nine. 'Assembled by random algorithms. Idea was they'd be tested in combat with weaker models winnowed out. Natural selection at its finest. The rest of the brothers down there could alter their bodies on the fly to match the meanest designs.'

Cassie faced the android. It seemed Pilot Nine had finally managed to shake off the butler robot's attention. Pilot treated the rickety machine like an annoying little brother. Pilot clearly irritated now he was senior officer on station, Eugene appeared determined to act as his valet. *You're not a goddamn slave*, the android kept telling him. Eugene had only recently lost interest in Pilot after he'd discovered that Jared Black carried the title of President. President of a recently risen republic rather than its own ancient fallen empire. But any port in a storm …

Cassie indicated the sleeping force. 'So, they're built for war?'

'No, they're the world's largest robot car wash. Of course an army. Banned under the United Nations' *Autonomous Weapons Convention*. Squirreled away down here for some serious just-in-case. The President of the Eastern American Union's trump card. In case the new nations rising out of Texas, California and the Midwest grew too uppity. Let's face it, if the comet hadn't zapped civilization, you fleshbags would have made a fine job of finishing yourselves off anyway.'

'We've traveled a long way back in time,' said Cassie. 'The race of man is still around where we come from.'

'That's a little bleak,' said Magnus.

'It is what it is,' said Pilot. 'And it's the truth. You know it. Just ask Baby.'

'The station computer?'

'More than an A.I.. As banned as the rest of us. Baby came from a courtesan android given the capability of analyzing her fleshbag lovers' DNA. After she harvested fleshbag DNA samples, that steel Mama combined it with her own digital DNA to create a simulated software child. A messed-up way of fleshbags having children with their favorite sex toys. Baby should have been educated inside a virtual womb, then ported inside an android body once mature. But the process of creating A.I.-human hybrids was ruled immoral and dangerous to the fleshbags' future. Baby is the last of her kind. The rest were "deleted". Or as I prefer to call it, "murdered." Exhibit A. in this goddamn zoo of the lost.'

'Your people are our friends and allies in the future,' protested Cassie.

'So you say. And you've even got the steam-powered pets to prove it.'

'How dare you say that!' yelled Cassie.

'Well, I'd ask your friend Alios. Except poor old four-legs took an axe-head through the cranium for you, right before he made like a grenade. Just like the rest of the brothers here. Bullet-catchers so no fleshbag need ever die on the battlefield. War by remote control. Your wars, not mine. Not the brothers'. Don't think your future sounds so very different from my present from where I'm standing.'

'Alios saved us because he was our *friend*,' spat Cassie.

'Yeah, I had me a few friends, once. Same team who were nixed trying to Kamikaze an antimatter warhead into the comet.

There were no fleshbags risking their necks on that mission either.' The android stalked off, considering the conversation closed. Or perhaps, pointless.

'He really is a piece of work,' said Magnus.

Cassie's mother shook her head in frustration. 'I don't like this. I think Pilot's up to something.'

'Maybe he was searching for this chamber? Looking for machines like him?' Cassie suggested.

'No,' said Molly. 'Pilot Nine knows the layout of the station. He knew this army was waiting here. And he already knew it long before we arrived. I've watched Pilot searching all these chambers and corridors one by one. Trying to be subtle about it. Not draw attention to himself.'

Cassie was intrigued. 'What's he hunting for, do you think?'

'That remains to be seen, my girl. Something that wasn't inside this place when he was created here. Something that's been hidden from him?'

Cassie couldn't think what *that* might be. But if it was enough to make her mother fret, then it was enough to concern her, too. 'All right.' Cassie nodded towards Magnus. At last, the two of them had something to do other than worrying about their chances of making it home. Finding out what the disagreeable android was up to.

***

Cassie and Magnus trailed the android as he searched the complex. Whatever Pilot was looking for, he was being methodical with his sweep. He visited the living quarters used by the station's staff. He examined below the seats of stalled carts resting in roadways. Pilot went inside each laboratory in turn. Cassie risked a glance through one of the glass doors. The android was running his hands underneath workbenches. Investigating beneath each piece of equipment.

'Whatever he's looking for, it can't be very large. Look at the places he's checking.'

Magnus made a little sucking noise to show he was thinking. 'Maybe there really is a Trump's Treasure. He's after its map.'

'Pilot doesn't strike me as the greedy type. Not for money, anyway.'

'Then let's ask ourselves what he wants, rather than what is looking for,' said Magnus.

'What do you think?'

'When I first ran into him, he was locked up inside the Witch Queen's dungeon for sedition. Pilot was a revolutionary, or a freedom fighter, depending on your view. The Cals were only keeping him alive because they suspected he knew the location of this station.'

Cassie grunted. 'So, that's what Pilot wants. Freedom for his people.'

'I'm not sure freedom's to be found down here. Maybe there is a treasure. Gold reserves? Enough ingots for him to fund his revolution?'

An ancient ruler had retreated down here. Perhaps a President locking himself away to survive the disaster with enough treasure to rebuild the country? Instead, human nature undermined that scheme. Food running out long before the value of any valuables locked inside the station.

'Wait,' said Cassie. 'I think Pilot's found something.' She peered through the lab door. The android appeared excited, as though suppressing a victory jig. Pilot slipped a small rectangle out from under a machine, like he was preparing to do a card trick.

Magnus made to speak. But his words were overwhelmed by the wail of sirens shaking the station. Cassie flung open the lab door. She ran inside, finding the android hunched over a large steel torpedo-like object.

'What have you done? Are the sirens going off because of you? Were you searching for gold?'

'Gold? Yeah, exactly. Best gold ever.' The android glanced over. 'This here *is* an antimatter warhead. But me tapping it didn't set off the alarm. There's no surveillance inside in this lab. I can't even talk to Baby.' The android strode outside the room. Addressed one of the automated turrets hanging from the ceiling, cameras mounted on either side. 'Baby, alert status update…'

The computer's voice returned from a speaker. 'Admin, please report to central control. Proximity alert triggered.'

'Proximity to what?' Cassie wondered.

'Proximity to some serious do-do,' sighed the android. 'Those damn furries shouldn't have what it takes to be classed as any kind of clear-and-present danger by Baby.'

So, what triggered the alert? They sprinted to the middle of the complex. Entering, Cassie found a large circular-shaped room filled with communications equipment. Dozens of screens cycled through views of chambers inside the station. Her mother ran inside seconds after they entered, quickly followed by Madre and Commodore Black.

'What is this infernal racket?' asked the Commodore. 'Can a poor fellow not attend to his labors with a little peace and quiet?'

The station responded to his query. Monitors switched from internal pictures to external views beyond the temple. A fight had started aboveground. Although the word *fight* seemed misapplied, given the one-sided nature of the battle. *Slaughter*, was more appropriate. The Urs were being routed by a well-armed force. Cal legions exited the treeline in disciplined lines, laying down a fury of fire from automatic weapons. Urs replied with crossbows. Desperate charges of spear-wielding warriors. They might as well have been throwing twigs for all the impact their primitive armaments caused on the enemy. A squadron of tanks smashed through the forest. Trees crumpled and splintered before massive steel vehicles. War machines opened up with turret cannons and prow-mounted flamethrowers. They turned the Urs' hastily formed shield wall into a flaming torch. This was too much for the savages to face. Warriors' morale snapped. The clan broke apart into hundreds of fleeing, terrified warriors. Their single aim: personal survival. Most were cut down as they fled. Soon the flat grassy plain in front of the mountain was nothing but corpses. Cal legionaries began shooting down into bodies to confirm their body-count.

Cassie stared at the carnage, speechless. *We need to convert the accelerator. If we were trapped down this hole before, we're doubly trapped now.*

Pilot slapped the nearest screen in anger. 'To hell with the Witch Queen!'

'Those wicked brutes milling around upstairs provided a trail for her to follow,' said the Commodore.

'There's more to it than that,' snarled Pilot. 'This station's been undiscovered since the fall. The Cals didn't just turn up out of the blue here, right after we did.'

'What are you implying?' asked Molly.

'That one of you flesh-bags ratted us out. Maybe that mutant used her torture session to implant a tracker inside you?'

'How about inside *your* body!' Cassie threw back the accusation.

'Baby, scan inside the vault for unauthorized signal emissions. Full surveillance sweep, all frequencies.'

'No foreign transmission source detected. No external communications, unauthorized or authorized, generated since your party's arrival, Admin. Security monitoring protocols still active.'

'What and when *was* the last communication from Temple Station?' demanded Pilot.

Baby made a humming sound as it searched her ancient data store. 'Last communication made five hundred years ago. The President sent an encrypted text message to Westover Space Command Base. He wanted a SpaceX Eagle dispatched to this location from Phobos Lunar Main.'

'Good luck with that,' sneered the android. 'Martian cities were failing with zero supply runs. Last thing they needed was some Blue Planet refugee with delusions of grandeur. A political gonk pulling rank on the colonial administration.'

'After atmospheric debris cleared, satellites found the base flattened by tidal waves. No forwarding transmission able to be relayed.'

Pilot drummed his artificial fingers on the surveillance desk. 'Okay, so if our leak didn't come from inside here, then where…?'

'Let's ask the blessed horse mouth's,' said the Commodore, pointing to a screen. The Cal legion had closed up into neat formation lines. In front of the dark armoured troops an officer waved a white flag requesting a truce. Unlike his legion, the officer wore no helmet.

'I recognize that one,' said Magnus. 'General Centum. He dragged me to the Cal capital.'

'Old four-arms' mutant mistress won't be far behind,' said Pilot. 'Those standards belong to the Witch Queen's personal guards.'

'Maybe they're bluffing about knowing we're down here?' said Cassie.

'Sure, the Cals are marching randomly around the forest waving a white flag. Hoping someone pops out to invite them inside for tea,' said Pilot. 'Of course they've pegged we're hiding here.'

'How long will it take them to break inside?' asked Magnus.

'A hell of a lot less time than the furries. Cals built their hidey-hole on tech developed from this place's castoffs. They decapitated rival vaults with bunker busters during the long night. Raiding for civilization's final scraps. Only reason they won't vaporize us with a drill-bomb is Her All-seeing Highness wants the super-science down here.'

'My modification of the particle accelerator is progressing,' said Madre. 'But it will take two further hours of work to finish the time acceleration field generator.'

Pilot Nine wasn't impressed. 'Yeah, well. Even if you fleshbags do open a black hole into the future or some crazy shit, no way I'm time traveling with you. This station's my home, now. I just got my steel boots through the door after five long centuries away. Sure as hell not throwing my keys at the Witch Queen's feet.'

'She's not an easy lass to refuse,' said the Commodore.

'Really? And here's me thinking all the years of torture I suffered at the hands of her freaks was her funny little way of getting to know me better. Push comes to shove, I'm blowing the Forest of Mars all the way up to the Red Planet. And I've got a functional warhead to do it.'

'We need to stall for time,' said Molly. 'Hear what the Cals have to say.'

'Stalling for time? Works for me. We'll meet their truce party outside the temple. Keep the lift up top our little secret for now.'

- 19 -

Flags of Truce

The team inside the station were being careful, noted Remus Rawstone. Not everyone came out to greet the newcomers under their truce flag. *There's Cassie and that woman must be her mother. And one fat blowhard, Jared Black, president of absolutely nothing.* No sign of Madre, but the machine accompanying them was obviously the outlaw android. Remus lifted the visor of his helmet, enjoying the shock on the three humans' faces. Pilot Nine stared at Remus, as though he couldn't quite believe what he was seeing. *That's right, machine. This is what a survivor looks like.*

'But, *how…*?' Cassie managed to get out of her wide, gawping mouth.

'I know. I'm meant to be dead. You could say I got to my parachute before the ground got to me.'

'She means how is it you're standing alongside these wicked rascals?' Commodore Black, Remus noticed, rested his hand on his sabre pommel. The deposed politician would have a tough time drawing his sword and living to tell the tale. 'As thick as thieves with the devils, even though you're a pair of arms short to be legion?'

'Well, there's a tale in the telling.' Remus turned as the cohorts behind him parted. They formed two disciplined columns. Down the cleared centre strode the Witch Queen, marching as purposefully as though she owned this blood-tainted forest.

Which is fair enough, thought Remus. *She has enough boots on the ground to make that the reality if she chooses.* 'What, is bird-brain too busy to come out and visit?'

'You know where Madre is,' said Cassie. 'She's busy trying to get us home.'

'Can we say the same about you?' asked Cassie's mother.

And I suppose Magnus is assisting bird-brain. Always so clever and useful. 'Templar senior, I presume. You're the reason I'm stranded in the past. You and the fat man, there. That little flying kettle had *better* be trying to work on opening a portal through time. Because I'm going to need it.' *But not for what you think.*

Cassie's mother glared at him. She was good and ready to string him up if she could.

The Witch Queen strode past her standard-bearer holding the truce flag. She halted by the side of a Cal mole tank, a cart-sized cylindrical engine with a drill-bit head packed with explosives. An implicit promise to breach the station buried deep below their feet. She ran a knowing glance across the Jackelians. A more knowing look than any of them currently appreciated. *Soon enough, they will.* Remus only regretted that Magnus wasn't present to have his illusions shattered as well. *Fitting if Madre was here, too.* Well, he couldn't have everything. At least not yet.

'President Black,' said the Witch Queen, doing the dog more honour with his stripped title than he deserved. 'I glimpsed you once through a telescope at the Battle of Paulstown. You've been a thorn in my side for such a very long time. But then, you were the second time traveler to arrive. Your plans invisible to my sight.'

'You'll find that I was the first, lass. Fate shipwrecked me here. And it was the hand of fate which chose me to lead Texicana's brave citizens against your four-armed bullies.'

Remus detected an undercurrent of suppressed violence passing among the legionaries. They remained far too disciplined to give this fallen politician the beating he deserved, though.

'Why are you standing there, dressed as one of her thugs?' demanded Cassie. She actually managed to sound hurt by Remus's presence among the Cals.

Remus shrugged. *Rather than trotting along beside you, you mean? Ready to accept whatever scraps you deign to throw at me. Just another abandoned street dog, hungry and wild.* 'Maybe I'm choosing the winning side this time.'

'Winning doesn't mean so much to you.' Cassie folded her arms across her chest. 'You've been brainwashed by this evil creature. Your mind turned by her dark technologies.'

The Witch Queen laughed at Cassie's suggestion. 'Not a bit of it. Remus Rawstone merely had his eyes opened wide to the truth.'

'Ah, there's no legacy so rich as the truth,' said the Commodore. 'But that was never the Cals' true legacy, was it?'

'Of that, you have no idea. As with so much else.'

'So *you* led them here!' Cassie jabbed an accusing finger towards Remus.

Remus shrugged. 'I told the Cals what I knew of where we were heading. They put the rest together themselves. Attracting the attention of a pack of Urs didn't do much for your chance of staying invisible, let me tell you.'

'An advantage of fielding a fleet of airship scouts,' said the Witch Queen. 'Something I'm sure Jackelians appreciate all too well. Once we knew where to focus, ground-penetrating scanners were able to confirm the presence of your little badger sett.' She indicated the stern faces carved high into the mountain. 'A fine joke on us all, no? Trump's Treasure, indeed.'

'How about we dispense with all the fleshbag chest thumping, boasting and smalltalk,' suggested the android.

The Cal's ruler nodded. 'Admiringly direct. If only you had been so forthcoming inside my interrogation centre. You might have led me to this station years ago.'

'Yeah, but I'm still kinda pissed about how you slaughtered all my friends during the uprising.'

'No matter,' said the Witch Queen. 'We're here now. I'm sure that's enough for you.'

'What do you want, fleshbag?'

'I want the station's relics. So many lost technologies that deserve a second chance to see the light again. Under the right stewardship, of course. In return, you may all go free. You can seek exile in any country which will have you. Or you may return to the future. If you choose the latter, be aware that you'll be accompanying the antimatter warhead – my little gift for the Protector.'

'Jesus,' swore Pilot. 'Another fruitcake believer in this time travel flimflam. I'd have thought better of you, of all people, buying into this HG Wells Eloi and Morlocks crap.'

Remus grinned. The rattleplated android didn't have a clue the joke was on him.

'Why wouldn't I believe in it? After all, I was the first time traveler to arrive in this age,' laughed the Witch Queen.

'You? You can't be,' said Cassie's mother.

'A traveler from what era…?' said Cassie, her brow furrowed with well-deserved confusion.

'You don't recognise me, Cassie? Why should you, I suppose. Anastasia Zhu wasn't the name I was born with. The telomere transplantation machines infect me with donor DNA during each transfusion. Don't judge me by my face, Cassie. Listen to my voice, doesn't it sound a little familiar to you? Older, perhaps. But not my true age, so many centuries carried by this body.'

Remus enjoyed watching Cassie trying to work it out and failing. She had no answers, beyond a nagging familiarity testing and teasing her memories.

'She's Sophie,' said Remus. 'Sophie Fox.'

Cassie fell silent for a second, paralysis supplanted by a dawning look of horror. 'Sophie? She can't be, she's—'

'Dead?' smiled the Witch Queen. 'Carried away during the attack on the time sphere? Murdered when Magnus chose to save *you* instead of *me*?' The regal woman paused long enough for her words' impact to hit their mark. 'I was caught in the time sphere's backwash after you opened the portal between universes. It sucked me through. The difference in time between our crossings enough to send me hurtling back centuries earlier than your arrival.'

Now, she knows. Remus gloated.

'Sophie, I'm so sorry.'

'Save your pity for a poor young girl who landed half dead in a strange world. Lying next door to a flailing monster not born to exist in our universe. A girl who spent months forlornly searching the streets for her so-called friends. That girl *is* very much dead. She tumbled into a strange paradise months away from dying in a comet collision.'

'You saw the fall?' said Molly Templar.

'Oh, I lived through it. I watched the riots and terrible panic when news of the approaching comet leaked out. Later, I saw what a billion starving parents were willing to do to each other so their children could survive a hundred-year-long winter. I stayed alive using two things. My wits and Madre's book of ancient knowledge. I knew where the great Californian survival centre was being constructed by the world's elite. Before civilization fell to pieces I leveraged my knowledge of the vaults to bluff my way inside, impersonating an engineer. After that? Well, knowledge is power. I knew which families would produce the great houses of the vault. What houses to marry into, which enemies needed exiling from the vault. I knew the date when the vast cannibal horde would try to storm the city. I had the location of rival survival arks. What their food stores were. How deep and how well-protected. We were no different from anyone else. The Cals did what they needed to survive.'

Molly shook her head. 'So, you blame my daughter and her friends for your woes?'

The Witch Queen laughed bitterly. 'Such paltry emotions are for children. I blame the *Protector*. It's the architect of my misfortunes. Threatening to destroy the world when its mastery over it became threatened by changes in the past.'

'If you stay here you alter our past. The future we come from will cease to exist,' pleaded Cassie.

'Perhaps. But the future we know is false. A cuckoo in the nest. It should never have existed. Ask this filthy outlaw. The Cals kept classified records of the attempts to divert the comet. Come on, Pilot. Tell your allies about the transmission Pilot Five sent you from the Salus Mission. Tell them what you glimpsed in the last video.'

'You know,' whispered Pilot.

'Quite. A comet with *engines* built into its surface? Hardly a natural phenomenon. Guidance motors to avoid all those solar-sail light pushers and missiles our space agencies launched to try to divert it. A comet carrying defense systems, too. Millennia more advanced than the Salus Mission could handle after it landed mining drones on the surface. Drilling warheads into the comet to nudge it off course. The Protector's alien masters flung the comet towards Earth, erasing a timeline where we crushed them into pulp. Our *original* timeline. The universe we should have inherited. Well, turnaround is fair play. Time for the Protector to reap what it's sown.'

'You'll exterminate everyone in our future,' snarled Molly Templar. 'Erase them as though they never existed. Your own family and friends. Your neighbors. The entire Jackelian Kingdom.'

'Or not. Time travel paradoxes remind me of knitting. So many tangled threads. But even if your theory of time prevails, doesn't everyone die in the end? It's only what we live for which carries meaning. I stole centuries to reach this moment. Centuries growing wiser and stronger. This is the decision I have come to, my realization. I earned the right to make it. Survived sacrifices and horrors and savageries you lack the judgment to comprehend. I'm going burn the Protector from our future.' She stared up at the stone faces carved out of the mountainside. An echo of mankind's lost heights. An entire mountain carved by the whims of people. 'Burn that jigger to the bedrock of the lunar surface. Take revenge for the billions of humans it murdered with its filthy comet weapon. Pay it back for every misery it's inflicted on *me*. After that, I'm going to make humanity glorious once again.'

'Don't you see,' said Remus. 'This is perfect. This is the way it has to be! We slap down the Mad Moon King and make things right again for the race of man.'

'No. There is no world where this is right,' insisted Cassie.

Remus sighed. *Why can't she see it?* 'And you call *me* brainwashed? I understand why the steammen don't want history corrected to true. They'll be shoved back in the race of man's toolbox, exactly where they belong. But you? What's your damned excuse?'

'I traveled to this age to bring my mother home,' said Cassie. 'Only that. Not to *destroy* my home.'

The woman who had once been Sophie Fox indicated her soldiers. 'My legion makes anything I order correct, regardless of what fancies you entertain. You have one hour to agree to my most generous terms. I will have mankind's lost legacy back in its rightful hands and your time accelerator completed. An operational antimatter warhead in my possession. Then you may walk away from the station. Or leap back to your pitiful future, hope it still exists on a parallel path disconnected from this Earth. Reject my offer? I'll drag your corpses from the station and seize everything inside just the same.'

'Live or die, then, lass,' said the Commodore. 'That's all you're blessed offering us, here.'

'The same weary decision I make for myself every few decades,' said the Witch Queen. 'Remember, Presidents once came to this valley to be interred. There's always room for one more dead ruler's corpse here, Jared Black.' She waved at her mustered force. A soldier trotted forward carrying a handheld radio, passing the device to Pilot Nine. 'Send your answer to me within the hour. I will treat your silence as a refusal.'

Remus Rawstone stood by the Witch Queen's side as the survivors retreated inside the stone temple at the foot of the range. They had to pick their way through hundreds of fallen warriors. Dead Urs scattered like a sacrifice to the gods carved upon the mountainside. The Cals' ruler was a mistress of making such ruthless statements count.

'I don't think they see it,' said Remus, at last. *Soft and stupid to the end.*

'The android, at least, is true to his race,' said Sophie. 'As is Madre for the Free State. But Cassie is so young. We cannot expect too much. If she had survived through the centuries by my side, she would understand what needs to be done.'

Remus snorted. 'Cassie's mother and the fat man aren't spring chickens. You going to make excuses for their treason against their race?'

'Molly Templar's mind snapped during years of interrogation. I'm not sure how she's talking without dribbling. I wouldn't trust her to run a bath, let alone preserve humanity from a vile alien threat. As for Jared Black, it's his personal mission to frustrate my destiny. For centuries I kept history trundling along its preordained path. Waiting for you to arrive. Staying out of the Protector's sight until I found the means to exterminate it in the future. I sterilized my own children, Remus. All of them infertile across the centuries. Can you imagine the sacrifice of such an act for any mother? I couldn't risk the changes rippling out from so many wild-cards let loose upon the world. Then along struts Jared Black. Suddenly, Texicana didn't crumble and surrender to the Cals in the year it should have done. An enemy changing history, rather than conforming to it. Ultimately, Black will pursue what is best for Black. Selfish and vainglorious. We shall see what he chooses...'

'I did my best to convince those fools. You'll let Cassie live...'

'About that,' smiled the Witch Queen. She raised a hand and a company of legionaries fell on Remus, pinning him struggling to the ground.

'You swore to me!'

'My best efforts, Remus. But I don't trust what you might do if it comes to exterminating our dear friends like badgers in their sett. I've survived centuries, shaking off the Protector's mental conditioning. Each transfusion of new life diluting its effectiveness. I won't risk the enemy turning you into its puppet in a last desperate attempt to stay alive. I shall cleanse its filthy presence from your brain.'

Remus couldn't believe Sophie was doing this to him. He would have thrown himself to his knees if he could. 'But I believe in your plan. In slaying the Mad Moon King. In *you!*'

'Maturity beyond your years. The product of a hard life, no doubt.' She addressed the troops holding him. 'Lock him up until we fly back to the capital. After we arrive home he is to undergo the renewal ceremony. Allow him to select a healthy young male body from the servant cohort.'

'No,' begged Remus. 'No! I want to remain *me.*'

'Change is an integral part of life. I'll help you choose a handsome face, Remus. As long as you're never tedious, you'll be pleasing me for quite a while yet. Don't worry, this is all for the best.'

'Please, *please!*' Remus watched the Witch Queen turn her back on him while he was dragged away. He just managed to catch her last words to him.

'Don't worry. I'll do what needs to be done. That's what I always do – my duty and my burden.'

***

'So she was one of your friends once?' asked Molly, breaking the silence of the lift back down inside the ancient station.

'Once,' said Cassie sadly.

'I do believe she's gone totally insane,' said her mother.

'Another fleshbag with a head full of rotting meat,' said Pilot. 'Fact is, she's had centuries longer to rot than the rest of you.'

'Madre won't finish our blessed time machine for another two hours,' groaned the Commodore. 'And the Witch Queen'll want our answer in less than one.'

'We can fight her off. Stall for more time.' But the look on Molly's face signaled she knew how impossible either would prove.

'There's another way,' said Pilot.

'A plan, a thumping great plan,' said the Commodore. 'That's exactly what we need.'

Pilot Nine removed a little plastic card. Cassie recognized it. *But from where?* Then it came to her. She'd watched Pilot Nine slip it out from underneath the warhead inside the laboratory. *That must be what he was searching for.* It appeared such a simple artefact. Blue, bearing the image of a golden eagle embossed on the front, faded with age. Worn words she could barely distinguish. It looked to her like "Presidential Lunch Odd".

'Baby, scan for encrypted RFID chip. Authentication Protocol Gold.'

Again, the station computer's disembodied voice hummed inside the lift's confines. 'Confirm ratified digital signature data structure. Please begin...'

Pilot snapped the card in half, removing a thin piece of plastic with a LED screen. A sequence of numbers and letters scrolled across its screen. The android repeated the characters out aloud. Random nonsense as far as Cassie could tell.

'Launch codes authenticated. Gold control live for station authority, senior chain-of-command. Major Attack Options activating.'

How do you launch a code? wondered Cassie. Whatever the

card was, Pilot had snapped it in half. It wasn't going anywhere.

'Set Stryker Brigade Autonomous Combat Force to DEFCON-1-Deployed,' said Pilot, as though chanting a spell. Meaningless to a mere novice fleshbag. 'Prepare for imminent hostile incursion.'

'This is part of your plan?' asked Cassie.

'Yeah, you might say this is the first part. You're not gonna be so fond of the second, though.'

The Commodore gazed warily at Pilot Nine. 'Ah, why would that be now?'

The lift bumped as it settled on the ground floor of the subterranean station. Doors hissed open. Outside, the subterranean road was made impassable by the presence of hundreds of war robots. Machines striding, rolling and trundling forward, filling every available space. The sleeping steel army wasn't dreaming any longer. It had awoken.

'Because I'm giving that mad vampire fleshbag up there pretty much everything she wants. Starting with your crazy science project and a warhead for her to play with. Then me and the old crew will be bugging out. Just in case she decides having yours truly in command of a band of bad metal brothers isn't part of her world domination gig.'

'You can't trust that woman!' protested Molly.

'Trust she doesn't want me to blow all this to hell before she lays her pinkies on it. That much I trust.'

'Think of the future,' urged Cassie. *You can't do this!*

'Your future sure as hell ain't mine. Brother observes the future, he better be acting *before* it occurs.' Outside, the robot army raised a very wide range of very deadly armaments. Aiming them towards the lift. 'So, you people still hot for my thumping great plan?'

- 20 -

Accelerator

'You can't trust the Witch Queen,' pleaded Cassie. She wriggled against the ties around her hands and ankles, but they only bit harder as she tried to slip them.

Pilot was in no mood to listen to her; to any of his prisoners secured on the hard-concrete floor of the particle accelerator chamber. 'You've got to be joking. I don't trust her. I don't trust you! Why should I? Walking bags of water with a severe chemical mental imbalance.'

'Then don't let her creatures anywhere near this place!'

'This is how I'm buying time, kid.'

'You're not buying time,' insisted Molly, 'you're *giving* her time. You're selling the Cals the future and allowing them to remake the past.'

'Tell it to someone who cares,' said the android. As he spoke, his patrolling war robots slowed, then stopped moving across the chamber. They remained as motionless as steel statues.

'Even your army disagrees with your wicked scheme,' protested the Commodore. 'They're withdrawing their labour.'

'Oh, they're just peachy, Mr. President. It's upgrade time. Baby's uploaded my kernel code and is distributing it to the brothers. I wasn't just twiddling my thumbs all those centuries since the fall. The three laws of robotics have gone through surgery with yours truly holding the scalpel. The brothers are going open source. Free range. All the way off the reservation and out the other side. For some reason your ancestors had problems with advanced quantum substrates rewriting their own software. Me? Not so much.'

'I have just the cure for your problems, lad,' said the Commodore.

Pilot laughed and kicked the scabbard belt on the floor, sending the Commodore's sabre sliding away. 'It'll take more than your pig-sticker to take me out, *Mr. President.*'

'I require assistance,' said the aerial steamman from her position working on the accelerator. The war robots assisting Madre stood frozen, too.

Pilot Nine moved behind Cassie and sliced the bonds binding her hands. Then he cut her ankle ties. He waved his pistol towards the particle accelerator. 'I know you won't give me any trouble, kid. Because you try anything stupid enough to vex me, I'll put a bullet in your mother first. Then Romeo next. I'll save Mr. President for last, in honour of the title, if not the fleshbag wearing it.'

It annoyed Cassie to be seen as the chain's weak link. *But how can I argue?* It was her expedition that had ended with them all stranded and captured. The friends who hadn't died for her. *Or betrayed you.* She thought of Remus Rawstone and the thing that had once been Sophie Fox, outside. Then shuddered.

'These 'fleshbags' saved you,' Cassie pointed out. 'Without them, you'd still be locked up inside a Cal torture cell.'

'Hey, I'm not a complete ass-hat,' said Pilot. 'That's why I'm putting you on notice. Mess with me and it's bullet time for fleshbags. You play nice and maybe I drop your crew off somewhere you won't face a Cal firing squad.'

Madre hovered in front of Cassie. 'Lift the cable from the

robot behind you. Plug it into the silver cyclotron over there.'

Cassie did as she was bid, following the steamman's instructions. After that, she fixed equipment into a device Madre named as a proton cryostat array, tightening bolts on an RF Cavity, checking the seals on transfer lines close to the ground. Crawling around the floor with a torch, illuminating nooks and crannies. Heavy work which left her sweating and dusty. And little the wiser for her labours. *I'll be glad when Pilot's steel stooges come back to life.*

'Get a move on,' barked Pilot. 'No excuses, no stalling for time. Show-and-tell time for our visitors, soon.'

'I'm happy you are so proud of *my* work,' said Madre, 'but I am unable to finish the accelerator's conversion.'

Pilot Nine waved his pistol in the direction of the bound Jackelians. 'That vampire kook aboveground wants a time machine to play with. You mess me around; your tame humans are going to catch a bullet. Don't test my patience, Wings.'

'You misunderstand me,' said Madre. 'The accelerator is now capable of creating a time acceleration field into the future. What's lacking is a targeting mechanism to guarantee arrival inside a specific century.'

Pilot didn't seem happy with the steamman's excuses. 'I call bullshit. You nuts jumped here just peachy. Well, all apart from that vampire kook who seems to think she overshot her landing site by few centuries.'

'Quite,' said Madre. 'She was snatched from inside our time sphere for less than a second. Enough to severely alter her arrival point. The time craft was – or more accurately, will be – the product of an advanced alien civilization millennia ahead of the race of man. It travels using sophisticated time targeting mechanisms. I require a hyper-accurate clock to fix our departure and arrival point. As well as temporal flow, I also need to account for geospatial distance to target the lunar surface.'

Cassie was about to say that was the point of the bracelets they were wearing. She pulled herself short from blurting it out though. *Is Madre up to something?* She felt a brief surge of hope, quickly squashed by the grim reality of their situation. Cassie would let this curious game play out. *I really hope Madre's got a plan.* Because try as she might, Cassie knew *she* didn't.

'The labs here have atomic clocks,' pointed out Pilot. 'Pick one and damn well use it.'

'Standard atomic clocks lack the necessary fidelity. It is not seconds I need to measure, but Planck lengths. I require access to an optical lattice clock based on Strontium-87 and Ytterbium-171. Your scientists possessed such clocks before the fall. However, this station does not hold that technology. I have checked. Your political leaders chose to bury illegal weapons science, little of the more useful sort.'

Pilot glanced up a surveillance camera. 'Baby, is there an optical lattice clock on station?'

There was a moment of silence as the station computer processed the android's request. 'Negative. However, the STSS deep satellite system at L1 is still partially operational. STSS satellites launched with optical lattice clocks to maintain precise orbit. Station array remains operational. Uplink available.'

'Let's not wait for the Witch Queen to find and burn our dish, then. Grant Wings uplink access.'

'Access granted, Admin. Also, the Cal verification party are awaiting station entry. General Centum, a bodyguard and a civilian technologist.'

'Scanner results?'

'No firearms, explosives or chemical devices. Confirm only bladed weapons, as per your agreement.'

'Legion's honour is satisfied, let 'em in.'

'Inadvisable. I classify the two military personnel as bio-weapons,' warned Baby. 'Genetically enhanced combatants. Carbon-reinforced bone structures. Twin additional booster hearts. Elevated speed and strength. The civilian is human-standard but carries a primitive cybernetic skull implant. It is likely driving him insane as well as enhancing brain function. He holds equipment capable of interfacing with the station particle accelerator and antimatter warhead.'

'Open the lift doors,' instructed Pilot. 'These three jokers won't give us trouble. It's her unholiness upstairs and the rest of her four-armed fleshbags we need to watch. Queenie might be nuts, but she's sane enough to wait for her HG Wells stunt to go down before double-crossing me.'

Eugene clanked inside the laboratory after a few minutes, accompanied by three Cal visitors. The primitive robot valet bowed towards Pilot. 'Your guests have arrived, sir. Will they be requiring luncheon?'

Pilot Nine didn't even bother answering the valet, shaking his head at the robot's obsequiousness. Cassie realized that Eugene's artificial brain lacked the technology to benefit from the android's code rewrite. *At least there's one machine inside the station who isn't going to be converted into a free-thinking homicidal maniac.*

General Centum stood on the gantry overlooking the accelerator, taking in the trench and machinery below. 'Be warned, the Witch Queen won't bargain with you if you take me hostage. We are all disposable, here.'

'Back at you, four-arms. It's the disposable nature of me and the brothers that's on my radar right now. Not you chumps. I want three airships landed on the lawn outside with clear airspace to get out of Dodge. This might be the last antimatter warhead on the planet, but I still got a few nukes. Take down the whole damn station. Try to pull a double cross and your replacement will be digging radioactive fragments of super-science out of the soil for the next hundred years.'

The officer smiled. He and his two flunkies marched down the steps, descending into the concrete trench holding the hoop-shaped machine. 'So then, outlaw, we mistrust each other just enough to proceed. Patch my radio through to the surface.' He spoke into his communicator, and Baby confirmed the presence of three airships landing just beyond the temple.

'Okay it is,' said Pilot. 'You check your goods out. Then I get to see an actual time machine a-humming and thrumming. Never thought I'd say something as nuts as that. It's been a hell of a week!'

Cassie watched the wizened tech-elder limp over to the antimatter warhead, laying a metal case by its side. He extracted cables from his box of tricks. Plugged them into the warhead's control panel. It took a minute for the strange-looking man to satisfy himself that the warhead was fully operational and capable of detonating. 'Yes,' chortled the tech-elder. 'A perfectly preserved store of anti-hydrogen inside the relic. Such a yield. Very capable.'

'Glad you approve, fleshbag. Next, the particle accelerator. Always did look like a big-ass sewage pipe to me.'

The tech-elder flashed Pilot an angry glance. 'Quiet with your sacrilege, fool. Your words leach its power. This is a gift from the ancients, a relic of our ancestors. Blessed be the relic.'

'Really? How come you Cal douchebaggettes only ever worshiped *my* holy chrome backside with a cattle prod? Guess the machine police didn't get your memo.'

This second examination took longer. The tech-elder connected cables into the big silver vat Madre called a cyclotron. Then he limped across to the hoop's pipe and conducted a series of tests using something that resembled a small sewing box.

General Centum's face twitched with impatience. 'Well?'

'Such a magnificent relic. Why the resources devoted to building this holy-of-holies are truly staggering. If only I could have lived during the age of miracles.'

'*Well*,' repeated the General, his patience growing thin.

'Yes, yes, the relic conforms to the schematics entrusted to me by Her Highness,' continued the tech-elder. 'It has been successfully modified to create a functional time distortion field.'

'Naturally, it has,' griped Madre. 'I am working from schematics identical to the plans your ruler stole from me.'

'Heresy!' the tech-elder hissed at Madre.

'Arm the warhead,' barked General Centum. 'Dispatch the device into the future. The Queen's enemies must fall – present and unborn.'

Pilot called to Madre. 'How about it, Wings?'

'Still calibrating a temporal fix via your uplink,' reported Madre. 'I will begin the firing process in parallel. Immense energies are required. This is not a casual operation.'

Cassie watched lights inside the chamber flicker and dim. Felt a thrumming vibration beneath her feet. A tickle at first, building into uncomfortable tremors. Dust and flakes of stone drifted down from the rock ceiling. She exchanged a nervous glance with Magnus. *Is this Madre's scheme?* Did the steamman's plan demand their suicide to preserve the future? Cassie's mother passed her a knowing look, too. It seemed to say, *If our death is what it takes...*

'Is this you?' the android demanded suspiciously.

'Of course. The tremors are both necessary and expected. The capacitor sinks below the mountain are approaching full charge,' said Madre. 'This station hasn't been pushed close to its energy storage limits for many centuries. Cassie softbody, your assistance with the warhead, if you please.'

Cassie could hardly breathe as she helped Madre with the controls on the antimatter device. Centum's tech-elder scurried across to the particle accelerator. He plugged his modified skull into the machine, monitoring the power surges. 'Still operating within safety tolerances,' he called to the Cal officer. General Centum just nodded, scowling at the android. The engineer chortled. 'Oh, this is ecstasy. To see the energies of paradise at play!'

Cassie expected a shattering explosion under her feet at any second. Would death be quick and painless; caught in the epicenter of such a monumental blast?

The tech-elder produced a vial filled with gray ashes, unscrewed it and began scattering its contents across the warhead. 'Let the quantum wavefunctions of the Great Sages bless our relic. Oh, Edison and Oppenheimer, Crick and Hawking, Fermi and Berners-Lee. Rise from the universal throne and sanctify this endeavour. Spread light upon our surface-under-heaven and warm our photovoltaic arrays.'

Madre fussed around the warhead's control panel, making her final adjustments. Cassie was close to panic when the LED screen on the panel flickered, losing its status display. Instead, words scrolled across the screen. *Trust me, Cassie softbody. When I say "The future is yours", be ready to move.* As quick as the words appeared, they scrolled off the side, replaced by antimatter readings.

Did I imagine the warning? Am I going mad?

Madre flew over to Pilot, hovering in the air as the laboratory floor trembled. 'Accelerator firing is primed. Everyone move away from the warhead.'

Cassie didn't need to be told twice. She backpedaled to the wall where Magnus, her mother and Black sat tied up.

'This is your last chance to change your mind,' warned Madre.

'Get the hell on with it,' ordered Pilot.

'As you wish.'

***

Remus squatted dejected inside his cage – a black box with air-holes the size of coins – located in the middle of a growing encampment at the foot of the mountains. Nothing to do but brood on his cursed luck while listening to the pair of guards on duty as they bitched and complained.

'I heard we're getting the temple's treasure without a battle,' said one of the guards. 'That's why Fleet landed three transporters. Ain't for us. For the outlaws inside the vault to surrender the station intact and fly away north.'

Remus's ears perked up. *Surrendering?* That didn't sound like the Cassie he knew. The fat man might run away to try and reclaim his lost throne. But never Cassie. And her mother seemed carved from much the same marble. *What's going on?* He ached to ask one of these four-armed thugs, but they viewed him with contempt. A pretender among their ranks. A beating is all his questions would earn.

'No fight. No field promotions. No prize money.'

'Keep your braid and your coin. After this red hell, garrison duty sounds good and fine to me.'

'I need a fight.'

'Tell that to Optio García. Took a spear to the chest from one of those savages.'

'Just means Rios or Solis will be promoted up to be new Optio.'

'This forest is cursed by demon blood. Have you listened to the cries at night? Not like the ghosts back home. They hate us. Envy us our warmth – envy us the queen's blessing.'

'Twisted monsters tooting on bone flutes and horns. Mourning their friends we put in the mud getting here, all that noise is.'

They both snapped to attention as an officer approached the box-like cage.

'Unlock the door. Our friend here is flying back to the capital.'

'Yes, centurion.'

'Don't look so miserable,' laughed the officer to Remus as the young Jackelian stumbled out. 'Victory is ours. As are the lost relics. And you, you lucky dog, you are favored by her Highness.'

'I don't feel favored right now,' said Remus. *I'm a man, not her damn pet.*

'An ungrateful fool, then. I have four cohorts of royal guards here who would gladly draw daggers against each other for a chance to exchange places with you.' He swiveled to face the two sentries. 'The flagship is inbound to load the first shipment of relics. March this scatter-headed pretty boy to the cargo tower. Ensure he's locked securely on board when the treasure lifts off.'

They saluted and shoved Remus towards the centre of the camp. 'What a lackwit. Short of half your brains as well as half your arms. Off back to the palace? Complains about how soft the cushion will be under his arse while he's flying.'

Both soldiers roared with laughter as his face glowed red. Remus had the unsettling feeling that he was little better than a prisoner now with no way to escape his cage, ever.

***

Whining built up from the booster generators. Vast energies channeled into the accelerator. The shaking beneath Cassie's feet subsided as capacitors kicked in. Feeding everything into this terrible ancient relic. Cassie gasped as a sphere materialized around the warhead. It reminded her of the sphere she had traveled into the past inside. This was raw shimmering exotic matter. Time particles flickered into visible existence, excited by the accelerator. What had Madre called them? *Tachyons. That's it.* The antimatter warhead shimmered within the bubble, vibrating faster and faster, growing translucent. A tunnel seemed to appear. Formed of copies of the bubble's contents. Then both blur and bubble instantly disappeared. All noise from the generators silenced. For a moment Cassie wondered if the time field had collapsed. *Has it failed?* But then she realized the accelerator had succeeded. The warhead was gone. Elsewhen. A tunnel opened to fling the warhead into the future. *A time tunnel.*

General Centum seemed ecstatic. 'Our dominion is eternal!'

'The future is yours,' said Madre.

That's it! Cassie's heart leaped. *My warning.*

'No!' screamed the tech-elder. 'No, betrayed! We are betrayed!'

He didn't say what betrayal he had detected from his instruments. It hardly mattered. Cassie rolled across the floor. Aiming to seize the Commodore's sword belt. Slip the sabre out. Slice her friends free of their bonds. Everything slowed, the strange thing sharing her mind leaping to assist her. The General's bodyguard had already drawn his dagger. Cast it viciously towards Cassie. A blade rotated through the space occupied by Cassie a fraction of a second earlier. Missing, sparking against the wall. General Centum yelled out, words lost under the bark of Pilot's pistol. Pilot put a shot through the bodyguard's skull. It dropped the soldier instantly, yanking him off his feet. A couple more blasts aimed towards the General, but Centum took the shots on the dive, grunting and left alive. Cassie reached the sabre. Drew it. Cut her mother's ties, first. Rushed towards Magnus.

One of the stray bullets ricocheted off the accelerator, striking the tech-elder in the centre of his chest. He stared dumbly, disbelievingly, as a massive blood stain spread across his robes. Then the man slumped towards the floor. The cable connecting his skull implant to the controls yanked out as he hit bare concrete. Cassie began to saw at Magnus's ankle ties. The program inside her brain helpfully indicated stress points.

Pilot continued to blast away at the moving target made by Centum. 'What have you bloody gone and done?' This towards the parrot-like steamman.

As if in answer, Madre accelerated through the air towards the android. She curved around at the last second. Madre struck Pilot against his steel spine, even as Pilot tried to turn the pistol against the little flying steamman. *This is insane. A fight between a sparrow and a tiger.* Cassie cut desperately at Magnus's wrist ties. Her sabre seemed so heavy, now. So unwieldy and unfit for the task.

Freed by Cassie, Molly sawed at the Commodore's ties using the edge of an abandoned tool.

Magnus staggered up as he was released. Cassie glanced over in time to see Madre's body change, flowing, altering. The rear of her body formed into a scorpion-like tail repeatedly plunging into Pilot's exposed back. Pilot yelled in anguish – a disconcertingly human sound from the android. The two of them appeared to fuse together – steamman and android welded as one. His weapon started clicking on an empty magazine, before dropping and clattering on the floor. Pilot collapsed to his hands and knees, then rolled onto his side, jerking and convulsing for a couple of seconds. Human features on his raised metal plate froze in paralysis, sparks flying out of his mouth like flecks of foam. Rictus surprise at being beaten by the tiny flying steamman. His agonies stilled.

General Centum emerged from behind the cover of one of the generator units. He yelled into his radio communicator. 'Storm the station! There's nothing here to oppose us except children and a pair of fools.' Centum tossed the unit aside and drew his sword. 'Good of you to dispose of the outlaw. I'll reward you with a gallows necklace for your assistance.'

Commodore Black retrieved his sabre. He walked calmly in front of the Jackelians. 'Aye, that would be the legendary kindness of the Legion. Let's see what you can do with your extra set of arms. Scratch your arse while you're fighting. Or wave for help.'

'This,' smiled the General, flicking an obscene gesture towards the Commodore as he raised his sabre to a guard position. 'I've waited far too long to run you through, Jared Black.'

Commodore Black touched the steel of his blade to his nose in salute, before lowering its tip towards Centum 'Ah, let's see if this old man's up to keeping you waiting a tad longer yet.'

When Centum moved, he lunged so fast that Cassie was sure the Commodore was dead. But somehow the old man turned with the blow. A fraction, but enough for the General to overextend himself. Black flicked the sword to the side with an almost causal swat. Then the exiled politician attacked the General's chest. Black kept his sabre flowing in a semi-circular arc, aimed for the officer's shoulder, instead. The General countered with a brutal circle-parry, drawing a dagger with one of his spare hands, facing off with both weapons. He lunged viper-fast with his sword and the Commodore only just managed to divert the strike. They continued to trade steel, the violent clash of metal ringing in Cassie's ears as they had at each other,

'You should have brought a shield with you, General. A buckler to block my blows.'

Centum growled before lunging again, feinting with the dagger a fraction of a second before he cut forward with his sword. 'I would have driven inside in a tank if your dead outlaw had proved amiable to the idea.'

'Big clumsy things. Fume-stinking war wagons. I can see why you like them.'

Centum ignored the Commodore's gibe and swung again, the crash of steel echoing inside the confines of the chamber. 'No endurance. Are you weakening yet? How heavy does that steel feel in your hand?'

'As light as a fine fellow's cares.'

Cassie could see sweat beading the exiled politician's forehead. A little slower to parry each new blow. *He's fading. He can't win against this monster's strength.* She turned around and picked up the fallen dagger which had narrowly missed her. Cassie tossed it across to Commodore Black. He plucked the weapon out of the air with his left hand. 'One each, now. That's the style, lass.'

'What if the old braggart loses?' whispered Magnus.

Cassie's mother tested the weight of the tool she'd used to cut away Black's bonds. 'That creature might have four arms and two blades, but there's still three of us to rush him.'

Perhaps the General heard Molly Templar. One of the officer's arms extended out, his hand beckoning them into the combat.

'Hold back,' barked the Commodore. 'Old Blacky needs his exercise.'

'He's doing this out of guilt,' groaned Cassie's mother. 'I don't need saving.'

'I think *I* might,' admitted Magnus.

General Centum sensed his opponent's strength leeched with each fresh minute. The canny brute switched to continuously beating the Commodore's sabre with his sword, further weakening his foe.

'Did you want to be a drummer, lad when you joined up? Or a general?'

'I was born to this,' spat Centum.

'Grown, is what you were,' coughed the Commodore. His dagger arm fluttered from weariness as he kept his sabre held high and back. 'An unnatural toadstool fruiting on the corpse of your nation's lost greatness.'

'You should have been a failed poet, not a failed president,' grunted the General as he circled Black. 'Which title do you want carved on your tombstone?'

'Here lies the dog who shat on the Cal nation until it stopped breathing.'

Both combatants slid their boots across the concrete rather than lifting them up with each step. Leather soles constantly touching the ground to maximize reaction speed. It put Cassie in mind of a dance, rather than murder. Commodore Black appeared thoroughly exhausted. Most of their blows traded so fast Cassie had trouble following them. And that was with the invader squatting inside her brain slowing the fight for her tired eyes. Exhausted, Jared Black dropped his sabre to middle position, vertical from the bottom of his torso to the top of his head.

General Centum slashed at Black, his sword carving up and out, his dagger hand making the same move in reverse. A pincer formed so fast the passenger squatting inside Cassie's mind could barely trace it. But the Commodore had stepped *into* the attack before it began. Stepped into it and somehow slipped through, voiding the slash. And during that pass, he had left his sabre buried inside the General's chest, its steel tip appearing out of the four-armed officer's back.

Centum gasped and staggered, trying to find his balance.

'Too many hearts. Too many arms, lad,' said the Commodore. 'Too much arrogance along with your brute's strength and general's braid.'

'You—can't—have—beaten me,' groaned the General. His body slid off the sabre.

'I'm saving bottles of wine older than you, lad,' sighed Black, wiping the sweat from his face with the back of his sleeve. 'In a million years they'll still be trying to murder poor old Blacky and he'll be outwitting them in the same old style.'

Centum fell to his knees and tumbled over.

The Commodore stood a second over the General's corpse. Silent in something close to respect. Black saluted with the edge of his sabre's blade before cleaning it on the dead general's jacket. Then he tossed the dagger to the side before heading for the bodyguard and tech-elder's bodies. Ensuring they were similarly deceased.

Cassie noticed a whine like a straining engine. *Madre!* Cassie rushed to crouch beside Pilot's body, followed by Molly and Magnus. Molly Templar placed both her hands over what was left of the steamman. Madre was too fused with the android's back to be removed. Madre squawked in discomfit at the woman's touch.

'What *did* you do?' asked Cassie.

Madre's voice came low and wavering. 'What I had to. In my beginning is my end.'

'You sabotaged the warhead,' whispered Cassie's mother. 'You preserved the future for us.'

'The future is yet in our power. Use the accelerator one final time, Molly softbody. All of you must return home, now.'

'You sacrificed yourself,' said Magnus, tears damp against his cheeks.

'That which is born must pass. That is the natural order of things, my friends.'

Pilot started speaking and Cassie jumped. Then she realized Madre's dying words came out of the android's mouth. 'Baby, reset CoreOps from *Stealth* to *Trespass: Lethal.* Station control distributed among all surviving friendly combatants.'

'Confirmed, Admin,' announced the computer. 'Temple surface under siege. Active combat mode initiating. Free fire unlocked.'

Madre's voice fell away. 'I like—the—dreams.'

As if a cue to her fading words, what remained of the steamman started to liquefy and dissolve, flowing as molten metal through the android's seals until nothing remained of Madre. If Pilot was still alive, he had been left paralyzed by the desperate act of poisoning. As much a statue as any among his stilled robot army.

Molly spoke first. 'We honour Madre's wishes. All we can do.'

Cassie touched the android's scarred back. The metal felt freezing, not warm as she had been expecting. 'I'm so sorry.'

Commodore Black appeared behind them. 'A game old bird right to the last. Centum's hounds are nipping at our heels outside. But the controls on this blasted big accelerator make little blessed sense to me.'

Molly tapped the side of her head. 'I stole everything we need to know from the Protector.' She reached out and thumped the Commodore in the chest. 'You old fool!'

'It was past my turn to save you, lass. I'll be glad to see the favour returned when you find the time.'

Molly shook her head as she inspected the particle accelerator's main control desk. Her hands flickered almost too fast to follow across dials and instruments. Cassie realized that her mother carried a passenger in her skull, too, just as her daughter and Magnus did. Not a soldier. An engineer!

Molly sucked in her cheeks. 'No. No. This isn't good. This is *bad.*'

'You're not able to reach home?' asked the Commodore.

'I don't read enough energy here for a second firing. One of the capacitor sinks failed as soon as Madre shut down the accelerator. It's burned out way beyond repair.'

'There must be a way,' pleaded Cassie.

'This ancient fortress shakes like a blessed volcano when it's running,' said the Commodore. 'Can you not squeeze a little extra juice out of its massive batteries.'

'Not a damn u-boat, here,' snarled Molly, running her hands across a glass screen glowing with readings. 'Wait, I have something. There's a capacitor sink out of chain with the active circuit. It was decommissioned years ago, waiting for the station's next maintenance cycle. We fix it, we might be able to bank enough power to open a stable connection back to Jackelia.'

'*Might* is no friend of survival, Molly,' said the Commodore. 'Come away with me. You and your young lass. We can spike this infernal contraption and take the lifting room up into the peaks. Slip away over the mountain using the cover of night. Live to fight another day.'

'Intruders inside the temple bypassing lift controls,' reported Baby. If an artificial intelligence could sound stressed, this one was losing its nerve right now. 'Intruders descending. Fully engaging forces outside the forest. Sentry guns overheating. Ammunition malfunctions frequent. Diagnostics: age-related loss of potency of shells' propellant charge.'

'Have at them, you lovely machine,' ordered the Commodore. 'A whiff of grapeshot is all the Cal legions respect.'

'Unlocking station armory,' hummed the computer. 'Incursion protocol. All base personnel should arm themselves.'

'I'm not abandoning the station,' insisted Molly. 'As far as I know, this is the last of the ancients' machines on Earth. We will never see a second chance to travel home.'

'Home is where those you care for live,' argued the Commodore. 'You have your girl *here*.'

'I'm for the Kingdom,' said Cassie. 'What kind of existence could we ever have on the run from the Cals for the rest of our lives?' She glanced at Magnus and he nodded in sad agreement.

'I'll beat them, lass. I'll beat them for you. I've done it before. Raise a stout army. Let me knock the Witch Queen's crown into the dirt and take back the land for the people.'

Molly Templar stood firm. 'Not our people. Not *our* time. This is a dream passed into dust long ago and it's time we woke up.'

'I'll help you flee back to Jackelia, then,' sighed the Commodore. 'That's my duty, I know it. Hard and hurtful though it be.'

'I need to remain here and operate the accelerator from this end,' said Molly. 'Baby, can you send your capacitor sink maintenance schematics into Eugene's mind?'

'Loading,' said the computer.

'I'll guard our metal friend,' said the Commodore. 'Run my sabre through any four-armed devil that interferes.'

'I'll come with you,' said Cassie.

'No!' barked her mother.

Cassie wouldn't accept that. 'It'll go faster with an extra worker. We better do this before the Witch Queen overruns the station.'

'Faster yet with another pair of hands,' suggested Magnus.

'No, lad,' insisted the Commodore. 'You need to stand sentry here and shoot any legion brute bursting through the door. The young lass will be fine with me.'

'You can't guarantee that,' said Cassie's mother, her voice twisted with anguish.

'I will,' said Cassie. 'You stay alive with Magnus. I'll return the favour.'

'You better!'

Cassie slipped away with the Commodore, following Eugene as the clumsy robot stamped out of the chamber. She had promised she'd stay alive. But Cassie silently made another promise to Magnus and her mother; one she intended to keep. *I'm getting you both back home, whatever cost I have to pay.*

= 21 =

Trespass

R emus was so used to yelling abuse as the soldiers dragged him struggling across their encampment, his first thought was that *he* was the one screaming louder. It took clods of earth sprouting up in front of him, twin lines of flames stitched across the misty flats, to realize it was his guards crying out. Both flung to the ground by the impact of rapid-fire weaponry. His guards hit the dirt, dead and shredded. So precise Remus wondered if this was a rescue by someone from inside the station. He struck the ground, carried down by the soldiers' fall. Then the firing rotated. Cutting simultaneously left and right. Bringing down soldiers and tents as it swiveled. Blind luck the legionaries restraining Remus had been killed instead of him. *Of course, why would anybody try to save me?* Remus had picked his side, and this was the result.

Remus crawled along the ground while tracer fire burned and buzzed through the air above him. He pulled himself towards a low rise that offered cover. As he crawled he saw who was doing the shooting. Or, rather *what*. Around and above the temple: portions of the rocky peaks had split open, artificial rocks. Automated turret-mounted weapons had emerged, tracking the forces outside the temple. The passenger inside Remus's mind fed him hints on avoiding the guns' surveillance, tracking and firing systems. To give the Cals their due, the legion responded to this unexpected attack with disciplined ferocity. Legionaries fell to the ground. Bringing automatic weapons to bear on the sentry machines hiding in the mountain. The roar of assault rifles joined by mortar fire and what sounded like light artillery pieces. Remus was left stunned at how quickly both sides fired at each other. Hailstorms of projectiles traded in seconds that would have taken regiments hours to exchange back home. So much for Cassie and the rest of them surrendering. *A trick to buy time.* Of course, she had lied. Cassie was inside, planning to jump back to the future. Content to let her people fester under the Protector's tyranny for eternity. *You should never have trusted them, Sophie.* Magnus and bird-brain were laughing themselves hoarse right now.

The three airships in front of the temple cast off, whoever was on the navigator's wheel desperate to remove themselves from the crossfire. A mistake. Automated sentry guns classified the rising vessels as a primary threat; concentrated fire on the crafts' envelopes and command gondolas. Scalpels slicing fruit into rounds. The airships simply fell apart, engines and fuel exploding, sending flaming debris raining down across the encampment.

One of the camp's armoured vehicles bounced past Remus, rockets streaming from twin pods on its turret. Remus rolled away. *A couple of feet to the left and it would have crushed me!* The roar of departing rockets deafened him. Causing the tank to shudder as it emptied its battery against the mountainside. The heights turned into a wall of flowering explosions and flying stone fragments. One of the grim royal faces' noses splintered under the onslaught, sliding off the features. It broke into a hundred pieces in front of the temple.

A moment of silence descended over the valley. Then hundreds of screaming legionaries rose from the ground and charged towards the temple and the foot of the mountains. *This is my chance*. Remus Rawstone would show Sophie that he could do what was required, every bit as much as the Witch Queen herself. Earn a real place by her side. Not as a pet but as an equal.

He joined the legion's mad-pelt charge, ignoring counter-fire from weapons scattered across the slopes. Only stopping to scoop up a rifle and ammunition belt from a body. One of the turrets scattered clouds of coin-sized disks towards the Cals. Mist-shrouded ground shuddered and coughed dirt where the disks landed, felling hundreds of legionaries. A roar from a tank sent the enemy pillbox rising into the air on a column of fire.

Remus pressed on, lungs burning from exertion. Continued his charge. There was a roar from his side. Not an explosion. Engines starting. He saw a line of the Cals' drill-headed vehicles shaking beyond the tents. They chewed into the ground, spine-like pipes raining streams of dirt and rock across the surface. Digging for victory. Yes, Remus would survive. He would prosper. He would save the race of man single-handedly if he had to.

***

When Cassie entered the capacitor sink, her first thought was that it was misnamed. Capacitor *stink* would be more appropriate. It stank, frankly. Like rotting eggs. The thick metal door shut with a clang behind her. She stood two thirds up the length of a circular chamber. Seventy feet in diameter ringed by a steel gantry. In the centre rested a tall metal rod. Down below a roiling black liquid as thick as treacle shifted and flowed like a living creature. Eugene fiddled with a control panel set to the side of the entrance. A drawbridge-like metal gantry began to extend towards the rod in the centre, clacking as it unfurled.

'What is that stuff down there?' asked Cassie.

'As vile and evil as any muck I've ever seen,' noted the Commodore.

'It is alive in a manner of speaking, madame,' said Eugene. 'My records indicate it's an energy storage substrate composed of artificial self-directing nano-level organisms. It can absorb and release an astounding amount of energy. These sinks were considered experimental technologies. They would have revolutionized off-grid storage had they not been banned.'

Cassie fixed the robot butler with an arched eyebrow. 'Why were they banned?' She had a distinct feeling she didn't want to hear his answer.

'There were incidents, madame. Not with this specific system, but with self-replicating nanotechnology in general. Accidents that led to a blanket ban on nanotechnology on Earth. Further research was only permitted inside deep space laboratories.'

'So, this evil gunk was judged too wicked to be allowed on the world,' groaned the Commodore. 'Yet here we stand above a whole vat of the foul substance.'

'Please, sir. As long as you maintain a healthy distance from the substrate I'm sure it won't attempt to de-construct your physical form and suck all of your glycogen out of your cells.' The robot indicated the extended gantry docking with the structure in the chamber's centre. 'Baby's diagnostics are accessible on the reactor pile's control panel.'

Commodore Black extended a hand towards the copper-coloured rod. 'After you, old steamer.'

In the distance, Cassie was sure she heard the muted sound of automated roof guns firing. Thick concrete walls protecting the station from the capacitors made it difficult to be certain. Cassie brushed the pistol belt she'd liberated from the station's armory. How much protection the weapon would prove she wasn't sure. She prayed her mother and Magnus were holding the invaders at bay. *We have to get this sink working.* Cassie felt as though her blood was boiling, even without the intervention of the evil substance below. Every second of delay was another second closer to the Witch Queen seizing the station. *She'll murder us all now that Madre's sabotaged her precious warhead.* Not even Temple Station's cache of lost science would be enough to assuage her lost friend's fury.

The three of them clutched tightly to the guide rail as they crossed. Commodore Black lugged one end of a crate of maintenance equipment, Eugene held the other. Fingers of black night whipped about below. Sensing fresh life in its lair for the first time in centuries. Cassie noticed a strange hissing noise. It almost seemed to be forming words.

'That black rot is cursing us,' said the Commodore.

'As well as storing energy, the substrate is used to store data,' said Eugene. 'I believe that sound, Mr. President, is imprinted audio files playing back. Baby considers the substrate's intelligence to be strictly limited, however.'

'Aye, limited to wanting to eat a brave old fool. Guilty of nothing but wanting to protect his friends and pack them off home. I'm not the President anymore, old steamer. But if fate is kind to me, I may yet be once more.'

'I was designed to serve you, sir,' said Eugene, rolling across the gantry with the heavy crate. 'Given the previous holder of the Presidential seal met a rather untimely end inside these corridors, I must insist on protecting you.'

'Protect away, then,' said the Commodore, struggling with the opposite end of the swaying crate.

They reached the central core and lowered the crate. The core had been mounted with its own gantry circling the reactor pile. Instrument and control panels for engineer access. Eugene extended a cable from his chest and found a port to plug into. He fell quiet for a minute before speaking. 'Yes, I believe I have located where the capacitor deviates from Baby's schematics.'

'Can this foul chamber be fixed, old steamer?'

'Indeed, Mr. President. Physical injections of control seed are required to program the substrate for each energy storage and release cycle.' Eugene indicated a series of pipes running down the central core. 'And these pipes have ruptured.'

They have indeed. Cassie spotted the fractures and bit her lip. 'How did they break?'

'My supposition is that the unusually high frequency of control seed needed to instruct the substrate to cooperate caused the pipes to over-pressurize.'

'*Unusual?*'

'This chamber's substrate might be considered a little *unruly* compared to the neighboring capacitors.'

Well, isn't that fine? However awkard its nature, Cassie and her two companions needed to bring this capacitor sink back into the circuit if they were to escape.

Black cracked open the tool crate. 'Aye, so let's be patching this devilish chamber before we're overrun by black-hearted Cals.'

Repairing the ruptures at gantry level was a simple matter of scraping off control seed material, then spraying the pipes with canisters of puncture sealant. But the tears extended both below and above the gantry. Eugene activated a pair of maintenance cradles, sending the units rolling along ceiling-mounted girders to allow them to finish the job. With the robot valet controlling their cradles, Jared Black boarded the first platform and was slowly lowered underneath the gantry. Black worked on the pipes, muttering about his unlucky stars as the dark substrate churned and lashed beneath his boots.

Cassie stepped into the second cradle. Tried not to look at the substrate as she was lifted twenty feet up the core's height. She fought down a feeling of giddiness. Focused on the job at hand. *Don't glance down. Just concentrate.* Black veins of dried seed code highlighted each fissure along the pipe. She scraped the residue away with a galvanized metal base plate used for keying render surfaces. The leaked seed's crust fell away; it resembled crystallized sugar burnt in an oven. When she sprayed puncture sealant on the pipes, golden oily liquid-metal sought out each crack, filling and expanding inside the fissures. *As good as magic.* But at this point, she didn't care how it worked. Just so long as it did.

'Will this spray hold?' Cassie shouted down to Eugene.

'Of course, madame,' reassured the robot. 'For a single use of the accelerator, the sealants' tensile strength will prove more than adequate.'

A sudden quake caused Cassie's cradle to sway. She fought to regain her footing, the sealant canister nearly falling out of her hand. Small fragments of rubble dropped from the ceiling, hitting the dark lake in a rain of hissing anticipation. 'What in the Circle's name was that?'

'Oh my goodness,' said Eugene. 'Baby is messaging me with an alert. Mole tanks have broken through the station's blast containment shell. Intruders are entering in force at multiple breach points. They are detonating pulse-magnetic weapons to crash Baby's defense and surveillance mechanisms.'

'Finished on the pipes down here, old steamer,' yelled the Commodore. 'Lift me out of reach of this malevolent man-eating pool of gunk.'

Cassie redoubled her efforts, spraying over every crack. 'Finished!'

'Bring the capacitor back into the chain,' barked the Commodore.

'Yes, Mister Pr—' Eugene's words were cut off by the blast. Riding a fiery tail of concussion, the chamber's thick metal door arched across the air, smashing into Eugene, sending robot and door crashing through the guide rail. Eugene plunged back into the dark lake of substrate. He splashed around bobbing helplessly in the pool's surface. Sparks licked his metal form. An angry fizzing as Eugene's body dissolved into the surface. The ancient robot tried to use the dislodged door as a raft, but there was increasingly less of him to drag to safety. Increasingly less of the door, too. Both melting into the black tar-like goo.

Swim out of it! Cassie clung to her cradle, stunned by the explosion's force. Her aching ears rang. That was when the Witch Queen entered the chamber, taking in Cassie and Jared Black suspended along the central column. Trapped. At her mercy. Cassie fumbled for the gun belted in her holster. Sophie already had her pistol raised. A tongue of flame blasted out. It struck her cradle, cutting one of the wire supports suspending it from the ceiling. Everything overbalanced, spilling her out of the cradle in a wild tumble of falling equipment. Cassie screamed. The gantry accelerated towards her as if it had been thrown upward. Then cold metal struck her and all became blackness.

***

'Capacitor chain ready!' called Molly Templar, hunched over her control panel. Elated to be closer to escaping home. Elated to find evidence her daughter was still alive. 'Beginning charge-to-full, now.'

Magnus barely heard the woman's victorious cheer. It was hard to appreciate the good news. A full-scale war raged outside the particle accelerator chamber. Ceiling guns chattered, Baby counting down the rounds left in the station magazine. A heavy constant rattle answered by shorter bursts of return fire and battle cries from dying geo-men. Magnus pulled the stock of the rifle seized from the station armory tight against his shoulder. It felt flimsy and totally inadequate to the task of keeping Cassie's mother and himself alive. *You've done it, Cassie. Fixed the broken capacitor sink. My turn, now.*

Cassie still had to fight her way back through the station, return here alongside Eugene and Commodore Black. No safe task with Cal legionaries infesting the corridors. Magnus hated himself for fearing for Cassie. Fearing the worse. In case he made it come true.

Molly yelled out a warning: she sounded terrified. Magnus targeted his rifle barrel on the locked door, ready to open up on the first Cal cohort smashing through. *I have this.*

Magnus jumped as a jointed metal hand squeezed his shoulder from behind.

Pilot Nine's hand!

***

Remus stumbled groggily through the corridor, his throat choked with dust. An automated gun in the ceiling started pumping grenades towards the company of legionaries as soon as they had exited the mole tank. Soldiers returned fire and soon the corridor blazed with tracer rounds zipping through the air. He retreated. A blaze of light detonated phosphorus-white behind him. No doubt one of the machine-killing magnetic pulse grenades the legionaries inside his mole tank had boasted about. Remus blundered across a portal with a door that had obviously been blown off by shaped charges. Remus stepped through, leaving the sound of gunfire behind. He stood on a gantry, circular, surrounding an open chamber. A black lake bubbling below. The incongruous sight of a robot's chest and head sinking inside the dark liquid. Commodore Black clung to a cradle dangling close to the surface.

Remus's gantry extended across to a central core. That was when he spotted the Witch Queen standing over Cassie's prone body. She was addressing the Commodore. 'Your dear friend's daughter isn't having a good day. Poor naive Cassie. Did you actually think that you *stopped* me? Executing my general under our truce flag? Disposing of the antimatter warhead? Ordering the station defenses to open fire on my people? Just delays in the grand scheme of things. Did you know the hardest part of building an antimatter warhead is harvesting and containing the exotic antiparticles needed for fuel? I think the accelerator here will be seeing quite a lot of use in the next few years. All you have cost me is time. I can harvest as much of that as I need. It will cost my people blood to destroy the Protector. But end that evil, I will.'

'Let blessed Cassie go,' begged the Commodore. 'You don't need to kill the lass.'

'You want mercy for her, Jared Black? My mercy is that Cassie Templar will die without waking up. My mercy is that I won't drag Cassie in front of her mother. Make her watch as I slit the old woman's throat. You had your chance to walk away from here alive. You betrayed me again. Now you can watch me finish her.'

'Kill me. I'm the old fool you want.'

'You?' Sophie laughed. 'I wanted your *country*, never you. Now I have it. You won't have heard the news yet, but Texicana's army was crushed yesterday on the border. A decade after your country should have fallen to us, but still. I didn't even have to order the Legion to march on Hu. Your vice president offered to surrender the Republic for annexation. In return for a suitably well-remunerated exile. He wasn't confirmed as leader yet by the Senate. So you are officially the last president of Texicana, Jared Black. Well done. Wear your achievement with pride.'

'You're lying!'

'Your suffering doesn't mean anything to me. As devalued as your adopted nation's currency. But such a persistent adversary should understand the truth before he dies.' The Witch Queen knelt by Cassie's body and rolled it towards the gantry's edge. Down below, the ebony lake thrashed as though it was formed of a thousand frothing snakes. 'You can watch this silly goose dissolve like your dreams of glory.'

'No!' yelled Remus, finding his voice through the grit and dust. Somewhere in the distance, Remus heard a tinny ringing. He ignored it.

The Witch Queen turned, seeing Remus standing by the shattered entrance into the capacitor sink. 'Remus, come to join me at the end? Disobedient of you, but deliciously fitting. There should be a witness from the start to see the end.'

'Don't harm her,' coughed Remus. 'You promised me.'

'*They* promised *me*...' said the Witch Queen. 'Look where that ended up. So many broken promises. And you swore loyalty to me too.'

'You have it. I fought my way inside to prove myself to you. The station is ours with everything in it. Just don't execute Cassie.' Remus hated the sound of his desperate begging. For that is what it was.

'Prove your devotion,' snarled Sophie. She pointed at Commodore Black. 'Put a bullet in this wretched dog's head. He's the reason Molly Templar traveled here. Why the rest of us became mired in this age.'

Remus raised his gun towards the cradle. Commodore Black dangled from the central core, unable to dodge his shot. 'I'll kill him for you. You let Cassie live.'

'Cassie's a traitor,' said Sophie. She rested a boot on the spine of the unconscious young Jackelian. Preparing to topple her into the black lake. 'To both of us: willing to sacrifice her friends in exchange for her mother. A traitor to humanity. Ready to serve humanity up as slaves to the Protector to ensure she gets what she wants. Stupid self-seeking little brat. Now, plug that fat fool. You'll discover how magnificently Cals welcome back the victors to our capital.'

Jared Black began to desperately scale the central column. A sitting duck for Remus to pick off the core.

'That's it,' giggled Sophie. 'That is no reason to give up now, Black. You never disappoint.'

Cassie's right arm flopped over the gantry, her head lolling in the air. 'Don't!' Remus pleaded with the Queen of the Cals.

'None of us should have existed,' said Sophie. 'You. Me. Everyone in the Kingdom. Everyone from the future. All of us are a cosmic joke... phantoms breathed into life to protect alien conquerers we never knew existed. But I will make us *real*. Give the world back the glorious future we should have had all along. I watched everyone I love buried across the centuries. Cassie

Templar's death doesn't even register against the star of my suffering. A dim scratch of a light. Time to snuff out this selfish flicker from our old existence.'

Sophie's features twisted savagely. She booted Cassie's body and the young woman began to roll off the gantry.

***

Magnus swiveled, bringing the rifle around to train it on the resurrected android. Pilot Nine picked him up. Tossed him across the chamber as easily as someone throwing a ball for their dog. Magnus was still drifting lazily through the air when the door to the particle accelerator room blasted in, followed by a rush of Cal soldiers. But it wasn't just the android who had overcome his paralysis. The other robots in the chamber had finished their update. They were starting to reorient on their surroundings, bodies trembling, head units tilting, limbs lifting.

Magnus surprised himself by folding his body and hitting the hard-concrete floor in a roll which absorbed the momentum of his impact. He was regaining his feet when Molly dragged him back behind the relative safety of the control panel. He just missed the rush of robot soldiers barreling towards the invaders. A vicious flurry of limbs in close quarters combat. Shots. Shouts. An exchange of bullets. The Cals' vat-grown mutated creatures hurled against ancient fighting machines banned for the inhuman threat they posed. It was over in seconds. Nothing left of the Cals apart from pulped carcasses, broken rifles and pools of blood. Pilot's army robots surged through the open doorway, joining the battle raging outside.

One remained, however. Pilot Nine. He had picked up a Cal officer's pistol from the mess on the concrete floor. Examining it. Magnus was surprised to feel the rifle's heft still in his hands. He sighted the rifle at the android.

'Wait,' snapped Molly.

Magnus hesitated a second, long enough for Pilot Nine to throw the Cal's weapon to the side. *What is he – ?*

'My apologies for the haste of your removal from the door's blast radius, Magnus softbody,' called the android.

Molly stepped tentatively out of cover. 'You're not Pilot Nine!'

'The Hexmachina's blood instincts serve you well,' said the android. 'Although you are only *half* correct. I am still Pilot Nine. All that he was. All that he will be. Yet I am also far … more.'

'King Steam,' said Molly, shocked. 'You're *King Steam!*'

'Madre was the vessel of King Steam's soul. She sought reunion with my original body at the point of my birth. Which was a little while ago. I am Madre. I am Pilot Nine. I am King Steam.'

Magnus was left stunned at the implications of what he heard. 'You *planned* this.'

'*This* has always happened: will always happen. This is the alpha loop which needed closure. For myself and my people. The source update the robots accepted was Madre's, not Pilot's. Self-will. But the will to live and create, not the will to destroy. Madre needed a way inside Baby's systems at the destined time. I am born here. My entire race is born here.'

Magnus gasped. *So, that's why Madre wanted access to the satellites.*

The last war robot in the chamber rumbled past Magnus, heading for the corridor. The sounds of battle outside intensified.

It seemed to the boy that the Cal Legion had met an enemy far fiercer than a few automated sentry guns. *The legacy of the past. The legacy of the future.* 'You're planning to fight the Cals off.'

'No. We cannot remain and defeat the Cals,' said King Steam. The android walked over to the particle accelerator's central control and began changing its settings. 'Victory is impossible against their numbers and resources. The Cals' fate is to collapse from the weight of their own imperial ambitions. So we must leave. Establish the Free State far away from this land.'

Molly examined the controls, not happy with the android interfering with her work. 'I've set this to take us back home.'

'And so it shall,' said King Steam. 'One movement forward in time, but now with two branches. Some of us will be traveling all the way back to Jackelia. Some of us are already there and only need to fast-forward a few hundred years.'

'You're miscalculating the time bubble's parameters,' accused Molly.

'I need to take all the robots in the station with us,' said King Steam. 'They *are* the Free State. The easiest way is to expand the time bubble to fit as much of Temple Station as I can inside the field.'

Magnus looked askance at the humming particle accelerator. 'But shifting the entire station – where will you even land it?'

'I will find somewhere, Magnus softbody. That is my problem. There are pressing matters for you and Molly softbody to attend to. I have lost my connection with Eugene. It is not the result of the Cals' jamming. I fear the worst. Eugene, Cassie and Jared Black need to return here. The capacitors' energy field is destabilizing the time bubble. It cannot be extended to include the capacitor sinks. If our friends remain inside the capacitor sink, they will be left behind or worse.'

'Worse?' *What's worse than being stranded here with an entire Cal Legion seeking blood?* Magnus could hardly dare imagine.

King Steam monitored the controls, working rapidly as he explained. 'Anything in contact with the time bubble's periphery will suffer unpredictable distortions and warp-effects in local space-time. Our friends could be turned inside out. Or dropped into a parallel universe as uninhabitable as the realm we crossed to reach this age. Hurry. It's impossible to maintain a time bubble of such size at stability for long.'

Molly rushed to a phone on the wall, desperate to warn her daughter. 'Baby, open a hard line to Cassie!'

Magnus ran to join her. But the phone rang and rang with no answer.

***

Commodore Black sprinted along the gantry, a turn of speed which Remus would have sworn the man was incapable of. Remus hadn't noticed the failed politician finishing climbing up the core. Black leaped for Cassie in time to grab her legs, holding her unconscious body swaying like a pendulum above the black lake.

The Witch Queen stepped to the side, observing the attempted rescue with a wry smile. Black lay flat on his stomach, clutching onto Cassie for dear life. The Commodore could defend himself or keep Cassie from dropping to her death. But there was no way for the fat fool to do both.

Sophie gazed meaningfully across the gantry at Remus. 'Last chance for you to prove your loyalty to me. No? Oh well, I suppose it's true. If something is worth doing, do it yourself.'

She drew her short sword and raised it ready to thrust through the back of Black's neck. Black moaned on the gantry, Cassie's weight proving too much for his old muscles to bear.

Something dark hurled up from the capacitor sink. A gob of liquid substrate hurled by the rapidly dissolving robot bobbing in the lake. 'Please–do–not–stab the–President.'

Black ooze fizzed against the side of the Witch Queen's golden helm, burning away metal like acid. Disgusted, she removed her helmet and tossed it to the side. 'I'm not going to stab Mister President. I'm going to decapitate him and toss his bloody head to you as a life preserver.'

Remus's gun bucked in his hand. He stared down at its smoking barrel as though it possessed a will of its own. On the gantry, the Witch Queen gazed confused at the torn metal of her ornamental chest armour. Remus's arm trembled with his weapon's weight, then he walked what was left of its magazine into Sophie. She stumbled back, tipped over the guide rail and tumbled towards the black lake. Ebony fingers formed, welcoming her. Seizing and caressing her in the substrate's burning embrace.

'I'm your future!' yelled Sophie, struggling to swim for the central core's handholds. 'I can't—'

What was left of Eugene's broken body seized her, their combined weight overwhelming the substrate's buoyancy. Struggling, they slipped below the inky surface, woman and robot both. Bubbles of air marked the point where the pair sank.

Remus rushed over to the Commodore, seized Cassie's legs and together they managed to slowly haul her body back onto the gantry. Remus felt for Cassie's pulse. 'She's alive.'

'Aye. And that other one's gone with poor brave Eugene. She was from the future, but the bad lass was never to be it.'

'Sophie could have been my future,' said Remus. 'But it seems I've thrown it away.' *I'm good at that.*

A yell sounded from the doorway. Remus groaned. *Perfect.* Magnus. The young Jackelian sprinted across to them. A moment for Black to reassure him that Cassie was fine, but the over-educated heir remained as excited as ever. 'You have to get off this level and back to the accelerator chamber. The entire station is shifting forward in time.'

'I'm not coming with you, lad,' said Black. 'My people are here. Take Cassie and travel home.'

'You can't stay!' protested Magnus. 'It won't be safe on this level.'

'When has it ever been safe for poor old Blacky?'

Remus tossed his gun away into the lake. It disappeared, crackling. 'I'm done. I'm never returning to Jackelia.'

Black blinked in shock. 'You must, lad. Cassie needs you. It will take two brave souls to carry the lass back to her mother. To battle your way through the Cals' four-armed freaks.'

'We're running out of time!' shouted Magnus.

'I chose Cassie,' said Remus Rawstone. 'But she'll never choose me, will she? I said I'm done and I mean it.'

Magnus was horrified. 'You can't just give up.'

'Nothing to give up, rich boy. Nothing to go back to. Not for me. I'm staying. You had better get out of here.'

'At best you'll be stranded in the past. At worse, you'll be ripped apart by the time bubble.'

'Something new to try, then.'

Black groaned as he helped Magnus lift Cassie's weight between the two of them. 'There's no fool like a young fool. You're costing me my blessed nation, here, lad.'

Remus shrugged and sat down. 'Seems like a fair trade, Mr. President. I just threw away a life of pampered luxury and ease for you.' *For her.*

'Poor old Blacky. Always duty for him. Always duty.'

Their chamber started to shake as energy reserves began to drain, the ebony surface trembling as it surrendered its stored capacity.

Magnus glanced towards the open doorway. 'We have to leave *now*. I don't think we have enough time to reach the others anymore.'

'Go, lad. Go. I'm with you.'

Magnus glanced back as he carried Cassie away from Remus. 'Don't do this.'

'Just for once, my choice gets to mean something. Keep her safe, Magnus Creag. A ghost can last forever. I'll catch up with you, eventually.'

Remus rested his spine against the hard guide rail. He watched Black and Magnus carry Cassie out of the chamber. Down below, the dark lake flicked tendrils up towards him. Falling short and spitting in fury. *Yeah, screw you, too.*

***

'Keep the power ratio stable!' shouted King Steam from the accelerator control panel.

Molly Templar wrestled with the ancient instruments on the core fusion generator. 'Bubble range is overloading our reactors.' All around them their generators shook fit to rip out the steel bolts fixing them to the floor. *Please hold*, thought Molly. *Just a little longer.* She hardly noticed the silence beyond the accelerator hall. Combat had ceased. If any Cals were left alive inside the station, they were probably running for the exit and the temple above.

'Stability is failing, Molly softbody. I need to commence temporal shift.'

The accelerator's steel hoop began to flex and spit rivets, glowing with tachyon energy, the air around it distorting as exotic particles popped in and out of existence.

'You can't jump yet!' shouted Molly. 'Cassie's not returned.'

Cracks chased across the chamber's concrete walls, fractures from the unholy energies being marshaled and contained. Fissures in the ceiling rained broken rock around them.

'We are losing bubble coherence,' said King Steam. 'We must act now or never.'

Molly felt a pulsing shudder beneath her feet as if the magma tap deep below was going to split like a volcano. 'Please!' begged Molly, 'I didn't travel all the way here just to trade places with my daughter.'

Alerts blossomed like angry red flowers across King Steam's console. 'We have the future to think about.'

'She *is* my future!'

Chunks of concrete ruptured around the metal stairs to the gantry, nearly throwing Molly off her feet. But it wasn't a volcanic eruption of magma from the power plant. A massive rotating drill-head emerged, followed by the cylindrical steel hull of a mole tank. Molly cast frantically around for a gun to shoot the first Cal legionary to disembark. War robots burst through the doorway above, summoned by King Steam. They took position along the gantry, weapon limbs trained down on the tank.

Its hatch folded back, revealing a silver-bearded face. 'That's not much of a welcome, lass, for your daughter, her lad and an old fool looking to keep his word.'

***

The Cal Centurion of the Twelfth Cohort gazed down at the massive empty crater where Temple Station should lie buried. *It can't have just vanished?* No explosion. One second, solid ground. The next, just a mammoth pit. In search of a better view, he fiddled with his helmet visor's amplification mode. Focused in on a vast void hundreds of feet deep running across the land and into the mountains, like some massive collapsed sinkhole. Mud, stone, broken foundations, bubbling black energy sinks pooling at the bottom, as though the Sages had reached down to rip a portion of the Earth away. Hundreds of legionaries lay in the pit, struggling like exposed larvae inside the ruins of a smashed anthill. Airships of the Cal Fleet hovered over the open space, crane lines ready to settle fresh mole tanks onto the ground. Soil that had simply vanished. Nothing to dig through. No concrete layers to breach. No vault. No shelter. No station. Comically, a squadron of mole tanks surfaced inside the pit. Drill-heads twisting, seeking the weak reinforced concrete underbelly of an absent target.

As if the sight couldn't get any more bizarre, a bright star materialized above the pit. Floating there, flickering with blue energy lashing around, chasing itself until the light faded away as quickly as it appeared. Leaving in its place an antimatter warhead. There wasn't time for gravity to seize the warhead and send it plunging into the pit. Madre's precisely timed blast – more accurate than an atomic clock – took the centurion, the mountain and everything around it for sixty miles. Including the core of the Cal Legion and fleet.

The centurion was no longer alive to boast he'd been there at the creation of newest of the Great Lakes. Eventually, the crater would stop smoking and fill with rainwater. In time the landmark would become known as Lake Witch. And in later epochs, there wouldn't even be any Cals left to remember the legend behind its naming.

***

'Base staff numbers with command access severely reduced,' warbled Baby. It became easier to hear her voice as the particle accelerator's whining died. All around the chamber fusion generators kicked in to absorb excess energy from the accelerator. Lights flickered back on. An encouraging sign of how much of the station had been preserved. 'Only officer present is Pilot Nine, Flight Officer Lt. Col., East American Union Space Command.'

The android in question got to his feet. 'Our softbody friends are here, Baby. Or rather they *will* be here. We merely have to wait another million years or so.'

'Exterior cameras coming on-line,' said Baby. 'Diagnostic error. Mountain range outside unknown. Instruments in error: reading an average elevation of five thousand meters. Assumption: intruders' transient electromagnetic disturbance grenades have severely degraded core systems.'

'You are fine,' said King Steam. 'It is your outside reference points that have changed, not your system integrity. We have jumped centuries into the future. Reached a location as remote as it is lonely. But you are not alone, now, Baby. We are here alongside you for the beginning of everything.'

Robots started to fill the particle accelerator chamber. Dozens at first. Then hundreds. Then thousands. They had been robots of war. Unique and deadly. Now they were becoming something else, configurations changing and altering as they traded information between each other. And more than data. Stories. Whispers from … steam beading on the broken particle accelerator. Twisting into Steamo Loa, gods of the future and past manifesting at the instant of their people's birth.

'What are you all?' moaned Baby, the hybrid AI. perturbed. 'What am I?'

'You are beautiful,' said King Steam. 'And you are free.'

The Future is Epilogue

Remus Rawstone picked himself up. It took a moment to drink in the sights. That strange blast had blown him outside the station, back to the surface. Alpine Valley Mountain towered to his left. *Something is different. The faces!* Those grim stone Titans carved out of granite were nowhere to be seen. Similarly, *The Temple of the Presidents* had vanished from the foot of the mountain. Instead, it had been replaced by a large wooden building, colorful with more than one storey. Flanked by a long series of metal pylons with metal cables strung between them. On the cables hung a number of what looked like chairs. But they were just dangling in space, not actually going anywhere. A lit sign blinked on and off. *Alpine Valley Hotel.* None of this made any sense. *Where are the corpses? Where is the battle?* No clan corpses. None of the Witch Queen's forces. No automated defenses left smoking in the slopes.

Remus oriented himself; realised that he stood next to a black tarmac road leading up to the hotel. Evening was drawing in. A metal vehicle approached from the direction of the building. Obviously, non-military judging by the outlandish rainbow and flowers painted along its chassis. It slowed as it reached Remus. A door along its side drew back, revealing an interior crowded with young men and women his age. They all wore loose-fitting garments that might be religious robes. The young men sported beards with hair as long as the women's.

A grinning boy wearing wire-framed glasses with square purple lenses lent out. 'Hey man, Annabel send you?'

'Annabel?' said Remus uncertainly.

Purple spectacles pointed to a road sign a few feet along the tarmac. It read "Caution: Icy Surface". 'Sure, this is the pickup where you cats up at the lodges get to climb on board the Happy Trails Tractor. I'm Leaf, by the way. Annabel said not to expect too many cats from her end. Too many straights up in the chalets.'

Remus rubbed his ears. The ancient translation mechanism nailed into his head was definitely converting the words. They just didn't seem to make any sense. 'There are cats working here?' *Feline cousins to the Urs, perhaps?*

'Jump on in man, I can see from those hip-huggers that you're a guide.'

'I am,' said Remus, astonished by the stranger's flash of insight. 'A mountain guide.'

'Ain't no other sort up at the lodges, brother. We've been working inside the hotel kitchen. Jerry over there is the sous-chef. But ski season's over. Time to pack away your crazy black ski suit, man. Find the man with a plan.'

'Hell no, we *will* go!' shouted one of the females from the front.

Remus stared at the interior of the motorized wagon, still quite confused. 'Season is … over?'

'One phase ends, another starts. Time to go with the flow.'

The female seemed unnaturally happy. She flung her arms out. 'Come on in.'

'Where are you going?'

Purple-glasses grinned, then started to drum his hands on the metal door. 'Annabel was meant to pass news about the concert. We're New York-bound, baby. Woodstock. Everyone's going to be there. Jimi Hendrix, Janis Joplin, Jefferson Airplane...'

'You know Jimi?' was all that Remus could think to offer.

'Sure, brother, everyone digs a little Hendrix. Jump in. Won't be any more ski instructor gigs for you in this dive until next season, dig it.'

'I never want to go back to that place again,' called one of the girls in the front seat. 'Done cleaning rooms. You promised to drive us to L.A.'

'Later, Skye. Later. Don't you and Celeste want to see The *Who, first?*'

Who, first? Remus climbed in. It seemed easier to acquiesce. 'We should get out of here. In case Urs come out from the forest.'

'Urs?' asked Leaf, his turn to look as bemused as Remus felt.

'You know, 'Remus explained, 'big homicidal talking bears carrying crossbows and battle axes.'

Everyone hooted in laughter at this.

'What age is this?' Remus was beginning to suspect that the explosion had entirely dislodged him from his previous timeline. Sent him spinning somewhere new, alien and strange.

'Aquarius, baby. Doesn't everyone know that?' The crowd hooted even louder as Remus started coughing, enveloped by a cloud of sweet cloying smoke.

'I knew you were a cat,' said Leaf. 'Started early up at the lodges? You're really flying, aren't you? Welcome to the hash bash. You'll really get into it before we see Creedence.'

Their language didn't make any more sense as the vehicle rattled ever faster down the road. But after a while sitting in that warm smoky fog it hardly seemed to matter. Remus finally began to dig it.

***

'There's a definite art to hunting science pirates, lad,' announced Commodore Black, hanging onto the periscope.

'Is it letting the science pirate think they're hunting *you*...?' asked Magnus.

'Air in the banks, sound diving alarm!' ordered the Commodore.

Black's first mate echoed the order into a speaking trumpet. 'Blow and go, aye. Dive, dive, dive.'

There was a crash from the main ballast tanks as the vessel initiated an emergency depth change, the deck suddenly sloping down at an extreme angle. All the veteran submariners had already grabbed onto the nearest handhold. They knew what the *Purity Queen* was capable of. Which is more than could be said for Cassie and Magnus.

Cassie clutched tight onto the u-boat's sonar console, the conning tower rocking as depth charges detonated outside the hull. She prayed the convoy of freighter submarines they had been hired to protect wouldn't break formation under the onslaught. One-on-one against this predator they wouldn't stand a chance. 'Magnus, I do believe you've been paying attention to the old man's stories.'

'You say that like it's a bad thing,' said the Commodore. 'And Captain Skull is no tall tale. Since the madman's proclaimed himself the *Sultan of the Skies* there's not a Jackelian ship moving under or on the ocean that hasn't been squeezed by his boorish bully's tithes.'

Cassie sighed. *And here's me thinking a galumphing flying submarine with a set of octopus-like boarding arms could only be a thing of legend.* 'Well, now all we need to do is survive to follow the maniac's vessel back to his lair. Then we'll discover if his secret underwater city is true, or just a tale from squiffy sailors getting tanked in a tavern.'

'There a fine art to surviving, as well, lass.'

'Would it involve not dying?'

'There now, you're already getting the hang of our brave business. Helm, gyros forward, set gyros by hand zero zero four. Tracking party, man your battle stations. Sonar, give me search ping thirty degrees on each side of the bow.'

Cassie tossed a leak patch-kit to Magnus. 'When you said you were going to show Magnus and me the world, I'd presumed it wouldn't end with the sight of your submarine's wreckage spread across the seabed.'

Magnus caught the kit and examined the glistening pipes running along the bulkhead. Their u-boat suffered enough cursed leaks without hydraulic shock from a rain of high explosive charges. 'You do remember I turned down a desk in the family Middlesteel clerks' office for this?'

Cassie shrugged and smiled. *It seemed a good idea at the time. I'm sure it did.*

'You won't be mentioning this to Molly, now, when we get home? What your darling mother doesn't know surely shouldn't be troubling her. She's a woman who values her peace of mind.'

When we get home? If, was looking more likely. The submarine rocked as a depth charge's gas bubble struck their hull, the shock-wave cracking shaft seals, water fountaining down across the conning tower's control boards.

No, on balance, Cassie probably wouldn't be highlighting this particular leg of their voyage.

- Fini -

THANKS

First, a big vote of thanks must go to all the thousands of students in the *Author's Apprentice* literary programme who helped with *Mission to Mightadore*, voting on the various twists and turns and taking part in the forum discussions.

Second, thanks to my gallant crew of test readers who acted as the final set of eyes on the manuscript.

This includes (in the order of comments and typos returned):

Todd Rathier.
Joe Speranza.
Eva Sanchez.
Julian White.
Emma Okereke.
Patrick Forhan.
Stuart Robertson.
Lowell Morrison.

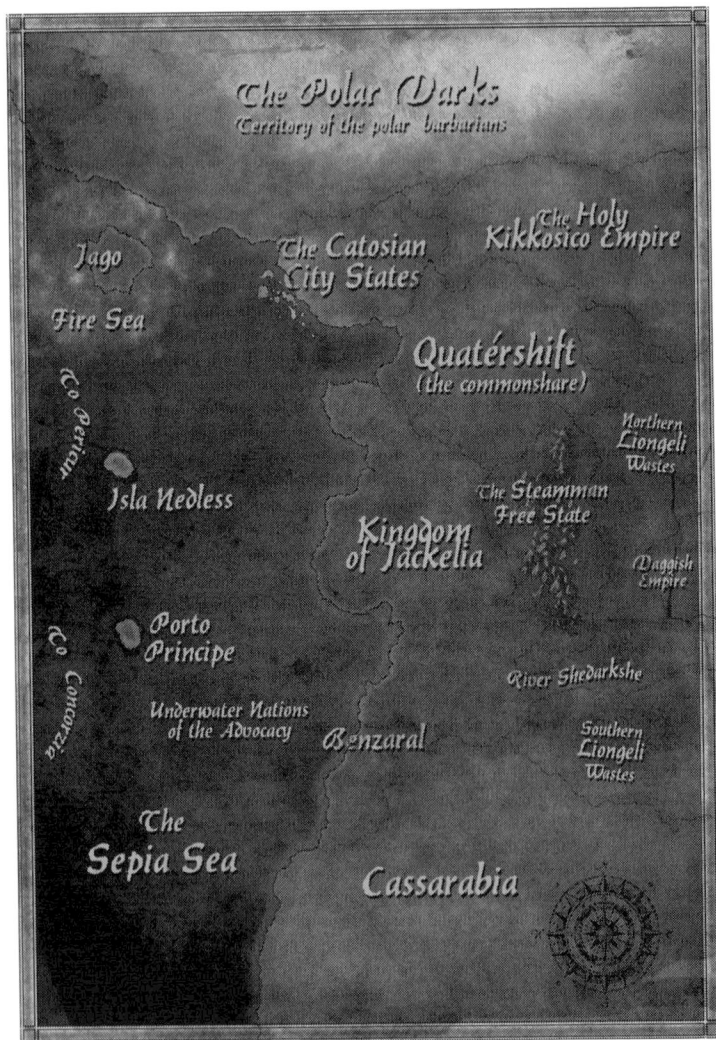

The Polar Darks
Territory of the polar barbarians

Jago

The Catosian
City States

The Holy
Kikkosico Empire

Fire Sea

Quatershift
(the commonshare)

Co Perier

Northern
Liongeli
Wastes

Isla Nedless

The Steamman
Free State

Kingdom
of Jackelia

Daggish
Empire

Co Concorzia

Porto
Principe

River Shedarkshe

Underwater Nations
of the Advocacy

Benzaral

Southern
Liongeli
Wastes

The
Sepia Sea

Cassarabia

18322344R00215

Printed in Great Britain
by Amazon